PRAISE FOR
AUDREY CARLAN

"FIVE STAR REVIEW! I recommend this book to anyone looking for a sweet, fierce love story. It takes a lot to write an original story that takes twists and turns you won't see coming."
~Abibliophobia Anonymous Book Reviews Blog

"DAMN! Audrey did it again! Made me smile, made me laugh & made me cry with her beautiful words! I am in love with these books."
~Hooks & Books Book Blog

"A sensual spiritual journey of two people meant for each other, heart and soul. Well-crafted and beautifully written."
~Carly Phillips, New York Times Bestselling Author

Limitless Love

A LOTUS HOUSE NOVEL: BOOK FOUR

Limitless Love

A LOTUS HOUSE NOVEL: BOOK FOUR

AUDREY CARLAN

WATERHOUSE PRESS

DEDICATION

To my sister Denise Pasion.

The woman who taught me...
The love of a good book.
It's okay to cry during movies.
Sisters are God-given best friends.
To follow your heart in all things.
And so much more.

My love for you is limitless.

NOTE TO THE READER

In previous Lotus House books, I've focused on both yoga and the chakras. Since this couple is driven by the heart chakra—in my opinion one of the most important—I felt it vital to focus on the chakra teachings, versus the practice of yoga. The chakra teachings were part of my official schooling with The Art of Yoga through Village Yoga Center in Northern California. Every chakra fact has been personally written by me and comes from my perspective and personal understanding of the teachings through hours of study and research.

I hope Limitless Love teaches you more about your heart chakra, the best ways to open it and prevent it from being closed, and how to experience each day keeping love and kindness at the forefront of your mind.

Namaste,

Audrey

CHAPTER ONE

HEART
C H A K R A

The Heart Chakra is the fourth of the seven primary chakras in the body. It represents our ability to love, the quality of our love, our past loves, and our future loves.

MONET

"There is no love without pain, for we wouldn't know the beauty of one without the other." I sat in my quilted leather chair, crossed my legs, and looked over the rim of my glasses at the man seated across from me.

He sighed, eased his broad shoulders back against the couch, and stretched out his arms. A rather open gesture for someone so jaded.

"That's deep, Doc."

I half smiled, set my legal pad across my thighs, and shifted forward to rest my elbows on my knees. "There is a natural yin and yang to all things in life. Love, pain, joy, grief. The universe organically seems to balance these things out."

He huffed. "Oh yeah? And what does it say about my cheating wife?"

"What does it say to you?" I bit the inside of my cheek so I didn't react the way my heart wanted to. I had been in the same position once. It hurt like hell. As this man's therapist, though, I needed to sympathize with him, not empathize, or we'd both go down a dark, winding, jagged path of grief.

He scowled. "That she has it coming to her?"

"And you don't believe that you leaving and walking away without so much as a discussion didn't hurt her?"

"Not even close. She fucked my best friend."

His words hit like a thousand tiny icicles across the bare skin of my arms. I swallowed against the dryness that suddenly took over my throat.

This is not your life, Moe. Don't put too much of your own experiences into your response.

"That's got to be hard to get past," I voiced sympathetically.

"You could say that again." Dave clenched his jaw and glanced over his shoulder. "I don't even know why I'm here."

That caught my attention. "Yes, you do."

He shook his head and placed his fists on his knees. "How could I ever trust her again? My best friend." Dave rubbed at his chin. The sound of his callused hands rubbing across his prickly jaw triggered an unwanted memory. Kyle used to rub his jaw in that exact same motion when he was hiding something. Turned out he hid a lot—the most unsettling of which was the long affair he had with my baby sister.

Moe, this is not about you. Let it go...

I inhaled and exhaled slowly, giving Dave and myself a minute to calm down.

"I thought maybe if I laid it all out there, you know, told all the gory details to a professional, I'd feel better." Dave sneered and picked at his fingernail.

"And do you?"

He shook his head. "No. Not at all. I'm still angry. So angry. I'm not sure if I can ever get past her betrayal." His jaw seemed to tighten when he continued. "Do you think it's possible? To get over it, I mean?"

No. I didn't, but I wanted to. I desperately wished my own circumstances were different. That I'd been different. Better somehow. A better wife. Mother. Friend to my husband. Then maybe he wouldn't have left me high and dry. Perhaps my sister wouldn't have looked like the perfect escape from a life he didn't want. A woman he didn't want. A child he couldn't even look at.

I pushed down my own secret desires and plastered on a smile. I looked at Dave with as much generosity and compassion as I could muster, and lied. Lied, because in this instance, my job was to be objective. "I think anything is possible."

Big. Fat. Lie.

After years in this line of work, I'd seen many cases of betrayal. Having gone through it myself made me feel like an expert on the subject. In my experiences, I've come to realize a person may forgive a transgression because of the love they have for the individual, but they never *ever* forget. I most certainly have not. Kyle leaving me the way he did still plagued my dreams. Sometimes I thought he might have taken a piece of my heart and destroyed it forever. If that was the case, I had a hole in my heart—one I wasn't sure could ever allow me to truly love again.

My phone chimed, reminding me that our hour was up. Instead of a buzzer, I used soft tinkling bells. It wasn't as jarring and didn't have the same rushed effect for the client.

"Our time is up, Dave. I know this was your first session, but if you'd like to continue with me, I'd be happy to take you on as a client."

"Do you think you can help me?" He stood up and clasped his hands in front of him.

I reached out a hand for him to shake. He took hold.

With truth in my statement and honor in my commitment, I responded, "Yes, I believe I can."

Dave nodded, sighed, and ran his fingers through his brown hair. "Okay, so what's next?"

At least he was eager to seek help. Who knew? Once we got into the reasons why his wife cheated and his feelings around it, perhaps there would be the option for reconciliation. For the first six months after Kyle left me, I held on to hope. Every situation is different. I still believed in love; I just wasn't sure it would ever happen for me again.

"Just schedule your next appointment with my receptionist in the lobby. She'll take care of you. And Dave?"

He stopped just as he grasped the doorknob.

"It gets easier over time. I promise." And it did. Every day I found new ways to be happy. My daughter. Mila, my best friend and confidant, was another. And last, the yoga she introduced me to. My hobby. I had things in my life that gave me joy.

He closed his eyes in what looked like relief. "Thanks, Doc. See you in a week or two?"

I nodded. "Whatever you need. I'll be here."

Dave left and I gathered my things. My phone buzzed on top of my planner.

"Hey, crazy, we still on for dinner?" I asked.

"Of course. Dinner doesn't make itself in my world," Mila scoffed dramatically.

I laughed and held the phone closer to my ear while I put my legal pad and laptop into my briefcase. "Atlas coming? Lily wants to see PowPow." I used the cutest of many nicknames my daughter had come up with for my best friend's boyfriend. Just thinking of my love bug made me smile.

"Yep. Lily told me if PowPow didn't come to dinner he could no longer be the Prince of Secret Garden Land. I reiterated this to Atlas, and the man practically teared up. Wuss." Her voice was playful, and I loved the sound of it.

Ever since Mila and Atlas became an item last year, my best friend had been happier than I'd ever seen her. They still bickered like an old married couple, but it worked for them. Two feisty personalities could manage if there was mutual love and respect. One day, I had hoped for that for myself. Of course, that would mean I'd have to do more than work, take care of Lily, and go to yoga. I sighed knowing how unlikely it was I would put myself out there again.

Without a beat, I changed my focus back to my friend. "I'll have to talk to Lily about empty threats."

Mila chuckled. "I don't know. She seems pretty serious. Aren't you, honey?"

My girl hollered through the phone. "Hi, Mommy!"

I grinned, thinking about my daughter's happy face. "Did Auntie surprise you and pick you up from daycare today?"

"Uh-huh, and she has a prize for me!"

"A *sur*prise?" I added more inflection on the "sur" part so she'd hear the difference.

"'S'wat I said! A prize."

I laughed and waved to my receptionist and Dave, who was still making his next appointment. The elevator dinged, and I hopped on. Luck was on my side tonight. Having an office on the twentieth floor of a building in downtown San Francisco usually meant waiting for an elevator.

"Yeah, well, she can't have her sur-prize until after dinner," Mila confirmed.

"Ah, Auntie bought you some sweet treats, I think."

"Yay!" I heard Lily clapping wildly.

"See you at home. You have a key still, right?"

Mila made a gurgling sound through the line. "I only moved out last month, Moe. And I'm never giving my key back. Though I do have one for you for our pad," Mila said with more happiness in her tone than I'd heard in a long time. It had taken the better part of a year for Atlas to get Mila to move in with him after their big blowup last year. Since she took over half ownership of the Second Chances Gallery his father and grandfather had owned before him and he went to work for the music label, life had been coming up roses for the two artists.

"Okay, well, make yourself at home. There's white wine chilling in the fridge. It will go best with the chicken dish I'm making."

"Oh, and I have a pretty exciting surprise for you too!" Mila taunted.

"Really?" I asked while stepping off the elevator and into the underground parking garage.

"Yep, and it's going to blow your saccharine-sweet mind."

"Please tell me Atlas proposed!" I squealed, wanting so much for my friend to take the ultimate plunge and put that man out of his misery.

"He does that almost every day since I moved in with him. I have a feeling a certain recent development is going to make it a lot harder for me to keep saying no."

"No way! Seriously?" My heart started thumping a mile a minute. Last I heard, Mila would only marry Atlas once he knocked her up. From what I understood, they were technically not trying to get pregnant, but not preventing it either. Oh my God. My insides were jumping for joy in anticipation. I crossed my fingers.

"Are you?" Tears pricked the back of my eyes. "Mila..." I gasped and swallowed down the emotions clogging my throat.

"Just come home. We want to tell you together." Her voice was loud and jovial, which meant I was probably right.

Chills raced up and down my spine, and a lightness filled me with such excitement I could hardly breathe. I wanted this for my friend. "Okay. Home. Thirty minutes if traffic is light."

"See you then. And Moe, be safe."

"I always am." I clicked off the phone and walked in a daze to my car.

If my assumption was correct, Mila was about to tell me that she was pregnant with Atlas's baby and they were getting married. Everything I could have ever hoped for my best friend was about to happen. Life could not get any better than this. *For her.*

"Stuck-up fucking cunt," a voice growled from a dark corner behind my car.

I spun around and came face-to-face with a masked man. I could only make out two holes for his eyes and one for his mouth. My hands shook, and I dropped my keys as I backed up toward the center of the garage, closer to the light. That's when

I saw the knife. A small blade, about four or five inches. The man walked toward me as I scrambled back on too-high heels. Each step sounded louder than the last.

"What do you want?" I pointed to my purse that I'd also dropped when I saw the man. "I've got money and credit cards in my purse. A couple hundred dollars. And my keys. Take my car. Just leave me alone." I put my hands up in front of me to show I wasn't going to be stupid.

"You think you're so smart. Rich and powerful. You're nothing but a filthy, greedy bitch."

"Wh-Wh-What do you want?" I backed up as he moved closer. The lights were directly overhead, and if anyone came down or drove up, they'd see me. Someone had to come. They just had to.

I stayed as calm as I could. "Please, just take whatever you want."

"Oh, I will. I'm going to take your life. Then all that money will go to the right person. Not you and that little fucking beaker baby."

Tears fell down my cheeks as the man advanced. His voice was familiar, but I couldn't quite place it through the roar of fear. He growled his words as if to mask them the way he did his face.

The man lifted up the knife in all its heinous glory. "Time to die, bitch!"

At those words, I screamed, turned, and ran as fast as I could. My pencil skirt was tight around my legs. I pulled it up a few inches to gain more speed. It wasn't enough.

With every step, he gained on me. "Run for your life. That's right. Run, bitch, run. There's nowhere you can go I won't find you!" he roared before getting so close I heard the heavy gusts of air bursting past his lips.

I tried to zigzag, but it was too late. A searing pain ripped through me as the knife pierced just above my hip. He yanked upward, the blade slicing up my back and knocking against my upper shoulder blade. The entire right side of my body had caught the blade, and I roared out as I crumbled to the ground in a ball of agony. The wound felt like an intense fire licking along the entire side of my back. Before I could react, my attacker was on top of me, straddling my sides and crushing my hips into the pavement.

He dug a forceful hand into my hair and tugged my head back hard. As I tried to push myself up, blood poured down my back and onto my hand. I screamed, kicked, and pushed off the concrete, but nothing would get him off me.

That's when I heard it. Laughter. He was laughing as he held me down. "Not so all-powerful now, are you, Monet..."

When he said my name, I knew who was hurting me.

Jesus. Lord no. Why?

"Kyle! Why are you doing this to me?" I pressed back, attempting to look at him and make eye contact, but my vision flickered in and out. Everything around me got darker around the edges.

He put the knife to my throat and dug the tip in. I cried out when I felt blood trickling down my neck.

My thoughts scattered. Lily. Kyle. Getting him off me. "Kyle, please, we have a daughter. Lily..."

"That beaker baby is not my daughter. Never was, never will be." His voice was angry, violence seeping off his tongue with each word.

"You're listed as the father on her birth certificate!" I groaned in pain, trying to remind him. We'd made that decision together. The two of us. I thought we'd wanted the same things, but no. He didn't. He'd wanted a child of his own. One I wasn't able to give him. But I wasn't the problem. It was his ineffective sperm that weren't capable of doing the job. I thought choosing donor sperm would settle the problem and bring us closer together. I had never been more wrong. It tore us apart beyond repair.

Kyle's spittle hit the side of my face when he sneered against my cheek. "Which will only make it easier to take all the money when you're dead and we put her up for adoption."

"No!"

"Yes!" he growled, pulling my head back so hard my back bent unnaturally and I thought for sure he'd break my spine. "Any last words?"

"Go to hell." I knew no matter what happened to me, Lily would end up with Mila and Atlas. She'd promised me when Kyle and I had divorced she'd be her guardian, and I had the legal papers in place to make it so. I knew Atlas and Mila would adopt her if the worst happened.

I'm so sorry, baby. Sorry to leave you.

"I'm already there," he mocked as he sliced the knife along my neck.

Pain shot through my system like a lightning bolt.

"Hey! You! Get the fuck off her!" I heard a voice yell out like an angel's call.

The knife left my throat and Kyle's weight floated off my back. My head felt so heavy I couldn't hold it up. I rested it on the concrete beneath me. Fire rippled along my back and down my neck.

Two strong arms lifted me up and turned me over. "Dr. Holland. Dr. Holland. Help is on the way." I vaguely recognized that voice.

I opened my eyes as much as I could and saw Dave, my client. "Call Mila..." I said on a whisper. "Call Mila."

"Okay, okay. Just stay with me. The paramedics are going to be here soon. Jesus, there's a lot of blood. Where is it all coming from?" His voice shook, and I closed my eyes. "No, no, no. They say on TV to keep the person awake. Dr. Holland. Stay awake. Dr. Holland." He patted the side of my face. "Please, don't die."

I blinked a few times and gripped his wrist as best I could. "Call Mila."

"I will. I promise," he spoke fast and loud.

"Has my daughter," I whispered.

He nodded. "Okay, yes."

Just then his head snapped up, and for a moment, I worried Kyle was back to finish me off.

"Thank fuck. The cops and ambulance are here. They're here," he said with unrestricted enthusiasm.

He lifted one of his arms and waved it above his head, jarring my side painfully. "Over here!" he screamed.

The paramedics got to me, and at some point I was shifted onto my side, and I felt hands working on my back.

"Oh my God. What did that fucker do to her?" Dave said from somewhere behind me.

"Ma'am. Where else are you hurt?" an unfamiliar voice asked.

"Back and neck. Knife," I mumbled before everything went black.

★ ★ ★

"Wildcat, you can't stay here all night," I heard Atlas murmur as if I was in a dream.

"Oh, yes, I can. You take Lily home. Put her in bed with you so she's not scared. I'm not leaving until Moe wakes up." Mila's voice was stern and direct.

I blinked a few times but couldn't open my eyes fully. A groan slipped from my throat as the pain in my back ricocheted down every nerve ending.

"Moe." I felt Mila's small hand run along my bicep. "Moe, wake up."

Again with the blinking. Darn, my lids felt like they had two-ton weights on them. Once I got them open, I looked into the worried chocolate-brown eyes of my best friend.

"So tired," I mumbled.

Mila grabbed a cup of water with a straw and held it to my lips.

I sipped until the dryness in my throat cleared. Absolute heaven. "Thank you."

Mila placed her hand on the side of my head and caressed my temple and hair soothingly. "You gave us quite a scare, Moe. What happened? All we know is that someone attacked you in the garage at your work." A tear slipped down her face. Atlas put his hand on her shoulder.

"It was Kyle," I croaked.

Mila's lips went white and flat. "Kyle?" she sneered.

I coughed. Sparks of pain slashed down my back as I adjusted to a more comfortable spot on my side. "Yeah, he had a mask on, but I could tell by his voice."

She shook her head. "Why? I uh..."

"He said something about wanting me dead for the money."

"Money? He tried to kill you for money?"

I swallowed, and the severity of what happened finally hit me. My entire body started to tremble, and tears fell down my cheeks like waterfalls.

"What did I ever do to him?" I focused on my best friend.

Mila put her face close to mine. "Nothing. You did absolutely nothing but give him everything a wife could ever give. He's a bastard and a lunatic, and now a criminal. Moe, he hurt you so bad."

"How bad?" I flinched and felt aches all over, realizing I'd been here sedated a while. I knew he'd cut me pretty bad, but I'd survived. I would live another day, and right then that was all that mattered.

"Don't worry about that now. You're fine. They were actually able to stop the bleeding pretty quickly. You were only in the OR for a little over two hours." She stroked my cheek with her thumb and wiped away the tears as they fell. I couldn't control them.

"Tell me everything now, Mila. Please."

Mila let out a long breath.

"The doctor will go over it with you when he comes back. You had to have some internal stitches that will dissolve naturally, but, um, you have eighty or so in your back and another twelve in the wound on your neck. He didn't hit any organs, but the slice up your back is pretty gnarly. If that client of yours hadn't come upon you..." She choked on a sob. "Moe, you're the only family I have besides Atlas. I can't lose you."

Mila pressed her forehead against mine, and together we cried. The evening's events started coming to me in flashes of memory.

Kyle in a mask approaching me.

The light hitting the knife and reflecting off its shiny surface.

Kyle's words so vile.

"You're nothing but a filthy, greedy bitch."

"That beaker baby is not my daughter. Never was, never will be."

"Take all the money and put her up for adoption when you're dead."

"What happens now?" I asked Mila.

Atlas placed a hand on my lower leg near my foot and rubbed from ankle to knee. "We take care of you and Lily. That bastard is never going to get to you with me around."

A knock on the door broke through our little huddle, and two men in suits walked in.

Atlas turned around, stood in front of me, and crossed his arms, making sure to show his brawn. I tried to smile at his possessive move but couldn't through the pounding ache throbbing everywhere. Even my feet hurt, and nothing had happened to them.

"Who are you and what do you want?" he demanded.

"We need a few words with the victim." One of the men looked down at a notepad. "A Ms. Holland?"

"That's Dr. Monet Holland, and I think she's dealt with enough tonight. Don't you?" Mila stood up next to Atlas, creating a wall in front of the men.

"We understand, but when it comes to these types of attacks, it's best to get the victim's statement when it's as fresh as possible."

Victim.

That was what I was now. A victim.

"It's fine, guys. I'll be okay." I'd rather get it over with. "Give me a few minutes, gentlemen." I gestured to the detectives. The two men nodded and made their way out of the room.

I grabbed Mila's wrist. "Who has Lily?"

"Uh, we had to move quick, and I was with a friend when Mila called," Atlas answered while rubbing at the back of his neck.

"A friend?" I queried.

"Yeah, Clay."

"Clayton Hart has my daughter?" I was unable to mask the shock in my voice.

Atlas looked down and away sheepishly. "He's reputable."

"That may be, but he's never met her. Wasn't she scared?" My goodness, my poor baby with a man she'd never met as her aunt and uncle left her to see her mom in the hospital. This was so messed up.

"Nope. It was the weirdest thing. I introduced her, and they stood in front of one another, squaring off, and then she grabbed his hand and asked if he liked secret gardens."

I closed my eyes.

"What can I say? Lily's easy to love." Atlas shrugged.

"Yes, she is. Can you please go relieve him and send my thanks?" I asked Atlas.

Atlas nodded. "Come on, baby."

Mila tugged her hand out of his. "No way. I'm not leaving the hospital until Moe leaves."

"Wildcat," he growled in what could only be taken as a warning. A man who didn't want to be separated from his woman. Lovely to witness.

"Curly, back off. This is my sister, lying in a hospital bed, skewered like a fish on a hook, with detectives staring at her. And let's not forget. She almost died. Died! I'm staying." Her face turned red and she fisted her hands at her sides.

Atlas lifted up her fists, smoothed out her fingers, and kissed each hand. "I'll be back in the morning with Lily and breakfast for both of you. Try to get some rest." He shifted forward and pecked her on the lips, and then he kissed his fingertips and placed them over her stomach.

I knew it.

The two men entered as Atlas made his way out the door. "Dr. Holland, can we please ask you a few questions now? Then we'll be out of your hair and you can rest."

I sighed and sank back into the pillow. "I'm ready. Let's get this over with."

CHAPTER TWO

HEART
C H A K R A

Anahata is Sanskrit for the fourth chakra in the chakra system. The word means "unhurt." The name implies that beneath the hurts and grievances of past experiences lies a pure and spiritual place where no hurt exists.

CLAYTON

I'd never been more scared in my thirty years on this earth than when I was sitting on the floor in a little girl's room while she pranced around in some type of fairy-ballerina-meets-Barbie-queen-of-hearts type getup.

"Clay, you're da king and I'm da queen, 'kay?" Lily plopped a plastic crown on my head. I blinked and sat silently until she spun around, put her hands on her hips, and frowned. "You're 'posed to say 'kay."

"Uh, okay?" This was some fucked-up shit. How I got conned into taking care of Monet's daughter, the one I absolutely did not want to even meet after finding out about her last year, was jacked. I wanted Monet back then. With her sexy body, flowing black hair, and unique features, I was all in with one glance. And we hit it off right away too. Until I found out she had a child. Then all bets were off. The last thing I needed was to be roped into a situation like I'd had with Stacey. Hell, no. That bitch did a number on me. One I'd spent years getting over.

Did I want children? Hell, yeah. Always had. I just didn't know how to fix that piece in me that died after Stacey's lies and betrayal. And yet there I sat, taking care of the child of the woman I'd brushed off, a plastic crown on my head, pretending to be a king.

A brilliant smile adorned Lily's face while she assessed me. Hell if I couldn't ward off the arrow that pierced straight through my gut. I rubbed at the tender spot, not understanding the new feeling.

Lily hummed and danced around her room. She had a wand in one hand that she fluttered in the air sporadically. For the life of me, I had no clue what the heck she was doing, but she seemed very serious about her dance, so I didn't ask.

"King Clay..." she started.

"My name is Clayton, sweetie." Shit. I'd given her a nickname already. I clenched my teeth and focused on the kid. Damn, she was cute. Just like her mother.

"'S'wat I said. Clay." She frowned and bopped me on one shoulder and then the other, blasting me into attention.

"Ouch!" I laughed and grabbed hold of her weapon.

"Dat's mine! I have to protect you with my spell!" Her

voice rose excitedly.

I couldn't help but chuckle and nod. "Okay, okay. Just do it softer." I used a low tone. Keep her happy while her mom dealt with whatever had gone down. Only thing I heard was that Monet was in the hospital and Atlas needed me to look after Lily while they checked it out.

She smiled and did it again, this time with less force. "You are now 'tected by the power of the Secret Garden Land!"

"What do I need to be protected from?" I asked, getting into the pretend game.

"Monsters."

I widened my eyes for effect, which she seemed to enjoy. "There are monsters in the garden?"

She snort-huffed. "No, silly. I've 'tected the Secret Garden Land. You're safe now, even when you leave my room!" Her corresponding smile and the pride that puffed her chest up was something to behold.

"Why would you protect me?" I asked softly, that uneasy feeling in my gut growing with each playful smile she bestowed.

Lily pursed her lips. "B'cuz I like you, and you like my mom."

I jerked my head back. What the...? "Now what would make you think that, sweetie?" I tickled her side, thinking it was the thing to do in that moment. Deflect. Deflect. Deflect. What was that thing Trent was saying about kids always knowing when something was up with people? They were like natural little private investigators.

Lily howled with laughter and jumped back.

"You looked at her pictures on the walls a lot and smiled. You like her." Lily's tone was matter-of-fact and more confident than I would have expected from a small child.

Observant little bugger. I did do that while checking out the house. When Atlas left, he asked me to drive Lily home and get her situated because they didn't know when they would be back. I took that time to take a gander at the beautiful woman I'd been attracted to last year.

"Well, your mommy is very pretty."

She nodded vigorously. "The prettiest princess in the *whole* world."

"And what about you?" I petted the top of her black hair, surprised at how soft it was. Lily was quite possibly the cutest little girl I'd ever seen. Not that I'd been exposed to that many kids. Only my buddy Trent's son, William. I'd've bet this kid could be on the cover of those parenting magazines. She took a lot after her mother's Asian side, but the unique blue eyes and lighter skin must have at least partly been from her father. My guess? A white guy with blue eyes. Probably the douchebag ex-husband.

Those pretty eyes of hers focused so intently on me I swore she could see right through to my guarded and tarnished soul. And just like a truly honest and forthright kid, she responded to my statement with one of her own.

"I'm the queen, don't ya know." She said the words so seriously I cracked.

I couldn't hold the façade anymore and laughed so hard I tumbled on my back, clutching at my abdomen until it wore off. Damn, this little girl was a hoot.

"'R'you hurt?" She put her hand on my forehead. "Not hot."

"You checking my temperature, Lily?"

She nodded and stuck out her tongue and lopped it to one side as she checked my entire face. "Yep. I'm gonna be a doctor and fix up all the people hurt in the world. Animals too."

I smiled. "Those are some lofty goals there, but if anyone can do it, it will be you." I poked her nose.

What was going on with me? This kid was bringing out a totally different side of me. One I didn't even know I had. I mean, I'd hoped I had it. When the shit went down with Stacey, I'd planned on doing everything in my power to be great with kids. Trent's son liked me. Only, there was something about this child. I wanted more from her. Acceptance. Attention.

I ran my hands through my hair, letting the strange feeling seep into my bones. I wasn't sure what else to do with it.

Lily stood and jumped up and down. "I'm really hungry. Mommy was gonna make chicken. Can I have Froot Loops?" She changed subjects faster than I could blink.

I shook my head and hopped up. When she grabbed my much larger hand with her tiny one, a zap of electricity zipped through my fingers. I was surprised by my natural reflex to hold her hand tighter. Something about it just felt good, like hope and joy perfectly fit in the palm of my hand. I shook off the weird feeling. My guy friends were always telling me kids did weird things, like tugging on their heartstrings better than any sexy woman ever could. I was beginning to think they were right.

"Come on, sweetie. Let's see what your mom has in the kitchen, though I don't think Froot Loops is a good dinner."

"But it is. It's *very* good. And tasty!"

"Oh, I have no doubt it's tasty. It's just not a balanced meal. You need a full belly of healthy food before bed. You have school tomorrow. You do have school tomorrow, right?"

She swung my arm and led me through the house to the kitchen. "Yep! I'm in kindergarten."

"Wow, that's a big girl. How old are you?" I took a second to mentally pat myself on the back. I could so do this kid thing, and so far, I thought I might even be good at. She hadn't cried. Seemed to enjoy my company. Yep, I had it in the bag.

"Six," she deadpanned.

I drew back and focused on her face. Her little lip was trembling and her eyes sparkled with mirth.

"Fibber! You are not. Besides, kindergartners are younger." At least I thought they were. I needed to Google that shit.

She smacked my thigh and squealed. "I'm five. Just had my birfday a week ago, but I'm kinda six."

"Birthday?" I repeated for her benefit.

"S'wat I said. Birf-day. You don't listen very good."

Man, this kid had me cracking up. We made it to the kitchen, and she crawled up onto the barstool and placed her chin into her hands to watch.

"What'cha gonna make me?"

Little did she know, I happened to be a very good cook. Being physically fit, eating healthy, and making a living as a personal trainer to the local celebs living in the Bay meant I needed to know how to give the body the best sustenance. However, this was a kid who apparently would rather have Froot Loops than chicken, which meant I needed to come up with something healthy that could compete with cereal.

I opened the fridge and scanned the items. Monet had a lot of food in her fridge for just two people. Tons of fresh veggies and fruit. The last woman I'd dated had little to no interest in shopping. Probably because I took care of all of that. And everything else under the sun. The unwanted reminders of that time in my life were coming up fast and furious. It had been years. I thought I'd gotten past it, but being in a domestic environment was bringing up all that crap again. All the things I'd pushed behind me. The dreams I let go of long ago rushed back to the surface while I stood in a strange kitchen, watching the daughter of a woman I'd hit on then bailed on a year ago.

Clay, you are reading too much into this situation. Relax, dude. Relax and feed the girl.

"Do you like carrots?" I finally asked.

She nodded, so I pulled a few mini ones out of the bag, washed them in the sink, and set them on a napkin. "Munch on that while I make you some grub."

Her eyebrows narrowed. "Grub?"

"Another way to say food."

Lily bit into a carrot and crunched loudly. "Gruba dub dub."

I snickered and pulled out the thawed chicken. Might as well cook it up so it didn't go bad. Then I found a few small blocks of cheese and came up with a great idea. Once I had the chicken in strips and sizzling in the pan, I shredded up three of the cheeses and poured a bag of noodles into a pot.

"I wuv pasta!" Lily spoke around a mouthful of carrot.

"You do?" I laughed. Something in me knew I could win over the kid. Atlas had been right when he gave me a pep talk before leaving her in my care. Lily was an easy child and fun to be around. My heart panged, reminding me that I too should have had this. Once upon a time...if my ex hadn't been a lying bitch.

I shook my head. Never again was I going to allow a woman to play me. No way. No how.

"Is that cheese?" Lily asked excitedly.

"It is. Have you figured out what I'm making?"

She shook her head but licked her lips while I picked a small chunk of the cheddar and held it over her mouth. She opened up and gobbled it, clapping her hands.

"Homemade mac and cheese with chicken thrown in for some protein."

Her mouth opened and her cheeks turned pink. She clapped again. "I love mac and cheese too! You da best, Clay!"

"Sweetie, it's Clayton. Clay-ton," I sounded out for her.

"'S'wat I said!" She pouted, and it was the cutest thing. Reminded me of when I first saw her mother the day Mila moved into this house over a year ago. At the time, I'd thought she was drop-dead gorgeous. Still did, but I'd been avoiding her like the plague. She represented exactly what I thought I would have had at that point in my life, and I straight up couldn't hack it once I had found out about her kid. Now, standing in front of Lily, my heart broke a little. I could have hung out with this cool-as-hell kid long ago. *Maybe by this time her mom and I would have...*

Nope. Not going there. No more what if. I couldn't live my life that way any longer. If I wanted something, I was going to go for it. Balls to the wall, go all out. Hanging out with Lily was giving me all kinds of ideas for the future.

While I plated a small amount of food for Lily in a bowl and a large portion for myself, I chastised myself for being so afraid to date a woman who had a child. Lily was amazing. Sweet and funny. Made me wonder what the deal was with Monet's ex. If he was part of her life, Atlas and Mila would have called him to get Lily and not had me cover for them.

"Hey, Lily, where's your daddy?" I asked, poking a noodle and a chunk of chicken.

She looked at me and shrugged. "Don't got one anymore."

I frowned, anger prodding at my chest. "Why's that?"

She answered around a mouthful of pasta. "He didn't want me."

Ice-cold fury slithered along my skin. "Is that what he told you?" I asked, realizing I was heading into territory I had no business getting into with a five-year-old.

"No. Mommy said he didn't want her anymore, but everyone loves Mommy. She's the bestest." She shoveled more pasta into her mouth.

Even if she didn't say it outright, she did in her own way—because her mother was loved by everyone, she figured that it must be her that her father didn't want.

Mother. Fucking. Cocksucker.

I clenched my jaw and turned as a shadowy figure stepped into the hall. Instinctively I jetted around the kitchen and stood in front of Lily with my fists up. I'd beat down any intruder with my bare hands before they got to this angel.

"Who are you?" I roared, making sure I sounded extra scary. Lily cowered into my back, her forehead against my shirt.

"Dude! It's me." Atlas laughed, stepping into the light of the kitchen and shrugging off his coat. "Man, by the size of those muscles on display and your chest all puffed out, I'm lucky you didn't charge me like a rhino!" He chuckled as he came up and clasped me on the shoulder. Tingles of anxiety slipped along my skin before petering out.

Atlas went around me, ruffled Lily's hair, and kissed the top of her head. "Hey, munchkin, what'cha got there?"

"Mac'n'cheese!" she responded again with her mouth full.

Okay, kids weren't always cute. They could be gross too.

"Got any more?" Atlas asked and rubbed his gut.

Silently I went around the bar countertop, pulled out another bowl, and loaded it up for my friend, letting the last dregs of irritation fade away.

Atlas turned on cartoons. "Hey, munchkin, you can watch TV in here while you eat. Clay and PowPow are going to go into the formal living room, okay?"

"'Kay!" Her eyes were already glued to a yellow square creature that lived under the water. I watched for a second as the square hit a starfish with a spatula.

I shook my head to clear the weirdness. Cartoons had definitely changed since my day.

Atlas grabbed the bowl I handed him, and we moved into the other room.

He scooped up a huge bite and ate for a few moments.

"How's Monet? What happened?" I asked in a speedy deluge of questions.

Atlas lifted a hand. "She's fine. Well, not fine. Had to have surgery, and the attacker... Dude, it was her ex, Kyle."

"You're kidding? He attacked her? How? Sexually?" The anger that had burned me earlier with Lily's words about her father came back with a vengeance.

He shook his head, and a wave of relief settled over me. "Naw, he knifed her."

I jerked my head back and my hands shook, almost making me drop the bowl. "What? Clarify." I said through clenched teeth. A man putting his hands on a woman was wrong, deserving of a beating and jail time. A man knifing a woman... There wasn't a space in hell hot enough for that type of scum.

"Guy had a mask on and threatened to kill her. When she ran, he chased after her. Then he caught up and sliced her open all down her back. Fileted her, man. She has over eighty stiches in her back alone."

"Jesus Christ," I blurted. Images of the stunning woman I'd seen around the yoga studio and all through the pictures of the house flickered in my mind along with the idea of her laid up in a hospital bed. A sour taste hit my tongue and my appetite disappeared.

"After he cut her, he tackled her to the pavement, which shredded her knees, elbows, and hands. Then he pierced her neck with the blade and sliced an almost three-inch-long shallow cut when someone intervened."

I sat my ass on the arm of her fabric couch, my knees shaking under me. "Fuck!" I wiped at the glistening sweat that formed on my brow. "Shit. That's serious." Every protective instinct inside me warred for attention, wanting to do something, beat the shit out of someone in her honor.

Atlas nodded. "Yeah, we're going to be staying here with them for a while. Make sure she's safe until they find the bastard. I swear to God, if I ever see him face-to-face..."

"I'm right there with you. He better skip town."

"So how did it go with Lily?" Atlas grinned.

I smiled automatically at the change in subject. "We had a good time. She's easy. I can see why you like the kid."

"Well, pretty soon here I'm going to have one of my own..." He scratched at the back of his neck and looked up at me through his curly brown mop of hair.

"Are you telling me you knocked up Mila Mercado?" I smirked.

"Fuck yeah I am! Confirmed with the doctor just today. Ten weeks along."

"That's awesome. I'm happy for you." And I was happy for

him that he had a woman he loved and was starting a family with her. And because Mila wasn't a lying skank who would take him to the cleaners and ruin his life.

Deftly, I gritted my teeth and reminded myself that Stacey was long gone and that it was okay—healthy, even—to be happy for my friend and his woman. Honestly, I was. More than anything, I wanted to be in a similar place in my own life. I was thirty. Time was flying by, the years merging into one another. I worked, I hung out with the guys, boxed with my buddy Nick when I had time, and did yoga. Women came in and out of my life, but I never offered more than a few dates and a few nights in the sack. It just never felt right to go for more after what I'd been through. Being here with Lily and hearing about another one of my best friends finding the right woman reminded me what I was missing out on.

"And now she has to marry me," Atlas said and scooped up some food, shimmying like a fool in love.

"You think you're going to get the spitfire to marry you because you knocked her up? Do you not know Trent and Genevieve? Took him a year to get her to walk down the aisle."

Atlas shook his head. "No way. Nuh-uh. Mila promised me that when she got pregnant she'd marry me. We'll probably visit the courthouse this week."

"No fuckin' way!" Marriage and a baby on the way...all in the same week. Some guys had all the luck.

He shrugged. "We don't have anyone besides the folks at Lotus House and Moe and Lily, so a quickie wedding feels right for us. I'd suggest Vegas, but she's become super sensitive around smoke and she'll just be mad she can't drink."

"I can see that. Well, whatever you guys decide, let me know. Congratulations are definitely in order one way or the other." I clapped him on the bicep and squeezed, showing my support.

"Too right."

"Are you excited or scared shitless?" I was curious how my longtime friend would take impending fatherhood.

Back when I thought I was going to be a father, I'd been ecstatic. I'd always wanted a big family. My brother and I were so far apart in age we might as well have been father and son. My parents had him when they were twenty and then didn't have me until they were in their late thirties. My brother was off to college when mom brought me home, so it'd mostly been me. We'd moved around a lot with my father being military, so I didn't see my brother much or have any long-term friends. All the friends I have, I'd made as an adult. Of the ones who lived around here, Trent and Atlas were the best of them.

"A little of both," he admitted. "Mila and I don't have any siblings and no fathers to speak of. But we have each other and our desire to make our own family. Moe and Lily are part of that. She's like a sister to me now, and God knows I love that little girl out there." He pointed to the kitchen, where I could hear Lily singing along with the cartoon. Something pirate-like.

I nodded. "I could see that. Growing your family is important."

"What about you?"

"What about me?" I responded on instinct.

"You ready to settle down?" His lips tipped up into a goofy smile.

For the first time ever, I looked into Atlas's eyes and laid out the truth. The real truth, not the player façade I'd lived under for the past six years. "Been ready."

His eyes widened. "Seriously?"

"Yeah. I've always wanted a family to call my own. Have roots somewhere. Since Trent has laid his roots here, I've stayed. Then I met you, Dash, Nicholas, and I've got a good core group of friends. My business is doing well here. I only travel with Trent if he needs me to work an injury or give him some extra attention due to that wife of his trying to fatten him up."

Atlas laughed. "Dude, that Genevieve. She can cook a mean meal!"

"True. I've sampled them many times myself. And since they've got Will, I'm making more of an effort to be present, take on the active uncle role, same as you with Lily."

"Crazy, huh?"

"What is?"

Atlas tipped his head to the side. "I don't know. How much having good people in your life changes you. I've never been happier. Except, of course, this shit with Moe."

Monet. My hand went into fists thinking about the woman being hurt.

"How long is the recovery?"

"Don't know yet. I left before she'd seen the doctor. Mila is with her. Won't leave. So it's me and the munchkin tonight. She's a cuddle bug, though, so I'll be okay."

"You're going to sleep with her?" I asked a bit shocked. Watching a kid was one thing; sleeping with one was another.

"Uh, yeah. Her mom's been hurt and her dad is a fucking psycho. There isn't an alarm on the house...yet. That little girl is our life. We're taking her mom's bed, and I'm barricading us in just in case that lunatic tries something with Lily."

The thought of Lily getting even a scratch made my skin

crawl like a hundred tiny ants were all over me. "Point well made. Mind if I stay and hang out until you guys go to bed?"

Truth was, I didn't want to admit I was hoping Mila would call and give Atlas an update on Monet's progress before I had to leave. Hell, maybe I'd even take the couch.

Once that thought hit, I couldn't let it go. "You know what? On second thought, maybe I should take the couch. Be an extra set of eyes tonight."

Atlas's corresponding grin was priceless. "You want info on Moe."

"Obviously, I want to make sure she's okay. Her and Lily."

"You're sweet on her. You were a year ago, and you still are. Something's changed though. Before you wouldn't even consider dating her. Now you want to sleep on her couch and make sure her kid is safe?"

"I like the kid, okay?" I shrugged.

"What's not to like? She's awesome, but that's not why. You like her mom too."

"She's hot and a friend of my friends. I want to make sure she pulls through. Can you just drop it?" I turned and headed back into the kitchen with my now cold pasta and chicken.

A manly chuckle and cough followed behind me. "Whatever, dude. Lie to yourself all you want, won't change a thing." He followed behind me. "Got any more chicken? This shit is amazing," he spoke through his lips as if he was still chewing.

"I hope you choke on it," I growled, and he laughed hard, coughing his way through.

Admittedly I felt a little better at his discomfort.

"Monet and Clayton kissing in a tree..."

"Grow up," I said.

"Don't want to."

"If you're going to be a dad, you'd better learn real quick!" I shot back and set my bowl in the microwave to reheat my dinner.

That got his attention. "Mila has already told me she'll make sure I'm a great one, and I believe anything that comes from the two of us is going to be good. With her, I'll be okay."

I slumped against the counter and looked at my friend. "I was just kidding. You're going to be awesome, Atlas. Mostly because you want to be, and that's all it takes. Caring for the little one more than yourself is what it's all about. You'll do fine. I have faith in you, man."

"Can I take a bubble bath?" Lily screeched from behind Atlas. She was standing with her hands together in a prayer position. "Puh-leeeeeeeze! You can take one wif me!" Her blue eyes sparkled as she bounced between Atlas and me.

Both of us went dead silent. I thought I was scared earlier; this request terrified me. Sleeping fully clothed next to a five-year-old was one thing when you were her guardian, but bathing her? Uh, nope!

"That's all you, buddy," I blurted.

Atlas winced. "Munchkin, that's not a good idea. When Auntie Mimi is here tomorrow, or when Mommy is back, you can take a bubble bath. I promise. Tonight, we're going to skip the bath altogether. How about some ice cream?" he offered.

"Smooth, Atlas. Redirection." I laughed. "Real smooth." I chuckled and clapped him on the back, silently thanking him for the quick thinking.

"Best. Uncle. Ever. Status. The struggle is real." He chuckled.

CHAPTER THREE

HEART
C H A K R A

When the heart chakra is open, we are able to forgive; our lungs are clear and our immune systems are healthy. The higher chakras cannot be accessed until we pass through the heart. A heavy heart is one that carries resentment and anger from denied emotions, as well as guilt.

MONET

"Dr. Holland, you're going to have to take it easy." The nurse gripped my bicep and helped me stand from my prone position on the bed. I winced and breathed several times, trying to cut through the agony splintering out every limb.

I'd been in the hospital the better part of two days and I was done. D-O-N-E. Done. Flying monkeys couldn't keep me here a second longer. I needed to be home, surrounded by my things, including my bed, my clothes, the solitude of my bedroom, and most important, my little girl. She needed her mommy. A pang of guilt fired through my heart as I thought about her being without me, probably worrying. And she'd been with Clayton Hart for most of last night. Ugh. That couldn't have been comfortable for either of them.

I stood shakily as white-hot pain ricocheted down my back, halting me into stillness. "My God, that hurts." The words blasted out of my lips on a surprising gust of air.

Mila held me by the other arm.

"Perhaps you should sit down," the doctor, standing at the other side of my bed, offered.

I shook my head. "No. I'm fine, just eager. You've already signed the release papers. Now please go over my discharge and recovery plans. I'm ready to go home."

"As you wish." The doctor looked down at his electronic tablet, scanned it for a moment, and then tucked it under his arm.

Mila set my loafers down on the ground in front of me, and I slipped into them slowly, being extra careful not to jostle anything.

"You'll have to come back in two weeks to have the stitches removed. They need to be kept dry for at least three more days. Sponge or sink bath for now. Do not submerge them in water. The wound was superficial, but the healing will be uncomfortable to say the least with a laceration that large. I've prescribed a broad-spectrum antibiotic to help prevent infection, a muscle relaxer, and a mild narcotic for pain. Use the last two sparingly and try to wean yourself off by next week."

I nodded, listening intently as Mila carefully laid a bulky

sweater over my shoulders. Pushing my arms into the sleeves was not an option. The warmth of the familiar fabric engulfed me, and I sighed, the solace of being home feeling near.

"Are we done?" I glanced up at the doctor.

He smiled softly, laid a hand over mine, and gave it a light squeeze. "You're going to make a full recovery. The scars shouldn't be too noticeable after a few months to a year."

Except for the fact that I'd always know they were there. Every time I wore a bathing suit or a strapless dress, people would see them. The one on my neck was not going to be easy to hide. Questions would arise, and what the heck was I supposed to say?

Yeah, my ex-husband hates me so much he wants me dead and gave me some stunning reminders to prove it.

As a psychiatrist, I knew it was going to be a long road to recovery for my mind and soul, not to mention my physical body. Though at that point, as a woman first, doctor second, I just wanted it all to go away. I wanted to go home, hug my daughter, wash my body of Kyle's filthy hands, get into my bed, and pretend none of this ever happened.

Pretend once and for all that I didn't love, marry, and ultimately divorce a psycho.

★ ★ ★

Mila held my hand as we eased up the two steps to my front door. It was late afternoon, closing in on six p.m. The vintage-style street lanterns flicked on, and the Bay breeze teased the leaves of the large oak tree shading my Berkeley home. I sucked in a full breath, reminding myself that I was alive, here, safe and sound. The stale antiseptic smell of the hospital still clung to me as Mila ushered me through the door, but I wouldn't let it affect my mood. Not when I was going to see my baby girl.

The scent of garlic floated on the air as we entered, and my mouth watered. Hospital food wasn't known for its palatable qualities, and my stay had been no different. Whatever was being cooked smelled heaven-sent.

A squeal of laughter bombarded my ears, and my heart began to pound. My love bug was close. The cloud of happiness and the comforts of home blazed like a healing balm across my ravaged soul. I held on to Mila as we walked into the kitchen, where I was stunned speechless.

I'd expected Atlas to be the one making my girl laugh like a hyena, but no. It was none other than Clayton Hart. The gorgeous man that I'd crushed on last year. We'd hit it off really well when we met, and then out of nowhere he bailed. Every time we'd see each other at Lotus House, he seemed to go out of his way to avoid me. I figured his feelings had changed, and yet...here he was, cooking up a storm, making my kid laugh. What in the world had I entered? The Twilight Zone?

Clayton faced the stove in a skin-tight black athletic tee and a pair of jeans that clung to every toned curve of his impressive backside. He hadn't realized we were there, so I looked my fill as he shimmied his hips from side to side to the beat of "Faith" by George Michael, which was blaring from a phone sitting on the counter. Of course, at the center of the party, engrossed in his dance, was my Lily, clapping along and screaming "Faith" every time the word was sung by the '80s pop star.

As we approached, Mila and I stared. Besides the fact that the song was highly inappropriate for a five-year-old—the man sung about touching bodies and being tied down—the way Mr.

Hart was shaking his groove thang would make any nun switch sides from worshipping the God above to worshipping this man right here on earth.

Sweet baby Jesus, he was sexy, and boy, did the man have moves!

On the chorus, Clayton swung around holding up a baguette and pretended to sing into it for my daughter's pleasure. I may have melted a little on the spot.

"King Clay is da bestest dancer!" She clapped and carried on, shifting her shoulders from left to right while she shook her little bootie on the barstool.

"And baaaaaabbbbbyyyyy..." Clayton belted and finally turned. His eyes widened and his eyebrows rose up toward his spiky blond hair when he realized we were standing there enjoying the show.

This was not what I expected to come home to. But on a scale of one to ten, this man's entertainment value scored an eleven. The man had definitely not lost his sex appeal. The tee he wore looked even better from the front, stretched across the miles of muscles of his chest and abdomen. I could even see the hint of a dent at each abdominal brick as the T-shirt fell to the top of his jeans. Even feeling like I'd been run over by a semi couldn't stop the carnal response of my body at seeing such a virile man. My nipples beaded against the flimsy top Mila had brought me to wear, sans bra. I wouldn't be wearing one of those for a while. My mouth went dry as sandpaper while my head throbbed along with the music.

Clayton openly stared. His eyes seemed to rove over every inch of me before stopping at my gaze. "I didn't think you'd be back yet."

"Translation, you didn't think you'd get caught singing

your heart out with a pop god while entertaining a princess." Mila blatantly stated the obvious.

"I'm da queen, Mimi!" Lily hooted, dancing like a loon.

"I mean the queen." She bowed dramatically. "Excuse me, Your Highness." Mila played along with my daughter's game.

Clayton, on the other hand, didn't so much as glance away. No, his entire focus was on me and me alone. "I decided to hang out and keep an eye on things while Atlas picked up clothes for him and Mila." He reached for his phone and shut off the music.

My pounding head thanked him, but I didn't respond. Instead, I swallowed the emotion welling up my throat and clung to the doorjamb for support. The weight of everything that had happened and what I was currently seeing sent a bout of exhaustion through me. I sucked in a breath and tried to be polite. "That was very nice of you. I, uh, can't thank you enough for your help and stepping in when everything went to hell...erm..."

With just a few steps Clayton stood before me, and he enclosed my hands in his. "Monet, I..." He stopped as if he couldn't find the right words before letting out a long breath. "I'm glad you're okay. I was happy to help. Lily is a wonderful kid." He smiled softly, and I watched his full lips spread apart, wondering in another life what it would have felt like to kiss those plump bits of flesh. Maybe if I'd pushed to talk to him at some point between last year and now, shown him I'd been interested, things would be different. Now there was no way he would want a divorcee who'd been damaged beyond repair by a psycho ex.

I shook off the daze and patted his hand, content to focus on my daughter. Anyone complimenting my baby got major kudos in my book. "Thank you. She is."

"Dang, Clay, what smells so good?" Mila lifted the lid off a pot on the stove and sniffed. "We need to keep this guy around, Moe. He can cook!"

Clayton didn't respond. He just continued to stare at me, his eyes traveling from my face to my neck and the bandage. Those crystal-blue eyes turned insanely dark in a second flat, and his jaw hardened.

I squeezed the hands still holding mine. "I'm okay. Thank you for your concern, but really, I'm going to be fine."

"Damn right you are, and I'm going to make sure of it," he growled. His eyes widened as if he didn't mean to voice the sentiment out loud. "I mean..."

I shook my head and patted his hand once more. "It's fine. There are a lot of good guys like you who want to take a jab at my ex right now." I tried to lighten the weight of the moment with a laugh but failed miserably. I just didn't have it in me.

Clayton cleared his throat. "You hungry? Lily and I made some turkey meatballs and spaghetti."

My mouth watered at the reminder of real food. "Yes, starved."

That simple comment seemed to make him happy, if his megawatt smile was anything to go by. "I'm glad, because I've made a feast! Come sit down. Get comfortable."

He curled a hand lightly around my shoulders and led me to the family room. He helped ease me onto the end of the couch where I could easily reach the side table with my left arm. A small gesture but a huge one to me. He'd taken in my condition and accommodated it, making sure I could take care of myself easily. Such a nice guy.

I closed my eyes and settled in slowly, making sure not

to let my stitches press against the back cushion. I should have braced, because the moment I sat down, Hurricane Lily slammed into my chest. Pain ripped through my back as she catapulted into my lap like she normally did.

"Mommy!" she screamed and bounced on me.

"Oomph, my God..." I clenched my teeth and closed my eyes to hold back tears.

Clayton was right there to help. He pulled Lily off me quickly and held her in his huge arms. "Hey, sweetie." He nuzzled her neck which shocked me. "Mommy hurt her back. Remember when Uncle Atlas told you that Mommy was in an accident and got hurt?"

She nodded a bunch of times.

"Well, she has boo-boos there, and they are really tender right now. So how about instead of jumping on Mommy, you try and see how softly you can hug her and give her a kiss, yeah?"

"'Kay, King Clay, I can do that!" She wiggled her body until he set her down in front of me.

She eased in between my legs and put her hands on my cheeks. "You hurt?"

"Yeah, love bug, I am." For the most part, I tried to be honest with Lily. She may have been five years old but I wanted her to know she could trust her mommy.

"I'm going to make you better," she promised in the way that only a child could.

I held her in my arms and glanced up at the man watching me reconnect with my girl. Our eyes met over my daughter's head, and I mouthed, "Thank you," so he'd know I appreciated his concern and patience with Lily.

He nodded and left to go to the kitchen.

"You heard me, Mommy. I gonna make you better. Queen Lily." This statement was more forceful and given with a conviction I understood very well, because she'd gotten that drive and determination from me.

"You already are, baby. You already are." I buried my nose into her neck. The oatmeal-and-lavender bath wash mixed with my daughter's natural scent soothed my senses, and I breathed her in. While I held her close, the last twenty-four hours came at me in a deluge of feelings.

Anger at Kyle for hurting me.

Fear that I could have not only lost my life but lost my daughter.

The injustice of this little girl not having a real father to care about her.

Unease that Kyle had gotten away. This wasn't over. Not even close.

Shivers wracked my frame and tears fell down my cheeks as I thought about the nasty things Kyle had said he planned to do to my daughter in the event of my death. I sent up a prayer to God that he'd shown me mercy and prayed he'd protect her, protect us both.

Kyle was right about one thing and one thing only. Lily was not his daughter and she never would be. I gripped her so tight she cried out.

"Mommy...you hurting me."

I swallowed and forced myself to let her go, my heart pounding a mile a minute. "Sorry, love bug. Mommy just loves you so much." My voice cracked, and I wiped away the tears quickly.

Lily kissed my forehead, smiled, and then scampered off. In that moment, I vowed my daughter would stay a normal, happy child without a care in the world. She didn't seem to have been bothered about the time I spent away or the fact that Clayton had taken care of her. A veritable stranger who had also stayed and made us all dinner. It was as if he'd quickly won her over, or she'd won him over.

Clayton entered the living room and set a dinner tray on the coffee table in front of me, placing the drink on the end table at my side. Then he moved the table closer so I wouldn't have to bend too far to reach it. I watched intently as the muscles of his biceps and forearms bunched and shifted with each lurch of the table. He lifted his face and caught me staring. Like a smooth operator, he winked and made a clicking sound with his tongue.

So sexy.

The pain meds must have been making me loopy. Maybe my hormones were just all over the place. I closed my eyes to dissipate the image of his male strength and block out his suave demeanor so I could focus on the here and now. Food, sponge bath, snuggle time with Lily, and bed, in that order.

When I opened my eyes he was gone, but he'd left a steaming plate of spaghetti and meatballs and a bowl of salad in front of me.

He came back with a napkin. "I didn't know how hungry you'd be, so I loaded you up. I made plenty, and enough sauce for extras, which I thought I'd put into a lasagna so there will be another meal you won't have to make."

What was going on? Why was he even here?

"Clayton, this is amazing, but I don't understand..." Tears filled my eyes and fell down my cheeks, my emotions getting the best of me again. There I sat, a pain-filled, torn-up mess, and this handsome man was being so...

"You don't understand what?" He kneeled down in front of me and placed his hand on my knee.

I winced and sucked in a breath through my teeth when his large palm landed on the abraded skin—still so sensitive, even covered by my pajamas and a bandage.

I gritted through the pain. "Why are you being so nice to me? You don't even know me, and before..."

"Before I was an idiot. I've cured myself of that condition," he murmured. With a delicate touch, Clayton focused on my loose pajama pants and inch by inch raised them up from the ankle until my knee was exposed. The bandages were soiled through.

Clayton groaned. "Jeez-us, Monet. I'm going to need to change these."

"You?" I choked out.

He nodded. "Unless Mila or Atlas has medical training."

"I have medical training," I reminded him.

"Yes, but you can't and shouldn't bend right now. My degree is in sports medicine and fitness. I even did a stint as a paramedic before I found my calling on the fitness side of health."

Now that I had not known. I wondered if Atlas or Mila knew that about him.

"I assure you, Clayton, I can take care of myself." The last thing I needed was this man to think I was weak. I'd been taking care of myself without a man for years and would do it through this situation too.

His head shot up from where he was inspecting my wound. "That you've proven by coming out of this alive. You're not alone. You've got a lot of people who want to help. Let us help you."

"But why do you want to help me? I'm nobody to you."

He pressed one of his hands high on my thigh and squeezed, a supportive, not sexual touch. "You, beautiful, are somebody. A somebody I'm very interested in getting to know more about." He offered a sexy smile.

He thinks I'm beautiful. Did I hear him right or were the drugs way better than I thought?

Mila walked in with Hurricane Lily behind her. "Uh, yeah, so is everything okay?" She put her hands on her hips and smirked at the scene before her.

Clayton didn't move his hand from my thigh. Instead, he rubbed it back and forth, reminding me it was there. "Just making sure our girl is all settled. You good?"

I swallowed and forced myself to stare into his eyes and nod. They were a dark blue that held a flash of excitement. I didn't want to know what that meant. Not right now when I didn't know which way was up, down, left, or right. He stood, winked again, and lifted Lily up into a fireman's carry.

"Queen Lily, you ready for some pasta and meatballs?"

"Yes! King Clay!" she squealed and held on to his ribcage as best she could.

The only other man I'd seen her this free with was Atlas, and he'd had to earn her affection. Of course, he'd done so in spades with his silly shenanigans and free spirit, but after two days, which really was only a handful of hours, Clayton had done the impossible. He'd managed to get my girl to open up to him. Nicholas, our friend from the yoga studio, had made strides with Lily, and she liked him, but mostly she could take or leave the guy. Clayton came in and overnight had won her over. I didn't know what that said about him as a man, but it didn't hurt his appeal. Not that it mattered. He didn't want me a year ago; he most certainly wouldn't want the mess I was now. After he left today, I'd probably not see him again.

The second they were out of the room, Mila swooped in. "I see you're *our girl* now. Hmmm, sounds intriguing."

I rolled my eyes at her. "Don't you start."

She jutted her head back and raised her arms in a placating gesture. "Who, me? I would never!" she mocked dramatically.

"Mila, stop. It's nothing. He's just being nice. Helpful to a broken woman who was attacked. Good guys do that sort of thing." I sighed knowing it was the truth. Clayton's sudden interest in me would wane the second he left. As it should.

"If that's nothing, then my ass is nothing, and we both know my ass is something. Something bangin'. What I just witnessed was a man falling over himself to take care of you. A sexy-as-fuck wall of muscle with insane blue eyes that didn't leave your face for a second."

I ignored her ramble and picked up my fork, cutting into a golf-ball-sized meatball. Steam puffed out of the center, sending a burst of garlic and oregano to my eager senses. I took a bite and moaned around the perfectly seasoned meat. It was soft, hot, and spiced to perfection.

"And he can cook. Let's not forget that little tidbit, not that I could."

Thoughtfully, I chewed and sampled several bites. "You are not wrong. The man can cook. But why is he here? I don't get it."

Mila raised her face to the sky. "Lord, please tell me my best friend isn't this dumb. Did you give her all the book smarts and none of the common-sense smarts?" She waited a moment, staring at the white expanse of the ceiling. "Nothing? You're telling me nothing. Fine." Mila sighed and pursed her lips, focusing on me. "Moe, when a man likes a girl, he does things for said girl. Like watch her kid, take care of her, cook her and her bestie dinner."

I pointed the fork at her. "I get where you're going with this, but frankly, it doesn't make sense. Last year he hit on me and then...poof...disappeared into thin air. And from what I heard from the gals at Lotus House, he's a bit of a player. I don't need that in my life. Lily doesn't need that in her life. And besides, now look at me." I bit down on my lip, not wanting to remember how Kyle had damaged me this time. As if leaving me brokenhearted and my daughter fatherless wasn't enough.

"I am looking at you. What are you trying to say?"

"Don't you see? Even after I heal, I'm always going to be scarred, always going to have an ex who tried to kill me and didn't want the daughter we created. I'm always going to be lacking. If it's not this new problem, it will be something else."

"Lily's father is a sperm donor. Let's not forget that."

"You're missing the point, Mila." I set the fork down and placed my shaky hands on my thighs, bracing through the pain and the devastation that rushed to the surface once more.

Mila eased over to me on the couch and grabbed my hand. "I do understand. But I'm here to tell you, you're going to be fine. The stitches are going to come out, the cops are going to get that rat bastard, and life will go on. Who's to say that life can't go on with a sexy fitness trainer type on the sidelines ready to be tagged in for the game of his life?"

I laughed and brought her hands up to my lips and kissed the back of each. "You're a good friend. Delusional, but the greatest."

"Well, yeah, I'm the bestest. Ask Lily, she'll tell you." She grinned, and I smiled in return.

Clayton walked back in holding a second steaming plate and set it on the table in front of Mila. "Soup's on for you," he said to Mila.

"If you don't keep him, can I have him?" Mila whispered, picking up her plate and practically drooling at the feast in front of her eyes.

The abrupt chuckle spilled from my lips, stopping Clayton on his trek back into the kitchen. He placed his large, warm hand on the ball of my good shoulder and squeezed. "Like hearing that, beautiful."

I closed my eyes and let that small touch sink in just enough to keep my strength up. When I was alone in my bed, I'd let it go, knowing that regardless of what was happening right now, it would all change. Eventually, he'd see I was no longer the catch he thought I was. Like last year, he'd up and leave the same way Kyle did, and then where would I be?

Where would Lily be?

No, it wasn't a good idea to go handing my heart to every sweet guy who lent me a hand.

Soon, Clayton would realize I wasn't worth the effort, and he'd back off. If I had to guess, under all his bravado was a gentle soul, one who wanted to take care of women, especially ones who'd been hurt. Probably in his genetic makeup, because even though I'd heard he dated a lot of women, I'd not heard that he'd been careless or hurtful to them.

We ate for a solid fifteen minutes until a wave of nausea and fatigue swept over me. Clayton entered just as I swayed, my body losing its battle with exhaustion.

"Whoa, whoa, hey there. You all right?"

I blinked a few times and shook my head. "Tired. So tired."

"Let's get you to your room. Mila, can you help her with

a sponge bath? I'll change her bandages." He took charge as if it was his duty as well as his right. I didn't have the strength or desire to argue.

Mila's eyes widened, and she put her plate down, wiped her hands over her thighs, and stood. "Yes, sir."

Dazed, I was led into the bathroom, where Clayton helped me get settled on the cushy stool tucked under the bathroom vanity. He made sure I was situated and turned on the water in the sink, testing it every few seconds until it was the right temperature. While the sink was filling, he moved through the bathroom as if he'd been doing so forever, opening and closing the cupboards until he found a washrag. The man was so capable. I could have told him where everything was, but my meds were finally kicking in. With the addition of a belly full of protein and carbs... I needed sleep, *real* sleep. The kind I could only get in my bed after such a horrendous experience.

Mila entered the bathroom and set a dark-purple pajama tank and a matching pair of skimpy silk shorts on the vanity. I wanted to groan at the choice she'd made but realized she hadn't chosen those to mess with me or make me look sexy for Clayton. They needed access to my wounds, and this would be the best option for frequent bandage changes.

"Okay, I'll step out while you wash her. Don't get the stitches wet. If you're uncomfortable, I can wash around them. Got it?" He addressed my best friend as if she was his soldier, not our friend.

Mila quietly nodded and submerged the cloth a few times in the soapy water. Clayton shut the door to give us privacy.

"Thank you for your help. I'm sure the last thing you want to be doing is giving your friend a bath." I frowned and lifted my good arm, which she took into her capable hand.

With precise, careful movements, Mila hummed and took to the task of cleansing me. I washed my privates and then eased into the panties and silk shorts with her help.

"What about the back?" Her voice shook and her eyes filled with tears. I held my hair over one shoulder.

I watched her reflection in the mirror as her gaze ran over every vile inch of the unbandaged surface of my once-flawless skin. She started at the top of my shoulder blade and then moved slowly down to my hip. Mila's entire body trembled as she half choked, half hiccupped. I watched her break in half in front of my eyes, her sorrow at what happened becoming too much for her. That's when she dropped the cloth in the sink, hovered over the vanity, both hands gripping the edge, and sobbed, her shoulders shaking mightily with the effort.

"I'm sorry." I clenched my teeth and let the emotional pain shred my insides until I could get my voice in check. "I'm okay. Really, I am." I wanted to sound confident and strong, but my words sounded weak and tired.

"No, Moe, you're not." Mila wiped at her eyes with both hands, grabbed a tissue, and blew her nose.

I clenched my hand into fists and tried to hold on to my composure. "No, but I will be."

More than anything, I hoped it was the truth.

CHAPTER FOUR

HEART
C H A K R A

The heart chakra is where the physical and spiritual meet. It's located at the center of the chest and includes the heart, cardiac plexus, thymus gland, lungs, and breasts. It also rules the lymphatic system.

CLAYTON

The second I heard the gut-wrenching sob echo through Monet's partially open bathroom door, I'd had enough of being separated. I couldn't say what catapulted me in there or what was keeping me in this house with this woman. All I knew was wild horses couldn't make me leave.

I *had* to be here.

Had to.

She needed me.

Slowly I opened the door, trying to remain as calm and collected as possible. Directly across from me, Monet clutched a towel to her bare torso with one hand. Her other hand was on Mila's back, soothing her. Of course she'd be comforting everyone else. Making sure the people who loved her were taken care of first.

Selfless.

The woman was so goddamned selfless. I'd never met a person quite like her, and the knowledge, the crushing intensity that I probably never would again, blasted me from the tips of my toes to the top of my spiky hair. I ground my teeth and patted Mila's shoulder.

"I'm sorry, honey. I'm okay. Really, I am," Monet cooed soft as a whisper to her friend.

"No, Moe, you're not." Her tone was hard and unrelenting.

Monet lifted her head and her coal-black eyes found mine. In that one look I gave her what I could. Friendship. Hope. Determination. I could have sworn those eyes answered back with gratitude.

Without wavering from my gaze she answered her friend. "No, but I will be."

Damn straight, I wanted to say but didn't. This situation was going nowhere fast, and my woman needed to sleep.

My woman.

Where the fuck that thought came from I didn't know. Everything about Monet called to me on a primal level. The need—no, freaking desperate desire—to help her and take care of her, wound around my chest like a vise and locked down. At that moment, I shoved it back into the recesses of my mind where I could bat at it later, when I could figure out why my feelings for this woman were so strong and sudden. Christ. I knew I had liked everything about her last year, but seeing her again, meeting her kid, spending time with this family... It was screwing with my head. Making me want things I didn't know were possible so soon. And that was the problem. It was all too soon. Too fast. I needed to cool my jets and take it easy with her.

Still, she needed to be fixed up, and I was the best person for the job. At least I kept telling myself that. "I've got her. Go on and take care of Lily," I suggested.

Mila sniffed, grabbed a tissue from the box, wiped her nose, and nodded. I led Monet back to the vanity, centered the stool in the middle of the large bathroom, and pointed at it. "Sit."

Her bare feet and mile-long legs moved elegantly in front of me. When she sat and I was sure she wouldn't fall off the chair, I grabbed the washcloth Mila had abandoned, sopped up some suds, and wrung it out. Then I went to Monet's back.

A long, somewhat jagged line scaled to the right of the sacral dimples near her lower back and trim waist all the way up her right side, curving crookedly at the very wing of her shoulder blade. Making a point not to wince—the last thing she needed to see right now—I ran the edge of the washcloth along the puffed-up skin and near the black sutures to clear the povidone the medical team had used.

Fire licked at the frayed edges of my nerves as I silently cleaned the length of her back. Monet sat ramrod straight and didn't so much as flinch. That courage and determination showed the strength of her character. Though, with enough adversity, even the strongest could fall. Eventually, the reality of what happened to her would fester like an open wound and drive her to a rocky edge. I wanted to be the one to catch her when she fell. *Would she let me?*

"How are you feeling?" I asked.

She sighed, her shoulders sinking with each pass of the cloth. "Fine."

I waited, knowing that her mind was probably working a mile a minute—or shutting down.

"No, that isn't right." Her voice cracked and rose with her ire. "I'm *not* fine. I'm tired. Bone tired. Weary. And so angry. Angry at Kyle and at myself."

I flinched and clenched my teeth, trying to take the edge off my frustration. "At yourself? You had nothing to do with this man's actions. You cannot take on that blame."

Monet shook her head and cringed as I dabbed lightly at what looked like a tender spot. Gooseflesh popped up all over her skin, and I wanted nothing more than to kiss every inch of her exposed back and neck. My instinct was to show her affection, ease her mind and body. Warm her up. Even after being attacked, with abrasions and scratches all over her olive skin, her hair tangled and dirty, she was still the most gorgeous woman I'd ever had the pleasure of looking at.

Her back was long, lean, and arched seductively. Her toned legs curved deliciously in the right places. An image of those limbs wrapped high around my hips as I pounded into her from above skittered across my mind—an unwanted but not unpleasant image.

Shit, Clay. Get your mind out of the gutter. The woman needed me to be there for her, not fantasize about her in the sack.

"But I can't help it," she continued. "I'm the one who married him. I'm the one he cheated on and left." She twined her fingers around one another in a nervous gesture.

I scoffed on a growl. She honest to God blamed herself. Had some kind of twisted rationale flapping around in her head that it was her fault. I groaned. She couldn't possibly believe she was unworthy of a good man. The concept of any man leaving this gorgeous woman and her adorable child did not seem anywhere near the realm of reality.

"Yeah." She blew out a fast breath through her lips. "And you know who he chose to cheat with and leave me for?"

Physically I braced, knowing that whatever she said was going to piss me off beyond compare. "Who?"

She lifted her face and met my gaze in the mirror. Her eyes were glassy saucers of hurt and pain. "My baby sister. The black sheep and soil on my family's good name. And I haven't spoken to her since." Her lip trembled, and I wanted so badly to kiss away that wound, give her something better to look forward to.

Jeez-us. Her douche ex-husband had left her for her sister. Proved the man was indeed insane. I considered myself a good judge of character and I knew a solid and beautiful woman when I saw one. Monet Holland was that and more. The whole enchilada.

"And Lily? He doesn't see his daughter?" A protective spur tightened the muscles of my free hand. I tried to loosen my fist, but the biting anger over a man leaving his child filled me with disgust. When I thought I was going to be a father, I couldn't have been happier. My buddy Trent lost his mind over Viv being pregnant with his baby, in a good way. Atlas just found out about his impending fatherhood, and he couldn't take his hands or eyes off his woman's stomach. The right man would feel pride in his young.

Monet shook her head. "That's just it. We couldn't conceive

naturally. We tried for two years, and it never happened. Then finally, I got him to agree to get checked out. Turned out his swimmers were few and far between."

"Okay...but it obviously worked because I've been hanging out with the queen for two days." I waggled my eyebrows dramatically in an attempt to lighten the heaviness of our chat.

Monet smiled at my nickname for Lily. Technically it was a nickname the little one had given herself.

"Yes, but Lily is a product of a sperm bank and me. At the time it seemed like the best option. Once Lily was born, Kyle didn't want anything to do with her. He rarely held her, never did any of the normal things fathers do, like rock her to sleep, change her diapers, or feed her. By the time she turned a year old, he hardly looked at her."

I closed my eyes and placed one hand at the nape of Monet's neck. "I'm sorry. There aren't words that can describe the level of revulsion I have for your ex."

"Get in line." She chuckled.

That small laugh filled my soul with happiness. Piece by piece, word by word, this woman was worming her way into my heart without even trying.

Realizing that I was getting far too close much too soon, I backed away and tossed the washrag into the sink, pulled the plug, and let the water drain out. "Now we need to bandage. Tomorrow, during the day, you may want to give the stitches some air time."

"Yeah, that's what the doctor said too." She clutched the towel in front of her chest.

I focused on all the hospital supplies Mila had placed on the counter. Gauze and medical tape for her back. Neosporin for her knees, elbows, and palms.

"I'm going to start with your back. I'll put them on pretty loose."

"Thank you, Clay. I don't know how to..." Her voice shook, as did her body. The woman needed rest and time. Time to heal and to deal with the severity of what had happened to her.

Once more, I placed my hand on the crook of her neck, only I brought my face eye level. With my thumb, I caressed the apple of her cheek. A spattering of freckles fanned across her nose and cheeks like a dusting of cinnamon. So pretty. "I want to be here. You do not need to keep thanking me. For reasons I can't explain, that I'm not exactly sure of...I just...uh... need to. Okay?"

Her eyes widened, and she licked her plump lips. They looked so soft and inviting. What I wouldn't give to press my own against them just once, but it wasn't the right time. When I kissed Monet Holland it would be because she was aching for it, and the look in her eyes would be one of excitement not uncertainty.

"Monet, not only are you part of the family of friends I've built in this area, you're a good woman. A kind, loving mother, and someone I want very much to get to know better. Is that okay with you?"

She swallowed and inhaled softly before answering. "Yes."

"You going to stop thanking me for doing what I feel is necessary?" I cocked one eyebrow for emphasis.

She licked her lips. "Yes."

"Is yes all you can say?"

Monet smiled huge, the first true smile I'd seen since I laid eyes on her earlier this evening. It was the same one that'd had my nuts in a twist when I met her last year.

"You're making me nervous." Her reply was breathy and

sexy as hell.

I inched closer, leaving only a dozen centimeters between our faces. I could feel her warm breath against my lips and chin. Her eyes were dark pools I wanted to gaze into forever. "Nervous good or nervous bad?"

"I don't know," she admitted. Honesty. I hadn't had many honest women catch my eye.

I grinned, and she bit into her bottom lip. *Jeez-us.* So sexy, and without even trying. Her beauty, honesty, and adorable mini-Moe running around... I knew without a doubt I was a goner. I'd take it easy and give her time, although frankly not a lot of it, because I wasn't a man who wasted precious weeks messing around when what I'd always wanted was sitting right in front of me.

"Beautiful, I think you do know. Do you feel safe?"

She sucked in a sharp breath. "Right now?"

I nodded.

"Yes."

"There is that one word again." I bent forward and laid a long kiss to the apple of her cheek right next to my thumb. "You never have to be afraid of me. Ever."

She held my hand against her face. "You make me feel safe."

"But nervous too?" I confirmed.

"Yeah."

I winked. "I can work with that." Needing to put my lips on her somewhere, touch her skin one more time, I pressed my mouth to her temple. I stayed a moment, taking in her natural jasmine scent and the soap Mila had used to bathe her. For a minute too long, I breathed her in, soaking in her presence, silently making a promise to protect her with my entire being.

Unwillingly, I pulled back. "Let's get you bandaged up and in bed."

She nodded and smiled. "Okay. Thank you for being here."

"Nowhere else I'd rather be."

★ ★ ★

After I bandaged her back, treated her knees, elbows, and hands, and bandaged those, I helped ease the sleep tank back over her head. I helped her into bed, noting the side she used was opposite the one I used at home. Interesting and weird to notice such a thing, but fuck if I cared. It was just one more aspect of her that made us seem like we'd be a perfect fit.

"Can you get Lily, please?" Monet asked once she was settled.

"Sure. Would you like some tea or anything? Do you have tea?" I remembered belatedly I wasn't in my own home.

"No, thank you. I'm about to drop, but I do want to say good night to my love bug."

"I'll be right back."

I found the queen wrestling with Atlas in the living room. Lily completed a complicated twist, and lying sideways over his abdomen, pinned Atlas on the floor.

"You got me, munchkin. You win." Atlas kicked his feet and waved his hands in pretend agony.

"Bingo!" she hollered, and I laughed.

"Excuse me, Queen Lily, your mother would like to see you in her room. She's about to go to bed."

"Oh, she is?" Mila jumped up. "I need to go back and tell her I'm sorry for breaking down like that." Her pretty face and brown eyes saddened as she worried her bottom lip.

I set an arm around her shoulder. "She knows you love her and worry about her. I don't think she needs an apology. But she probably does want to give you instructions about Lily for the night."

Atlas stood and scoffed. "Dude, not like we don't already know, man. We practically lived here on and off for a year. We don't need to be instructed by you."

For a second, a flicker of irritation sizzled at the base of my neck before it dawned on me he had a point. Not realizing how far I'd gone, I was taking charge of this woman's life, and I didn't exactly have that clout. Not yet anyway. I definitely planned on gaining access and soon. Something inside me was going straight caveman possessive over this woman. Hell, now that I'd spent two days with Lily, I felt downright possessive of her too.

I rubbed the back of my neck where the irritation at the situation and my reaction sat. "Shit, man, I'm sorry. I don't know what's gotten into me." I did know, but I wasn't ready or willing to admit it to my buddy just then.

Atlas's curls flopped over his forehead as he made his way from his impromptu wresting match with Lily. "It's cool." He clapped me on the back. "You care for her. You did a while ago, and apparently this tragedy is pushing your buttons and giving you a much-needed kick to the nuts." He smirked.

I chuckled. "Think so?" It made sense. Tragedy brings up a variety of responses in people. Some handle it well, others not so much. I, apparently, turned into Tarzan, and Monet was my Jane.

"Know so. If anything like that had happened to Mila, I'd have lost my shit, and that's after being with her for a year. Does this mean you're going to become a regular fixture around the

Holland household?"

Atlas's question was direct and no-nonsense. I appreciated that side of him. No-holds-barred all the time.

I didn't even take a second to consider it. My answer flew out of my mouth unfiltered and honest. "Yes, it does."

"Cool. She needs a good guy giving a shit about her. It's been a while for her, and after what happened, I don't know how easy it is going to be for her to trust again."

Trust.

I tipped my head and checked out my Nikes. "Good thing I know a little something about that particular issue."

Atlas nodded but didn't question me further. Now was not the time to dredge up old wounds with my friend.

"Should I expect this to mean you're going to drop your one-nighters and cling-ons?"

I frowned and gritted my teeth. "Look, my bedroom activities are not up for debate here." He didn't know jack shit. Just because I didn't bring women around my friends didn't mean I'd only had one-nighters. Most of the women I dated I saw at least three or four times, but the last several were gold-digging trophy women. They didn't want to settle down, have a family. I was thirty years old, had a steady career, a secure future, and I wanted a woman to share it with. Build on.

Atlas scowled. "Fuck if they're not. If you're going to go after a woman I consider my sister, you're going to look me in the eye and promise me she's the only one you'll be seeing. Moe deserves that. She is not a button on your speed-dial list of hotties to hook up with. Feel me?" Atlas's tone had turned hard and acidic.

I couldn't blame the guy for being protective. She brought that shit out in a guy. I'd been in her house two days and was half-gone for the woman and her kid. Besides, I agreed with him. Monet was not the type of woman to be strung along. "Wouldn't do that to her, man. And yeah, she's going to be the only woman on my mind for a good long while...okay?"

He stared me down, not letting up. Damn, he had this brother role on lock. "And you're going to take it slow," he stated, not questioned.

I frowned. "What is this, therapy hour with Atlas? What happened to bros before hoes?"

Wrong thing to say. Atlas's eyes turned as hard as steel. "Don't ever refer to Moe in that manner."

"Christ, dude. I was joking. Lighten up."

Atlas shrugged. "Can't. She's important to me and my future wife. What happens to her directly affects us. As you can see." He displayed an arm out and around the room. This was a home away from home for them. Something I wanted for myself. I couldn't blame him.

"Man, I'm not going to hurt her. Any numbers in my phone will lie uncalled while Monet and I feel this out."

"And you'll take it slow?" he asked again.

"I'm not an asshole. I was just in there cleaning and bandaging her wounds. That ex of hers did a number on her. She hasn't even entered the first stage of her mental recovery. She's too busy dealing with the physical pain and making sure everyone else is okay. But I'm not a stranger to this. She's going to flip her lid and soon. Once she allows herself to deal with what happened, truly understand that she almost died and that her ex-husband tried to kill her, she's going to need every one of us to help her through."

"We'll be there," Atlas proclaimed.

"So will I." I glared, making sure he understood how

serious I was about this woman.

"Fair enough. I'm gonna go say good night and get Lily settled for bed. You heading out?"

Was I heading out? Fuck. I didn't want to, but they needed time alone together as a family.

"Yeah, I'll follow you and say good night."

As we approached Monet's bedroom, I finally took a moment to take this side of the house in. The hallway was lined with pictures of Monet and Lily, Mila and Atlas, and some of the yoga staff too. Another wall had black-and-white photos of people I assumed were Monet's parents and grandparents. Where were they in all this? I'd have to ask Monet when she was feeling better. A spark of excitement skittered around my chest. For the first time in a long time, I wanted to know more about a woman. Was looking forward to hearing about her past and her family as well as sharing my own. Hell, if this went the way I thought it was headed, I'd be taking her and Lily home to my own family one day. My mother would be ecstatic.

Both Mila and Lily were in bed with Monet. She was lying on her good side, with Lily in the center telling them a story and Mila looking on.

I took that time to enjoy the sight of the three ladies on the bed. If Monet hadn't been hurt, the scene would have been right out of a family movie. Atlas went over, sat next to Monet's feet, and put a hand on her ankle.

"How you doing, sis?" he asked.

"I'm good. Really good now that I'm clean, bandaged, and in bed with my girls." She blinked sleepily.

The bed had a bright-white comforter, but the walls were a deep burgundy. Above her bed was a mirror with a gilded frame. The center of the ceiling was inset and had a small dangling chandelier that splintered sparkles of soft light around the ceiling in a flower-like shape. The carpet was soft beige, and she had a Turkish-style area rug under the bed. A comfortable-looking pinkish-colored ottoman spanned the bottom of the bed. A pair of slippers were tucked neatly under it. The furniture was dark cherry with gold knobs that complemented the style of the room. Monet definitely had good taste. Elegant and classy but not overdone.

Made me wonder what she'd think of my bachelor pad. It definitely wasn't a home but more a place to crash, with all the creature comforts a guy needed. Black leather sofas, TVs, stereo, game system, and after Atlas had moved out, I converted my spare bedroom to a home gym.

While I scanned the top of Monet's dressers, mostly finding pictures of Lily and Mila, I thought about how much I'd like coming home from a long day to a bedroom like this. To a charming woman like the one lying in bed. My gaze landed on hers.

"You all settled?" I asked lamely.

"Yes. Again, thank you."

I groaned. "Stop thanking me. You've used up your allotment of that word this week."

She smiled and rested her head on the pillow. Unable to stop my forward motion, I made it to the side of her bed, tunneled my hand in the crook of her neck and shoulder, and kissed her forehead and then her cheek. I may have pressed my lips to her face a little too long, because out of nowhere, Lily had reached over and bonked my head.

"Ouch!" I laughed, rubbing at my temple.

"Where's my kiss, Clay?" Lily blinked several times, her sweet little face innocent and happy.

I laughed, got close, and kissed the pretty girl on the forehead.

Her brow furrowed and she pointed at her cheek. "And here. Like on Mommy."

Again, I kissed her cheek. "You good, Queen Lily?"

She nodded and flailed back.

"You remember what I said about being really careful around Mommy?"

"I 'member."

"You re-mem-ber," I sounded out for her.

"'S'wat I said." She frowned. "I 'member. Be careful wif Mommy 'cuz she's hurt."

"That's right, sweetie."

"Will you come back tomorrow and make dinner? I want mac and cheese." Her demand was succinct and thoughtful.

I laughed. "You've had pasta two days in a row."

Her nose crinkled when she responded. "I luv pasta!"

She smiled huge, and it melted my heart. Yep, this little girl had me wrapped around her pinky finger already.

"Yes, I gathered that." I ruffled her dark hair. "How about I come over and make tacos? Does that sound good to everyone?"

Mila and Atlas chimed in at the same time. "Hell yes!" Then they laughed, and Atlas covered Mila's hand.

"Uh, before Clay goes, Mila, I believe you had something you wanted to tell the family yesterday," Atlas prompted, sitting up straighter.

My eyes widened. "I, uh, I can go." I moved backward a couple steps to head out, and Atlas grabbed my wrist.

"No, man. Stay. This is the good part." He winked. I already knew what she was going to say because he'd told me, but being included and hearing it officially, in a family environment, made my heart pound double time.

Mila kneeled ceremoniously on the bed, placed both hands over her belly, and looked at Monet. "You're going to be an auntie! We're pregnant," she said happily.

Monet grabbed Mila's hand and squeezed. "I'm so excited for you guys."

Atlas grinned so wide I could see his gums. Lucky bastard. At least he had a woman who wouldn't lie about carrying his child and take him for a ride. Mila loved him and was good people. They both were. Still, it grinded my gears when I was reminded of that time in my life years ago.

"What's pweg-nant mean?" Lily asked.

"Means Auntie Mimi is going to have a baby," Monet offered to Lily. "I'm so happy for you two. This is amazing news."

Monet yawned sleepily. I could tell she was about to fall asleep any minute.

Lily's blue eyes widened so big I could have gone swimming in those excited pools. "You got a baby? Where? I wanna see it!" She jumped on the bed, ready to bolt to wherever this magical baby was.

We all laughed while Mila tugged an arm around Lily's waist, pulled her into a hug, and kissed her neck a bunch of times until Lily squealed in delight. "No, silly. The baby is growing in my belly. We have to wait for just about seven months before the baby is here."

Lily pushed back and scrambled down to put her face near Mila's abdomen. She poked it experimentally. "It's in there?"

"Yep. And I'm going to get all round and big!"

Her lips pursed as she placed her ear to it.

"What are you doing, love bug?" Monet asked.

"Trying to hear it. Be quiet," she admonished. Then her eyes got big again. "I think I hearded a swish swish. My baby is in there!"

"Already laying claim, munchkin? I think that's *my baby* in there," Atlas said proudly.

A spike of jealousy slammed into me once again. Several years ago that had been me. Happy and elated that I was going to be a father. Until the lying bitch took the dream away.

I shook off the old wound and focused on the group in front of me. Lily was still arguing with Atlas about who got the baby when it was born as I came back to the here and now.

"Well, congrats, guys. I'm going to head out. I'll be back with the fixings for dinner tomorrow. Give you guys a break. Monet, I can change your bandages then too."

She smiled and closed her eyes. With her eyes closed, looking like she did not have a care in the world, she was unearthly exquisite. Maybe one day I could be the one to see that look on her face while I was lying in bed beside her.

CHAPTER FIVE

HEART
C H A K R A

You may have a closed heart chakra if you are feeling bitterness and anger toward those you have perceived as having wronged you. In order to open your heart chakra you must release that anger, forgive yourself and others without condition, and truly let go.

MONET

I adored Mila and Atlas. *Loved* them. So much so I couldn't imagine not having them as part of my life. But with my heart shredded and my psyche having taken the motherlode of hits, the last thing I wanted to see was a couple in love flaunting their happy selves all over my house.

I was wretched. A horrible friend. Downright loser material.

As I made my way through the kitchen and past the couple canoodling on my couch, I physically gagged. This was not like me. I'd always been the world's biggest proponent of love. Finding it. Keeping it. Working hard at relationships because I believed wholeheartedly that anything worth having took work. Love was no different. And I know I did my best with Kyle. Doted on him the way a loving wife should. Only, he never returned that affection.

But when it came right down to it, I'd failed at love. Failed miserably. A shot of guilt warring with anger sliced straight through my back where a tender patch of my wound stung. Not the first painful reminder that the man I had loved more than my next breath didn't love me back. In fact, he loved me so little he'd taken a knife to me in hate.

For what?

I lifted up a coffee cup and filled it with the nectar of the gods. My hands shook like I was a frail hundred-year-old woman. I set the cup down and rested my arms on the counter in front of me, bracing myself for the onslaught of emotions that tore me apart one flash of memory at a time.

Kyle tried to kill me.

Breathe, Moe. Calm down.

He tried to kill me for money. Money.

Anger and disgust coated my heart, and I broke out in a misting of fine sweat. I could feel a tremble start in my toes and work its way up my legs, through my body, and out to my fingertips. I gripped the rounded edge of the counter.

What was it he'd said? So the money would go to the right person? He must have been talking about my sister, Matisse.

A shiver catapulted me into the past.

★ ★ ★

Kyle entered the lawyer's office. At first I was surprised to see him. Hopeful, even, that he'd come at such a sad time in my life. My grandparents had both passed, and I was the lone living relative sitting in their lawyer's office for the reading of the will. I'd gotten everything. My family had not intended anything for Matisse. But I had a plan. I'd create a separate trust for her. I had more money than I needed or could ever use in this lifetime. Maybe if she didn't have to worry about money, we could focus on building our relationship. With our dad somewhere working, focusing on himself as usual, pretending he didn't have a family he'd left behind, Matisse was all I had left.

And then she walked in behind Kyle, holding his hand. They both stopped in front of me, smarmy grins on their faces. To say I was shocked to see Matisse with my ex-husband would have been putting it mildly. I knew he'd been fond of her, but not this fond.

"Matisse? Kyle? What are you doing here?" I questioned, tearfully watching their body language, trying to vanquish any negative thoughts before they could rise to the surface.

"Don't be dense, Moe. I'm with Kyle." She laid a hand over his abdomen and nestled in close. He wrapped an arm around her shoulders. "Once he left your sorry ass, I picked up the pieces of his broken heart and made him mine." She blinked flirtatiously.

The weight that hit my chest was devastating. "No." I shook my head, not wanting to believe it was true. My sister wouldn't betray me like that. Not after everything I'd done for her over the years.

Kyle smirked. "You knew I liked Matisse. Hell, I was

fucking her the entire time we were married. Why did you think I always wanted her to come visit? So I could crawl between her sexy thighs while you were sleeping." He snorted. *"I had Matisse on every surface of our home before I left you to trade up for a better model. And look at her. She's everything you could never be. Now it's time to get her back the money she deserves. Excuse us while we talk to the lawyer."*

★ ★ ★

Vomit crawled up my throat, and I barely staved it off as I gripped the tile. My stomach churned with the vile memory.

Breathe, Monet. Let it all go. That was the past; this is the present. You don't want Kyle. He's not the right man for you, and if you think back, he never was.

I had pushed her, their betrayal, and every attachment I'd had to my sister to the darkest recesses of my mind the second she walked into our lawyer's office with my ex-husband's hand in hers. Except it didn't work.

Matisse was my father's illegitimate child. I only learned of her existence when I was eleven years old and she was eight. For years, my father lived two lives. He had Mom and me, and at some point a couple years after they had me, my father wooed and impregnated his mistress. For a decade, he'd been unfaithful to our mother. Until that fateful day when Matisse's mother died in a car accident. All our lives changed in an instant. My father admitted his transgressions, explained the circumstances to my mother and me, and apologized profusely. Then he asked my mother to take in Matisse and raise her as her own.

My mother, saint that she was, took in his daughter and

lavished her with love. My mother's parents, on the other hand, had not accepted her. They were very old-fashioned and strict about familial ties. Matisse was not welcomed into their arms or their estate. She didn't share blood with my mother, nor did my mother adopt her; therefore, she was not included in the will. The lawyer correctly pointed out that Matisse had no standing to challenge the will. This infuriated Matisse and Kyle.

My hand shook as I lifted the coffee to my lips and took a sip. The smooth Columbian flavor settled over my tongue, and I sighed, thankful to be alive.

Alive.

Just the other night I was close to death on the cold black pavement of the parking garage. My knees and elbows throbbed with the beat of my heart at the memory. I practiced my yoga breathing as the visions took over.

Kyle's knees pressing into my lower back felt like an anchor holding me down.

The forceful tug of my hair so tight, pieces ripped out from the roots.

Blood oozing down around my hands, sticking to my clothes, and pooling around my body.

The first bite of the knife as it pierced the skin of my neck.

Screaming.

"Help me! Please!" I opened my mouth and screamed at the top of my lungs.

"Monet! Moe! Please, please come back!" Someone was yelling. At first it sounded far away. The sound echoed down a long length, like it was traveling down a tunnel to reach me.

"Mommy, Mommy!"

Oh my God, my daughter. I looked around but couldn't

see anything but the garage. "Lily!" I cried out. "Where's my daughter?"

"Mommy! Please, Mommy!" I couldn't see her. Kyle must have had her. He took her like he said he would.

No. No. No.

"Moe!"

Hands around my shoulders. Fingers digging into my biceps.

"Monet! Honey, please!"

Hands around my neck. I can't breathe. He's killing me!

"No, no, let me go. Don't touch me!" I screeched until a burning sensation and a crash around my feet broke me out of my hallucination. Kyle had been here, holding me down, trying to get to me again. Only, he was gone, the dark garage replaced with the bright light of my kitchen. I blinked several times trying to rid my mind of the fear and anxiety ricocheting through me.

I trembled hard as my vision wavered. A burning sensation sizzled against my bare feet. I looked around and found Mila, with tears running down her cheeks, holding a crying Lily to her chest. Atlas was standing in front of me with his arms out, as if he was about to wrestle a wild animal but was trying to calm it first.

My body shook as if I was being vibrated from the inside out by a giant machine. Then my teeth started to chatter, and I couldn't catch my breath.

Atlas moved closer, his arms and hands extended in front of him. "That's it, Monet. It's just me. Atlas. You're safe. We're here for you, honey. And you're safe. Kyle is not here. He's not here. No one is going to touch you or hurt you."

"Mommy!" Lily cried out again.

I looked down at the coffee splattered all over the ground, the porcelain cup shattered in tiny pieces everywhere.

"I think I just had a panic attack," I said right before blackness swept into my vision and blurred out the edges. Atlas locked an arm around my waist before I completely lost it. He led me to the couch and sat me down. Once I was seated, he kneeled and pressed his forehead to mine.

"Breathe, sis, and watch me. Keep your eyes open and look at me. Inhale for four beats, and then exhale for four beats. Follow my breathing." He used the same voice he used in the yoga classes he once taught. Melodic, tranquil. I followed along willingly.

For a few minutes, we breathed together until I felt my heart rate decrease, the sweat on my neck and brow cool, and the trembling abate.

"Mommy?" Lily said from across the room.

I inhaled slowly and pushed back from Atlas. "Thank you. I'm better now."

"Flashback?" He stood and stepped away.

"I think so, but it was more random and disjointed. Honestly, I'm not really sure what that was exactly." The fact that it was on the heels of the memory of Kyle and Matisse at the law office made it worse. I knew between the betrayal of my sister and the attack from Kyle, I was no longer operating on a healthy level.

"Mommy?" Lily said again in her small voice, a hint of fear and concern making it sound deeper.

"Come here, baby," I said, holding my arms out.

She flew into my arms, and the pain of her embrace blasted through me, but I choked back the cry and instead gritted my teeth waiting for the pain to abate. Lily was more important. She pushed her tear-stained, stricken face directly into my neck.

I petted her hair slowly and hummed the way I did when she was scared. Same as I'd done while rocking her as a baby. "I'm okay, honey. Mommy just had a bad daydream."

"Like a monster dream? Did you see a scary one?" She pulled her face back, and her blue eyes widened as she focused on me.

"Yeah, baby. Scariest monster ever." A tremor skittered down my spine.

"And his name was Kyle?" she asked.

Crap. I didn't want her knowing what had happened and who had hurt me. That was the last connection I ever wanted her to make, not that she remembered Kyle anyway.

"Don't worry your pretty little head about Mommy's monster, okay? Just know that sometimes mommies get scared too. But having you in my arms makes it all better."

My daughter offered a wide, toothy smile. "Can I have pam cakes?" she asked out of nowhere. It only took a child to bring things right back to the here and now, with her easy dismissal of this uncomfortable moment as if it'd happened last week and not within the past few minutes.

I chuckled and kissed her forehead. "Yes, love bug. You can have pancakes. Let Mommy get the floor cleaned up and I'll make you some."

"No need, I've got this!" Atlas hollered over his shoulder. He was already in the kitchen, and Mila was already tossing away the last of the glass I'd broken.

"Thanks, guys."

"Hey, it's what families are for. We're here for you, Moe," Mila reminded me of the obvious.

And thank God for them.

★ ★ ★

Sometime later, I woke to the mouthwatering smell of spiced meat cooking. Easing out of bed slowly, like an eighty-year-old woman might, I took one small, calculated move at a time. Being careful was paramount to healing. Maneuvering out of bed cautiously, I pressed a hand against my side and curved my body until my heels rested on the floor to limit the stretch of my back. Like yesterday, music was playing in the kitchen, only this time it wasn't George Michael blaring. Atlas was playing acoustic guitar on the couch next to the kitchen.

He plucked at the strings like a professional, playing something Latin-inspired, slapping his hand against the soundboard to add a bit of beat every few seconds. Lily was in the center of the kitchen being spun around in circles by long, muscled arms that I recognized instantly. I allowed myself the pleasure of watching Clayton interact with Lily. He was a natural with her. After she'd whirled too many times, he scooped her up and placed her on the counter close to the stove but not so close that she could harm herself on the burners or pots.

"Now, Queen Lily, you have to pour the red sauce over the rice like so."

"Ohhh, and then it makes the rice colored. Why you want it red and not lellow or white?"

"Yell-o? Yellow?" he repeated for her benefit.

I knew it was coming even before she opened her mouth. Her small nose scrunched up defiantly and her eyes blazed. "'S'wat I said." She placed both fists on her hips and looked very put out.

Clayton bowed low. "Pardon me, my queen. I shan't correct you again." He mimicked an English accent.

"No, don't stop correcting her, or she'll never learn the proper way to pronounce the words," I added from across the room.

"Hey, beautiful, you're awake. I hope we didn't wake you up with the noise."

I shook my head. "No, just resting. The meds take a lot out of me."

He nodded. "You hungry?"

I smiled and slowly made my way over to the stove and placed my hand on his bicep. It flexed, either to impress me or on instinct. Something made me think it was the latter. Clayton didn't have to go out of his way to impress a woman. He was literally God's gift to womankind. His physique was unreal. Hard slabs of muscle everywhere I could see, and that wasn't saying much since I hadn't seen him naked.

Of course, the thought of seeing him sans his clothing sent a thrill of arousal through my body that landed directly on my clit. A gentle pulse woke that bundle of nerves as I took in all that was Clayton Hart. Even with every bone in my body weighed down with medicine, his appeal still had the ability to affect me.

The man was tall, very tall, and I was not a short woman at five foot six. He had close to a foot of height on me. He wore a pair of loose-fitting black track pants with two white stripes running down the side seams. His upper body was covered by only a white ribbed tank.

"Did you, uh, just come from the gym?" I asked, my mouth salivating at the bulging muscles of his shoulders. His hair was spiked in every direction, making me think he hadn't yet had a shower. I wondered if I got close enough if I could smell his natural musk. As soon as the thought hit, I mentally smacked myself and smashed it down. A relationship was so not what I needed right now. Painkillers, food, sleep, and my kid to be healthy and happy. That was on the menu tonight. And tacos, because Clayton was back again making dinner. Why was he here again? I couldn't fathom why he'd want to be near me, especially right now. It didn't make any sense. Not only did I look ghastly, I was cut up from hip to shoulder. My neck was a mess of visible stitches, a reminder that Kyle's wrath wasn't far. He could come after me again at any time. Then what? He'd definitely hurt Clayton. Mila. Atlas. None of them were safe here. Why was he here?

All those thoughts slammed into my mind, adding to the throbbing at my temples. My head was still tender to the touch from its repeated tug of war with Kyle's hand.

A shiver of dread rippled along my skin, and I crossed my arms over my chest and held myself.

Clayton watched the move and squinted before responding to my earlier question. "Yeah, I had a late client, but I didn't want to take too long. I know the queen needed to eat at a reasonable hour, and you have medications to take that require food."

I opened my mouth to say something but then closed it. I tipped my head and planned to ask why he was doing all of this. Why would he want to be here cooking for a single mother who was attacked, but the words flew right out of my head as he watched my inner turmoil play out. Instead of responding, he hooked a hand low around my hips, avoiding my wounds, eased me near him, and plastered my front to his chest. I looked up at him, not understanding what was happening. Fearing it but at the same time needing comfort. This man's comfort. Something I was learning might be unique only to him. He tunneled one of his hands into the hair at my nape and lightly turned my head so my cheek rested directly over his heart. Going with the flow, I looped my arms around him in a full-body hug.

I held on as tight as I could and breathed him in. His natural scent enveloped me with notes of the mountains, pine trees, and something richer. Frankincense, perhaps. A full-body sense of peace coated my high-strung form. After the flashback and panic attack, the meds taking their toll, and my body hurting everywhere...he knew what I needed. A simple hug from a safe, secure man who I knew would never do anything to harm me. I relished the heat of his body and the serenity I allowed in at that moment.

Clayton didn't miss a beat. He wrapped a thick forearm around my waist and held me close, making sure to steer clear of my back wound. The other hand curled around my shoulder and into my hair, where he massaged the back of my neck and head. I groaned, turned my forehead against his sternum, and breathed through the bliss of his hands working out the tension in my muscles. I hadn't realized how sore I was after the attack because I'd been focusing on the knife wounds and abrasions. As he worked out a particularly painful knot, I did the unthinkable, acting so far out of character I wouldn't have believed it was me if I hadn't caught myself doing it.

I bit him. Nuzzled his chest until my mouth encountered a chunk of muscle, his pec, and I sank my teeth in. Through the tank. Right into his flesh. I probably left a mark. *Holy mother of God, I'm a twisted woman. What in the ever-loving hell is wrong with me? How could I do this?* Acting like a horned-up teenager when in reality I just got so overwhelmed with the sensual nature of his embrace, the warmth of his arms, a carnal response bled out of my system.

Right as I was about to apologize profusely for my stupidity and callousness, Clayton groaned and thrust his hips against me, showing exactly how he felt about that lapse in judgment. When I felt the hard shaft wedged against my pelvis, the budding arousal I'd had turned into embarrassment and panic. I moved back a few inches as quickly as my body would allow, but Clayton wouldn't allow me to go too far. His hand stayed firmly at the back of my head, and he dipped his chin low, leveling his face with mine. Our gazes met and an undeniable energy speared through us as if we'd been struck by lightning. I felt the magnetism, the push and pull between our forms, as we stood close together. It was wrong, but my goodness did it feel so right.

Clayton whispered close to my ear, tickling the wisp of hair there. "You can't move back right away. It wouldn't be decent. Feel me?"

Did I feel him? Was he insane? There was a steel pipe between us. Of course I felt it.

"I shouldn't have done that," I whispered, remembering that little ears were not that far away, although at some point she must have jumped off the counter, because I heard her laughing at Atlas somewhere behind us.

Again, I tried to back up, but Clayton tightened his grip on my hips. "Don't you dare take that back. It was the single best hug I've ever had in my life. Besides, you reacted naturally. Never be afraid to respond with me."

"But..." Mortification simmered around each breath I

took, making it hard to respond. I'd never acted like that with any man before. Clayton seemed to bring out an entirely new side of me—one that was more willing and confident. Then again, it could very well have been the drugs. I figured that was a much better reason for my extreme lack in judgment.

"I liked it, beautiful." He licked his lips, and his nostrils flared. "A fuck of a lot, in case you didn't notice." He gyrated his hips in a small circle, allowing me to experience every blessed inch of his proof. And it was a lot of inches. A *lot*. More than enough. *Oh sweet baby Jesus, I'm in a heap of trouble with this man.*

"We can't..." I gasped, remembering how messed up I was, how I still had my ex after me, and that everyone near me, including Clayton, was in danger.

He chuckled. "No, we can't. Wrong place, wrong time, but not the wrong person. I'm here, Monet, and I intend to see this thing through."

I frowned. Thing. "What thing?"

He smirked, and I swore his face was more handsome when he gave off the cocky vibe in spades. "The spark. The chemistry we have. I want to let it play out and see where it goes."

For the love of God, why did this have to happen now? Last year was the right time, when I'd felt confident and strong, and he didn't want me then. Now I was broken and wounded. Worse, I'd been branded by my ex, who wanted me dead. Everything I knew and felt about myself and my ability to judge men and relationships was broken. Just like me physically. I didn't know what was up, down, or all around, let alone how to handle a "thing" between me and the sexiest man alive.

I shook my head and abruptly backed up. He frowned, his

arms falling to his sides. My guess was he probably sensed my confusion at what was taking place between us.

"Clayton, I'm not sure I can do that. I'm not even sure I'm capable of giving anything right now." The words were honest and heartbreaking at the same time. Mostly because in another place and time I would have jumped at the chance to be this man's girl. To experience the chemistry and spark, as he put it. To live it every day, be excited about every call. Planning meals, dressing up, trying to impress him. Now, like this, I didn't even know who I was anymore. Kyle had taken that from me. My confidence was black and wasted like a piece of burnt toast. I had no idea when it would come back around, or when I would. He didn't deserve to wait, put his life on hold for what might be.

Clayton inclined against the counter, his muscles bunching seductively. Ugh, why did he have to be so attractive?

"Do what?" He flattened his lips and narrowed his eyes.

I licked my lips, distracted by his beauty regardless of his obvious irritation. What I wouldn't have given to be whole. "I don't think it's fair for us to let it play out."

He sighed and crossed his arms over his chest in a defensive posture. "Care to tell me why?"

Honesty. He deserved that. "Look, Clayton, you are an amazing man, but you don't need this." I pointed to my chest. "I'm messed up. My ex is after me and could hurt anyone in my path, including you. I have a child..." I could have gone on and on, but really, it wasn't necessary. My baggage was obvious and far heavier than any one man should have to endure entering a new relationship. Not that this was a relationship.

Clayton shook his head, turned, and flicked the burners on once more. With efficient movements, he stirred and prepped the rest of the food. I noted a pan full of succulent spiced ground meat, a pot of beans, another pan with homemade Mexican rice, and a cast-iron skillet with a stack of corn tortillas sitting on the counter next to it. He'd done all of this for me, and here I was telling him he should step back. Practically begging him to.

"Why don't you let me decide what it is I need, huh?" he shot off as he tossed a tortilla on the hot skillet. The corn disc sizzled and popped instantly. Methodically he flipped it.

"Clay, you're an impressive, handsome man who deserves a good woman. A whole woman. Not one who's broken and damaged. Between Kyle, Lily...the attack." The line of stitches running down my back smarted, causing me to pause and breathe through it. I closed my eyes tight. "I'm not what you need. I don't know if what I have, what I am, even well and healthy would be good enough." The truth burned like acid against my lips with each word. "You're so much more than this, and I don't know when I'll be better. I'm certainly not worth the wait or the wasted time." I clasped my fingers together and worried my sweater's sleeve, which fell over the top of my hand. My throat was dry, and the admission of how jacked up my life had become was nauseating.

Clayton spun around, slamming the spatula down on the counter. I jumped a bit at the crack of the plastic as it landed on the marble. Anger tightened around his lips, and a hardness I hadn't seen before entered his eyes. I bristled at this new side of Clayton but wouldn't allow it to outwardly affect me. He didn't deserve that. I wasn't scared of him. He'd never hurt me. I knew that with my entire being.

"Spending time with you, with Lily, and Atlas and Mila is not *wasted*." His voice was low and even-tempered. He inhaled sharply through his nose. "If you haven't noticed, I've been enjoying myself. *For once.*" He groaned, sounding frustrated, possibly even disappointed.

"For once?" I blinked, desperately trying to figure out where he was going with this.

His tone rose. "Yeah, for once I got off work and had a home to go to. Not an empty bachelor pad, but a *real home* with people in it I care about. People who I thought wanted to see me. Are you telling me you don't want me here?" His eyes blazed with an emotion I couldn't pin down, but seeing it made me feel ugly and uncomfortable.

Was I? That wasn't my intention. "I'm saying everything all wrong." I flicked my hands, trying to ease the worry and instability I felt roaring through my veins. Damned meds. I couldn't get my mouth around what I wanted to express, and I was a doctor for crying out loud. I talked people off cliffs for a living, and I couldn't share with one man why his interest in me wasn't a good choice. I took a slow breath and tried again. "Of course we want you here. You've been nothing but helpful, and you're our friend. What I said came out wrong, and you're misinterpreting."

"Yeah?" His eyebrows rose in question.

"Yes," I blurted, not knowing what else to say to make things better, to show him that he mattered but not lead him down a slippery path I wasn't sure I could take with him. Not now, maybe not ever.

"There's that word again."

I pursed my lips and placed my hands on my hips. "Well, you are."

He ran a hand through his hair and looked over my shoulder. I did as well and noted Lily happily watching cartoons. Atlas was on the couch next to her, plucking at his guitar and writing things down in a small notepad, totally oblivious to the strange smackdown of wills we were having in the kitchen.

"You know what, beautiful?" His eyes were a bonfire of heat when he looked me up and down, taking in my loose pajamas, my disheveled hair, and finally my face. He seemed to zero in on my mouth.

"Misinterpret this!" he said on a growl before his face was in front of mine, his hand tunneled into my hair, and his lips slanted over mine.

"Oh!" I moaned a second before his tongue dipped in and tangled with mine. I couldn't help but respond. His entire presence enveloped me in a cocoon of warmth and heat. He tasted of spice and mint and luscious man. I had absolutely no willpower with his lips on mine.

Clayton cocked his head to the side and eased my face up with his thumb at my jaw. He didn't have to. I'd have gone like a horse to water. His lips were warm as they pressed against mine. For a moment, I allowed him to stun me with his kiss... until I'd had enough of sitting on the sidelines and I wanted more. So much more. With both hands, I cupped his cheeks and sucked on his bottom lip, taking control.

"Fuck," he whispered, easing me forward until he was against the counter and I was pressing against the hard wall of muscles again. We were back in the position that had gotten us into our heavy discussion in the first place. What the hell was it between the two of us? I didn't know, but with his mouth on mine, his tongue lapping and flicking against my teeth, I didn't give a flying fig.

I moaned into his mouth until I twisted my upper body

too far and a jolt of pain fired from every nerve ending.

"Oh God!" I cried out and backed away, pushing my hair from my face and gritting my teeth. The torment of each stitch pulling against one another throbbed and banged through my entire body. The kiss ended, and in its place a new sense of dread. Even a simple kiss hurt like hell. Kyle had done that to me. He'd taken my first kiss with Clayton Hart and made it painful. God this situation was torture, but the kiss...nothing but pure beauty.

"What's the matter? Shit, Monet. I wasn't thinking. I lost it the second I kissed you." He held my biceps and craned his neck to look into my eyes.

I lifted my hand to my mouth, feeling the swollen flesh. Screw the pain. The kiss won out. I'd take the pain any day of the week to feel that bliss again. I peered over my shoulder to check on Lily. She was still watching cartoons, oblivious, but Atlas was openly gawking. Much to my dismay, he raised his hands and offered a slow clap for the show.

I closed my eyes and clenched my teeth. This was not happening. This could not happen. "Um..."

"You okay?" Clayton's normally light-blue eyes had darkened with the shadow of worry. Again, all my fault. Usually when a man kissed a woman, the last thing he worried about was whether she was in pain.

Needing to brush it off and not take away from one of the loveliest moments between Clayton and myself, I fibbed. "I'm fine. I just twisted weird for a second."

"You mean when you were trying to suck my tonsils out of my throat?" He cocked an eyebrow and smirked.

I narrowed my gaze, giving a death glare in reply as I backed away from his body a few steps.

He put a hand over his abdomen and laughed heartily. "Just kidding, beautiful. You need to lighten up. Besides, that kiss said everything you couldn't." He turned and placed a tortilla on the skillet to warm.

"Which is what, exactly?"

"That you think I'm hot." His confidence was just barely this side of arrogant.

I rolled my eyes. How we went from he shouldn't bother with me and my baggage to kissing to him knowing I thought he was hot was like a case of whiplash. My emotions and feelings were bouncing all over the place. Trying to take a note from his levity, I responded, "Everyone thinks you're hot. The entire female population would admit that. It's not a stretch."

He smiled and winked over his shoulder.

"Annnndddd..." he drew out the word. "You like me," he added, his voice laced with humor.

I cringed. "What is this? Seventh grade? Yes, I like you." Easy enough to admit. He was a likable guy.

"That you liked kissing me," he continued.

A wave of heat flashed over my cheeks. Uh-huh. I saw where he was going with his jabs, and I decided I'd play along. "Maybe."

"That you felt the spark."

I sighed. Infuriating man! "I will admit there were some definite sparks."

"And we have chemistry." He just blazed ahead, no stopping at Go, no collecting his two hundred dollars as though we were playing Monopoly.

"Clayton..." I warned. Why couldn't he see I was all wrong for him? He deserved so much more than what I could offer him.

"What do you have to lose trying this out with me?" His voice was low enough that only I could hear him.

There was so much I could say to that loaded question. I could lose my sanity. I could fall in love and risk having my heart broken. My daughter could get used to him and have *her* heart broken. He could realize I was not worth the trouble. Kyle could hurt him, me, any of us, and he shouldn't get involved. I was a divorced single mom who'd been cut mentally and physically. Besides all of that, it could all go to hell in a handbasket. Then Atlas would be angry with Clayton, and it would affect their friendship. Honestly, I could come up with far more reasons against this "thing" between us than I could for it.

I didn't say any of that. Instead, I fired back the one thing I needed to know more than anything. The question that would tip the scales one way or the other. It was the only way I could risk it all.

"What do you have to gain?" I heard how tired, lost, and everything in between I sounded. My mind was mush, on complete and utter overload.

His next words floored me.

"Can't you see? I have everything to gain. Lily, and all of this." He gestured around the general vicinity of my home, the warmth I knew he found there. "Mostly though, it's...you."

CHAPTER SIX

HEART
C H A K R A

The heart chakra and the body need love. The best way to receive love is to give it freely. Kiss and embrace often. A gentle pat to the back, a kind word of affirmation, even a hand to the shoulder provides a peaceful energy exchange. Making another smile will make you smile. Happiness is contagious.

CLAYTON

Monet was warming to me. For the first week of her recovery, I went to the Holland home each night to make the clan dinner. To some it might have sounded like work or a pansy-ass attempt at getting close to the raven-haired, freckle-nosed beauty, but I didn't care. Monet was getting stronger every day. Arm movement seemed easier. She winced less when handling things or hugging her child. Sure signs she was on the road to recovery.

And as always there was Ms. Lily.

The things that kid said had me laughing up a storm. I couldn't get enough of the little bugger. Atlas said that proved I was indeed ready to settle down. Of course he'd say that. He had a baby on the way and walked through his days beaming like a spotlight was on him, smiling for the world to see. I was happy for Atlas and Mila. They'd each had rough childhoods, and the beginning of their relationship hadn't been easy. I didn't begrudge them their piece of the proverbial American dream. Selfishly, I also wanted a piece for myself.

Monet could very well be that crucial fit I'd been looking for. My attraction to her was off the charts. Even wounded, makeup-free, and dressed in house clothes, the woman was still the most splendid thing I'd ever seen. From the tip of her dainty feet to the top of her head of silky black hair, she was perfection. I didn't care about the scar that ran up her back, but I knew she did. It would take a while for her to come to terms with that change to her appearance. Even more so would be the impact the experience had on her life. I imagined that as a therapist, she knew what was coming. So far she hadn't made any mention of therapy for herself. Just spoke often about when she planned on going back to work.

What was that saying again? Doctors made the worst patients? I had a strong feeling Monet was going to crumble at some point if she didn't talk about what had happened. Mila and Atlas were content to let her push it aside and pretend it didn't happen. I, on the other hand, knew from experience—hiding from this would not be possible. The vulgarity and viciousness of what Kyle did would creep up to the surface in one way or another. I just hoped I'd be there to help her through. If she'd let me.

In just over a week, I'd wheedled my way into a groove with this family. It had been so seamless too. I hadn't been kidding when I told Monet I wanted to let the spark between us play out. And over the past week it had...in spades. Even while healing, the woman was strong and determined to be a good mother and provide a solid, healthy home for her daughter. I'd caught her trying to pick up toys off the floor, lift a laundry basket, and more. Several times, Mila, Atlas, and even I scolded her. None of us wanted the healing process impeded because of her endless drive and determination. The woman was a machine. She'd taken on healing and taking care of others like it was her job. And I guess in a way, it was.

Things had changed between us too. I went out of my way to touch her, hold her hand, kiss her cheek, and I was getting to know Lily better. Monet was responsive if not a bit skittish, but my goal was set. Win her over with kindness and stability. Show her I could be the type of man she could count on for the long term.

I pulled up to the Holland home, bags of food at the ready. Tonight, I'd planned on pleasing the queen with homemade pizzas and salad. Instead of grabbing the bags, I jumped out of my car and used the key Mila had given me to open the door first. No sense in waking Monet by knocking or ringing the bell if she was taking one of her naps before dinner.

Atlas strolled past as I opened it.

"Hey, man, what's on for tonight?" he asked, following me out to my car.

"Homemade pizzas and salad." I walked to the back of my SUV, lifted the hatch, and the two of us organized the bags.

"Dude, this is more than the fixings for tonight."

I shrugged. "Got enough for a couple days and some breakfast items and lunch. Wanted to make sure you were all set for a while."

Atlas frowned. "Because you're not coming back?" His voice was lower than normal and carried a slight strain I hadn't heard before.

"No!" I shook my head. "I wanted to make sure Monet and Lily have everything they need for every meal. That's all."

His frown turned upside down quicker than a snap. He slapped my back with a harsh man-pat. "Atta boy. Making sure your girls are set. I get you."

"How's about you help me get these bags in? Unless you'd rather make your own dinners again?" I stated sarcastically.

Atlas's eyes rounded. "Right-o. Message received. Oh, but hey, some of the gang is coming over tomorrow after work. Genevieve, Trent, the baby, and Amber and Dash. Should we plan to order in?"

"You know, Atlas, subtlety was never your strong suit."

He ran his hand through his hair. "What the fuck am I supposed to say? You've been coming over every night, making dinner for everyone, which I hella appreciate by the way. Not gonna lie, I've never eaten better. But I know Moe doesn't expect you to keep doing it. Especially with more people coming over. I just thought I should... I don't know what the fuck I thought. You've put me in a weird spot. You're Moe's man but not..."

"I am."

"You are what?" He struggled to cinch a few bags.

"I definitely am Monet's man." There was zero hesitation in my statement. Then doubt wiggled its way into my thoughts. "Well, I'm attempting to be."

Atlas cringed. "Does she know that?"

"Working on it." And hell if I knew a faster way to get her over that hump. I knew I needed to give her time. I'd read up a bit on post-traumatic stress. I could try my best to get into her headspace and give her what she needed to help her heal mentally, but I wasn't the professional. All I could do was show her that I wasn't going anywhere and that I was into her for the long haul. However long it took.

Atlas sighed, mimicking my own feelings. We hauled all the bags out of the car at once so we didn't have to make a second trip.

"I wish you had entered the picture a year ago. Then we wouldn't be dealing with this awkward shit." He walked into the house in front of me, shifting sideways so the bags didn't bang into the walls. I followed his lead.

"Me too. I'm paying for that mistake now. But I'm here and I'm not going anywhere." It would be up to me to prove that to Monet. Just the thought of that woman had me smiling, and her kid... Shit, she might as well be my happiness meter. When Lily smiled, the entire world smiled with her.

My friend nodded while we filed into the kitchen. Lily was spinning in a circle in the open living room in front of Mila and Monet, who watched her every move.

"Hey, beautiful...Your Majesty," I called to Monet and then Lily.

"King Clay. Finally! I've been waitin' all day for you."

"Really? Why's that?" I asked, setting my bags on the counter next to the ones Atlas had put down.

"I have a 'prize for you."

"A prize? What did I win?" I removed several cans of tomato sauce and spices, set them to the side, and continued to unload while Atlas put everything else away.

Lily pursed her lips. "You didn't win somefing. I made you a 'prize."

"Oh, you have a sur-prise for me."

Her nose crinkled as I expected it would. "'S'wat I said. A 'prize!" She shook her head. "I gotta get it." And then she was off, a blur of purple and blue fabric racing down the hallway.

I shook my head. "That girl is a ball of fun."

Monet came over and leaned into me, pressing her good side against mine. I curled my hand around the back of her neck and into her hair. Soft as fucking silk. I couldn't wait to hold on to the satiny strands while I fucked her. My mouth watered at the thought of taking her.

Visions of my hands cupping Monet's head as I pounded into her from above, relentless in my pursuit of her pleasure, flashed across my mind. She'd tip her head back and offer her neck, which I'd take like a greedy beast.

Monet nuzzled against the side of my chest and inhaled long and slow, knocking me from the mini-daydream. I'd been having those kind of thoughts more and more every day I saw her but couldn't have her.

"You smell so good," she whispered.

Monet openly showing affection without me leading the charge. Hallelujah. I wanted to jump for joy and fist pump the air. Instead, I played it cool and ran my hands through her silky tresses. "Haven't showered yet, beautiful. You're smelling stinky man. Went to the store right after my last three clients." I kissed the crown of her head.

She made a sound low in her throat, inhaled again, and closed her eyes as if she was truly taking me in. A thrill of excitement and arousal slinked down my spine, but I didn't let it reach its target. No way was I going to get hard while she initiated affection on her own. Usually it was me touching her in small ways, helping her up, changing her bandages, caressing her cheek and arm. I'd been very careful not to go too far past the intense kiss we'd had last week.

She'd run hot and cold with her emotions since our heated kiss, and I was leery of pushing her too much further outside her comfort zone so soon after the attack. The last thing I wanted was to hurt her. I still believe she needed the time to process what happened as well as come to terms with the idea that I wasn't going anywhere, that I *wanted* to be with her and Lily.

"You know, you don't have to buy groceries, come over, and cook every night." Her tone held a note of concern, and the hand that was lying flat against my abdomen fisted and fell to her side.

Not wanting her to start backtracking, I moved on her, forcing her to look into my eyes. "I want to. Frankly, babe, I love having you guys to come home to after a full day at work. It gives me something to look forward to." Her eyes were honest and reactive. I knew what I was dealing with when I looked into them. Right then she was open, welcoming, and appreciative of my presence. Fuck if I didn't love seeing that look on her face and holding her in the crook of my arms. Gave me the little bit of hope I needed to keep working toward more.

I ran the pad of my thumb across her bottom lip. Her expression darkened and heated in the seconds I touched her. Then a smile brightened her pretty face.

"Monet, feeding you, being with this family... It's what I want. Do you want me here?" I asked the question I'd been dying to ask. If she didn't want me to be a part of all of this,

I'd have to respect it, lick my wounds, and leave them be. At this point it would hurt like hell. I already felt connected and engaged in the day-to-day, and I had no desire to stop it anytime soon.

"Yes." She winked. Winked. My chest filled with pride and a little something else I wasn't ready to deal with. This stunning woman was burrowing into my heart and soul with every one of her smiles.

"There's that word again, beautiful." I smirked. "One day it's going to get you into trouble, young lady."

She snickered as I got a few inches closer, making my intention clear.

"I'm going to kiss you now. Is that okay?" I arched a brow, waiting, wanting, but giving her enough time to decide for herself.

Monet stared at me, myriad emotions rushing across her face as she took in my features. When her eyes landed on my lips, she bit down on hers, and I knew she wanted it. Wanted me.

"Yes."

I laid my lips over hers, gently at first. I reached around her hip to bring her closer. With small movements, I varied the pressure of my lips against hers. She opened her mouth and sucked my bottom lip. I didn't take the bait. Instead of taking her deep and wet, I rubbed my lips against hers, nibbling on the top lip, then the bottom. She followed my lead, running a hand from my abdomen up and over my chest to my neck, where she held me. God, I wanted her hands all over me.

"King Clay!" Lily screamed. I heard her feet pounding down the hallway coming closer.

I expected Monet to pull back as if burned, hiding our

moment from prying little eyes, and was pleasantly surprised when she didn't.

I was the one who pulled a few inches back. Her eyes were filled with delight. Not only was Monet stunning, exotic with her Asian-American features, she was breathtaking. Her lips were swollen from my kisses, reddened and succulent as a ripe berry. Not being able to hold back, I kissed her again, enjoying the pleasure of having this woman near.

Within moments a bundle of energy plowed into my legs from behind. "Stop kissing Mommy. I got a 'prize for you!" Lily hopped up and down, trying to pull me away from her mom.

I didn't budge. I shifted away only after pecking her lips a couple more times, lost to the sensation of kissing Monet and having her so willing to kiss me back. It was a huge step in the direction I wanted us to go. "We'll come back to this another time I hope."

Her cheeks turned a rosy hue—which I liked seeing a fuck of a lot—before she answered. "Definitely."

Finally, my woman was coming around. I felt like a million bucks.

"Clay!" Lily yanked at my forearm.

I turned around and kneeled. "What's up, Your Majesty?"

She held up a big sheet of blank paper, about twelve by twelve inches in size.

"Honey, I don't see anything." I frowned.

She looked at me, then down at the paper. "It's backward." She giggled with glee and then turned the paper around.

Drawn on the page was a house with pointed rooftops and lots of trees around it. Had to be a castle in her garden.

"That's a really cool castle. And is that your secret garden?" I asked, encouraging her.

Her entire face lit up, her smile leading the charge. "Yes! And there we are." She pointed to three stick figures at the bottom of the page. The tallest one had yellow hair and what I think was an orange crown.

"Is that the king?"

"That's you, King Clay!"

My heart constricted as I looked at the stick figure. A pair of black squares haphazardly colored in were his pants. He had no shirt and just a stick for a body. Most surprising was that he was in the center with his stick arms stretched out holding the hands of two other stick figures.

"And who are these two?" I knew the answer but needed to hear it anyway.

"That's Mommy. She's the princess. See her long hair?" She pointed at one of the figures in a triangle-shaped red dress with black hair so long it reached the hem of the dress. Then she pointed to the smallest one with a pink triangle for clothes. "That's me. The queen."

Again that pang knocked against my chest, and I rubbed at it. "This is awesome, sweetie. I love it. You're an excellent artist like your Auntie Mila."

She nodded ecstatically and said the one thing I would never have expected. "It's our new family."

As if my brain wasn't in control, my head shot up and I looked at Monet. A kink speared into my neck like an icepick. Monet's mouth opened in what I could only assume was shock. Had to be, because I felt those four words Lily said as if I'd been tazed.

"Can we put it on the fridge, Mommy?" Lily asked innocently.

Monet swallowed and stared at her daughter for a

moment, and then she coughed and went into action. "Sure, honey."

Fuck. Fuck. *Fuck.*

As much as I loved that Lily was adding me into the mix, into the family, it was too soon. *Way too fucking soon.* I knew I had hit the nail on the head when I saw Monet take the drawing from her daughter and put it on the fridge almost robotically, not saying a word.

"Hey, Lil, can you go draw another picture of your family, one with Atlas and Mila and the new baby coming? We can add that one to the fridge too."

Her eyes got big, and she spun in a circle. "So fun!" she squealed and ran off back down the hall.

Once Lily was out of earshot, I approached Monet with a hand to her shoulder. "I don't know what to say." She flinched at my touch. A far cry from where we were two minutes before.

She flattened her lips. "I knew this was going to happen with you around every day." She shook her hands in the air while starting to pace. "She's attached to you. I can't believe it."

"Ouch, that hurt. Why wouldn't she be attached to me? I'm a cool guy." I stayed on the opposite side of the counter, allowing her some space to freak out. I'd rather she did it in front of me than go inside her head and push me away slowly.

Her head lifted and her gaze shot daggers. "Clay, she's never attached to anyone this fast. *Ever!*" She spun around too fast, her arms shifting more quickly than I'd seen her move yet. A wince stole across her face, and she braced the counter to steady herself, breathing in through her nose and out through her mouth. I could tell her movement had twisted her back too far.

I sighed and reclined against the counter, gripping the

rounded edge while I watched the woman I cared about pushing through her pain. It killed me not to go to her and comfort her, but I didn't think that was what she needed or wanted just then.

"Look, I like Lily. Love her, even," I said, allowing the truth of the words to roll around in my head.

"She's easy to love," Monet sighed, using the words Atlas always had when it came to the sweet little girl. "But I have to protect her." She sucked in a harsh breath, and her head fell forward. "When you leave us, it will destroy her."

When you leave us. When, not if.

I cringed and clenched my teeth at the severity of what she'd said. "Let's get this straight, right now. Nothing in life is guaranteed, Monet. Fucking *nothing*. I've learned that the hard way too many times. I've had everything I've ever wanted dangled right before my eyes and then snatched away in an instant." I clenched my teeth, remembering how much it hurt when Stacey's lies were revealed. If I'd gotten through that— granted, it had taken years—there was no way I wasn't going to fight for Monet, for what we were on the cusp of having together.

She lifted her shoulders and turned around to face me. Her posture exuded sadness and regret. I wanted so badly to scoop her into my arms and hold her, tell her it would be okay, because I had no intention of not seeing this through. Every day I came here put me one step closer to never wanting to leave.

"Beautiful, we have to take risks in life. No risk means no reward."

Monet closed her eyes and slumped against the counter. "I don't know if I can take that risk. It's not just me in the picture.

Not just my heart at stake here, Clay." Her voice shook, and I could see the weight of concern and fear pressing down on her.

"I get that you're a mother protecting your daughter. What you're not seeing is that you don't need to protect her from *me*." I reached out but she backed away. The move hurt like a hundred bees stinging me at once.

She needed space, but fuck all if I wanted to give it to her. The metallic taste of blood hit my taste buds as I clenched my teeth around the inside of my cheek to hold back my frustration. My anger was not going to help her see the light.

A puff of air left her mouth, and she ran a shaky hand through her hair. "Her own father left. Didn't want anything to do with her. You've known her just over a week. One week. He had *two* years."

Everything she said was true, yet it still shoved a knife through my soul. I couldn't imagine ever leaving Lily or Monet now that I'd had a small taste. I only wanted more.

Deciding to go for broke, I laid myself out there. "And in the past week, I've already fallen in love with her. No matter what happens to us, I'd never just bail on her."

She shook her head and looked down at the floor. "You say that now, but..."

I couldn't stop the forward momentum of my legs. They were going to her led by my heart, not my head. Moving slowly I put my arms on each side of the counter, trapping her in, forcing her to be inside the bubble of what I was feeling. "Monet, I'm saying I love her and I mean it. Don't confuse me with your douchebag ex-husband. I've been here every day since what he did to you, and I'm *not* going anywhere."

Her eyes filled with tears and she swallowed. "You barely know me," she whispered, agony coating her tone.

"I know enough," I fired back with a conviction I felt down to my toes. "Be in this *with me*. Take a chance." The plea slipped from my tongue with no thought to hold it back. I needed her to find it inside of herself to commit. To take a chance on me.

Her chin trembled and her voice splintered. "You're asking me to risk my heart. My *daughter's* heart."

I shook my head, cupped her cheek, and gave her everything I was capable of giving. "No. I'm asking you to allow a little room in that heart for me. Just a little for now. I'll work toward filling it up so full you'll be bursting with it."

At my words, she curved her lips into a small smile, and I could see the fear fading from her eyes. It wasn't much, but I'd take the tiny reprieve for what it was. A foot in the door.

"I'm scared," she admitted.

Scared I could handle. Being pushed away...no. I licked my lips. "With reason. You have a lot at risk." I'd give her that because she did. "Just know that I'm going to take what little you give and work to build on it. Regardless of what happens, I'll be here, and I'll sure as hell be here for Lily. You can count on that."

She closed her eyes and a tear slipped from one and eased down her face. I swept it away with my thumb as she said, "You do love her." It was a statement not a question.

I mentally did a jig knowing she was coming around. "She's easy to love, remember?" I lifted my hand and ran a finger down Monet's temple and then tunneled my fingers into her silky hair. I caressed her lower lip with my thumb. "Her mom's not so hard to love either."

She gulped, her eyes flying open. "Clay, don't say things you don't mean."

"I wouldn't do that. I know where things are headed, and

I know they're headed there fast. I can't stop that train from moving full speed ahead, but I can try to pump the breaks a bit." I shifted forward and kissed her softly, with enough pressure to know I meant every word. Just over a week in and I was falling hard and fast for Monet and her daughter.

"You could hurt me so easily," she whispered against my lips.

God, don't let me hurt her, I prayed softly. "I could, but I won't." I kissed her again with more intent, wanting her to *feel* my truth.

"Promise me you'll go slow." Her words sounded like a plea, not a demand. I would absolutely heed her request if that's what it took for her to accept me as part of her world, as the man in her life.

"No reason to rush, beautiful." I focused on her eyes, making sure she knew the magnitude with which I held this conversation.

She closed her eyes, cupped my cheeks with both hands, and pressed her forehead to mine. "Okay."

"Okay, you're going to take a chance on me?" I needed to hear the words. Her commitment to what was happening between us.

"Yes." Her voice shook. "Yes," she said again with more power and strength.

"And you're going to trust me to be careful with you and Lily?" No matter what, I'd prove to her I was worthy of that trust.

She said that one word I was beginning to love. "Yes."

I had to push it a little further just to make sure. "You're going to start believing in *this*. In *us*?"

No hesitation this time when she replied, "Yes."

"Can I have a million dollars?"

I felt her frown against my forehead and her fingers dig into my hair. "What?"

Thank God, she was following. I laughed, easing the tension between us. "Just making sure you were paying attention. With all those yeses, I had to be certain."

She chuckled, and I took the opportunity to kiss her. Really *kiss her*. I laid my lips over hers and delved deep with my tongue. She was hesitant at first but soon got lost in the kiss and moaned, allowing me to go deeper. I couldn't get deep enough, close enough. After a few minutes of kissing the living heck out of her, I ran my lips down her jaw and kissed along the column of her neck. I placed my mouth over the spot where her shoulder and neck met and licked and sucked. My special spot. I nibbled on the tasty flesh, and Monet pulled me closer, wrapping her nimble fingers around my neck, encouraging. Once I'd licked, kissed, and nibbled my way across her collarbone, I came back up, making sure to avoid the three-inch span of uncovered stiches.

Needing air, I pulled away from her mouth. "Christ, Monet, you're the most radiant woman I've ever seen. You smell like jasmine and sunshine and taste like mint and heaven. I want to put my mouth on every inch of you. One day, when you're better, I will. You hear me?"

"Clayton." A solitary tear fell down her cheek.

I kissed it away. "You're beautiful, and as of today, you're mine."

"I don't know why you want me."

Her words broke my fucking heart in half. I cupped her cheek again and looked hard into her soulful eyes. "Because you're everything I've ever wanted in a woman."

"I'm not."

"You are." I pressed more firmly against her forehead and gave her the words I'd been dying to say. "You're beautiful. Intelligent. Driven. Kind. Generous. Loving. An amazing mother. Monet, I could go on and on."

She sucked in a quick breath. "This doesn't seem real. You can't be real." Her body shook in my arms as her fingers tightened around me.

Another tear ran down her cheek. Once more I kissed it away, the salt tingling on my tongue. "I'm going to prove to you that I am. That what's between us is very real."

I cupped her face and stared into her eyes, trying to sear the truth of my statement into her psyche. I'd do whatever it took to make her see I was in this for the long haul and had zero intention of walking away. At that point, I didn't think I could. Everywhere I looked, I saw my future staring back at me. A graceful woman I wanted more than anything. A little girl who needed a father figure. A man to take care of her. Of both of them. I wanted to be that man. I *would* be that man.

"Thought we were making pizzas, bro!" Atlas's voice boomed from around the corner. He walked into the kitchen and then stopped cold. "Um, yeah, I can see you're busy."

I shook my head and chuckled, squeezing Monet to me so she could hide her tears and burrow into my chest while she pulled herself together. "Nope. We're all good. Monet and I were just getting some facts straight. Right, beautiful?"

Atlas coughed. "Ooookaaay. So then you want me to go?"

"Naw, man, we're cool. Why don't you get some beers for me and you? I'll take care of dinner for the family," I said, making my statement very clear to the woman I held.

I kissed her once, then twice, and let her go.

Atlas placed an open beer next to me and turned to leave the kitchen, probably realizing we needed another minute.

"Hey, could you tell the queen to get in here? I promised her a royal meal, and she's going to help make it."

Atlas chuckled and went to find Lily.

The second he was out of earshot, I couldn't help but push her a little harder. "You believe me? You going to give this an actual shot? Stop thinking I'm going to walk away or disappear any second?"

"I'll try, Clayton. I want this to be real. I really do. For me. For Lily. For all of us. But I've been hurt before. Goodness, I've had my heart shattered, and I'm wearing the stitches to prove how badly I've been hurt by love." Her lips trembled and it took everything I had to keep my distance.

I nodded. "Then, like I said, it's up to me to prove it."

Right then, Lily barreled into the kitchen and ran right into my legs for the second time that night. Her eagerness to please me slammed into my heart. "Ready for chef duty, King Clay!" She raised her arms, and I lifted her up and held her close, allowing her warmth to lead me through.

"I will prove this is real, beautiful. Just give it a chance. It's all I'm asking." I set Lily on the counter and held a bag in front of her, leaving Monet to her thoughts. She needed to process all of this, wrap her head around it, and start living in it the way I already was.

Lily held her hands to her chest and bit her lip. "What are we making?" Cutest fuckin' kid ever.

"Homemade pizzas!" I showed her the cheese, pepperoni, and additional fixings.

Lily clapped wildly. "I wuv pizza!"

I laughed and kissed her nose. She grabbed my cheeks

and kissed mine in return. "Mommy, are you gonna help?"

Monet saddled up to my back, placed her hand in the center, and ran it down to the small indention above my ass. I shivered at her simple touch, letting the awareness of her palm seep deep into me. She moved against my side, kissed my bicep, and then pressed her cheek to it before looking up.

"I want to try," she said softly. I knew those words weren't for Lily but for me. For the budding relationship I wanted—that we both wanted but she was afraid to enter. Elation mixed with excitement rushed through me.

"That's all anyone can ever expect," I said before leaning down toward her face. She lifted her head and I kissed her lips. "Thank you."

She kissed me once more. "No. Thank you."

Finally, a real start. I could put all the shit of the past behind me and start fresh with Monet and Lily. The number of people I cared about was growing by leaps and bounds, and at the front of the pack were these two raven-haired beauties. I was one lucky bastard, and I intended to hold on to that luck for as long as possible.

CHAPTER SEVEN

HEART
C H A K R A

Heart-centered females tend to appear more calm and collected. Others seek them out due to their serene nature. However, if a heart-centered female has a closed heart chakra due to an extreme physical or emotional setback, they may react irrationally and out of character until the chakra is opened once more.

MONET

I'd given myself yet another sponge bath in two inches of water, as a person would an eight-month-old baby. Stepping out of the tub, I stopped in front of the mirror. I'd purposely not looked at the damage Kyle had caused to my back. Every time I tried, I went back there, back to where he held me down against my will, threatening to kill me.

I knew the wound was extensive and ran the length of my back from shoulder blade to hip, but I hadn't gotten up the courage to actually look at it. Now that it had been a week and a half since it happened and I was getting the stitches out in a few days, I needed to woman up. Rip off the Band-Aid and move on.

With shaking fingers, I dried the rest of my body, bending incrementally so I didn't stretch the stitches and skin that was newly fused together. The doctor had encouraged me to move around but to take things slow.

Take things slow.

The phrase was my new motto and the exact pace I'd requested of Clayton. And so far, he had. I wouldn't call him a knight in shining track pants or anything, but he'd made his intentions with me very clear. He wanted me. No matter how hard I'd tried to come up with a good rationale, I couldn't figure out why. Sure, I wasn't hard to look at normally, but when it came to baggage, I had heaps of it. Most men I'd met since Kyle didn't want anything to do with a thirty-year-old woman with a child. And now that I'd been attacked by my ex-husband? Irreparably scarred for life? Just another load in the already full trunk of crap I carried around.

So why did Clayton want to be with me? I agreed we had chemistry and some serious sparks. His essence spoke to me. The way he tenderly helped with my bandages, his intense kisses...and that didn't even cover his body. I closed my eyes and hugged myself, clutching the towel tightly. The man was sex incarnate. Everything in me wanted to lay him out flat and take advantage of all those bulging, toned muscles and the miles of tanned skin, but I just couldn't. Physically I was sure I wasn't ready. Mentally, I was a straight up mess of mixed emotions and contradictions.

I shook my head. So stupid. Fantasizing about a man I couldn't even have sex with yet. Yet. That was the one word that glimmered like a ray of hope in my subconscious. *When I'm better, when the stitches are removed and I'm healed, he's going to want to have sex with me.* Eventually. Hopefully.

Uggh. It felt as though I was head-shrinking myself. The back and forth, the what ifs, the will he or won't he, was making me crazy. Certifiable. Why couldn't I just believe the words he'd said to me?

He enjoyed our family.

He wanted me.

He loved Lily.

Take the risk.

Try.

Setting the towel down on the vanity, I glanced at my naked form. Everything about me from the front seemed so average. Normal B-cup breasts, slim figure, shapely hips, a small, rounded belly I hadn't been able to lose since having Lily. Still, I wore a bikini confidently. Well, I used to be able to. Then again, maybe the damage wasn't so bad. I shifted to the side, just barely catching sight of the small wisps of strings from the black sutures in my shoulder blades.

Fear tingled up my spine and closed around my throat as I reached for the hand mirror. I closed my eyes, took a deep breath, turned around, and held up the mirror so I could see my back. Cotton coated my throat as I warred with myself to open my eyes.

Just open your stupid eyes. It's easy. Open them, look at the wound, and be done. Over. Simple.

I opened my eyes and focused on the mirror. My hand

shook, and my entire body trembled as I took in the carnage reflected back at me. From my hip up to my shoulder blade was a long, jagged, puffy pink line, held together with black sutures. It reminded me of those dressing gowns from the olden days, where a set of black buttons ran from the waist all the way up the spine to the neck. Only, these were no buttons and not nearly as pretty. It was ghastly.

The more I took in, the more acid swirled in my stomach. My mouth watered and I tried to swallow it back, but I couldn't. My chest heaved and I covered my mouth. I barely made it to the toilet, where I threw up violently. The images of my disgusting back flashed at me like a camera lens clicking madly. The sexy line of my back, the one feature I'd always appreciated about myself, had been destroyed forever.

Every heave shredded the tender stitches, but I couldn't stop. For long minutes I gagged and expelled every scrap of food and drink I'd put into my body until there was nothing but bile, yet I still choked. The rolling waves didn't stop, though I did my best to breathe through them, tears running down my cheeks, my nose and throat burning like white-hot fire.

Eventually I got control of my stomach and the violent physical response and pushed back onto my heels. For a long time I let the tears fall, cuddled my legs to my chest, and cried.

The man I'd loved, married, chose to bring a child into the world with did this to me. He hurt me. Repeatedly. The anger inside me threaded with the revulsion to make a heady mix of sheer hate. Kyle was still out there. He hadn't been caught. And me... I'd been holed up in my house healing from what that bastard did to me. And then there was Clayton. Good, masculine, kind, caring, handsome Clayton. The man I promised to try with. Try and be what he needed. But what if I couldn't? What then? Would he leave too? Kyle had no problem leaving me for my sister. Leaving Lily. Would Clayton do the same when he figured out I wasn't what he needed? When I couldn't give him the perfect woman?

Self-loathing slithered up my throat, but I choked it back down. No. I wouldn't cry another tear. No more. I was stronger than that, and it was time I proved it to everyone. Proved it to myself.

Slowly I eased up, rinsed out my mouth, and brushed my teeth. I stared unseeing into the mirror, not recognizing the woman standing there. She was pale, her cheeks sunken in, her hair a tangled mess. Pink blotches ran up and down her chest.

I wiped my mouth and tossed the towel at the image; I hated her. This wasn't me. But it was. The new body I'd have to live with.

On instinct I threw a camisole over my head and rushed to my closet. I slapped at each hanger until I reached my designer dresses.

"You're gone." I pulled out a white dress with an open back, dropped it to the floor, and kicked it aside. I grabbed another, a red number I absolutely loved. I'd worn it to one of Mila's gallery showings.

"You too!" I practically screamed, tears forming and spilling over my cheeks, even though I'd sworn I wouldn't shed another. It was like the hate was pouring out of me. The disgust urged my forward motion.

"Moe?" I heard Mila's voice from the entrance of my room, a good distance from where I stood in my walk-in closet. I ignored her, set on the task ahead.

My fingers wrapped around a sexy little black dress with a cowl in the front and the back. "Fuck you!" I ripped the dress off the hanger and tossed it to the floor.

"Moe, what on earth is going on?" Mila sounded worried and strained as she took in the growing pile of clothes around my feet.

I laughed heartily but didn't feel joy. No, all I felt was hate. And anger. Lots of anger. A bright-blue summer dress was next. I'd worn it to Genevieve and Trent's wedding. An amazing day filled with love, laughter, and hope for the future. It was a gorgeous piece that had looked better on me than it did on the hanger. Only, it had spaghetti straps, and now that I would have a scar up the right side of my back, it would be hideous.

"No one wants to see the disgusting part of my back, so this dress is out!" I hollered at no one in particular and tossed the dress on the floor. That one hurt. Not physically but emotionally, because I'd worn it on a great day I would have liked to remember the next time I wore it.

"You're not throwing that dress away. It looks amazing on you, and you love it." Mila frowned and reclined against the doorjamb.

"Correction!" I pointed the hanger at my best friend. "It used to look good on me. Those days are over."

I grabbed another random dress. This one had a cutout in the center of the back that was shaped like a diamond. I didn't know if it would show the new feature my ex had so lovingly carved into me, but I wasn't thinking straight and didn't care. It had an open spot on the back so it had to go. "You're out!" I flung it over my shoulder.

"Moe." Mila approached me and placed her hand on my wrist. "Please stop this."

"What? I'm just cleaning house. Getting rid of all the

things I can no longer wear now that I'm hideous!"

Mila clenched her teeth. "You are not hideous. You have been injured, but you will heal."

I laughed hysterically, more tears flowing down my cheeks, much to my dismay. "I'll never be the same."

"No, you won't."

I jolted back and looked at my best friend's sorrowful brown eyes.

"You won't be the same again. Everything that happens to us in life changes us in one way or another. We learn to live with those changes in whatever way we need to."

"And this is my way!" I pointed at the dresses and decided to grab all of them in a heaping armful and yank them off the rod. Pain splintered in my back but I didn't care. They had to *go*.

Mila let me throw the whole lot on the ground. "This isn't the way, Moe, and you know it. What would you tell your clients in a situation like this?"

I narrowed my eyes at her. "Don't you use psychiatry on me. I'm the one with the degree." I ground my teeth, ire burning hot under the surface of my skin.

Mila, being my best friend, didn't even flinch. "You're acting irrationally, and someone has to tell it to you straight."

"So tell it to me straight. Go ahead, give it to me!" I growled, clenching my hands into fists, waiting for the blow that was sure to come.

Mila shook her head. "Moe, you need help. You have to talk to someone about what happened. You're not talking to me, or Atlas, or even Clay."

I sucked in a huge breath and wiped my wet cheeks. "I'm fine."

"You're not," she fired back.

"Let me be the judge of that."

"You're not capable of judging your actions right now."

"Mila...you're walking on dangerous ground here," I warned.

Mila threw her hand up out in front of me in a stop gesture. "Shut up. You would never allow me to lose my shit like this, and I'm not going to allow you to either. When's the next time going to happen? When you have Lily with you? Huh? What if she wasn't at school and saw you like this right now? Do you think it's okay for her to see you like this? A sobbing mess, throwing away perfectly good clothes, acting irrationally?"

I scowled. "Are you telling me that I'd hurt my daughter?"

"Intentionally? Never. But you not taking care of you will ultimately hurt her. Look at yourself."

"I did. In the mirror!" I screeched like an evil banshee. "I finally looked at myself, Mila! I saw what he did to me. I saw it, and it's disgusting. Repulsive!" My legs gave out, and I landed on the floor of my closet, shaking, sweaty, destroyed.

Mila rushed to me, went to her knees, and put her hands on my shoulders. "I swear it will heal. It will look better, but it takes time. Honey, it just takes time."

I lifted my head. My eyes were like faucets, tears coming so fast I couldn't stop them. The only time I'd ever cried this hard was when Kyle left me for my sister. "What am I going to do?" I choked on a sob.

Mila put her arms loosely around me, and I nestled my face against her neck. I cried so hard while my best friend held me. "You're going to cry it out. You're going to get the stitches removed and let your body heal. I'll get some essential oils to help reduce the scarring. You are going to make an appointment to talk to someone."

"Mila..." I gasped through the tears. She made it sound so easy, when it felt like an avalanche was pressing me down into the ground.

"No. You're going to do what I say because you know I love you. Right now, you're going to lean on me, Atlas, and Clay. The three of us are going to get you through this. I promise. One day, this will not crush you."

"He already did. He crushed my heart when he cheated and left; now he's destroyed my body. What else is there?"

She held me tighter. I didn't tell her she was hurting my wound, because I needed to feel the pain, feel *something* instead of the bone-crushing grief over what I'd become.

"Moe, life has just begun. A woman I adore, love more than anything, once told me every day life starts over with new things to appreciate and love."

I closed my eyes, remembering when I'd said those very words to Mila when she was scared to commit to Atlas. She'd been hurt by the past and by him but needed to let go in order to move on. And there they were; my words had come back to haunt me.

"Please focus on what's ahead. Lily. The new baby. Clayton."

Those three things alone were pretty damn great, and I did have them. Right now, even. I had those now.

For long minutes, we sat on the floor in silence. I let all the things she'd said burrow deep and plant seeds of hope back into my heart.

"Are you going to do what I said?" Mila finally asked in a hushed tone.

I nodded.

"I need to hear the words from your mouth that you're going to talk to someone."

I nuzzled into her shoulder and sighed. "Okay, I'll call someone."

Her arms tightened around me again. "I love you, Monet."

"I love you too." She would never know just how much her being there for me meant, but I'd try to find ways to show her.

Mila kissed the top of my head. "You feel better?"

"Can I plan the baby shower?" I changed the topic, wanting something good to focus on.

"I'd be bummed if you didn't," she said automatically.

"Can I plan the wedding?" I pushed.

Her entire body stilled, then suddenly, her chest shook with her laughter. "Is this emotional blackmail?"

I sat up and wiped at my eyes. "You deserve a real wedding, Mila. Not something big, just the Lotus House people, us, Atlas's mom. Maybe some of Atlas's new friends at work?"

"Would this make you happy, really?" She dipped her head, focusing on my eyes.

"Yeah. Planning a wedding for my best friend would give me something amazing to look forward to."

She shrugged. "Okay. We were just going to go to the courthouse once you were healed, but a small party couldn't hurt. I'm talking small. And we pay."

I opened my mouth to object, but she pressed her finger to my lips.

"We pay. You buy your own maid of honor dress and Lily's flower girl dress." Her smile was infectious.

"This is going to be great. Lily will love wearing a frilly dress." A renewed sense of purpose rippled through my chest and squeezed my heart. My best friend was a goddess.

Mila nodded. "Get her the most obnoxious fairytale dress ever. Frankly, I don't care as long as she's in it."

"Thank you." I grabbed Mila's hand.

She stood up and helped me stand. It hurt but didn't seem so bad with the new plans I had for the future.

"When you slip over the edge, I'm always going to help you climb back up. Same as what you do for me. That's what best friends are for. Making sure you don't go completely off the deep end." She winked and then left me alone in the closet.

I looked down at the pile of dresses on which I'd taken out my rage. One by one, I picked them up and hung them where they were supposed to go. I ran my fingers down the blue summer dress that reminded me of better times.

I fingered the flowing fabric. "Maybe one day I'll be brave enough to wear you again."

Mind set on new horizons, I went over to my bedside and pulled out my phone. I scrolled through my business contacts and settled on the one I needed.

The phone rang three times until a cheery voice answered. "Dr. Shelby Batchelor here."

I smiled, thinking of my sweet friend. We'd gone to college and then medical school together but had gone our separate ways since entering the field of psychiatry. I knew she mostly taught at UC Berkeley but saw clients twice a week to keep her clinical skills fresh.

"Hi, Shelby. It's Monet. I was wondering if I could make an appointment to see you."

"Oh, it's so good to hear your voice, Monet. Would this be for pleasure or business?"

I swallowed, pushed down the anxiety, and laid it out. "This would be personal. I need someone to talk to. Someone objective."

Once I had the words out, I allowed them to sink in and realized that Mila was right. Just as my clients needed someone to talk to about their trials and tribulations, so did I. Especially now.

This was one step in taking back what my ex stole from me.

★ ★ ★

Clayton arrived before the rest of the crew. As usual, his arms were filled with grocery bags.

"Didn't you get enough yesterday?" I asked, poking my head in.

"Today's special. I needed some wine for the ladies and some brewskies for the guys. You're allowed only a little since you're still taking medication."

I harrumphed dramatically. "I'll have you know, I have weened myself off the pain pills. I think that earns me at least two glasses."

Clayton shoved the bags to the side, gripped both of my hips, and pressed the long length of his body against mine. "Does it? Maybe if that request came with a kiss for your man, he could be persuaded to break the rules, just this once." His blue eyes blazed with heat, sending a shimmer of arousal through me.

"My man?" I sucked in a quick breath as he invaded my space more fully.

I set my hands on his ribs lightly and then decided against a light touch and went for bold. I held on to his body, which smarted against my healing muscles but was well worth it when he rewarded me with a sexy growl. Clay dipped his head to the curve of my neck and laid a series of long kisses there.

"Yes, your man. Me. The guy who's been making you dinner every day going on two weeks. The man who's got the wine." He waggled his eyebrows.

I giggled, feeling lighter than I had since the accident. He nipped his way up my neck, across my jaw to my lips. His face hovered over mine, our lips barely touching.

"The man who's been taking care of me." I inched my lower body closer, allowing the full length of our bodies to touch.

"Fuck yeah, that man is me. Your man," he reiterated.

My man. It sounded so foreign. "Hmm...time will tell," I whispered, not wanting to promise too much, even though each day Clayton was indeed making it clear the position he intended to have in my life and in this household.

"Fuck time. You're mine." He tunneled a hand into my hair and pressed our lips together.

We kissed hot and heavy like a pair of horny teenagers until the doorbell rang and Lily came screaming through the kitchen bumping into us on her way to let in our guests.

"Showtime." He dug his hands into my skin.

Clayton jerked his hips against my pelvis, letting me feel exactly what being pressed against him did to his anatomy. "You're so lucky we have guests," he said, his voice thick with lust and desire.

"Oh, yeah? If we didn't, you'd ravish me right here?" I toyed with his belt loop, trying to play coy even though the thought of things moving further excited and scared the hell out of me.

He winked and pushed back. "Something like that."

"Looking forward to that something," I quipped with a saucy little sway to my hips, feeling more womanly than I had in months. Clayton brought out a spicy side I didn't know I had but was starting to connect with more and more as the days went by. Yes, I feared Kyle. The ups and downs of my healing physically and mentally wasn't fun to deal with, but having Clayton in my life eased that burden. For all of us. Knowing he'd be there every night somehow made it all more bearable. Gave me a stronger motivation to find that peace inside of me. The happy place I'd been in before the attack.

I held the door open as Trent and Genevieve entered, little Will on Trent's hip. When Trent was home he seemed to always have his son close. He was a good father who took his role seriously, unlike the bastard ex of mine.

"Hey, man, you cooking?" Trent asked Clayton, a hint of hope in his tone.

"Yep. Been doing so every day since Monet came home."

Genevieve's eyebrows rose toward her hairline. "Really? Looks like I have some chatting to do with our friend Moe. Excuse me, guys." She turned around, her shiny blond hair bopping around her shoulders, her hips swaying. Genevieve was undeniably a lovely woman and a dead ringer for a young Gwen Stefani, complete with platinum hair and bright lips.

"Stop looking at my wife's ass before I slug you," Trent growled at Clay as he set a kicking Will down. He was just learning how to walk.

"I can't help that she has a nice ass, man," Clayton teased Trent, and I tried not to let their conversation bother me. I knew it was male posturing and bonding, not because Clayton was genuinely interested in Viv.

"Try." Trent gritted his teeth like the over-possessive man

we all knew him to be.

Clay waved a hand in surrender. "Okay, okay. Sorry, man. Want a beer?"

"Fuck yeah!"

"I'll get it," I said. Clayton nodded.

Genevieve approached me and pulled me into a light hug. "You okay? I mean, I know we've talked on the phone, but how are you really doing?"

I squeezed her hand. "I'm good. Really good. Mila, Atlas, and Clay have been taking care of me, and it's been hard, but..." I sighed. "I'm getting there. Every day is better than the last."

"I'm so glad. We've all been really worried. Hearing that Clay's on point makes me feel better. He'd never let anything happen to you under his watch."

I glanced over at the big man while he tended to the snacks and drinks. His smile was wide, and he seemed so at ease in my home. More than that, I was more at ease with him here.

"Yes, I believe you're right." I smiled and let her run off after some banging sounds echoed down the hall where the kids were playing. I turned to get a beer for Trent when the doorbell rang. Lily flew from around the corner of her room, running once again. Dash Alexander and his wife, Amber, entered. Amber held a chocolate cake in her hands.

"We brought dessert." She smiled sweetly, her brown hair falling prettily to both sides of her cheeks.

"No, you brought sex on a plate." Clayton looked at the dessert as if the triple-layer chocolate decadence was a naked woman ready to be taken. "Looks like a thousand calories in a single slice," he continued, looking at the treat. "Shit, guess I'll be doing double time in the gym tomorrow," he grumbled but licked his lips.

That single bit of tongue peeking out made my heart hammer in my chest. Thinking about Clay at the gym did not help the heat curling up my chest. I waved at my face, not prepared for how hot and bothered he'd been making me lately. I don't know if it was partly due to the fact that I'd weened myself off the pain pills or his sheer presence every day, or the fact that he kissed and touched me...often. My hormones were on overload, and I wanted a piece of Clayton far more than I wanted a piece of Amber's decadent cake.

Dash laughed. "Can't say I never gave you anything. My wife is amazing at everything she does." He grinned.

I rolled my eyes. "Beer?" I asked Dash, not wanting the tantric yoga god to start talking sex, as he often did. To Dash, a person's sexuality was always open for commentary. He just couldn't help himself.

Dash surveyed the counter. "Wine?"

"Pussy," Clay mumbled before getting the corkscrew and opening a bottle of red he'd bought.

Amber set the cake down and came straight toward me. She pulled me in for a hug and asked me how I was, immediately checking out my neck sutures and confirming the doctor did a great job. I wasn't ready to show her my back, even though I knew she wanted to see the extent of the injury. The resident in her was always on the surface, but like her husband with sex, she was passionate about what she did—she helped people. I just didn't want her to focus on it here tonight.

"Hey, Doc, you want a glass of red or white?" Clay asked Amber as she walked over and sat on the couch.

"Same as Dash, please." She cuddled against her husband's side.

"Of course," he deadpanned.

"Don't knock it till you try it," Dash warned and grinned like a loon.

"Believe me. I'm trying." His gaze slashed to mine and burned with a thousand unspoken words of want and need. My knees weakened at the heat burning in his baby blues.

He continued to stare as I got close. He put a hand on my back. "Genevieve would like a beer. I'll take the wine though," I murmured shyly to my guy. My guy. A flush of excitement sprang to my chest.

"Now that's my wife." Trent's chest puffed with pride as Genevieve sidled up to him.

"What?" she asked.

He looked down and kissed her nose. "Nothing, gumdrop. You're just perfect for me."

She petted his cheek. "Don't you forget it."

"Not possible." He smiled and kissed her quickly.

My cheeks flamed red-hot when Clay put a proprietary arm around my shoulders. Dash clocked the move right away, lifting his head in approval. Amber's mouth opened in what was likely shock. Dash's hand went for her mouth to cover it, but she grabbed his wrist and tucked it to her breasts. He immediately copped a feel.

"No way! Monet, you and Clayton! This is so awesome!" she gushed.

Without realizing it, I stiffened in Clay's arms. I knew he felt it because he pressed me closer and rubbed at my neck, trying to provide a little comfort to the part of the evening we had to get out of the way. Our friends would eventually find out we were seeing each other, and at least it came from the source and not through the gossip mill.

Clayton spoke, his voice sure and strong. "It's new," he

hedged. "And now that everyone knows we're seeing each other, we can move on to other things."

"Yes, please." I placed my wine glass in front of the bottle. He poured half a glass, and I lifted my gaze to his and pouted. Clay cocked an eyebrow in response.

I let it go and lifted the glass to my mouth, taking a sip and enjoying the berry notes floating tantalizingly over my tongue. A soft moan left my mouth at the luscious taste. Clayton didn't miss a beat. He tunneled his hand into my hair and kissed the essence of the wine right from my lips in front of everyone.

When he was done kissing the daylights out of me, I was dazed and probably glassy-eyed, not able to see anything but him.

The couples around us didn't say a word. Clayton grinned, turned, and tucked me to his side once more, where I planted my face to hide my flaming-hot cheeks.

"How do grilled steaks, potatoes, and salad sound to everyone?" he offered the room.

A round of approved grunts and yummies from the women sliced through the silence. The awkwardness evaporated as he grabbed the steaks, kissed my forehead, and headed to the backyard to fire up the grill and hang out with Mila and Atlas.

We'd survived the uncomfortable moment of each person checking on me and us updating our friends about our new relationship. None of them seemed all that taken by the news, which not only made me feel more secure in my decision to move forward but paved the way for the idea of future barbeques, birthdays, holidays, and more as one big happy group to resonate through my mind. Nothing but love and light seemed to be ahead. One day at a time. Things were starting to fall into place.

CHAPTER EIGHT

HEART
C H A K R A

A heart-centered couple will experience challenges just like any other, but these struggles tend to strengthen their relationship, not weaken it. Each new challenge faced will have their love growing and expanding in time.

CLAYTON

Damn, that woman was going to kill me. Not being able to touch her the way I wanted to, hold her, make love to her. Fuck! I ran my hands through my spikey hair and did some yoga breathing in order to cool my jets.

Soon. I'd have her all to myself soon. I just had to be patient and let this play out. Give her more time to heal. She was just starting to come around. Rushing her more than I had wouldn't do either of us any favors.

Slow. I'd promised slow, and that was what I'd give her. Besides, it was no hardship to touch, flirt, and kiss Monet Holland. The anticipation of more might be killing me, but it definitely wasn't a bad way to go.

Heart and head in check, I refilled her wine—another half glass—and grabbed a handful of beers for the crew. We had settled into the formal living room, where Monet had several couches, tables, and low lighting. It was perfect for chilling with so many couples. Atlas and Mila were hanging out on the floor, him plucking at his guitar while she, eyes closed, hummed and swayed to the rhythm he set. They were perfectly content with one another, and I privately applauded them. They'd stuck with it through thick and thin and had worked out their differences when many would have just gone their separate ways.

Kind of like I did when I met Monet a year ago. The insane attraction was there even then, but my mind was still obliterated by fear. The thought of Monet having a child when my ex, Stacey, had fucked me over so bad had me backtracking fast. At the time, I was frightened of what it might mean to fall for someone who had a child. I'd worried it would bring up the old wounds and anger for what I'd lost out on. So I'd shied away. Out of fear, I had bailed on the budding connection Monet and I had. Now that I'd gotten a taste of Monet and this life, I wanted to shake my earlier self. I could have had this happiness for over a year. A year I'd wasted on bimbos and beers. Working hard and ignoring what I desperately craved...a family. Settling down with the right woman, trying again for a future I had always wanted—one that Stacey had taken away from me so abruptly. That particular sore was still raw. However, Monet eased that ache. The prospect of having Monet and Lily and a future together healed the hole Stacey left in my heart. I knew my feelings for her were coming fast and furious, but I didn't care. I was a thirty-year-old man who had finally gotten a small nibble of what I wanted, and there was no way in hell I was backing away from it. Not now, not ever. Monet would come around. I'd work toward healing the hurt Kyle left behind and teach her she could trust me.

I surveyed the room, appreciating the chill vibe this crew brought to the space. Not only did it make me feel comfortable, but I welcomed this change in my life. Being surrounded by couples who were settled and moving into their futures together was exactly what I wanted—and hoped I could have with Monet.

I handed Trent a fresh cold one.

"Thanks, man."

I pointed one toward Genevieve, or Viv, as most of us called her. She shook her head. "I have to drive."

Keeping my pace, I set a fresh beer on the brick next to the fireplace where Atlas sat. He lifted his head in thanks and kept strumming on his guitar. I clicked my tongue in reply.

Scoping out the table, I noted that Dash's and Amber's wine glasses were still half full. I brought a new half glass to Monet. She reached out for it and winced, sucking in a fast breath through her teeth. I sat next to her and rubbed along the back of her head and through the silky tresses of her hair. She hummed.

"You okay?"

She made a noncommittal sound. "Yeah, just sore today. I did more than I have been. Trying to push myself."

"When are you getting the stitches out?" Trent asked.

"Monday."

"I'd be happy to go with you," Amber said, her eyes lighting up at the idea of seeing a medical procedure. The woman had just started her third year of medical school and was eager to expose herself to all things medicine, even though she'd chosen to practice in pediatrics.

Dash chuckled and rubbed a hand down his wife's back. "Little bird, I'm not sure our friend wants an audience."

Amber frowned. "But why not?"

Viv chuckled and patted Amber's knee. "We'll talk later."

"But you had a baby and let me see the whole thing," Amber fired back. "It was absolutely amazing, you guys." Her face lit with excitement.

"We know, we know!" Atlas and Mila said at the same time. Both of them looked at each other and started laughing and then kissing like two lovebirds.

"What?" Amber scowled, not getting the joke at her expense.

"Amber honey, you've told Will's birth story at least a hundred times." Viv stated it in a placating tone but still patted her hand lovingly.

She shrugged. "I can't help it. Seeing my nephew brought into the world was like..." Smiling wide, she looked up to the ceiling.

"Watching a miracle come to life." Almost the entire room finished her statement, having literally heard her say it more times than any of us had fingers and maybe even toes.

Everyone burst into raucous laughter, joy and friendship spilling out around the room. I genuinely enjoyed the camaraderie of the group. Usually I hung out with Trent and Atlas, sometimes Dash, but mostly when we were at the gym or shooting the shit at the local pub. Sitting in a room full of couples and being one of those couples gave me a sense of rightness, of purpose. A new sensation I'd twist my arm to get more of. It had been too long since I was in a relationship or been one of the crew. I had to admit I wanted it long term.

"Aw honey, come here." Dash nuzzled his wife's cheek and brought her close. "You can tell me the miracle of life story a million times." He nibbled at her ear sweetly.

She pouted and mumbled, "It was pretty incredible seeing God's love like that."

Dash stroked his wife's hair and kissed her cheek. "I know, I know. How about you tell me the story again tonight while my fingers are so far up your..." He lowered his voice and continued whispering into his wife's ear.

Amber's cheeks turned a bright crimson, and she crossed her legs and gripped her knees with both hands, all ten knuckles on her fingers turning a bright white. She swallowed and moved back, fanning her face. "I think we have to go," she muttered, her voice cracking.

That time, Monet and I howled.

Dash stood up, holding his wife's hand. "We must take our leave. I have a woman's needs to tend to this evening." He grinned wickedly, and Amber laid her head against his chest, letting the veil of her hair hide her face.

Monet went to get up but I stayed her movement. "I'll walk them out."

She smiled and squeezed my hand.

Once they left, I checked on Lily and Will. The baby was already asleep on a pallet of blankets on the floor in front of the TV. Lily was lying next to him. She turned her head and lifted a finger to her lips and made a shushing sound.

"Baby's sweeping."

"Sleeping. He's sleeping, not sweeping."

"Shhh, King Clay."

I chuckled, ruffled her hair, and went back to our friends. Atlas was now singing a song he'd just written for an up-and-coming male singer Knight & Day Productions had signed. The guy he was writing for had a grunge approach and alternative appeal that hadn't been given a go in the music industry for a solid twenty years.

Atlas belted out the chorus of the new song.

Take me away from here...
From the things that harm.
It's cold and strange...
alone...
Never warm.
Take me away from here, bring me home.

His voice flowed and ebbed like a wave, and when he finished, the character's fear and anxiety fell away with the lyrics of the song.

"Damn, Curly, you're so talented." Mila grabbed Atlas's face and laid a wet kiss on his lips. "That song is going to be a hit when that new kid sings it and works with you to put his spin on it."

He smiled. "I think so."

"Man, it's really great," Trent added.

"You can tell the guy is tortured and searching for something more out of life. A home. Something we all need to feel at peace," Genevieve contributed.

Boy, Viv hit the nail on the head with her insightful comment. I could relate to the guy in the song. He wanted to get away from the world that made him feel out of place. He wanted to find a home where he could be at peace within his soul. I too had been looking for that very thing. I glanced at Monet, her skin glowing against the light of the lamp behind her. Her lips glistened and I watched her pucker them in thought. Her beauty floored me, but in that moment, sitting around our friends, being touched by a song that could tell the story of my life, she was so much more. She was my future.

"I like the part about him wanting to be brought home. I can relate to that," Monet said, her body flush against the arm of the couch, one hand holding up her head.

For a while we all just sat, sipping our drinks and listening to Atlas entertain us, until the phone rang.

Monet grabbed the handheld sitting on the table near her side. She looked at the display and frowned before bringing it to her ear. "Hello?" she said and walked out of the room, probably to hear better. I watched as she stopped midstride in the entry to the kitchen. One of her hands flew out to the wall as if she needed to hold herself up.

A sense of dread prickled against my spine as I watched her body bow and shoulders fall. Her head turned toward me, her eyes flat and lifeless. Her entire face went white as a sheet. Shit!

★ ★ ★

"You think you can hide away in your house and I wouldn't know where you were, huh? You stupid bitch." An angry, hateful voice ripped through the line.

My heart started pounding and the hair on the back of my neck stood up.

"You think what I did to you was the worst of it? Oh no. I

have so much more planned for you." Again that voice, hateful and ugly, but I recognized it.

It took me several moments, though, to understand what I was hearing.

"Kyle?" I knew it deep down to my soul that my ex, my attacker, was on the line. The sensation of acid burning my skin filtered through every pore as I held the receiver tighter and tried not to be frightened.

Breathe, Monet. Breathe. He doesn't control you.

"You know, Monet, I have dreamed every night about slitting your throat and watching you bleed out onto the concrete floor of that garage."

I reached for my neck on instinct. My throat tightened and I slammed my hand against the wall, trying to breathe and calm down. "No, Kyle, no. Why?" The words were small, childlike, and filled with sorrow.

He chuckled as though what he was doing was nothing more than a sick game. "Monet, you stupid cunt. I told you. That money you have should have been ours. You're just wasting it away on that beaker baby and that fucktard friend of yours. You're probably buying her bullshit art now too."

I clenched my teeth, my entire body now shaking uncontrollably. "I gave you everything," I choked out, gripping the phone as hard as I could even though I wanted to smash it against the wall. He'd been my husband, the man I opened my heart and body to. At one point, he'd been everything to me. I thought I was to him, too. We'd been happy. For a time.

He laughed manically, the sound cold and toxic—a laugh I'd never heard from his lips before. "You gave me nothing but a limp dick. That's why I couldn't get you pregnant. Then you had to go and stuff your cunt full of someone else's sperm.

Good fucking riddance."

"Monet..." I heard Clayton's voice from behind me. "Who's on the phone?" he demanded.

I ignored Clay and focused on my ex. "Kyle, you can't possibly hate me this much. I didn't do anything. I was a good wife." God, I gave him *everything*. Made dinner every night, provided us a home, a child. I'd supported all that he loved and encouraged him to do what he wanted to do. Never demeaned him or his manhood.

"You were a good-for-nothing boring bitch of a wife. I hated every day of being married to you. I have more fun in the sack with your sister than I ever had with you. You disgust me. And the second you leave your house and you're all alone," he taunted, "I'll get you back under me. Only, this time, I'll be having all the fun." His promise slithered up my spine and clenched around my heart so tight I could barely breathe.

A sob tore through me. "No." I shook my head and fell to my knees, the cold tile and harsh fall barely registering.

"Fuck, babe!" Clayton was there, curving protectively around me and trying to grab for the phone.

I shook my head and shivers racked my frame violently.

"Yes!" His tone was confident, bordering on arrogant. "And when you're dead, Matisse will get your child and all the money she should have had. Sleep with one eye open, Monet. I'm coming for you," he sneered and laughed hard before the line went dead.

I dropped the phone, and it clacked to the ground and bounced, a piece flying off it. Strong arms came around me from behind.

"Monet, baby, please. Get up."

I couldn't move. The tears poured from my eyes, my

fingers grasped for anything to hold on to, but instead there was nothing. Nothing but the cold, hard tile below my palms.

"He's going to get me. He's going to kill me. Oh my God." The words left my mouth on a screech. But Clayton was there. He pulled me into his arms so we faced each other. I wrapped my legs around his waist, and he lifted me off the ground as if he'd had practice doing it. He moved smoothly, taking care not to jerk or jostle my body too much.

"Moe..." Mila said, her hand grasping for mine.

I pulled my hands away and fisted them. "No, he'll get you too. Don't touch me!" I cried out, attempting to kick and push off the steel bands that had me wrapped up.

"Stop struggling. Stop it, Monet. It's me. Clayton. Beautiful, I'm here. I've got you."

I shook my head, his words not hitting their mark. "No. He's going to kill me."

His head pressed against mine so his lips were touching my ear. I shivered.

"Atlas, see to our guests while I take care of Moe and put her to bed."

"Got it," he called out.

"He's going to kill me. He's going to kill me. He's going to kill me." The words fell from my lips over and over as Clayton held me and walked through the house and down the hall.

His hand locked around the nape of my neck while he rested his head alongside mine. "No one's going to kill you. No one is going to so much as touch a hair on your head. I fucking swear it!" he growled as he pushed open my bedroom door and kicked it shut.

With harsher strides than he'd used before, he stomped over to my bed, turned, sat down, and pushed back until we were against my pillows, where he laid us both out flat. Me on top of his body. I shook uncontrollably, every word Kyle said running through my system like hot lava. Clayton tugged the side of the comforter up and covered us with it. A blanket of warmth shrouded over me, and I tucked my body in tighter, bringing up my knees alongside Clayton's hips and cowering into his body.

Clayton whispered words of comfort, caressed my sides, my arms, and head as I shook.

"You're okay, beautiful."

He ran a hand down my side. I trembled, trying to let go, but failed.

"I'm here." A promise.

I shook my head against his chest as tears leaked out and wet his shirt. The sobs tore through my lungs as Kyle's words shredded my battered psyche once more.

Clayton held me through it all, allowing me to get it out.

I'm not sure how long I lay there and cried while he comforted me. I didn't even hear everything he said to me until the following words entered my emotional haze.

"You're safe." Another promise I couldn't dare to believe.

He pressed his lips against my temple as I gripped his ribs and focused on his heart.

Thump thump. Thump thump. Thump thump.

"I'll protect you."

A long, heavy breath left my lungs as I warmed, the tears drying up and Kyle's words fading out while Clayton's seeped in. His heartbeat, his caress, and his words lulled me into a dreamlike state until I finally relaxed. The trembling stopped, my muscles twitching and easing along with the rest of me.

Clayton paired his breathing with mine and I nuzzled into

his form, rubbing along his solid frame. He was safety. As long as I stayed with him, I had nothing to fear.

"What did he say to you?" he asked after what had to be at least thirty minutes of us lying there.

I mulled over the conversation, trying to use a blind perspective as I would when giving therapy to my clients. Remain separate from the equation, don't step into the client's shoes, be thoughtful but considerate. Give the client something to think about, tools to figure out their own problems and manage their lives in a healthy way. That's what I was supposed to do. Needed to do in order to get through this and find perspective.

Do not let Kyle control you. You are in control of your reactions.

I cleared the scratchiness from my throat after my mental pep talk. "He said he was going to kill me." *Just the facts, Monet. Don't put yourself in the picture.* I continued. "Promised to take my baby and all of my money." The agony at the mere thought of losing Lily shredded my therapeutic approach, and the tears formed again.

No, no, no! Stay strong.

"Keep going. I need to know." Clayton rubbed my scalp, and I listened to his heartbeat get stronger. He wasn't unaffected, even though his attempt at being cool and calm was commendable.

I swallowed down the fear that had crept up my throat. "Said I couldn't hide forever in this house."

Clayton's arms tightened almost painfully around my body.

"Do you believe what he said?"

For a couple minutes, I thought about everything. The

cops were after him for attempted murder and wanted to question my half sister. Logic flew out the window as I spoke. "Clay, he *did* get to me. He almost killed me once. Who's to say he won't get me when I'm alone? Mila and Atlas can't stay here forever. Eventually we all have to go back to work, live our lives. What then?"

Clayton pushed me to my good side and faced me on the bed. He lifted one of my legs and wrapped it around his waist so we were glued together. In another world during another time, I'd rejoice in the splendor that was being wrapped around this man. A man I'd lusted after for over a year.

His tone was adamant. "I'm not going to let anything happen to you. We'll make sure you're covered at all times. One of the first things we need to do is call the police. Update the detectives on your case so they can find out where that call originated. If he's close, they need to have units trolling."

Tears slipped out of my eyes as I remembered all the horrible things Kyle had said.

"He told me I was a horrible wife." A fresh bout of sadness struck.

Clayton cupped my cheek and waited until I'd opened my eyes to look at him. "I don't believe that's possible. I've been here every day for over a week, and I never want to leave. No man in his right mind could spend time with you, glory in your beauty every day, and not want to own it for himself. I'd be one lucky son of a bitch to have you forever."

More tears spilled out. God, so many tears. For a long, long time, I let his words penetrate and cried into his chest. Cried for the injustice of it all. Cried for the pain my ex caused. For Lily. For the fact that Clayton deserved my best and was continually saving me.

Eventually, the tears subsided and I realized I was warm. So warm. Content to be held in this man's arms as I let myself completely lose it. And he stayed. Held me through it all. Whispered his admiration for me, told me repeatedly how pretty, funny, and smart I was. How he loved my daughter and that I was an amazing mother. He did that for me.

Clayton's lips pressed against my temple.

"Are you feeling better?" he asked.

I nodded against his chest, where I'd kept my ear to his heart. Its beat was melodic, calming, the best sound in the world. I'd fall asleep to it every night if I could.

Clayton groaned and stretched his limbs out. That's when it dawned on me that I had moved my hand under his shirt, stroking his chest, running my fingertips in patterns across the ridges of his muscles. Each indentation was perfectly defined and fit each of my fingers as though I was drawing lines in the sand.

"I'm sorry." I stopped moving my hand, leaving it flat against his abdomen.

He chuckled, the sound manly and sexy. "Don't be sorry for putting your hands on me, beautiful. I love it."

I nuzzled his chest, hiding my face. "I like your muscles. You're warm and so...defined. Feels nice against my fingertips," I admitted rather shyly.

He put a hand on my booty, reached down to cup the cheek, and squeezed. "And you've got a stellar ass. I've wanted to get my hands on it for a while. So how's about we make a deal. You can run your fingers all over my chest and stomach if I can cop feels of this ass." He squeezed the underside, nudging me closer to him. A burst of arousal rippled down to center hotly between my thighs. On instinct, I rubbed my thigh against his, putting my sex in contact with his muscular leg. A sizzle of excitement zipped through me, taking away every ounce of melancholy and fear I'd had an hour ago and replacing it with scorching-hard lust. This—being with this man, feeling alive inside—that's what I needed. I was tired, so tired of being scared, of crying. I wanted to live. Feel alive.

"Mmm, I like when you rub along me like a content little kitty cat. You gonna purr for me?"

"Isn't it your job to make me purr?" I said boldly, not believing the words as they left my mouth.

I chanced a glance up at Clayton and found his blue eyes dark and dangerous. He bit into his bottom lip.

"Mouth, up here. Now," he growled.

I inched up and plastered my lips to his. One of his hands held the back of my head, controlling the kiss as he liked to do. He slid his other hand to the cheek of my ass and lifted, shifting me fully on top of him. Boldly, Clayton ran his hand down the center of my body and cupped my sex from behind. I moaned into his mouth, pleasure replacing the hate and horror of what happened earlier. I responded to his touch by delving my tongue deep inside his mouth. With my good arm, I held myself so that I could rub my lower half against him.

"Are we doing this?" I whispered into his mouth, sucking on his bottom lip, showing with my actions that I wanted to.

He nudged my head up and sucked his favorite spot on the side of my neck. "No. Just taking the edge off."

I hummed and rubbed my pelvis against his. The steel length of his erection slid perfectly against the tender bundle of nerves seeking friction.

"What if I want more?" I pressed harder and gasped at the bliss shooting through every nerve ending.

"You'll get what I give when I give it," Clayton growled, lifting his hips and thrusting against me. I was losing my mind to this man, and I never wanted it to end.

CHAPTER NINE

HEART
CHAKRA

Couples with open heart chakras don't usually experience major problems understanding one another. Their principal nature wanting to bring joy and peace to their partner and not pain, they tend to avoid hurting one another with careless jabs or snide commentary.

CLAYTON

Her body was over mine, and the sweet connection of her pussy rubbing along the hard edge of my dick through our clothes was unbelievable. Fucking magical. I felt like I was in high school again, out of my mind with lust for the hot cheerleader. Only, Monet was no naïve teen. She was a goddess.

Shifting us together so as to not hurt her, I backed toward the head of the bed, Monet in my lap, until my back rested against the headboard. She moaned when the full length of my erection rubbed along the edge of her seam. With slow movements, I unbuttoned the loose silk blouse she'd worn for the get-together and tossed it over the side of the bed. Underneath she'd worn a camisole sans bra. I could see her pert nipples poking into the silk, and I wanted to bite them through the fabric. On her lower half she was wearing a thin pair of yoga pants and nothing else.

Once I centered her over my lap, I took her mouth in a searing kiss. She held my head and hummed her appreciation around my tongue. Fuck. That sound made me wonder what it would feel like with my dick shoved down her pretty throat while she sucked me into oblivion.

Later. We had time. Right now it was my job to take her mind off what happened this evening. Show her how much she was desired. Wanted. Needed. And fuck, did I need her.

"You're so damn beautiful," I whispered along her neck, sucking and nibbling, her jasmine scent surrounding me.

She sighed and thrust her hips against my cock. A searing jolt of desire shot up my spine, urging me on.

"Fuck yeah, you feel that?" I ground her down on my cock. "You do that to me, Monet. Your sexy-as-fuck body, elegant face, and unending kindness. I want to own it. Kiss it. Suck it into my body until I'm drowning in you."

"Clayton..." She moaned, kissing along my neck. Her tongue came out and lapped at my collar from one side to the other. I pushed her back a few inches, just enough to lift my shirt over my head and let her look and touch her fill. "You're so hard and soft at the same time," she said, running her fingers across my chest.

Her touch was a white-hot brand. I wanted her hands all

over me all the time.

I tunneled one hand into her hair and used my thumb to lift her chin. "I'm going to take your shirt off because I want to see your pretty tits. Is that okay?" I asked, because I knew that getting naked in front of a man after the type of injury she endured could be frightening. The last thing I'd ever want was for Monet to be scared of being close to me in bed.

"I trust you." Her words were spoken like a prayer.

I lifted her camisole slowly and let her slip both arms through the armholes, then eased it over her head. I licked my lips and cupped both breasts in my hands, swiping her erect nipples with my thumbs. She gasped and arched slowly into my hold.

"Perfect for my hands. Look, baby. Just right for me." I circled each tip again.

Her breath quickened, and I curved forward, taking one brown tip into my mouth. Monet wrapped both of her hands into my hair, holding me close. Like I'd leave her tit. I swirled my tongue around the tight peak until it was nice and pointed, practically stabbing my tongue. I flicked and then pressed my teeth down over the erect nub to worry it a little more forcefully. She seemed to like that a lot. Her entire body tightened like a rubber band stretched to capacity and ready to break. Then she pressed down hard, grinding into my crotch, getting herself off.

Fuck yeah, my woman was primed.

Dragging my mouth away from one tip, I took in the other, licking and sucking it the same way I did the first. Monet's hips stirred over my cock. I knew if I put my hands into her pants, they'd be soaked.

"Clay...oh God. You're going to make me come."

I grinned around her pretty titty, sucking it and biting down. Her body went ramrod straight, as if she was going to soar at any second. Not wanting her to just yet, I backed off and stayed her hips.

I shifted her back enough that I could look at her tits and her face. She groaned and opened her eyes. They were glassy and filled with desire. Just the way I wanted her. Her lips were a berry red as she bit into the bottom one.

"God, I want to fuck you so hard, beautiful." I petted each breast and squeezed her nipples simultaneously between thumb and forefinger.

She let out a breath of air. "Then do it," she goaded.

My girl was gone for me. I grinned wickedly. "Baby, when I fuck you, *make love* to you, we're going to be alone and need at least twenty-four hours of uninterrupted time. And I want your back healed so I can pound into you from above." I ran my hands to her tiny waist, letting my thumbs caress down each side.

"Clayton..." She stirred her hips and lifted her hands to her breasts, cupping them and plucking at the nipples.

Fuck yeah. My dick surged at the sight, seeking her heat.

While I watched her tweak her nipples, I took my right hand and slid it inside the front of her yoga pants. She wasn't wearing any panties, but I'd known that since I grabbed her ass earlier and felt no panty lines.

"Just as I suspected." I rubbed all four fingers across her wet pussy. "Fucking soaked."

She moaned as I rubbed, then cried out when I inserted two long digits into her heat. I used my thumb to swirl around the tight knot of her clit. It was hard as a pebble and aching for attention.

"Oh my God. Oh my God." Her hands flew to my shoulders to balance herself.

"Ride my hand, babe. I want to feel you come all over my fingers while I suck your pretty tits."

I curved toward one succulent breast and sucked to my heart's content. I wanted nothing more than to mark her tits, a hickey to each globe, but my woman had been marked enough by a man. Fucking bastard. Right now, she deserved nothing but a nice hard orgasm given by me, the man who was going to take care of her. Hopefully for a good long while, maybe even forever.

She rode my hand, circling her hips as I plunged deep. It was a tight fit for my hand between her yoga pants, but I was up for the challenge. Moving to the other breast, I flicked the tight tip with my tongue, teasing the sensitive bud.

Monet rode my hand, pressing against my dick in a dizzying pattern, and I thrusted into her movements. I knew I was likely to blow my load in my pants, but I didn't fucking care. My woman was half naked, my mouth on her glistening tits, my fingers in her pussy. Nothing could be better.

Her pussy contracted around my fingers, and I grinned. "Mouth, beautiful. When you come, I want to taste your tongue."

She panted, closed her eyes, and nodded, focusing on her pleasure. Up and down, her legs moved as she rode. Her hips swayed side to side, grinding my dick with every rotation. Plunging deep, I added a third finger to her heat. Her eyes opened wide, her mouth keening on a silent cry. The walls of her sex locked down like a vise around me. I used my free hand to bring her head close so I could take her mouth. I delved my tongue in and kissed her while her body locked around mine, going impossibly tight.

A soft cry left her mouth around my lips, and I swallowed it down. My balls drew up tight to my groin, the crown of my dick wedged against my hand and her pussy, aching for more friction. A searing heat blasted through my loins, and my cock jerked as I thrusted hard, my release shooting up and out as we rode one another to orgasm.

As she calmed her movements, I removed my fingers but continued to pet her clit lightly. I could feel the twinges of her sex as a few tremors rocked through her.

She sighed into my mouth, and her body became a deadweight against my chest. I removed my hand and licked the digits clean. She tasted so good I couldn't wait to get a taste direct from the source. Nevertheless, I continued with my new mantra. We had all the time in the world. I'd put that activity off until later.

Once I'd licked her arousal off my fingers, I wrapped her up in my arms, firmly holding her around the hips. The sticky mess in my briefs would have to wait because there was no way in hell I was moving until my dark-haired goddess was ready.

"Clayton, that was..."

"Magnificent? Fucking hot? Pure bliss?" I offered.

"Yummy," was her innocent reply.

I laughed against her silky hair as the strands spread out across my chest. I loved feeling those velvety strands all over my naked body. One day soon I looked forward to feeling it in other areas, like my thighs, abdomen, and across my dick.

"Yummy?" I whispered against her neck, kissing my spot, licking the salt from the fine mist of sweat covering her skin.

She hummed, that sound going straight to my dick. The woman made me insane with lust. Her body was lying across mine, snuggled in close.

"Yeah, yummy." She licked a line across my shoulder. "Yep. Yummy," she mumbled, sounding sleepy.

My girl had to be tired. After the emotional turmoil of that call, the long day with friends, the wine, and now a solid orgasm, she needed rest. And I needed to call the cops and update the detectives on her case.

I shifted her body so she lay on her good side. I pulled off her yoga pants and groaned. Fuck, her bottom half was just as sexy as her upper half.

"You getting me naked?" she murmured, pressing her hands into a prayer position under her cheek.

She looked so alluring, her black hair spread out on the white sheet, her olive skin a stunning contrast to the white. If I didn't know better, I'd swear she was my very own angel. I didn't think I'd ever seen anything so ethereal, magical. Straight up living art. Now I understood why Mila painted so many nudes. If she painted Monet, she'd make millions.

I took a breath and covered her with the blanket. "Yeah, beautiful, those pants of yours are soiled."

Instead of finding her something else to wear, I picked up my shirt and helped ease her into it. She barely stirred. Once covered, the shirt going to mid-thigh, I surveyed my woman. Yep, still sexy as fuck, but now she was wrapped up in something that was mine. The Neanderthal in me perked up with male pride. Except my gym bag was in the car, and I was shirtless with a sticky pair of briefs under my track pants.

Gross didn't cover it. I was downright filthy.

The filth did not prevent me from grinning my ass silly while in the bathroom. I took a fast shower and put the track pants back on, sans sticky briefs, so I could go get my bag and check on Atlas and Mila. I was sure they had taken care of business like I'd asked.

When I exited Monet's room and entered the kitchen, Mila and Atlas were sitting at the bar, chatting.

"Trent and Genevieve leave okay?" I asked.

Atlas nodded. "Yeah, they were uncomfortable with what happened. Promised them you'd take care of Moe and we had this covered. Told the crew I'd check in tomorrow after we had a chance to brief the cops."

I nodded and ran a hand through my hair, remembering again I was in nothing but my track pants.

Atlas quickly ran his gaze over me from head to toe. "So, you guys were in there a *long* time."

I didn't address the amount of time we were gone. The time it took me to take care of my woman didn't matter to anyone but me. As long as she was okay, safe and sound in her bed, wearing my shirt after having what I considered a pretty stellar orgasm, anyone else could fuck right off.

"Monet okay?" Mila asked. She scanned down my bare chest, one eyebrow cocked in what I could only assume was intrigue.

"I take care of what's mine," I declared.

"Is that so? You going to be doing that until she's completely healed or until they catch Kyle?" She crossed her arms over her chest.

Knowing what Mila was really asking, I decided it was time she was in on my intentions with Monet. "I'm in a relationship with your best friend. She's my responsibility now. Not that you aren't important to her or me. But her safety and happiness rest on my shoulders. You feel me?"

Mila smiled. "Couldn't ask for better."

I liked that Mila thought I was good for Monet. It wouldn't have mattered if she didn't, but it sure as hell made things easier if her best friend, the woman who was like a sister to her, approved.

"Did you put Lily to bed?" I asked, glancing around the dark room, seeing that the pallet she'd been lying on was gone, the blankets folded up and placed in the basket in the corner. The rooms were clean of any mess, all the wine glasses were washed and in the strainer, and the beer bottles had been removed.

"Of course we did." Atlas cringed. "Dude, do I need to remind you that we've been family long before you came around?"

I clenched my teeth, realizing he was right. Still, I couldn't help the need to protect crawling up my spine. It made me downright overbearing. "Yeah, well, now I'm here. And like I said, I'll be taking care of my girls." I made sure what I said was direct and to the point. There would be no questioning my position in this household or with Monet and Lily anymore. Not even from her best friends.

"Your girls?" Mila's tone carried a hint of amusement.

"Damn straight."

"Right on," Mila said with mildly smug satisfaction.

I smiled and clasped her shoulder in thanks for her support. "As you can see, I need a shirt."

Again Mila's gaze ran up and down my form. "Don't put on a shirt on my account." She grinned and waggled her eyebrows. "You're built. I could look at you all day." Mila had never been a shy woman.

I laughed and Atlas frowned. "Do I need to put you over my knee and spank your ass, wildcat?"

She grinned and winked at me before turning around. "Oh, I'd like to see you try!" she fired off before leaping from the stool and running down the opposite hall toward the guest bedroom.

Atlas turned to me and placed a hand on my shoulder. "Like the way you took care of Moe. Happy you're here for them. They need a good man in their lives."

"And I'll try to be that man with everything I've got in me."

"Fuckin' A. Now I've got a hot little Latina to nail down, with an emphasis on the nailing." He waggled his own eyebrows, his curly hair flopping over his forehead.

I laughed. "You do that. Just don't wake Lily. I'm going to update the detectives, get them over here in the morning. And I'm spending the night." I let that hang out in the open. This would be the first time I'd be staying the night, and I didn't want any flack.

"Figured as much," he said and sauntered off to his woman.

I shook my head, retrieved my bag from my car, and stopped when I got back to the front door. I turned and stared off into the night, clocking every car on the street, surveying the ones in the driveways, which houses had lights on and off. I didn't see anything suspicious or any place someone watching might hide. Made me think he was lying.

Maybe Kyle was just trying to scare her. Either way, tomorrow we'd be dealing with the detectives. And that security system she said she didn't need would be installed immediately; I'd make sure of it. She had no choice in the matter. Same went for changing the locks and her phone numbers.

Fucker messed with the wrong woman.

MONET

I woke with warmth blanketed all around me. A steady beat entered my consciousness, and I smelled fresh pine and musky man. I hummed and snuggled in before it dawned on me that my face was planted against a very hard, very real male chest.

Slowly I eased my head up, resting my chin on the firm flesh.

A hand wrapped around my nape as I lifted my gaze to meet the clear blue eyes of the man I'd been dreaming about.

"Mornin', beautiful." Clayton rubbed at the back of my head, and I practically purred. I stretched my leg higher, coming into contact with a hard, very impressive bit of his anatomy.

He grunted and tried to shift away, but I wouldn't allow it. Nope, instead I ran my hand down his muscled chest, feeling every slab until I encountered a pair of cotton briefs. I kept going. Clayton's eyes heated in the morning light, golden flecks bouncing in every direction mixing with the blue as I wrapped my hand around the stiff length. The tip nudged the very top of his underwear.

"If you're going to wake me with your hand on my cock, beautiful, I'm never going to leave. Gives a man ideas."

I grinned, feeling feminine and sultry in the quiet and stillness of the morning. Brave, even. I could tell the entire house was still sleeping, including my daughter, or she'd already be bouncing in the room. As she'd gotten older, she liked to sleep in, and growing girls needed their beauty sleep. I rubbed my hand up and down Clayton's steely length. Looked like growing boys needed something else.

My mouth watered at the idea of pulling his briefs down

and wrapping my lips around the plush head of his cock. Would he allow it? Did men turn down a willing woman ready to blow them? I didn't think so. I'd been out of the game a long while, but I couldn't imagine he'd reject me.

Getting up the nerve, I shifted up and straddled the lower half of Clayton's legs. I rubbed up and down his length and raised my gaze to his face. "This for me?" I asked, trying my best to sound sultry and sexy.

He hummed, raised one hand over his head, and rested the other just above the line of his underwear on his hips.

"Do you want it?" he asked smugly.

I licked my lips, got bold, and tugged the material down past his protruding cock.

"I asked if it was for me." I scratched my nails down his legs as I pulled off his underwear, getting him fully naked.

"You know it is. Having your gorgeous body draped over me all night, a man can't help but be hard as stone when he's got you half naked in bed."

His words filled me with pride and a sense of sexual freedom. This sinfully attractive man wanted me. Me. Monet Holland, boring therapist, divorced, and single mother to a five-year-old. And now I had what would be a nasty scar marring my entire back, yet he was hard as a rock. He didn't care about what Kyle had done, other than wanting to kill him. He only cared about me. About Lily.

"Do you want my mouth on you?" I asked, running one finger down his naked length. His dick bounced up a full inch, as if reaching for my touch. His cock was thick, long, and hard. More than I'd had in the past. And it had been so long since I'd had intercourse. Knowing I had this to look forward to made arousal tingle through my entire body with anticipation.

Clayton's eyebrows came together. "Is that a trick question? Look at me. I'm fucking weeping for you." He thrust his hips up.

As I looked down, I noticed the pearl of pre-cum dripping from the slit at the top. Easing down into a comfortable position that didn't put too much strain on my back, I flicked my tongue at that drop and took the first taste. I moaned in appreciation.

He jerked his hips, bonking my mouth with the crown. "Don't tease me, beautiful. A man could go crazy when the gift of heaven is knocking at the door."

I sighed, curled my fist around his impressive girth, lifted it straight up, and took him in my mouth.

"Fuuuuucccckkkkkkk," he growled.

He tasted of soap and salt, a unique combination I found I liked very much as I sucked him like a lollipop. Then, swirling my tongue around the head, I shimmied my hips lower to get in a more direct position with his manhood.

"Babe, no. Don't go lower. Turn around. Straddle my chest so I can taste you too."

I let his cock slip from my lips and it slapped wetly against his cut abdomen. It was so long and thick it almost reached his belly button. Nestled at the root were neatly cropped, dark-blond curls of hair. Proved he took care of his manhood the same way he took care of the rest of his body.

"Monet...I asked you to come here. Take off your shirt and bring that pink pussy down over my face. I want to eat you while you swallow me."

A shiver raced down my spine at the lewd request, and arousal coated my thighs. Swallow. I'd never swallowed a man, not even my husband. He'd warned me every time he came. And I most certainly had never before straddled a man's face.

It sounded lewd and tawdry as well as absolutely scandalous. A new bout of excitement raced to my sex, making my clit throb.

"You want me to put my"—I pointed down between my legs—"over your, um, face?" The position flashed in my mind again, looking positively raunchy and decadent at the same time.

He grinned. "You've never ridden a man's face? Oh, beautiful, the things I'm going to teach you and do to you. Now take off my shirt."

I glanced down and realized I was in fact wearing his shirt from last night. How in the world did it get there?

"I put it on you after I made you come. Put the knockout juice on you."

I snickered. The knockout juice. If that's what he meant by giving me an orgasm after which I fell asleep, he had another thing coming. When Kyle used to make me come—those times were few and far between—usually he rolled over and fell asleep. Not me, though. I was wired.

"What? You don't believe me?" He grinned and lifted his hips. "Come here. Let me give it to you again." His confidence was staggering and infectious. I wanted to feel as confident in the bedroom as he obviously was. Maybe he'd bring out that side of me. One could only hope.

Easing my arms out of the shirt, I slowly removed it from my head. The stitches smarted but not enough to drown out my excitement.

Finally, completely naked, I shimmied across the bed on my knees. When I got close to him, he gripped my hips with a strength I hadn't anticipated and tugged me over his upper body. My knees rested on the bed on each side of his head. I braced my hands on either side of his hips.

"Now that's more like it. Put your mouth on me, beautiful," he encouraged, and I shifted forward, testing out the position with my back and finding that it didn't hurt. Actually, it felt good to curve my spine a bit.

Just as I got my mouth around the wide, knobbed head of his cock, he lifted his head and his mouth was on me. All over. He eased my hips down until my pussy was smashed against his face.

He growled, held my hips aloft just enough until I found where he wanted me to keep them, and I planted them there. He used the flat of his tongue and lapped at me from clit to anus and back.

"Holy shit." I gasped around his cock, my entire body feeling every lick as though it was a full-body caress. Goosebumps broke out over the surface of my skin as I panted with pleasure.

For a bit, I circled my hips, enjoying the feel of his tongue all over me. God, it had been so long since I'd been taken this way. Kyle hated going down on me and would only do so when he was drunk. I should have known then he didn't want me.

The sourness of that memory caused me to try to lift away from Clay's mouth. His grip tightened, and he stuck his tongue inside me as far as he could and made a sound like he was eating the best dessert and loving every bite.

He sucked and licked and then suddenly bit down hard on the sensitive flesh of my inner thigh. I jerked dramatically but stayed in place.

"Get out of your head. Wrap your lips around your man's cock and go to town. It's you and me in this bed. Just us, baby." He flicked his tongue at my clit and I jolted again, needles of excitement rippling up my back, urging me to move.

Clayton's hips gyrated, and his dick positively reached out for my touch. I wrapped my hand around him once more. When I covered his length with my lips and sucked, he groaned and buried his mouth against my slit, delving his tongue deep.

While I circled my tongue around the sensitive head of his cock, he mimicked my move, circling his own against my clit and then rubbing back and forth. He had me panting and wiggling, grinding down onto his face like a hussy. I became wanton, sucking and jerking his cock wildly.

"Fuck yeah!" He lifted his hips, going deep into my throat, stabbing at the back. "Suck me while I eat you. Tastes so... fucking...good. I can't get enough of you." He licked all around my sex, gorging on my flesh, pulling at my lower lips, and gripping my ass in both hands so he could sink his tongue deep. And I was right there with him. I humped his face as he thrust into my mouth. Together we made what I could imagine was an erotic picture, rocking back and forth like a teeter-totter. Giving and taking.

"Monet, baby, I'm going to come. You need to pull off," he warned.

I shook my head and went at him like a tigress. Sucking hard until my cheeks hollowed out.

"Oh fuck, you're going to take me down your throat. Sweet hell. Perfect woman. I swear." He jerked his hips once, twice, and then thumbed my lower lips, opening me wider, thrust up, and then stilled.

His cock jerked in my mouth, his release shooting down my throat. I swallowed everything right before he put the lockdown over my clit. He sucked so hard I screamed out. Literally screamed through my orgasm riding his face, just barely holding myself up with my knees. I lifted up, still coming, needing to take the pressure off my back, and placed one hand on his abdomen. The other I wrapped around the base of his scruff so he couldn't move from my pussy. He sucked me through one orgasm and kept at me until another swirled and charged, barreling through my body, hitting me like a two-ton wrecking ball.

I couldn't hold myself up any longer, but I shouldn't have worried. He locked his fingers around my hips and fucked me with his tongue, growling into my slit as he ate. As the final tremors were spilling out of me, I looked down at his jerking cock, his hips lifting into the air wildly as he came again. I wanted to wrap my lips around his shaft and suck him down again, but I couldn't. The lock he had as he devoured me was fierce, possessive, and unrelenting. His essence spilled white and creamy all over his happy trail and abdomen. We finished our second orgasm at the same time. His mouth lightly lapping at my sex while my entire body shook like a leaf, coming down from my high.

I eased off Clayton slowly and shifted around to my side, and I planted my head on his chest.

I swallowed around a completely dry mouth. "Is it always like that?" I asked, dazed, having never had a sexual experience that profound. And we hadn't even had intercourse yet. I almost feared that day would literally kill me. Then again, it would be the best way to go. Sexual bliss.

Clayton rubbed a hand down my side. "Beautiful, nothing has ever been that intense. Can only mean one thing."

"Which is what?" I kissed his pec.

"You're made for me. For me to kiss. To fuck. To make love to."

"Huh." I let the idea roll around in my head. The

experience had been pretty intense.

"What do you mean, huh?" His tone was concerned.

I shrugged, and he stilled until I finally spit out what I was thinking. "I guess when it's right, it's right."

He beamed. "Kiss your man, then I'm going to shower off the best orgasm of my life before I get up and make my girls breakfast."

I rose up and kissed him, tasting myself there. Tasting our lovemaking was exotic and not repulsive as I'd once thought it might be.

He held my head to his and looked at me. "You good?"

I rubbed my forehead to his, feeling content. "Yummy." I kissed his lips for another taste.

"Yummy again?" He smirked.

I nodded. "Yummy." And then I closed my eyes and lay back down. A moment later, my guy covered me with the blanket and kissed me on the temple.

"You're pretty damn yummy too, beautiful," he said before leaving me another kiss and running his fingers through my hair. The last thing I heard was the shower going off and feeling his presence over the bed. I was too tired to open my eyes.

"Knockout juice," he murmured.

I wanted to respond but I was already falling into a lovely snooze. At some point, he left and I slept.

CHAPTER TEN

HEART
C H A K R A

The mantra sound corresponding to the fourth chakra is the sound YUM. A special mantra to help expand love and compassion is OM MANI PADME HUM. You can repeat this mantra in meditation to gain greater access to these qualities.

CLAYTON

The rest of the weekend came and went. Atlas and I agreed that he and Mila would go back to their home and I'd stay with the girls until Kyle was caught. I had a security guy come and change the locks and begin implementing a full-home system complete with alarms and panic buttons in every room. Monet balked at that, but she finally let me have my way. When I say let me have my way, what I mean was I wrangled her into her room, slid down her pants, went to my knees, lifted a thigh over my shoulder, and ate her until she acquiesced.

My woman was hot for my mouth, and I figured out real quick that I could basically get her to agree to anything when an orgasm was within reach. Not gonna lie, that was a fat fucking plus in the perfect-woman column. So far, Monet was turning out to be everything a man like me could ever want. To hell with *want*... She's the woman men dream of having *long term*. The whole package.

I'd moved my schedule around so that I could be with Monet and Lily all week. Next week would be another story, but I'd talked to the guys. Trent, Dash, Atlas, and Nicholas from Lotus House would all be on point for a day or two to stay with Monet when I had clients. With that psycho on the loose, she couldn't be alone. And that included when she went back to work. Trent offered to hire a bodyguard, and I had to admit the idea held merit, but right now I wanted her protected by men who cared about her and Lily.

Lily was another concern. I put the smackdown on her going to daycare. That was not happening, which Monet agreed to pretty easily. Her daughter's welfare was more important than her own. Even if Monet was the target, we both knew that Kyle was unstable, and we couldn't put anything past him. We decided to take Lily into school this week and pick her up directly from the teacher's classroom. Monet had a talk with the principal and the teacher to give them a heads-up on the situation and insisted that no one except Mila, Atlas, her, or me was allowed at any time to pick Lily up from school.

I met the security guys first thing in the morning on Monday to continue work on the house. They were up on the situation and knew to keep the house on lockdown as they worked. We had to take Lily to school and then go directly to Monet's doctor for the removal of the stitches. I was not looking forward to watching my girl in pain. There were a fuck of a lot of stitches that needed to be removed.

I finished up the rest of the dishes for the pancakes I'd made Lily. Monet was too nervous to eat, which rankled my nerves, but I let it go. The protective side of me wanted to make sure she ate, but I also had to cut her some slack. She had a big day ahead of her, not to mention this would be the first time she'd be leaving the house since the hospital stay. I didn't even hear the bastard's words to her, and I knew she was hearing them over and over in her head. Made me positively violent thinking about the threats he'd made to her and Lily.

"Done, King Clay." Lily pushed her plate toward me.

"Come on over and wash your hands, sweetie."

"No need." She methodically put each finger into her mouth one at a time and licked them. "See, all clean!" She smiled.

I shook my head, wet a washcloth, and came around the counter. "No, they're not clean." I grabbed each of her little hands and wiped at them until I knew for sure there wasn't any syrup on them. Then I leaned forward and kissed each one while she laughed hysterically. They still smelled of syrup, even though there wasn't a trace left.

There was something special about this little girl's laugh that struck me in the chest and filled me with such glee. Now that I had it, I couldn't imagine not hearing it regularly, and I didn't plan on ever going without it. It was my job now to see that her face was filled with smiles every day. Same with her mother's.

Speaking of my goddess, she entered wearing a purple tank

and a bulky gray knit cardigan pulled around her shoulders. A worry line appeared deeply etched into her forehead between her brows. I went over to her, cupped both cheeks, and kissed that line. She closed her eyes and took a deep breath.

"I'm going to be there every step of the way, beautiful. You're not alone. You got me?"

She nodded, her chin trembling as she bit into her bottom lip. I rubbed along that lip with the pad of my thumb and then kissed it.

"Time to go. Lily's eaten, I've made her lunch, and we're set. Car's in the garage so we don't have to go out the front door. We'll take my SUV, yeah?"

She nodded again but didn't say anything. Her silence worried me. Still, she needed to deal with her thoughts in her own way.

Before I moved away, she wrapped her arms around my waist and rested her forehead against my chest. I hugged her and propped my cheek on the crown of her head. "Monet..."

"Thank you for being there for me...for us." Her words broke as she took a calming breath. "I don't know what I'd do if we didn't have you here..." She stopped there.

"Good thing you're never going to have to worry about that. I'm here, Monet, and I'm not going anywhere. Not now. Not ever." I made the statement, and more than anything, I *meant* it. Believed it with my whole heart. Shit like this didn't happen to me. Feeling for a woman the way I felt for Monet, for Lily... The only thing that had ever come close was Stacey. What I had with them was so much more. It didn't even fucking compare, and at one time I had thought I was going to spend the rest of my life with that woman.

Lily slammed into our legs, hugging us both. "Love you,

Mommy. Love you, Clay."

Monet stiffened in my arms.

"I love you too, Lily," I declared loud and fucking proud, because I did. And if I wasn't such a pussy, I'd admit that I was falling for her mother too. Far faster than I thought possible.

Only problem was that I'd been in this position before and I wasn't going to spill my guts if Monet wasn't right there with me. No, we needed more time. Time to just be together as a couple without the threat of her ex hurting her or her daughter.

"How's about you grab your backpack, sweetie, and we'll head out, okay?"

"Pack pack. Got it."

I chuckled and so did her mother, breaking the tension of the moment.

"Back. Pack, sweetie. Backpack," I corrected.

She grabbed her backpack off the couch and twirled, fire in her eyes. "S'wat I said. Pack pack! You didn't listen to me!"

"Go get in the car, Your Majesty." I grinned, wrapping an arm around Monet.

She stomped toward the garage. "No one listens me," she continued to grumble on her way out of the room.

"Seriously, Monet, I love that kid," I admitted, holding her close.

"She loves you too. Really loves you." She frowned and then pursed her lips.

"And that's a bad thing?" I wanted her to really think about it.

Monet lifted up on her toes, wrapped her arms around my neck, and kissed me softly. "No, it's a very good thing, provided you're staying around."

I tunneled my hand into her silky tresses. Fuck, I loved her hair. "I'm here, aren't I? I told you, I'm not going anywhere."

She looked down and let her arms fall. "Yeah, that's what Kyle said when he promised to love me forever. Now he wants me dead."

Man, I wanted to hurt the bastard. Smash his jaw with my bare fists as many times as I could until the anger at the torment he'd put Monet under abated in my mind. Letting those thoughts simmer for now, I reached for her hand and squeezed. "I'm not Kyle."

Her gaze lifted to mine. Worry and fear were coating the happiness I'd seen the past couple days since we'd taken our relationship to a more physical level.

"No, you're not. You're better. But you leaving Lily— leaving me—after the past two weeks would destroy us. Please think about that. Really think about that before you commit to me, to what we have started." She let go of my neck and helped her daughter get settled in the car.

Instead of a witty comeback or a quick retort, I held my tongue. I would think about it, long and hard, but I didn't see anything changing. I wanted this. A family. Monet and Lily. Wanted it more than I wanted my next breath. I'd just have to show her, prove it to her, to Lily, to every-fucking-body. I was in it to win it, and they were my grand prize.

★ ★ ★

Dropping off Lily was easy. I met her teacher and the principal, and Monet signed some forms and confirmed the instructions they'd discussed late last week. They knew about the threat and would keep an extra eye on Lily and the classroom. The teacher promised she'd never leave her sight, though I didn't think it would be an issue. Kyle hopefully wasn't stupid enough to kidnap a child from her school. Moreover, the day after Kyle's call, we met with the detectives about what had happened. They promised they'd have a patrol car circling the school and Monet's house for additional protection, as well as make it known they were on the lookout for Kyle. It gave Monet and me some semblance of peace. It would have to be enough until he was caught.

Monet was quiet as we waited for the doctor to come into the room and remove her stitches. She was instructed to lie on her belly in a flimsy gown that left the back open. I sat next to her, petting her back up and down where there wasn't an injury, to hopefully soothe her.

Next to the bed were a couple pairs of surgical scissors, tweezers, a bottle of hospital-grade alcohol, cotton balls, gauze, medical tape, and a few other things. I'd been stitched up before when I'd cut open my arm pretty good mountain biking at New Melones Lake a couple years back, but I only received twelve stitches, not eighty.

The doctor entered, dark hair with sprinkles of white dotting his temples. He had a salt-and-pepper short-cropped beard to match, kind eyes, and a soft smile. He bent over toward Monet's face and placed his hand over hers.

"You ready to get the stitches removed?" he asked softly as a petite blonde with pink scrubs entered with what I guessed was Monet's medical file on a tablet.

"Are you doing the removal?" Monet asked.

He nodded and went over to the in-room sink and washed his hands. "With this large a wound, I'd feel better doing it myself. Mandy here will assist."

"You're in good hands, Dr. Holland," the nurse added and

then washed her hands as well.

Both medical professionals donned gloves. The nurse went behind the table closest to where the tray was. I moved out of the way toward the front of the table where there was a bit more room. No fucking way was I not going to hold her hand or pet her hair while they tended to her.

I tucked the small chair next to her head and put one hand on her hair and the other on her hand. She gripped it firmly as the doctor poked and prodded at her back, checking the wound.

"Looks really good, Dr. Holland. I see you've heeded our instructions. The seal looks tight, but I'll remove the stitches and then we'll place some adhesive strips in strategic locations that might be at a higher risk of opening when you're moving around and more active. You'll still want to be careful for the next couple weeks, but you should be able to continue normal movement, go to work, resume sexual activities..." He glanced at me and then back to the wound.

Monet's cheeks pinked prettily. I kissed her temple, letting her know the embarrassment wasn't just on her. I squeezed her hand and stroked her hair.

"All right, Mandy, let's clean the entire area."

Mandy opened the alcohol and poured a healthy dose onto a stack of gauze. She ran the wet gauze all over Monet's back. Instantly gooseflesh prickled against her skin.

"Are you in pain?" My heart pounded and I held her hand firmly.

"No, just cold."

Mandy used the smaller cotton balls on the stitches, wetting and cleansing them at the same time.

"Okay, Mandy, hand me the scissors. Dr. Holland, I'll snip

them all first. Then both Mandy and I will ease each stitch out from the knot side and do our best not to tug too hard or open the wound. Everything looks really great and your healing process is stellar. I don't anticipate any problems."

"Thank you, Doctor."

With every snip I flinched. Eighty fucking times. Monet, on the other hand, held perfectly still and stared at the wall across the room. I wanted to do something for her, say something that would make this easier. I was at a total fucking loss.

The doctor and nurse started at opposite ends of Monet's wound with their tweezers and scissors, snipping and tugging each string out.

Monet's eyes closed tight.

"Hey, let's try Dara's chant. Om Mani Padme Hum. You know that one?" I asked softly.

Her eyes flickered open. "Yeah, okay."

"First, breathe with me, beautiful. In for four beats and out for four like in Dara's classes. Okay?" We both knew the yoga breathing process from taking regular classes at Lotus House. I'd taken Dara's meditation classes a few times but never thought I was any good at letting go of the monkey mind. Still, chanting helped get me in a better headspace. For Moe, I'd try anything to get her to stay relaxed and not focused on the procedure.

Monet followed along with my breathing, pairing our breaths. I placed my face directly in front of hers and ran my fingers through her hair. Her gaze stayed on mine as we breathed together, our faces only a scant few inches apart.

I inhaled long and full before letting out the words along with my breath. "Om Mani Padme Hum..." I let the last word run long, humming until all the breath inside my lungs was gone. Then together we breathed in again and continued to chant softly. "Om Mani Padme Hum." Every so often she'd wince and lose her place, but I'd bring her back to our combined meditation and she'd relax into it once more.

It felt like the process took hours when it probably was only twenty minutes or so.

"Now we're going to apply the tape. As you know, it will fall off on its own. Don't help it. Just take normal showers and let it ease off over time."

"I will," she whispered.

For another ten minutes, the doctor applied the tape and inspected the wound. "Looks really good. You've been a great patient. If you have to wear a bra over the next week, I'd suggest something really light with no elastic."

"You could try those camisole bras. Those are pretty good," the nurse offered.

Monet nodded, her eyes still pained and weary.

"We need to remove the ones from your neck now. Can you sit up?"

I helped Monet get up and twist her legs around to the side.

The doctor grabbed a light hanging near the wall, flicked it on, and adjusted it near Monet's upper body. "Almost done." He looked at the neck wound as she lifted her head.

"This will be quick. The wound is perfectly closed, though tugging on the sutures will hurt a bit since the area is so thin and sensitive."

"Please, let's just get this over with. I'm fine. Carry on."

The strength she manifested was staggering. In that moment, I couldn't have been more proud to call her mine.

Strong, gorgeous, intelligent. This woman absolutely had me by the balls.

The doctor did the neck on his own after his nurse cleaned the wound. Monet didn't move a muscle, but she held my hand so tight I worried she was in more pain than she let on. Still, the doctor moved quickly and efficiently. He applied a couple of butterflies and then gave her an antibiotic ointment to put over the entire area for a couple days.

"Vitamin E will be best to fight off the scarring."

"We'll get her some right away." I patted her hand.

"Good man." The doctor removed his gloves and washed his hands again. Once done, he shook Monet's hand then mine.

The nurse typed notes on her tablet and they both took their leave.

Monet's shoulders fell as she stared at her feet.

"Baby, I'm so proud of you." I cupped her cheeks and kissed her forehead. "So damn proud. A grown man would have teared up, and you were so strong."

A tiny smile slipped across her lips. "That sucked," she deadpanned. "It stung, it hurt, and it just...sucked. But it's such a relief. It actually feels better without the constant tug of the thread."

"Good. And now it's over. Oh, and bonus!" I smiled wide. "You can take a *real* shower."

Her coal-black eyes lit up for the first time all day. "I can."

"And I'll be there to wash your hair for you." I grinned wickedly. "And other things." I waggled my brows comically.

She chuckled and placed her hands loosely around my waist as I shimmied in between her spread thighs. The loose drape she'd worn dropped down to display her bare breasts. I groaned and tightened my hold on her thighs at the sight.

"Will you?" She dug her fingers into the tender skin around my ribs eagerly.

Not being able to help myself, I licked my lips and sucked a brown tip into my mouth, swirling my tongue around it until it tightened into an erect peak. Fuck, so good.

Wanting more than anything to keep my mouth on her pretty tips and her mind off her experience, I continued playing our game. "Oh yeah. Someone has to make sure your back is washed and these tits are tended to." I kissed my way to her other breast and wrapped my lips around it.

She hummed, arched into my luscious kiss, and scratched her fingernails through my hair. "We really shouldn't be doing this here," she murmured but didn't lessen her hold on my head.

I bit down on her nipple and flicked my tongue against the tip. "Yeah, but it's a really great way to celebrate your accomplishment." I grinned around her nipple, shifted her ass toward my cock, and rubbed my hardness against her crotch.

She moaned and wrapped her arms around my neck. "Clay..." she whispered dreamily.

"You want to come, beautiful, right here in your doctor's office?" I bit down on her other nipple and she moaned enthusiastically. We were both losing our minds, but after what she'd just endured, she needed to feel good.

A little something I'd learned about my woman was that she was all lady on the street and a freak in the sheets. The lithe beauty had a sensual and sexual side that rivaled my own. We hadn't had full-on intercourse yet, but one thing I noticed after this past weekend was her stellar libido. I liked to think my mad skills were the culprit, but not even those could bring out such a vixen.

"Oh yeah…" She thrust her hips against my pelvis.

I grinned and turned on the filthy talk. "Then you need to be quiet while I dry hump you."

Her fingers tightened in my hair, and she rubbed along my length in desperate strokes. She was close already, and it hadn't taken much. Then again, she'd been in pain; her endorphins were already high.

"Fuck. My woman likes the idea of getting caught with her top off, her man's mouth on her pretty titties, and her legs wrapped around my hips, doesn't she?"

Her body jolted, she sucked in a hard breath, and her legging-covered crotch grated wildly along the seam of my jeans.

"Clayton…" I knew that tone. My girl was going to come and come hard.

I wrapped one hand around her ass and ground into her over and over as hard as I could offer without making a racket. With my other hand, I pinched and plucked at her elongated nipple, working her into oblivion.

"Come for me, beautiful. Hurry up. You don't want to get caught," I said, reminding her where we were.

Her eyes flashed with heat, and her mouth opened. I knew she was going to scream through her orgasm. My woman was not a quiet lover, which I considered a goddamned blessing to the highest degree. However, no one but me was going to hear her climax. No one.

I slammed my mouth over hers and swallowed her cry as she trembled in my arms. I rubbed her long and hard, digging my hand into her ass, pressing her against me. Still, I wouldn't allow myself release. Not here. This was about her letting go. Getting a good memory from something necessary but downright unpleasant.

Eventually, her body calmed, but she still clung to me, arms and legs wrapped around me like an octopus. I chuckled against her neck and then kissed my spot until she relaxed.

"You going to fall asleep?" I whispered in her ear.

She sighed happily. My woman just got eighty stitches removed from her back, another dozen from her neck, and she was smiling. Yeah, my job was fucking done and done right.

"No. But I am sleepy and hungry."

I pulled back, kissing her long and slow before grabbing her tank and helping get it over her head. Next, I eased the sweater over her arms.

"How do you feel otherwise?"

"Mmm, yummy."

Again I chuckled and helped her off the table.

"No, babe. I mean where they removed the stitches?" I asked while leading her out of the office.

We didn't run into anyone on the way out, which meant no questions as to why it took so long to leave the room, and I thanked the big man above for the small favor. She didn't need to feel embarrassed after what was a priceless moment for the both of us. I'd never forget getting her off in the doctor's office, and I didn't think she would either. Mission accomplished.

"I think I feel pretty good. Of course, it's sore and it did hurt, but afterward was pretty darn great." Her cheeks flushed a rosy pink. I'd pay good money to see that blush on her face regularly.

"Darn great?" I laughed while buckling her into my SUV then rushing around the other side.

"Yeah, darn great."

I maneuvered my body over the console and kissed her

long, hard, and so wet she sighed sleepily when I finished. When I pulled back, I focused on the dreamy quality in her gaze and opened my heart to her.

"I am *so* into you."

Her return smile was huge, bright, and so fucking brilliant. "I'm into you too, Clay. Very into you." She beamed and then blushed again.

God, I loved that look on my woman. Pretty and pink.

"Where do you want to eat? Anywhere. Fancy, expensive, you name it; I'm buying you whatever you want because I'm so proud of you taking on that procedure the way you did. Blew my mind, beautiful."

She placed her hand over mine. "Honestly, I was thinking a bowl of soup and a sandwich at Rainy Day Café followed up with a treat from Sunflower Bakery would be awesome."

I put the car in gear and headed to the normal haunt near Lotus House. I shook my head.

"What?" she asked, a smile to her voice.

"I offer you anything and you want to go to a café where your entire meal won't even cost fifteen bucks, and that includes the treat at Sunflower. And that's if they charge you."

"I love Rainy Day and Sunflower." She shrugged. "Why go overboard when simple is just right?"

"Why indeed? Well, what my girl wants, she gets. We can even pick up some glittery cookies for the queen to have when we pick her up. She'd like that."

I glanced over when she squeezed my hand. "So. Very. Into. You."

CHAPTER ELEVEN

HEART
CHAKRA

When the heart chakra is open, an individual has a desire to bring happiness and joy to others, including their partners, friends, and acquaintances. Finding peace in all things is a guiding nature for this individual.

MONET

Clayton found us a table at the back of Rainy Day Café. I loved coming here, because just walking into the café gave patrons the feeling of entering a rainforest. Living potted plants dotted the environment, their vines stretching across the ceiling and walls. Coree and Bethany, the sisters who owned the place, did a great job of keeping the hippy, organic vibe of the street and served food worth eating. Hearty, healthy, and delicious. Not a combination every restaurant was capable of, but they'd found a balance.

"You seem happy," Clayton said while pulling out my chair. I couldn't remember the last time I'd had a man pull out my chair. Kyle never did in the years we were dating or when we were married. The simple act made me feel special.

I smiled and sat, making sure not to lean my sore back against the rungs of the chair. "I am. Being here is normal. Feels good to be out and around people I know and the things that make me feel like myself."

"Makes sense." He scooted his chair a bit closer to my side of the table so he could put a hand on my knee. The warmth from his palm seeped into my muscles, instantly giving me a serenity I hadn't anticipated feeling. His touches did that. Warmed me. Gifted the sensation of being safe. *Coveted.*

"I'm going to work tomorrow," I announced firmly.

Clayton's gaze slashed to mine. I could easily see concern etched into the fine lines around his sky-blue eyes.

I placed my hand over his where it rested on my knee. "I can't hide in my house forever. Who knows when they are going to catch Kyle, if ever. He could be long gone..."

"You don't know that," he growled angrily.

Licking my lips, I thought about how to best address what I wanted to say. He needed some semblance of security. "Look, I cannot allow my ex to control my life any more than he already has. I did it for too long when I was married to him. Now I've done it for over two weeks. The stitches are removed and I have clients to tend to. People who need me. Count on me."

Clayton's jaw hardened, and a muscle ticked in his cheek. "*I* need you. *Lily* needs you. *Alive.*"

His words arrowed into my heart. I closed my eyes against

the pain, the concern I knew was leading his fear. "The building has security. I'll leave before it gets dark. Whatever it takes."

"Whatever it takes?" He cleared his throat and squeezed my knee.

I nodded. "Yes. Whatever it takes."

"Then I'll be with you. And if it's not me there it will be Atlas, Dash, Trent, Nicholas, or a hired guard."

"Seriously, Clay..."

He lifted his hand and curled it around my nape. His hand chakras were fire-hot against my skin. "No way in hell I'm taking a chance with your safety. Not now. Not ever. You mean too much."

I pressed forward until our foreheads met. "For now, I'll accept your terms. In the meantime, I'll pray that they catch Kyle quickly so we can all move on with our lives."

"God willing," he growled in a surly timber.

Coree, the strawberry-blond owner, popped over and delivered our food. A hot cup of minestrone soup and a turkey on rye for me, a full turkey cranberry chock-full of sprouts and a side salad for the big guy. My mouth watered as the steam from the soup reached my nose.

"Let me know if you need anything else." Coree put a hand to my shoulder. "Glad to see you're doing well, Moe. We were all worried."

"I'm good. Thank you. Tell your sister I said hello."

She smiled and left us alone with our food.

Clayton tucked in right away, taking a huge monster bite. I snickered and blew on my soup.

"What's so funny?"

"You."

"Me?" He grinned and took another bite.

"Yeah you. It's always interesting to watch you eat." I sampled the first bite of my soup. The veggies were perfectly cooked and the broth a pure delight. The addition of Parmesan on top of the soup gave it an earthy, rich quality I adored.

Clay finished his mouthful and wiped his lips with a napkin. "Why's that?"

I twisted and then winced. The stitches were no longer there, but the subtle move still tugged on the butterflies that now secured my wound.

"You okay?" He placed his hand on my forearm.

"Fine. Anyway, what I was saying was that you're fun to watch when you eat because you eat like it could disappear at any moment."

He chuckled, and the sound banged around in my chest happily. His laugh was deep and full. A real manly man laugh.

"Growing up, we didn't have much in the way of money. If you didn't eat fast, you didn't get seconds." His eyes gleamed with a hint of mirth. "Survival of the fittest and all."

"Everything good now?" I asked, taking a bite of my sandwich. It tasted like heaven on a plate. The turkey, mayo, mustard, and rye combination with the fresh thick lettuce chunks and tomato coalesced together to hit the spot. So good.

He swatted at the air. "Water under the bridge. With school I scored scholarships and paid my own way. When I made it big in sports medicine and fitness, I started making a mint. Took care of paying off my parents' home, and now my mom putters around reading and volunteering while my dad is an accountant working from home. They have money in their retirement plans and a stable, good life. No complaints."

"Sounds fantastic. It's really good that you could do that for your parents."

He focused all his attention on me. "I take care of my own."

I felt my cheeks heat as his eyes zeroed in on my mouth followed by the rest of my face. He lifted a hand and stroked the apple of my cheek with his thumb. "You blush so pretty, Monet. You're like living art."

I rolled my eyes and let my hair fall in front of my face and focused on my soup. He took the hint to leave it alone and continued our conversation by asking some questions of his own.

"Where are your parents and grandparents? All you've mentioned is Kyle and your sister, Matisse."

Talking about my family was never easy, but if we were going to continue down a more serious path—and Clayton gave me every indication we were—I needed to lay out all my demons.

I took a heavy breath and put my elbows on the table so I could rest my head in my hand. "You know my father cheated on my mother and kept another family on the side."

He nodded.

"Well, eventually my mother found out that not only did he keep Matisse's mother a secret, he was having extramarital relations with anything in a skirt all across the globe. He worked for my grandparents' import-export business. Ran the customer development and business relationships department. That had him going all over the world. Apparently, he didn't keep his indiscretions secret." I fiddled with my napkin, forcing myself to stay the course. "On one trip, my mother followed him. First to Paris, then Italy, and last to New York. He had a different woman on his arm and in his hotel room in each city. She was devastated."

Clayton completely stopped eating. He put down his sandwich as if he was disgusted with it. "How could he do that?"

A choking sound left my throat on instinct. "Why would my husband cheat on me with my sister?"

Because men couldn't be trusted. At least that's what my mother always told me. I pursed my lips, glanced down at my soup, and took a few slow breaths. Clayton wasn't like Kyle or my father. He was the exact opposite.

Don't compare them, Moe.

"I'm sorry, beautiful." He cleared his throat and took a sip of his water. "What happened after she found out?"

Bolstering my courage to finish the story, I kept going. "Left his sorry ass. I'm not even sure where he is now. He'd always cared more for himself than either of his daughters, and he definitely didn't respect his wife." I pushed a kidney bean around in my soup with my spoon. "My grandfather fired him from the company, but he'd made so many contacts he had the pick of where he wanted to go. He was always a stellar businessman. Just a crappy husband and father."

"Jesus, Monet."

"It gets worse, I'm afraid."

He closed his eyes, took a fortifying breath, and released it. "Lay it on me, beautiful. This is your life, your past, and I need to know it. All of it."

He did have a right to know, but that didn't change how hard it was for me to talk about it. Sweat tickled at my nape as I swallowed down the sour taste in my mouth. "Mom couldn't take the blatant betrayal. She believed it was her fault somehow. Through my early teenage years, she was severely depressed, so much so that she took a lot of medication for it.

One day she took too much."

His hand flew to mine, and he clasped our fingers. "She took her own life?" He gasped.

I nodded, allowing the hurt to swirl around me but not pierce the armor I'd built around myself. "Technically an overdose. The doctors didn't say it was intentional because it's not like she purposely swallowed a bottle of pills. She just took some, probably forgot, took some more, and then followed it with a half gallon of vodka."

"Monet..."

I shook my head and pressed a hand out to show my appreciation for his concern but also made known my desire to not be touched right now. "I've had a lot of time to deal with it. I'm okay."

And I was. Okay. My mother had been weakened by the love of her life. I understood that better than most. I just didn't want to follow in her footsteps by letting that same decision control my life.

"And your grandparents?" he asked.

"My mother's parents raised me in my late teens and took in Matisse, even though they never treated her like part of the family. Mostly because she wasn't blood. They didn't blame her and never treated her poorly, but we both knew they did it for me out of obligation. Regardless of what my father did, she was my sister. They gave her every opportunity they gave me, even willingly paid for her schooling."

I ran my finger around the rim of my water glass, watching the condensation from the ice drip down the glass in mesmerizing rivulets. "Matisse got a liberal arts degree and promptly disappeared from my life for the better part of a decade. Only popping up now and then—for my wedding, again when I had Lily. Brief encounters where she'd stay with us for a few days and then be gone at sunup, not to be heard from again for another year or so."

"Except she came back when your grandparents died."

I snorted unbecomingly. "Yep. Out of the blue, she walks into the attorney's office holding my ex-husband's hand, attempting to contest the will."

"I can't imagine what that kind of betrayal feels like." Clayton's arms were lined with muscles, the veins standing out as if he was holding back his own strength. His hands were fisted where they rested on the table.

I let out a fast breath, the image searing through my mind. "It feels like blinding white-hot fire courses from the tips of your toes and out the ends of your hair. Nothing hurt more than that moment. Not even when Kyle left me originally. At least then I believed it was because we just weren't happy with one another, not that he had a piece on the side. Turns out he'd been seeing my sister all along."

"Fuck," he grated through clenched teeth. "I'd love to have five minutes in a room alone with your ex. Just five freakin' minutes is all I'd need. Hell, I'd stand for two."

That had me chuckling. An overall sensation of relief settled over the moment. Right then and there I realized for the first time in a long time I wasn't alone. I reached for Clayton's fisted hand and peeled his fingers open.

"It's okay. Everything happens for a reason, right? My marriage failed, and Kyle wants me dead, but at least I have Lily and now you." No truer words had ever left my mouth. The concept seeped deep into my subconscious.

Clayton's eyes twinkled with mirth before he tipped his head back and started laughing. Hard. "Only you, beautiful, would find a silver lining to this shit. Come here." He curled his hand around my neck and eased me forward so our lips could meet. He kissed me slow but with meaning.

"You're not alone in this. Not anymore." The words were whispered against my neck before he pulled back.

"See... You're my silver lining." I gave him my happiest smile.

He shook his head and grinned. "Fuckin' stunning woman. And all mine. You done? Ready for some sweetness?"

I wanted to tell him he was all the sweet I could ever need, but I figured that was going overboard on the cheesy romance. Instead, I eased up and grabbed his hand while connecting with his side, our half-eaten lunch forgotten.

"Lead the way."

★ ★ ★

As usual, Sunflower Bakery was absolutely hopping with people when we entered.

"Sweet Mother Nature and all things living. Moe!" I heard the sweet voice of none other than Crystal Nightingale, one of the owners of Lotus House.

I smiled and headed for her table back in the corner. She was sitting with Jewel Marigold, the other owner. The two of them were the same in morals, values, and spiritual thought processes but couldn't be more different physically. Crystal looked like an angel, with golden-blond hair, sky-blue eyes, and knockout curves. For a sixty-year-old woman, she had it going on. Jewel was a slip of a woman and reminded me of a fairy. Curly fire-red hair, a pair of tortoiseshell glasses perched on her button nose, and a welcoming smile.

Crystal's arms wrapped around me tight, and I stiffened as pain rippled down my spine. Her eyes widened, and she released me as if I'd burned her. "Oh my, I knew you'd gotten hurt, but I had not been informed of the extent. Are you okay?"

I squeezed her hand and held on. "I'm fine. I just had the stitches removed today. My injury runs along most of my back."

Both women's mouths opened then tightened into firm white lines. Crystal's hold on my hand eased and she lifted it between both of hers at her heart center. "I'm going to pray very hard that you heal quickly. We miss your presence at the studio."

"Me too. And as soon as I'm able, I'll be back taking classes. Right now, I need to be careful not to tweak anything."

"If there is anything we can do to help you heal, you must let us know. Perhaps I can do a chakra realignment using the singing bowls or crystals?" Jewel pressed her glasses farther up her nose and focused on my face.

Singing bowls. I grinned. "That's very kind. Maybe I'll take you up on that, if the need arises." Of course I wouldn't be taking her up on that because I didn't think my chakras were out of alignment. Not that I really knew one way or the other.

Jewel clicked her tongue and put her hands out in front of me. "Give me your hands, my darling."

I smiled and placed both of mine into hers. A sizzle of magnetism shot through my palms from hers. She closed her eyes, right in the middle of the bakery, not caring who might be watching. Crystal followed her lead and came around behind me and placed her hands next to the spot where my shoulder and neck met. Clayton's spot.

"Close your eyes," Crystal whispered into my ear.

"Right here?" I glanced around but couldn't really see

much of anything but Jewel standing in front of me, holding me in place.

"Yes. We're off to the side. No one's paying any attention anyway. Just let everything slip away for a single minute."

Not wanting to hurt their feelings, I played along and closed my eyes. I had no idea where Clayton was or what he thought might be taking place, but I imagined he'd ask about it later.

"Breathe in through your nose and let it out your mouth," Crystal instructed.

Following her orders, I inhaled fully, closed my eyes, and exhaled until all the air had left my lungs. I did it a few more times until everything around me completely faded away.

The sounds of the bakery, gone.

People moving around me, gone.

Jewel's presence, gone.

Crystal behind me, gone.

For one single minute I connected with my true self. Relief. Stress. Anxiety. Fear. All those things left me while I breathed, grounded by two women I truly believed must have a direct line to the Man Upstairs.

A simmering wave of love and solidarity speared through my body, welcoming me, tethering my spirit to the moment, and filling me with a love so intense I thought it might burst from my chest in a rocket of blinding green light. I opened my eyes. "Whoa!" I gripped Jewel's hands to keep upright.

Jewel's serene smile greeted me. Crystal chuckled from behind, gave my neck a little squeeze, and then let me go.

"Feel better?" Jewel grinned.

I blinked a few times, realizing I actually did feel a ton better—lighter somehow. Either it was the power of suggestion or these women were spiritual healers of the highest degree.

"I actually do. I'm not sure what you did, but I don't know"—I ran my hand through my hair and looked down—"somehow I'm lighter."

Crystal grinned. "We helped ground you. Sometimes when we're stressed and situations are controlling our every thought, we lose our footing."

Made complete and perfect sense. Only, in the medical and psychiatric community, "grounding" had a different description. In my world, grounding was a coping strategy that helped the patient immediately connect to the present. I personally used it a lot when dealing with my post-traumatic stress patients. Some of my veterans needed grounding therapy to help with flashbacks and dissociation.

"And your heart chakra is hurting right now." Jewel frowned and ran a finger from my temple to my chin. "I sense that you're working on it, but there's still much more to be done."

"My heart chakra? How so?"

Jewel smiled. "In order to have a healthy heart chakra, darling, you must love yourself and be able to forgive yourself and others. I'm sensing there are some things you are not letting go of. Perhaps a person who wronged you. One you allowed in your life. Someone who continues to hurt you? Could be a variety of things piling up."

Nail on head, anyone?

I opened my mouth to speak but the anvil pressing down on my chest wouldn't allow for it.

She patted my hand the way my mother used to. Another brick added to the emotional baggage weighing me down.

"No worries, darling. You're going to find the way. I suggest you attend Dara's meditation classes for a bit. Become more in tune with your inner self. Hmm?"

I nodded numbly, not sure how to respond. Thank God I didn't have to or I might have burst into tears. Clayton picked that moment to curl his hand around my neck in the possessive way I'd become obsessed with. "You good, beautiful?" He had eyes only for me, and they were an assessing darker blue.

"Uh, yeah. Perfect as a peach," I stuttered, and he frowned.

"We were just suggesting that our Monet work on clearing her heart chakra and spend a little quality time with Dara, our meditation expert." Jewel looked over my shoulder to where Dara was serving the myriad customers lined up.

Clayton chuckled. "Her heart chakra needs clearing?" He shook his head and sighed.

"You don't believe in aligning and cleansing your chakras?" Crystal asked in a way that was questioning, rather than judgmental.

I worked on perfecting that particular talent daily with my clients, and she had the natural gift in spades.

The big guy set down a tray filled with a variety of treats and what looked like a couple of lattes. My mouth watered at the sight, especially since I hadn't eaten much of my lunch. He must have caught on to that because there were enough treats on his plate to feed an army.

"I don't *not* believe." Clayton held out a chair for me to sit in. It was catty-corner to the yogis' table. "I say, to each his own." He shrugged, not exactly dismissing the conversation but showing that he didn't really concern himself with such things.

Jewel glanced at Crystal and then back at me. "Perhaps you both need a little cleansing. Though I've got the feeling that between the two of you, that heart chakra blockage is going to soon be a thing of the past."

Crystal nodded and beamed, her entire face lighting up as if the sun shone directly down on her in a blinding ray of light. Definitely one of God's angels.

Clayton sat down next to me, grabbed my hand, and kissed my fingertips. "I'll be taking good care of her heart, so you needn't worry, ladies. Isn't that right, Monet?"

My cheeks warmed, and I nodded. Everything inside me filled with optimism. Without laying my heart fully on the line, I would give what I could.

"I hope so."

CHAPTER TWELVE

HEART
C H A K R A

A heart chakra couple will have more opportunities for happiness than opportunities for unhappiness. Typically, marriages driven by the heart chakra are long lasting. Together they work through their karma and cleanse their consciousness of negativity.

CLAYTON

Over the next couple weeks, we fell into a routine. We'd pick up Lily from school, do homework, play games, and watch movies. This morning, Monet informed me that the last of her tape from her injury had fallen away. A month had passed since the attack, and she was doing really well. Amazingly so. In celebration, we'd picked up *The Lego Movie*, which I found rather awesome. The new graphics in these films were way beyond my day. And the fact that Lily chose what she considered a "boy movie" just for me made my heart swell. I had to admit, it was a damn good movie. The story was sound and the antics between the Lego characters pretty funny. While we watched, Monet cuddled along my side. Both my girls snuggled right up next to me. It was a surreal moment— one I'd take with me to my grave as one of the best.

While Monet put Lily to bed, I devised my plan for seduction. I wanted *inside* my woman fully. We'd held off on the more robust sexual activities due to the stitches and her discomfort. The stitches had been out for two weeks now, and the tape was gone. She was free and clear to be ravished and I could not wait. We needed to surpass this last physical hurdle. Tonight, I planned on touching every inch of her body and making her mine. No more worries, just the two of us connecting in the most honest way possible. She needed to know how amazing I found her, scars and all.

While Monet led Lily to her room, I locked up the house, closed all the blinds, started the dishwasher, and made sure everything was put away for the evening.

Walking through the house, it dawned on me how at ease I was in Monet's home. I hadn't spent a night in my own apartment in a long time and I did not miss it. Not even a little. My woman had a way of making me feel welcome. Even the decorating was conducive to hanging out and staying a while. The entire house felt like a home; it didn't just look like one. She had deep, comfortable couches and plenty of pillows that were often thrown to the floor for relaxing on. Blankets in baskets were within reach. Side tables and end tables we put our feet on without worrying about scratching the surfaces. I also appreciated the art on the walls with the muted and cheery vibe.

As I made my way down the long hall to her master bedroom, I noted all the pictures on the walls. Family was important to Monet, even if she didn't have much anymore. Pictures of her grandparents, her mother, half sister, and an entire wall of Lily from birth to now spanned the long pathway. Mila as well as Atlas had been added to the "wall of fame" as I called it. I fingered the last picture that depicted Mila, Atlas, Monet, and Lily at a pumpkin patch and wondered when I'd be added to her wall. Soon, I hoped.

I entered Monet's bedroom and tugged off my T-shirt, tossing it toward the hamper but not quite making it in. Sitting next to it I noticed a folded basket of clothes. All mine and all clean. She'd done my laundry and had placed it neatly into the basket. As much as I liked seeing my clean clothes in here, a hell of a lot, it burned that they weren't inside a drawer or hanging in the closet.

Cringing, I picked up the basket and set it on the bed. Then I went over to the closet, flicked on the light, and walked in. Monet had a lot of clothes, as I imagined any woman would. Suits, skirts, and dresses hung to the far back and blouses on another side. To the right was an open space that had shelving about four feet high where Monet's shoes were lined up neatly and efficiently. Above that space were jewelry boxes and various knickknacks, but higher up, a solid three feet of hanger bar was empty. It ran along the entire space and would be perfect. For me.

I grabbed the basket from the bed, reentered the closet, and set it on the floor. I hung all my shirts and jeans. I kept aside my boxer briefs and socks. I'd find a place for those too.

"Clay?" I heard Monet enter the bedroom.

"In here, beautiful," I called out.

She entered the closet and leaned against the doorjamb. I looked at her while I snapped the buttons on a dress shirt. My God, the woman was gorgeous. Her black hair fell in loose waves around her face, the strands a shining, silky ebony, like wet river rock when the mountain water rushes over it. She wore a simple tank with no bra. Her small nipples poked against the thin cotton fabric, making my mouth water. She tucked one of her heels against her ankle, giving me a sweet view of her bare legs in her sleep shorts. The woman was dressed for bed, but she could have been ready for the runway. I was one lucky son of a bitch.

"What are you doing?" Her nose crinkled up the exact same way Lily's did, only Lily did hers in irritation. Monet's showed uncertainty.

"Hanging my clothes up."

She nodded. "I can see that."

"Thank you for washing them. You didn't have to do that, but I'm grateful." I winked at her while folding a pair of jeans longwise before looping it through the hanger and placing it on the rack.

Monet took a full breath. "You're welcome, but, I can't help but notice you're hanging them in my closet."

I grinned and hung the second to last one up before finding an additional hanger for the last. "Observant, my girl," I joked.

Again, nose crinkle. "And why are you hanging them there?"

I hung the last and picked up the basket. "Because that's where I want them to be."

She backed up as I exited the closet. She moved to the ottoman at the end of the bed and fingered a chunk of her hair.

Her fingers moved in circles around the hair while I opened and closed a bunch of her drawers.

"Uh...Clay?"

"Just a second, babe." I found a drawer that was less full about two drawers down. It was where she kept her sexy nighties. As much as I didn't want to touch that drawer but rather fill it up with more silk and lace, I needed somewhere to put my socks and underwear. So I took the sexy things from there, shoved over the nightshirts in the second drawer and placed them to the side. I gathered my socks and underwear and put them in the new drawer. "Perfect."

Monet watched me with widened eyes while I took the basket and put it in the closet. Then I picked up my stray T-shirt and chucked it into the hamper. It went right in. "Score! Now what's up?"

"Clay..." Monet's voice was strained.

I went over to her, grabbed her hands, and lifted her to stand until her front was smashed against mine. Her pretty fingers splayed out against my bare chest, and she played with the little bit of chest hair I had.

I kissed her forehead.

"Did you just move in?" she asked, tipping her head up so I could stare into her coal-black eyes.

Without saying anything, I took her mouth in a searing kiss. After a few moments, she relaxed into the kiss and moaned her pleasure. I pulled away and rested my head on her neck, laying sloppy kisses on my spot. "Yeah, beautiful, I kind of did."

"Why?" She ran her hands up and down my back. I wanted her hands on me all the time. Her touch made everything better, more focused. Knowing I had her to touch and hold, to come home to... It eased me. I wanted that more than I'd ever been able to truly admit before meeting her. I never realized how much I desired it until now.

"Tired of seeing my stuff in a basket or on the floor and living out of a gym bag."

Her body seemed to jerk as she processed what I'd said. "Clayton...we have to talk about this."

I curled a hand around her nape. "*Do we really?* I'm here. Do you like me here every day?"

"Yes." Her reply was instant.

"Does it bother Lily?"

She shook her head. "My goodness, no. She loves you and you're so good with her. More than I ever could have hoped."

That sunk in and seared me deep. That little girl was quickly becoming everything to me, but hearing her mom say it went both ways...did not suck. "And I love her. And more than that..." Beads of sweat tingled around my hairline, my palms got sweaty, and my chest felt nailed down with so much pressure. I just had to get it out. Put it out there no matter what the repercussions. "I love you."

Monet gasped and her head dropped forward. "It's too soon, Clayton. We've only been together a month, and two of those weeks I was healing." She shook her head against my chest. "It's too soon...right?"

I cringed and lifted her face with my thumbs. "Beautiful, are you seriously going to stand there, wrapped in my arms, looking into my eyes, and tell me you don't love me back? It's written all over your face. In every glance. Every smile. Every sweet kiss. You can't hide from me. From this. I don't care if it's only been a short time. Who decides how long it takes to fall in love with someone? I'm in love with you, and I don't care what anyone but you thinks about it."

She swallowed and licked her lips.

"Say what you want to say. Don't leave me hanging alone. Not now."

"I..." Her voice shook like a leaf dangling in the wind.

The fear and anxiety she displayed shredded my heart and sat like lead in my gut. I never wanted to see my woman so lost. I softened my tone. "What are you so afraid of?"

Her eyes filled with unshed tears, and I cupped both of her cheeks. One tear slid down and another followed. I swiped them away with my thumbs.

She sniffled but continued. "One day you won't like what you see, or I'll do something wrong, and then..." She choked on her words.

A twenty-pound weight falling on my foot wouldn't have hurt as badly as what I saw in her eyes. The demons of her past were a heavy burden on her soul, on her future. Demons I needed—no, *would*—work to obliterate for good.

Finally, she laid it out. "You'll leave me. Us. Me and Lily." She sounded gutted, ravaged by something that could destroy her, which hadn't even happened yet.

Somehow, I had to get it through to her that it never would. I shook my head furiously and pulled her mouth to mine. I kissed her hard, harder than I ever had. She needed to *feel* what I'd say next, in her mind, heart, and all the way down to her fucking marrow.

I brought our faces so close together our noses practically touched. "Listen to me and listen good. I'm *here* now. I'll be *here* tomorrow. And I'll be *here* every day after that. You and Lily, you're mine now. My responsibility. I'll spend every day of my life worshipping that gift."

More tears fell from her cheeks, and she licked her lips.

Our mouths were so close I could feel the slip of her tongue and the moisture it left in its wake.

My grip on her tightened. "You hear me? Let it sink in, Monet, because I'm not going anywhere." I gritted my teeth and then took her mouth again.

She sobbed into the kiss and wrapped her arms around my neck, pulling me closer until our bodies melded into one another. Time ceased to exist as we gave and took from one another, sealing our commitment the only way we knew how.

I walked her to the bathroom, never letting her go, my lips glued to hers along the way. When I stopped and sucked in a harsh breath, her eyes were giant pools of love and desire. She closed them for a moment and then opened them dazedly. Determination and grit stared back at me.

"Clayton, I love you too."

There was no stopping the giant smile that spread across my face and the behemoth of fear that dissipated around us.

I hugged her to me and kissed her neck. "You love me?"

She nodded and placed her own face into the crook of my shoulder and neck. I could feel her smile against my bare skin. "Yeah, I do."

★ ★ ★

Steam billowed around the shower stall as I held my love's hand and led her in. Monet had an enormous shower with two heads that blasted mightily against the dark multicolored tile, which gave the impression of walking into a heated private cave. Hot water sluiced down my back as I grabbed the shower gel and poufy sponge. I poured a liberal amount and set the bottle on the shelf. Monet plastered herself against my back, her lips a welcome pressure between my shoulder blades. Tiny kisses rained down my spine and back up. My cock hardened painfully, a vortex of need following the line of her lips and imprinting everywhere those plump bits of flesh touched down.

Monet's voice was but a murmur through the sound of the water coming down. "You know, you always call me beautiful, but you're absolutely magnificent, Clayton." She ran her fingertips along my back and down each arm, caressing the muscles as if committing them to memory. "Most men don't look the way you do. Not even close."

Damn straight. I worked fucking hard in the gym and kept my body fit, toned, and packed with lean muscles. I grinned and turned around, looping my arms and crossing my wrists at her lower back. She was gloriously naked, and her pretty brown nipples puckered sweetly against my chest. I lifted one hand and cupped a breast, watching the tip tighten further as I rubbed my thumb across it. She shivered in my arms, her pelvis slamming against my cock.

"Cold?" I smirked.

"No, the opposite." She half moaned as I sucked the wet tip into my mouth and tugged with my teeth. "I'm so hot," she finished, tipping her head back and arching toward me. The second showerhead drenched the black waves of her hair, transforming it into a long flat sheet of flowing black silk.

I took the invitation from her body and sucked on her tits, nipping and pinching the way I knew she liked. I'd learned a bit about her body in the past month, and my girl loved nipple play. It got her wet almost instantly. After I toyed with her breasts, getting her nice and worked up, I moved a step back and rubbed the poufy thing across each sensitive peak.

"Mmm..." She sighed, her chest rising and falling with her breathing, which became more labored with each pass. I squirted more soap on the pouf and swirled it around her belly. I kneeled down and started at her feet. I scrubbed each leg thoroughly, wanting to show her how much I loved her.

Once I'd soaped her legs so they were nice and slippery, I ran my hands up and down them. On the pass up the back, I gripped her ass and squeezed each globe, bringing her pussy forward to hover a scant few inches away from my mouth.

Monet slapped her hands on my shoulders, and her chin shifted toward her chest. Her eyes were dark pools of lust. She licked at the trickling water running down her face and onto mine below.

"What do you want, beautiful?"

She bit down on that bottom lip, and for a moment, I was jealous. I wanted to bite her lips, suck them into my mouth until they were as red as little cherries.

Widening my stance so I was at the perfect height, I sank forward until my nose was an inch from the perfect landing strip of black hair at the apex of her thighs.

"I'm waiting..." I rubbed my hands up and down the backs of her thighs.

"I want you to make love to me." Her words were soft and sweet, the loveliest thing she's ever said to me.

I grinned. "And I will. But right now...is there something else I can do for you?"

She nodded but didn't speak. She pushed her hips forward so that her clit bounced against my chin. "Please," she begged.

Instead of responding, I gripped her ass hard and buried my face in her cleft. She was slick and sweet. Water ran down her body and mixed with her natural taste, allowing me to physically drink from the heart of her. The experience was exhilarating and exotic. I spread her lips with my thumbs until her pink parts darkened, and then I went to town. I'd never been so animalistic in my desire to please a woman orally, but something about knowing this was my pussy...for life...fuck. It changed everything. She tasted sweeter, her skin was silkier, and when my tongue fluttered over and over her clit, she came *harder*. I sucked her honey down my throat and went back for seconds until she rocked against my face like a bucking bronco, practically screaming out her second orgasm.

My cock was so hard it could have pounded nails through concrete. I stood, wrapped my hand in her wet hair, and slammed my mouth over hers. She opened immediately, rubbing her succulent body all over my rock-hard dick. I groaned, my knees weak when she wrapped not one but both hands around my cock. The crown stuck out at the top of her hold, but that didn't stop her from jacking me until my balls tightened and my hips jerked along with her movements. I was too far gone. I needed to come.

"Baby, if you keep that up, I'm going to come."

"Then come," she stated flippantly before sucking the flat disk of my right nipple. I also liked a little nipple play, and my girl knew exactly the right combination between suction and biting to drive me wild.

A fire built in my groin and spiraled up my spine from my lower back. "Wanted to come inside you," I growled angrily while still pumping into her slick hands.

Without a word, my goddess dropped to her knees, wrapped her perfect lips around my cockhead, and sucked the daylights out of me. I slammed one hand to the tile wall to hold my weight and the other to the back of her neck. She was not going slow. Something untamed had ignited within and seemed to give her the clearance to lay the hoover down on my cock. I gripped her hair in my hands, tugged at the roots, and fucked her face. She mewled and bounced along with each thrust. At one point, I saw her small hand go down between her legs and start circling. That's when our lovemaking turned to straight fucking.

"You like touching your hard little clit while I fuck your mouth? Christ," I rambled. "So sexy on your knees, taking my cock." I thrust until I slipped down the tight channel. Her eyes widened but she didn't stop. They were glazed and lust-drunk. I'm sure mine were a perfect match.

"Yeah, you like it when I take you hard." I pulled back so she could flick her tongue against the tip while I watched. She closed her eyes and hummed, her hand moving at the speed of light between her thighs. "Does sucking your man off make you hot?"

She nodded around my cock and then sucked me back down. "Fuck yeah it does! Take your man. This is your cock now. All yours."

Her suction got stronger, and I lost the ability to think straight. My mind was focused solely on the woman I loved giving me the best head of my fucking life. As I started to lose what little bit of focus I had been able to maintain, I wrapped both hands around her head, one on her cheek, keeping her mouth nice and opened wide for me, and the other behind her head so I could go deep. She took it all like a champ. Then I became a sap and started up with the filthy sweet nothings.

"You suck me so good, Monet," I groaned.

"I'm going to come hard for you." A trail of fire licked up my spine.

"Love your mouth. So fucking tight."

"Pinch that clit like I would. Yeah, like that," I moaned, losing another ounce of control.

"Oh Jesus, your fucking mouth," I grated through clenched teeth.

"Going to come down your throat."

"Mark you as mine."

Once she'd gone over the edge, she clamped her hands on my ass and worked the same finger she'd used to get herself off between my cheeks until she found the pucker of my anus and pushed it deep inside me. She followed that move up by swallowing me *all the way* down her throat. I tipped my head back and roared my release, shooting what felt like weeks of pent-up tension down her throat. She took it all, sucking me until I had nothing left to give.

Complete and utter nirvana coated every pore and nerve ending.

Slowly she stood and rested her head against my chest. "Best. Shower. Ever," she announced and kissed me over my heart.

Damn perfect woman. I'd scored the perfect woman. I laughed, holding her close. "Yeah, it was. Now I need to take care of you."

"But you already did...three times." She winked saucily and shimmied her hips.

I kissed her mouth in several hard pecks. "I want to wash your hair for you."

"That sounds almost as good as you talking dirty to me." She turned around, presenting me with her back. The wound looked a lot better without the stark black stitches.

"Looks really good. I think you'll be pleased with how well

it's healing." I kissed the ball of her shoulder.

"I'm trying to gear up to look again, but I'm scared," she admitted.

I wrapped my arms around her upper body and let her back rest against my chest softly. "It's normal to be scared. But I promise you, it will heal every single day. The line will get lighter. You will have a battle scar, but we all have those. It's part of what you've survived up to now."

She nodded. "It's just hard. I keep thinking that I'll be too ugly to wear tank tops or spaghetti-strap dresses. And if Lily sees it"—her head tipped down—"I won't even know how to explain that."

I shifted her hair to one side, soaped up the pouf, and ran it down the spots that hadn't been wounded. Then I poured more soap in my hand and lightly ran it down the wound. Monet stayed perfectly still but let me tend to her.

"She's going to understand that Mommy got hurt. Mommy is fine now, but she has a scar. I'll show her some of my scars and explain it to her. It will be fine. Kids are resilient like that. And she's really smart."

I could feel the tension pouring off her as I poured shampoo in my palms, rubbed them together, and got to work on her long hair. She groaned a sexy, scintillating sound that made my dick harden again.

"What else?" I murmured into her ear and nibbled the curve down her neck until she relaxed.

Her voice was but a whisper. "I don't want to be ugly to you. You're so perfect, and I didn't really have a body-image issue before, but now..."

I tossed the pouf to the floor and turned my girl around. "Let's get this straight right now, Monet. I fell in love with you *after* you were wounded, not before. Sure, I was absolutely attracted to you before. You're drop-dead gorgeous. Any man with eyes wants you. Period. And they still will. That isn't going to change because you have a scar."

"You say that now—" she started, but I cut her off.

"No. I'll say that a year from now too when I'm tracing your naked back in our marital bed."

Her gaze flew to mine, the truth in my words hitting her upside the head. I waited to see if she'd call me on it, but I didn't think she was ready for that admission. Because I *did* see us married in the future—in the not-too-distant future. Tonight we'd already laid some heavy shit on one another and admitted our love. Now was the time to rejoice and focus on the good we had.

She still seemed down, and I didn't want that for us after what we'd confided. Her fingers traced my side where my tattoo resided. "What do these letters mean?"

"You're Chinese. Don't you know?" I quipped.

Her nose crinkled up and she frowned. "I'm a Chinese and Caucasian... *American*. I don't know Chinese."

I laughed hard, knowing she was going to come at me fast, but she needed a subject change to get her out of her funk. I kissed her pretty nose in apology. "I know you are. I'm messing with you. Relax."

"Seriously, though, what does it mean?" Her fingers traced each of my ribs in a sensual assault. I sucked in a calming breath and let it out.

"Pursuit of happiness."

Her gaze ran over the symbols, and it gave me an idea.

"You know, if you don't like your scar when it heals, you could just get a tattoo to cover it. Make something you despise into something you love, something you made your own."

She blinked a few times, smiled widely, and then kissed me hard once. "You are so smart!"

I shrugged and turned off the water. "I try."

As we dried one another, our hands strayed. I tickled her, finding the spots that made her laugh. She pulled back the bedsheets as I stepped into a pair of clean underwear I'd taken from the drawer I'd confiscated. That's when I heard a blood-curdling scream and the home-alarm system blare. The scream came from inside the house.

Monet's head snapped up where she stood naked. "Lily!" she cried out.

I was out the door and down the hall as fast as my feet could carry me. Her bedroom door was open, and she was screaming at the top of her lungs while pointing at the window. The alarm blared, sounding like a banshee piercing the quiet of the night. I scooped up Lily and held her to my chest. She wrapped her legs and arms around me like a monkey.

"Baby, what happened?" I tried to use a calm voice, but her fear and the alarm had my adrenaline pumping and my heart pounding.

"A man, a man! He broked my window!" she cried into my chest. I could see the curtains moving across the room.

I flicked on the lights and handed the sobbing little girl to Monet, who'd just run into the room wearing my dirty T-shirt from earlier. I stomped over to the window and opened the curtains with a snap. Nothing was there but a hole the size of a person's hand near the lock. There was glass on the windowsill inside, as if someone had used a hammer or a tool of some kind to break it.

The phone rang as the alarm continued to blare, adding to

the overwhelming onslaught to our senses.

I stroked Lily's head and kissed her temple, and then her mother's, before walking into the kitchen, both girls hot on my heels. I picked up the phone and gave the alarm code.

"Yeah, send the police out. We had an attempted burglary and possible attempted kidnapping since it was a child's room that was breached."

Tears rolled down Monet's face as she whispered to her daughter. Blessedly, the alarm shut off.

I curled a hand around Monet's nape and squeezed. "Be strong, beautiful," I reminded her. "I'm here, and nothing is going to happen to my girls on my watch. Nothing."

She nodded furiously.

"I'm going to grab some clothes really quick. Stay here for a minute." I ran back to the room, tugged on a pair of plaid pajama pants and a white T-shirt, and then hightailed it back to the kitchen. Monet had Lily on the counter and was holding her close. Fuck, she probably hurt herself carrying her. A knock on the door startled both my girls, causing Lily to cry out in fear.

"That will be the cops. Just stay behind me as I check."

I looked through the peephole and then opened the door to two cops in uniform on the porch. A cruiser was parked in the drive.

"Thanks for coming so fast." I opened the door wider and let them in. "Guy tried to break into my little girl's room. It's down that way."

"Okay, we'll check it out. This way?" One of the officers pointed and I nodded.

"You might want to call Detectives Richardson and Bolinsky. They're already on the case. My girlfriend here was attacked about a month ago."

One of the police officers pushed a button on his shoulder mic and started speaking.

"Come with me." I tucked my arm around Monet. She still held Lily, who had her thumb in her mouth and her face buried against her mom's chest.

A rage like I'd never known simmered in my veins as I took Lily into my arms and led my girls to the safety of the back bedroom. My little girl's room had been broken into. If I hadn't had the alarm system installed, that fucker could have taken her, hurt her, or worse. I didn't want to even imagine the unthinkable.

If I ever saw Kyle, he was a dead man.

CHAPTER THIRTEEN

HEART
CHAKRA

When the heart chakra is functioning well in a child, she tends to be more nurturing and caring. She easily shows compassion to others and is contented in her life. If the heart chakra is overactive in a child, she may become possessive, divisive, or act melodramatically.

MONET

I petted my daughter's black hair, pushing a lock behind her ear and soothing my fingers down her face. She'd finally fallen asleep in between Clayton and me about twenty minutes ago. I couldn't stop touching her. It was as though my mothering instinct wouldn't let her go after what'd happened tonight. The two detectives were kind and gentle when asking their questions. At first, Clayton refused to allow them to speak to

Lily, not wanting her to have to remember what had happened, but they needed to know as much as possible in order to find the person responsible. I knew in my heart it was Kyle. Lily's room hadn't changed since he lived here, and he knew she'd be the easiest target. What he must not have expected was the alarm system Clayton had put in shortly after my attack. Thank God he had.

A shudder rippled through me as I briefly imagined what it could have been like had Kyle made it into the house. Clayton and I were occupied with one another and Lily was a defenseless little girl. I'd praised her so many times tonight for screaming the way she did. Still, it took the cops leaving and Clayton holding my girl against his chest for a long time in order for her to settle down. Even in sleep, she clung to his hand.

Clayton was on his side, his big arm curled completely around my daughter. Her head rested on his pillow and her back was against his chest. It was a position a father would take to protect his young, and Clayton hadn't thought twice about providing her what she needed to feel safe.

"Thank you," I whispered over her head.

He blinked open his eyes and tightened his hold on Lily, his forearm muscles flexing. She sighed and nuzzled her head into his hand.

"For what?"

I placed both my hands in a prayer position under my head. "Taking care of us. Of Lily. Being what she needs. She feels safe with you."

A gentleness passed over his features. "I'm never going to let any harm come to this little girl. Monet, I was scared as fuck when I heard her scream..." He kissed the top of her head as if he couldn't stop showing her affection either. "It gutted me. I can't lose you girls, and I'll do anything...*anything*, to keep the two of you safe."

His words and the honesty with which he gave them reached into my heart and settled there. I believed him. One hundred percent. Clayton was all in. Somewhere over the past few weeks, he'd fallen in love with Lily and me and decided we were it for him. The shocking thing was that I too finally allowed myself to believe it was real. That the three of us together could actually be the real deal. And boy did I want it. Him. Everything that included. His bossiness, caveman-like attitude, his sweet and tender side when it was just the two of us or when I'd hear him talking just to Lily. Clayton Hart had woven so deeply into the threads of my existence that I never wanted him to leave. And maybe, just maybe, I had a chance to hold on to him, on to this, for the rest of our lives.

"You did keep us safe. You being here, putting in that alarm..." My voice cracked. "Clay, it could have been so bad."

His jaw went hard, and a flicker of anger passed over his eyes. "But it wasn't."

I shook my head. "No, it wasn't. Because you took care of us."

He sighed, tucked Lily close, pulled the blanket up over her shoulders, and ran his fingers through his spikey hair.

"The detectives are no closer to finding Kyle. The only thing they can surmise now is that he's still in town. They're going to put a car on the house again, but they've got nothing. No leads. He hasn't gone to any of his old haunts you mentioned, and his family hasn't heard from him. Or they're lying about it," he hissed. "It's so goddamned frustrating. I want him locked up."

I reached a hand out and wiped it across his forehead before raking my fingers through his hair. "I know. Me too. We just have to believe it will happen. In the meantime, we're being vigilant."

He sighed, and it sounded like the entire weight of the city was lying on his chest.

"Monet, we need to get you some training." His voice was a low, tired rumble like a storm slowly moving in.

I frowned. "Training in what?"

"Self-defense. Nicholas offered to teach you. Says he's taught it in the past. I asked him to do it at Lotus House in one of the private rooms."

Self-defense. I lifted a shoulder and dropped it. "I mean, it couldn't hurt. If it would make you feel better, I'll do it. Not sure I'd be any good at it."

His blue eyes shot to mine. "It would make me *ecstatic*. I also need to know how you feel about firearms."

The mention of firearms made me shift up and onto my elbow so I could see him better. "I don't know anything about guns, Clay, and I'm not sure I want to." Guns killed people. My stance had always been that if a person wasn't a trained professional—say a soldier or a police officer—there really wasn't a reason for them to have a gun. I could see people living off their land owning guns, needing it to hunt and eat. But in the city? In a hippieville college town like Berkeley? Nope, just didn't add up for me.

Clay bit into his bottom lip. "I own a gun. It's back at my pad. Want you to know I'm planning on bringing it here and putting it in a locked box in the closet. If for some godawful reason Kyle gets into the house, I want you to be protected regardless of where I might be."

I narrowed my eyes and focused a hard stare on his face. "And where would you be?"

He lifted his arms showing his hands. "Fuck, I don't know. In the garage, reading to Lily, cooking dinner, checking the mail, running to the store. Beautiful, I have to know at the very least I've left you the tools and skills needed to protect yourself in the event that he gets to you first."

"Clay..."

He shook his head frantically. "I'm not going to bend on this. Tonight was a huge wake-up call." He sat up, put his fingers into his hair, and rested his elbows on his bent knees. "We need to be extra careful, and that means me protecting my family by whatever method I deem necessary." He glanced over his shoulder, the depth of sincerity in his eyes flooring me. As worried as I had been tonight, I think it hit Clayton even harder.

"Do you understand, Monet? I'm your man. I'm this little girl's male role model. I'm nothing if I can't protect the two of you. *Nothing*." Clayton's voice trembled when he spoke next. "And I'll have nothing if something happens to you. You get me?"

I didn't exactly *get him*, but I understood where he was coming from. This thing between us was new. Hell, just tonight we'd admitted our love for one another, and he'd practically shoved his way through moving in with me, another issue we hadn't talked about.

Not that I minded, though. I liked having him here. I wanted him here. Lily would love the heck out of him being with us full-time. My love bug was attached. Attached in a way a person doesn't come back from, which scared and excited me to no end. But Clayton's declaration of being the man of the house, the man in our lives, washed over me in a pleasurable yet again frightening way, because of what it would mean if we lost him.

I sat up, went around the bed, and crawled into his lap, careful not to wake Lily. He held me close as I hugged him, allowing our hearts to meld and speak for us. His head dipped low and he placed his lips against my neck. "I wanted tonight to go so differently. I'd planned on seducing you in the shower and then spending the rest of the night making love to you."

Not being able to stop, I grinned against his warm shoulder. "That would have been nice. Still, we had a great shower."

He chuckled, and just the sound loosened some of the tension still lingering from the evening's happenings.

"We have so much time to cross that final barrier. It's kind of fun enjoying the ride, don't you think?" I clung to his broad shoulders as he rubbed his hands up and down my ribs, over my thighs and back. I think the repetitive motion was calming him as much as it was soothing me.

"We need to go to sleep. Lily's got school."

I shook my head. "No, I'm keeping her home tomorrow. It's been a really hard night, and she's going to need some time with us to get past it before going back to school. I think I need that too."

He nodded, cupped my cheeks, and kissed me. He kissed me for so long that when we stopped, I was in a sleepy love haze. As if I weighed nothing, he lifted me and walked around the bed, putting me back on my side, where he tucked me in. He locked the bedroom door, cracked the door on the bathroom so there would be light enough to see through the shadows in the dark—especially if Lily needed to get up—and then went around to the other side.

Clayton maneuvered his big body under the comforter, scooted close to Lily, wrapped his arm back around her, and kissed her head. "I love you, sweetie," he whispered against her hair. I held back the tears but only just. He hunkered down into the bed, grabbed my hand, and held it across the bed, my daughter safely tucked against his broad chest. Usually that was my spot, but tonight my daughter needed the security, and he gave it to her, almost as if he needed it himself. She'd had a scary night, and as the protector, he wrapped her up and gave her his love.

In that moment, I loved him more, because he loved her more.

★ ★ ★

"What in the ever-loving fuck happened last night!" Mila's words were shrill through the phone receiver. There wasn't enough coffee in the world to handle this woman's wrath.

"Calm down. We're fine. The police were here, Clayton is boarding up the window now until the window-replacement guy can come and fix it."

Mila groaned. "He broke into Lily's room?" she asked for the tenth time.

"Yes, but again, the alarm Clayton installed scared him off. He won't be trying that again. I'm certain of it."

Mila sniffed a few times, and her voice shook. "I think maybe you guys should move in with us, or move into Clay's apartment, or maybe we'll come back and move in with you..."

I shook my head in frustration at her declaration. "Stop. Mila. Clayton is taking care of us. We're safe. I promise. I'm going to start a self-defense class with Nicholas next week. Clay wants me to be able to defend myself. And he's also going to be taking me to the gun range tomorrow when Lily is at school."

"The gun range... What the... *Seriously*? My God. Moe, this is crazy. Why the hell can't the cops find this bastard? I mean, it's not like he's some sort of mastermind. He's a blond-haired, thin white guy who used to sell cars! As far as we know, he doesn't even have a job. What money is he living off of? I don't even think they're trying."

I sighed. The same thoughts had run through my mind repeatedly. However, I had the distinct advantage of having lived with Kyle. He played dumb and lackadaisical often. In reality, he was extremely observant, manipulative, and cunning. It's how he got me to marry him in the first place. After a lot of self-loathing and thinking back over the years we were married, I'd come to the conclusion that he'd just married me for money. I never cared much about monetary things except for a home, car, and the usual comforts a woman wanted to have in her life.

Kyle liked to have the best of everything. When we went out it was always to the swankiest locations. He'd buy expensive clothes, even though he rarely had a job. I even let him leave with the top-of-the-line Porsche he'd bought with my inheritance. Still, none of that even put a dent in the bankroll I had. My grandparents had left me hundreds of millions. The interest off the money alone was too much for me to spend each month. Besides, I had a great job and made a decent income as psychiatrist. The court mediation I did mainly as a civic duty, not because it paid well, because it absolutely did not.

"I don't know, Mila. All I know is, today we're making

cupcakes, watching movies, and maybe hitting the local bookstore for a few new titles. Clay's going to make homemade pizzas if the two of you want to come over."

"Mmmm, pizza. I could eat that now."

I laughed out loud. "Mila, it's nine in the morning."

"Yeah. I wonder if there is a place that would deliver early?"

"Pregnancy cravings?" I wondered. When I was pregnant my cravings started early. As in the second I found out I was pregnant I wanted pickles, olives, and balsamic dressing all the time.

"Maybe. You think?" she asked.

"Honey, have you been reading the books I ordered and had shipped to your house?" I personally patted myself on the back for that one. Best friend status secure.

"Um...not exactly."

"Mila..." I chided.

She laughed heartily. "Atlas has taken on being the encyclopedia of my pregnancy. If I want to know something, I just ask him. He's read all of the books you sent—twice!" She snorted and laughed. "He says since it's not happening to him, he's going to find a way to be involved. When I ask for the book, he asks me what I want to know. It's irritating and cute at the same time. Damn curly-headed punk!"

I snickered. "That is cute though. He wants to be involved. Kyle never did. He didn't want anything to do with my pregnancy."

"Because he's a pencil-dicked, card-carrying member of the supreme bastards club."

"Well, that is true." Without warning the thought of Kyle's dick size in comparison to Clayton's was hysterical, and I burst out laughing.

I laughed so hard I couldn't catch my breath, and my eyes watered.

"What? Tell me! What's so funny?"

After several deep inhalations where I attempted and failed to catch my breath, I said, "I was comparing Kyle's and Clay's dick sizes..." I kept laughing.

"Oh wow. That bad, huh?"

"So bad. Clayton's got a monster co—" I covered my mouth as Lily burst into my bedroom holding her wand, wearing a princess gown and a pair of my dress shoes.

Mila groaned. "Don't leave me hanging. *Hanging*! Get it?" She busted up laughing through the line.

"Lily honey, you look cute as a button, but Mommy is having a private conversation with Auntie Mimi. Go see what Clay is doing. I think he's measuring the window in your room," I offered.

"Oooh...maybe I could use my wand and make magic!"

"Sounds great, honey!" I plastered on a smile for her as she teetered on my heels and clopped her way down the hall.

"King Clay! I'm gonna fix the window wif magic!" she hollered, her voice getting softer the farther away she got.

I waited until I couldn't hear her anymore.

"Moe...I'm dying."

"You know that saying, he's hung like a horse?" I offered with a saucy lilt to my voice.

"Mmm-hmm."

I grinned, loving that I was finally able to have real God's-honest girl talk with my best friend about a guy. When Mila was dating Atlas and had finally committed to being his girlfriend, she didn't shut up about all the ways he made her scream in the bedroom. Now it was my turn, and a giddiness overcame me.

I whispered, "He's that times a hundred!" and giggled.

A hoot and holler blasted through the line and was so loud I had to hold the receiver back away from my face. "Praise Jesus, halleluiah! Can I get an amen for my sisters out there who deserve some good hard lovin'!"

We both fell into a fit of laughter. Once we had ourselves under control, Mila's tone changed, a seriousness overtaking the levity.

"Moe, I'm really happy for you. I like Clayton, a lot. He's a good guy."

"The best," I said, awe coating my tone.

"And you gotta know he loves you. I mean, it's written all over his face and the way he dotes on you and Lily—"

I cut her off. "He told me he loved me last night."

"Holy shit. Okay...um... And what did you say?"

"The truth."

"Which is..." She let her question peter out.

"That it was too soon..."

"Ugh. Moe! Goddamnit!" She blasted me with her frustration.

"But that I loved him too!" I finished, but it was too late. She'd already started in on her lecture.

"You have to let him in. He's the right man... Wait? What?" Her argument stopped immediately.

I chuckled and raised my head when the door opened and Clay entered. I had taken a seat in one of my high-back reading chairs near the window in my bedroom. One of my knees was cocked up against my chest, and I had most of my weight on one hip to relieve any pressure from my back. Watching him watch me, I knew a rosy hue was crossing my cheeks because they warmed shamelessly.

With a boldness I felt deep in my heart, I looked right at him but kept speaking into the phone. "I told Clay I loved him too. And I do. So much."

Clay's chest lifted and fell as he breathed, watching me from across the room as though I was his prey and he could pounce on me at any minute.

I straightened my spine and blew him a kiss. He shook his head, his face filled with happiness.

"Fuckin' love that, woman," he mumbled low, turning around and heading back out to leave me to my call.

He'd only come to check on me. I'd been gone a solid thirty minutes, and something inside his protective nature made him look in to ensure I was safe. Another piece of the wall I'd erected around my heart after Kyle fell away, and the space filled in with Clay's love and affection. Soon, he'd own it all. My body, my heart, and my soul.

"Moe, I'm so proud of you. This is big. Huge. Oh! I know, we need to commemorate this! I need to paint you guys! Together! Oooohh naked!"

"Mila, I'm not so sure Clayton would be okay with that." I didn't know if I was okay with that. My best friend seeing my man's business. A snarl of jealousy teased at my senses.

"Why not! I've seen him naked tons of times in Atlas's classes, and you have nothing to be ashamed of. That man is built, and I mean *built*! And you've seen Atlas naked a bazillion times. You can't tell me that it would be uncomfortable. I call bullshit on that."

Would it be uncomfortable? I honestly wouldn't know unless we were put in the position. "I don't know, Mila. We'll see. Right now, I'm healing, and I need to focus on my gun training and self-defense classes. As well as the chaperones I'll be taking to work for a while."

Remembering I had a handful of my male friends planning to act as bodyguards for me while I worked was enough to make me hate Kyle and wish him dead. And I'd never wished a single soul dead. Until now.

"Yeah…" Mila mumbled around eating what sounded like a potato chip. She crunched in my ear several times before continuing. "Atlas signed on for Fridays. Told Silas about what happened, and he offered to take a turn on watch."

I rolled my eyes. "Seriously? I've only met Silas once, and that was at one of Atlas's release parties."

More crunching. "He's a really good guy. And I'm not sure why you're surprised. People love you, Moe. You're pretty, nice, and no one wants to see you get hurt. Least of all me or Atlas. You're our family. I offered to take a day of watch, because who would mess with a hormonal Latina preggo, but Atlas lost his shit. We fought it out, then fucked it out. It was epic. Thank you for that."

And I was back to laughing. Thank God I had such an amazing best friend. "I'm glad my situation is allowing you some make-up sex."

"Oh no. We always have make-up sex. That was normal sex for us. Fighting and fucking is kind of our thing. Keeps us honest."

I shook my head even though she couldn't see it. "Okay. On that note, I'm going to bid you adieu and get back to my princess and my own hunk."

"You do that. Dinner this weekend?"

"Sure, what are you thinking?"

She snorted. "Whatever you and Mr. Muscles are

cooking, I'm eating. So far, this baby is not picky. And I have a new ultrasound picture to share. So you have that to look forward to."

"Yes! I want to see. Maybe you should take a picture with your phone and send it to me?" A maternal ache kicked up inside me, reminding me that I was not getting any younger, and I wanted Lily to have a sibling.

"Nuh-uh. You have to wait. It will be sweeter when you see the baby's cute little nub arms and legs and big-ass head. I can already hear you getting all swoony, and I have so few things to look forward to with this pregnancy. Your sweetness, tons of carbs, and hopefully a second-trimester crazy libido. Atlas says it's coming. I'm all ready for it when it hits!"

"You are too much, but I love you." And I really did love Mila. Sadly, more than my very own sister. I'd be lost without her. But Matisse, after everything she'd done... I shook my head and ran my hand through the heavy layers of my hair, sliding them away from my face. No more thoughts of her. It only did more damage than good.

"I love you too," Mila said and hung up.

I ended the call, took a deep breath, and wondered if my own sister knew about Kyle's attempted murder and break-in. She may have been coldhearted about being with him on the sly while we were married, but I couldn't imagine she'd want me or my daughter dead. He had to be keeping his plans from Matisse. I couldn't entertain the thought that a woman who shared my blood would want my daughter and me gone from existence. He had to be doing it behind her back. He had to be.

CHAPTER FOURTEEN

HEART
C H A K R A

Emotional, physical, and existential issues may arise when the energy of the heart chakra does not flow. By healing the heart chakra, one may experience a boost in energy, positivity, love, and compassion, and an increased sense of connectedness to life. There are a variety of different yoga poses, breathing techniques, stones, crystals, and therapy that you can do to heal your heart chakra. Speak to a Registered Yoga Teacher for yoga tips or do a little research online. Deepak Chopra is a known guru on the subject.

MONET

"Angel. The first thing you need to know about self-defense are the soft targets. Regardless of what position an attacker gets you into, these are gold."

I nodded, standing across from Nicholas Salerno in a pair of black yoga pants and a royal-blue ribbed tank top that said "Love Me a Latte" on the front. Every time I wore the tank, I snickered, and today I needed some humor, mostly because the situation with my ex was not humorous at all.

"We're going to start with the eyes, ears, nose, mouth, and throat moves."

"Okay." I jerked my head back and put up my arms like I've seen in kung fu movies.

He grinned and shook his head but took his stance across from me. He wore a pair of black lounge pants and nothing else. Magnificently bare chested. His torso was what women all over the Lotus House facility were drooling over. Now I personally understood what the hubbub was about. Nick had a large defined chest packed with muscles, with smooth skin all the way to his belly button, where a smattering of hair met the V of his waistline. I'd bet many had lost their minds over that happy trail. Under no duress, I'd happily admit the man was sex on a stick. Still, his chest had nothing on my man's.

An image of Clayton's broad golden chest entered my mind. Thank goodness I had my own man whose chest bested Nick's, but not by much. Not by a long shot. Nicholas Salerno was ridiculously attractive. His hair shined a dark cappuccino like a new coffee bean. However, his eyes were the most incredible feature by far. My goodness, it was as if they were translucent. Kind of like looking through sea glass. The palest blue with a thin line of yellow around the edge. Stunning. I'd bet the right woman could look into those eyes and see her future. Probably many had tried. He hadn't committed to any that I knew of.

Unaware of my musings, Nick continued. "Now, if your

attacker goes for your upper body from the front, there are a variety of things you can do to ward him off. Start with the soft limits though. Those tend to be the easiest to remember. As he comes close, go for his face with your hands. Use your thumbs to jab straight into his eye sockets. Like so." He placed his hands on the side of my cheeks and moved his thumbs right in front of my eyes but didn't penetrate.

"Oh, okay. I get it." The position made sense. It would definitely hurt if someone used their thumbs to poke into an opponent's eyes.

"You try."

I repeated his move and felt rather proud of myself for getting it right the first time.

"Awesome. You can also go for the eyes with a spade-like shape, meshing of your fingers, or even knuckles first. I'd recommend the thumbs though because using them seems to be easier for women in the heat of the moment. And remember, you're not trying to bruise them. You're trying to blind them. Take away their sight so they can't see you and they let you go. Ears up next. I'm going to come at you, and you're going to grab both of my ears. Just not too hard!" He grinned. "This is pretend."

I chuckled, and as he placed a hand on my shoulder and got close, I grabbed both his ears.

"Good. You can use this position to grip with all your might and bring me down and into your knee. Or, you can just twist the ears and my head will automatically jerk back to protect myself. This will give you precious moments to hopefully escape. Still, I'd go for the knee to the face if at all possible, because it will hurt more and give you more time. Let's practice."

For several rounds, we practiced the move until he thought I had it just right. Sweat prickled at my hairline and my shoulders were tense. My back ached a bit but not bad enough to call a halt. I enjoyed the overuse. The skin where my stitches had healed had been feeling stretched tight and itchy. The doctor mentioned it would as it healed. However, I wasn't ready to call it quits due to a little discomfort. Clay wanted me to learn this training, and I needed to for my own safety. Protecting myself didn't come naturally. I was a giver by nature, but I hoped the tools Nick and Clay bestowed would take hold and I'd be better for it—more prepared in the event Kyle came at me again.

Nick went over to a table, grabbed a sports bottle, and sucked back some water. I did the same with my own that I'd set in the corner near my stuff.

"You're a natural at this, angel."

Nick's compliment and a sense of accomplishment made my heart feel full.

"Remember, doing this is going to ensure that if you're ever stuck in a position with that asshole again, you can defend yourself and get away. Yeah?"

"Yeah, I know. It's hard though." I looked down and focused on my neatly pedicured pink toes and gathered my thoughts. "I hear about cases all the time where a man beats his wife and vice versa, and their relationship is not only volatile but destructive. Then other cases with child abuse, as well as women being sexually assaulted or attacked. I've always been one of the ones who thought it could never happen to me."

"But it can happen to anyone." His voice was soft and gentle.

"Intellectually that makes sense, only, Nick, he could have

killed me. Had my client not come down to the exact same level on the garage, he would have slit my throat and left me for dead. That stuff doesn't happen. Not to me!" The tears I'd been holding back flowed to the surface, and I shook my hands and shoulders, trying to push the emotional blast out of my mind.

Nick was beside me in a couple of seconds. He curled a hand around my nape and got close to my face. "You did nothing wrong. You hear me? Nothing."

"But what if I egged him on in some way? Asked for it by not being a good wife and mother?" Some of my biggest fears spewed out of my mouth like a vile gas that had built up and couldn't be contained. The last month I'd been working hard with my therapist, and God knows between Mila and Clay I'd conquered some demons, but that little voice inside—the one that told me how insignificant and worthless I was—that voice was still there. I hadn't been able to vanquish it, and I worried I never would.

"Bullshit!" Nick's words were as abrasive as sandpaper over tender skin. "I've known you for years now. Years!" He punctuated his words by dipping his face closer. I could smell the musk of sweaty man, soap, and a hint of cologne. "No woman asks for what he did to you. He's twisted, Moe. Seriously messed up in the head. You do not take that on. It's not your cross to bear. What you do is focus on how you can protect yourself in the future. What do you say?"

I sniffled, closed my eyes, and wiped at the lone tear I wasn't able to push back. When I opened them again, my resolve was in place.

Fuck him.

Screw him and the horse he rode in on.

I had been a good wife. The *best* wife! Doting, loving, and considerate. Always.

Scowling, I narrowed my gaze until Nick was nothing but a blur. All I saw was red.

"You're right. And I'm ready. Let's continue. Show me how to be a badass!"

Nick squeezed my neck before pulling back. "Then it's time to get a little dirty."

I cocked an eyebrow, and he chuckled.

"Not *that* kind of dirty. *Mama mia*! I'm going to show you how to attack his nose, mouth, and throat."

"Goody. Let's do this."

"Goody." He rolled his eyes and chuckled. "Get settled in the stance I showed you. These are still the soft targets but definitely require closer range. You see this spot on my neck?"

He pointed to the divot at the top of his chest, in between the clavicles and below the Adam's apple. "This indentation is often referred to as the tracheal well. There's only a thin layer of skin protecting this vital organ. If your attacker comes at you with both arms out, or even one arm, move in toward him and shove your thumbs right into that indent the same way you do the eye gouge. Now come at me."

I went for him fast, trying to impress the teacher. He got a lock on my shoulders, and then I shoved my hands between his, gripped his shoulders, and pressed my thumbs to the area. He let go immediately.

"Yes! Perfect. You've got it. The best part about this hold is that it puts you in an awesome position to pull the man down lower than your hips and knee that sucker in the face!"

He shifted forward until I got the hint and pulled him low and then brought up my knee in slow motion.

"Nice, Moe. You attack that the same way you attack the

eyes. Thumbs right to the indentation. There's also the carotid arteries that run on either side of the trachea here." He grabbed my hand and placed it on his neck, pressing his fingers into the sides of the cylindrical shape of his neck. Just that hold made me uncomfortable, and I was the one touching it. His Adam's apple bobbed and I let go.

"Take a claw-like approach with thumb and forefingers around the cylindrical shape. Press in and squeeze to your heart's content. The goal here is to get his hands off you. His goal may change when you attack these sensitive places to getting your hands off *him*." He chuckled manically, his slick hair falling forward across his forehead. Nick had thick well-groomed eyebrows that arched beautifully but also had a very sinister appearance when he contorted his face the way he was now.

I squinted at him and snarled dramatically. "Don't be scary, Nick. It won't work on me!"

We both laughed and backed up into position. I glanced at the clock. It had already been almost an hour, and I hadn't even thrown him to the ground the way I'd seen in the movies.

"When do I get to flip you over my shoulder?"

He blinked, smirked, and then shook his head. "Angel, you are not going to throw me over your shoulder. You, sweetheart, are being taught practical defense today. We may get into the crazier moves months down the road when you're an expert on these."

I pouted. "Bummer."

"What I will teach you, though, is how to get out of a hold if your attacker is trying to rape you," he clarified meaningfully.

Rape.

The thought of rape had never even crossed my mind,

which was utterly asinine because, really, any woman was at risk at any given time. I just didn't believe Kyle had that type of attack in mind when it came to me. No, he'd gone straight for the jugular so he could get to the pocketbook.

"I tell all the folks in my self-defense classes that the ultimate goal is to always stay standing. That way, you can strike your attacker and run away. Unfortunately, that isn't always the case. If you're in the unfortunate situation of being brought to the ground..." Nick swiped my legs out from under me so fast I lost my breath. He hovered over me. His hands went straight for my neck and looped around it loosely. Fire rippled up my sore back where I'd fallen to the mat. Luckily this was practice instruction and I was on thick padding, or I would've been in a world of hurt.

"If you're ever stuck with a man on top of you, I'm going to show you how to get yourself out of it."

I flashed on Kyle straddling me, pulling my hair, and forcing my head back so that my back arched unnaturally. I had been completely immobilized.

"But what if he has me facing down?"

"Turn around fast. Shove and twist until you can." I nodded and he smiled. "Now what would you do in this particular position? Don't think. Use your instincts!" he encouraged.

Squirming around, I shoved my arms up and against his chest. He grinned wickedly and shook his head.

"Nope, angel. Wrong. That would allow him to slam your head into the ground and punch and choke you like so." He lifted my head and it flopped back onto the mat, and then he pretended to punch me. "Instead, what you want to do is wrap your hands around my neck and bring me down against your chest."

I frowned. "That's counterintuitive. I want to bring you close to my lady bits?" I gasped in shock.

He chuckled. "Just go with it."

"Fine." I sighed, brought my hands around Nick's thick neck, and pulled him toward my chest. He rested his forehead between my breasts. "What next?"

"You let his ass go and you have your instructor switch places with your boyfriend." Clayton's deep rumble broke through our concentration. "Nick, I see you've got yourself in a great position."

Nick being Nick, as in the epitome of an Italian Stallion, pressed up and onto his fists while still hovering over me. "That I do. My job is awesome. Being on top of a sexy woman... What could be bad about that?"

"Her boyfriend could kick your ass from here to kingdom come?" Clay deadpanned, but Nick wasn't having any of it.

Nick ruffled the top of my head, messing up my hair for the hell of it the same way a big brother would. Nick had a bunch of sisters, and he was the only boy in the family. That made him keenly overprotective when it came to those he cared about, and his big-brother side came out easily. We had that type of relationship, and it was the same with all of the female teachers at Lotus House and the regulars like me. He and Mila were really good friends too, and because of my relationship with her, he also put me in the friend category.

Nick shifted up and onto one hand before kneeling and standing.

"Come on, Clay. You may be big, but I teach boxers for a living, and you haven't been in the ring in a long time. I'd wipe the floor with you," he goaded good-naturedly.

Men were weird. I could hardly tell if they were kidding

or being serious until Clayton finally smiled. "Touché. Now what do you want me to do?" His expression turned a bit on the serious side, his blue eyes flashing with interest, regardless of the serious nature of what I was learning. He came over to me and kneeled between my legs.

"Hi, beautiful. You working hard or hardly working?" He cocked a sexy eyebrow.

I preened and ran my hands from his wrists up his corded arms until I could caress his face. I stroked his bottom lip with my thumb. I wanted so badly to rise up and kiss that lip. Instead, I answered with a breathy, "Working hard."

"Well, you look good doing it." He winked.

"Blah, blah, blah, let's get on with it. I was about to teach her how to get out of a rape situation. *Rape*. I'm assuming you want your woman up to speed on that?" Nick taunted.

"Fuck yes!" Clay growled, all hints of the humor he'd shown a moment ago long gone. "Let's do this, baby."

I nodded.

"Okay, so I'd told her not to push against her attacker but to bring him closer."

I took the instruction and wrapped my hands around Clayton's neck and brought his face in between my breasts. He took that moment to bite down on one through my tank.

"Ouch!" Cheeky bastard.

"An attacker might do that. I'm just keeping it real." He smirked, and I wanted nothing more than to kiss his full lips again; instead, I narrowed my eyes.

"Pay attention!" I chastised.

Nick chuckled. "All right, Moe, so what you want to do is wrap your legs around his waist and lock your heels."

I followed his instruction perfectly.

"Now we're getting somewhere," Clayton joked.

"Once he's secure, bring your hands around his head and press your thumbs into his eye sockets, doing the eye gouge."

I moved fast, having already learned this move. Clayton veered back as I pretended and startled him, pushing his head up and back.

"Nice, Moe. Perfect. As you can see, he braced himself above you when you shoved him up. Right now, he'd probably be screaming and spitting mad about his eyes. Use that moment to lock one of your arms around his and press into the side of his face, pushing him away from you. Let go of your leg guard around his waist, bend a knee, and twist with the scissor sweep until you're on top of him and have the upper hand."

I used the moves he'd taught me and flipped Clayton over onto his back, where I straddled his waist. A fist pump and trophy arms was totally in order, but I didn't think either of the men would appreciate it like a woman would. Mila would high-five me for that move alone. I couldn't wait to show it to her using Atlas as my lackey.

"Okay, here you'd go for one of your soft targets again like the carotid or the eye gouge, or you could straight up wail on his ass with some punches."

Wrapping my left hand around his trachea, I lightly compressed his carotid and pretended to punch him in the face with my right.

"Damn, woman! You're a badass!" Clayton sat up and hugged me to his chest, then laid a mess of kisses all along my neck. His loving embrace soothed my soul and aching form. I wrapped my legs around his waist and sat back so I could look at his smile.

"Really great, right? Nick taught me so many cool

moves, and I'm convinced I could do them if the need arose." I positively preened for my man. What was that saying about being silly in love?

"Yes, I did teach you a lot. Still, your sweet ass is going to be in here on Thursday at least one more time. I want you to go home and practice with Clay until then," Nick instructed.

Clay stood up, again hefting me around like I was a feather before letting me slide down his delectable body until I was standing. Yum. My skin tingled at the contact, wanting more. I always wanted more of Clayton's touch and nearness. That's what made our falling in love so fast not seem so ridiculous. We both felt it deep. The connection. As if when Kyle broke my heart, Clayton filled that broken half with his own, making me whole again.

My guy tipped his head down and took my mouth in a sweet, quick, but still meaningful kiss. After he'd had enough of my lips, he slid his nose along mine in a touching gesture that was somehow more lovely than the kiss.

Clay pulled away and went over to Nick, where he was gathering his things. He held out his hand. "Appreciate you doing this for her, Nick."

Nick frowned. "No thanks necessary. We all love your girl. If I can teach her some moves to protect herself against that dirtbag, I can sleep easy tonight."

"Still, I appreciate it, man." He squeezed Nick's hand and gripped him on the shoulder. Clayton turned to me as I was zipping up my white hoodie. "You ready? Want to pick up the queen and get working on our project."

I pursed my lips and grabbed his hand. "Which would be what?" He hadn't mentioned that we'd be doing anything handy around the house. Not since he had the window fixed and the security system installed.

"Getting Lily back in her own bed. That defense position reminded me your back is finally good to go. It is good, right?"

I twirled my hair with my free hand. "Maybe..."

He nudged my arm with his. "Don't tease me with the prospect of heaven, beautiful. It's just cruel." He dipped his head close to mine and whispered in my ear. "I want you flat on your back, legs spread, showing me all your sweetness."

My voice lowered, sounding desperate even to my ears. "Clayton..."

"Not waiting any longer, Monet. It's been over a month. I want in." His words brooked no argument, not that he would get one from me. We wanted the same thing.

It still shocked me that it had been over a month since my attack and our rapid pairing. Even though we'd basically done everything else in the bedroom, we hadn't consummated our relationship—our love—through intercourse. It was the final step toward our unity. In that moment, it seemed crucial, vital to moving forward with our forever.

"I want you in too," I whispered back, a girlie sense of anticipation fluttering in my stomach like a dozen flapping butterflies.

"Then let's get a move on."

"Bye, Nick, and thank you for everything." I waved.

"You got it, angel. See you on Thursday for the follow-up session. At that one, I'll be teaching you the bear hug, the hammer grip, and the wrist sweeps!"

He sounded honestly excited about it. Made me wonder if he should be teaching this class regularly at Lotus House. I'd bet Crystal and Jewel wouldn't think twice about adding a class to the schedule.

"Have you approached the owners about adding this class to the Lotus House regular schedule? It seems like a pretty important subject and something all women and men alike should learn."

Nick tipped his head and rubbed a hand along his jaw. "You know what, I think you're right. You being attacked really woke up the staff here. I'm going to chat with Crystal and Jewel. See if it's something they're interested in. Regardless, I should definitely open a session at my boxing gym. There's no reason I couldn't. Heck, the boxers alone have enough girlfriends and wives who would probably want to learn how to protect themselves too. Thanks for planting the seed, Moe."

I grinned. "Thank you for teaching me the ropes. I'll see you Thursday for sure!"

"You got it, angel. Keep your man honest, yeah?"

Clay looped an arm around my shoulders. "Always, man. Always."

"I'll just bet." Nick grinned, and Clay gave him one of those super cool three-fingered waves that totally said tough guy.

"So, our project?" I niggled at Clay.

He tipped his head back and smiled. "Yes!" The word came out as a hiss. "You already know I'm so into you. Can't wait to bury myself deep inside."

My cheeks flamed. "I do. And I'm so into you too!" Admittedly we were being super cheesy, but I was having fun with it. Something I hadn't had in a relationship before.

"Now it's time to physically get *there*." He nipped at the shell of my ear, sending a spark of lust spiraling right between my thighs.

I physically ached for his touch *there*. Heck, everywhere.

"We'll make it happen."

"Tonight?"

"Tonight."

"Halle-fucking-lujah."

CHAPTER FIFTEEN

HEART
CHAKRA

The heart chakra couple will often follow the same moral principles and uphold the same family values. This will allow for peace and happiness in the home.

CLAYTON

"And this little piggy went wee wee weeeee all the way home." I shook Lily's pinky toe, making her squeal with laughter.

Her breath came in ragged gasps as I situated her in bed, covered her up, and tucked her in on all sides around her small form. I was pretty proud of myself for remembering one of the nursery stories my mom used to humor me with as a kid.

Lily's black hair, so like her mother's, spread out on her pink sheets. I swept a lock off her forehead, and that's when she nailed me with it.

"Clay, are you gonna be my daddy now?"

Just like in the cartoons with the roadrunner and the coyote, a giant proverbial anvil landed right on my chest, pressing my ribcage against my heart. A whoosh of air left my lungs as I blinked and inhaled slowly, trying to calm my rapidly beating heart. This was not a conversation I could take lightly. I glanced around to see if Monet's mommy radar had magically sent out a homing beacon. Maybe she could zero in from afar and show up and do mommy things that would change the subject and make everyone happy all at the same time. Unfortunately, none of that happened.

Against my normal inclination, I decided to go the coward route since I hadn't had this conversation with Monet. As much as I would've liked to claim this little girl and her mother, we were not officially at that place. We'd need a church, an officiant, a horde of yogis, my family, and a badass party before anything became official.

"Why would you ask that, sweetie?" I sat on the edge of her bed and eased closer so she could play with the leather bracelet I'd worn since college. Trent and I had bought them on a whim in hippie central down on Telegraph Avenue, where the street vendors always set up their homemade wares for selling to tourists and locals. I guess maybe it could be considered a friendship bracelet of sorts.

Lily's shoulders bounced up and down, but her eyes stayed on the bracelet. "I don't have a daddy, and I can't have PowPow because he's Auntie Mimi's and not Mommy's husband. That's what Mimi said. But you like Mommy. A lot. I see you kissin' her all the time."

I grinned. "I do like your mommy very much. In fact, I

love your mommy. And you know what?"

Her dark-blue eyes flashed to mine. "What?" There was awe in her tone, as if I was about to impart a big secret to her.

"I love you too." I tapped her nose.

She smiled huge. "Good. Then you're my daddy. Great. I'll tell my friends. Oh!" Her eyes widened to the size of tennis balls. "I'll tell my teacher too and PowPow and Mimi. Great. Just great."

My gut twisted painfully. "No, baby, I'm not your daddy... yet," I added because I couldn't not.

Her nose crinkled up in the way that I knew she was not happy.

"But you said you love Mommy and you love me. Then you can be my daddy." There literally was no gray area for a five-year-old. None at all.

I was pretty sure I physically felt my heart rip in two knowing that without even trying, I was going to hurt this little girl. I never wanted to hurt her. Ever. I wished more than anything I could be everything she wanted, but I couldn't make those promises. I had a good idea where things were leading with Monet, and right now, between the two of us, we were awesome. Still, we had to deal with Kyle; we had to have some peace to be a couple and some time being a family of three that was not tainted by the threat of someone trying to hurt either of my girls. It did not, however, change that an ache filled my chest, wanting more right this second but knowing I had to wait. We all did.

"One day, sweetie, I'd like nothing more than to call you my own, but for now we need to take our time. If your mom and I get married, then I can officially adopt you."

"A-bop me?" she repeated.

"Ah-dop-t you." I sounded out the syllables and exaggerated the t so she could hear the variance.

"'S'wat I said. A-bopt me."

I inhaled full and deep and hovered over my girl with my forearms on each side of her little body and brought my face close to hers. "Sweetie, let's focus on being happy today, okay? We'll worry about the rest another time."

Her response was to wrap her tiny arms around my neck and plaster her forehead to mine. She smelled of that baby-wash stuff and lotion her mom put on her after her bath, with a hint of jasmine just like her mother. I closed my eyes, content to be embraced by an amazing child. It was a new feeling, something I hoped I'd never get used to.

"I love you, King Clay." She squeezed my neck, kissed my cheek, and then let go.

"I love you too, Queen Lily." I kissed her forehead. "You gonna stay in bed all night this time? You've got the super cool new salt rock lamp light we got you. And see that white thing there?"

She nodded.

"That's a monitor. We will hear and be able to *see* you while you sleep, and Mommy and King Clay will be checking on you regularly. Okay?"

She glanced at the monitor, then the salt rock lamp that glowed a soft orangey yellow throughout the room. Our little love was not willing to sleep in the dark after the attempted break-in, and we wouldn't make her.

"Also, you can see that your window now has a super big lock." I pointed to the new lock we'd installed. And this stick?" I pulled it out of the window track so she could see. "There is no way anything can fit through that window unless you personally remove it yourself. And the best ever is this super-secret *magical* covering. Nothing is getting through this magic wall." I dragged down the blackout blind we'd installed.

Monet felt if we put in new window coverings, mentally, her little mind would block out some of the fear of the window. Reiterating the extra locks were in place and showing her the monitor would hopefully ease any additional fears.

"What do you think?"

She snuggled into her bed, her eyes getting drowsy.

"I like magical walls."

Of course she did. And she believed they were real and they'd protect her. Monet was a freaking genius. Another reason to show my appreciation to my woman tonight.

Once more, I tucked Lily in and kissed her forehead. Her eyes were closed and her breath was already evening out as I stood above her. Resilient little girl. Just like her mother.

Closing Lily's door just enough to leave a crack of light from the hallway, I made my way into the kitchen. Monet was finishing up the dishes from dinner. I cooked, she cleaned. If she cooked, I cleaned. We'd only been living with one another for a little while, but we'd happily found our own system with the nightly duties. On the nights that I did the chores, she put Lily to bed. Over the past couple weeks, much to our dismay, that had been in our bed.

"She down?" Her voice was calm yet concerned.

"Yeah, beautiful. You'll never believe what she asked me, though. I almost called out for a life raft."

Monet cocked a hip against the island, picked up her half-full glass of red wine and took a sip. A drop of wine sat like a pomegranate seed right on her bottom lip. Before I could move, she licked the drop away. I grunted but stayed strong, picking up my own glass of wine and crossing my arms.

"Really? What was it about?"

I took a sip of wine, allowing its flavors to roll across my taste buds while I thought how to broach the sensitive subject for the second time. "She asked if I was her daddy now."

Monet's eyes grew to twice their size. "She didn't."

I chuckled, took another sip, and then stretched back. "Yep."

"Well...uh..." She cleared her throat and looked down. "What did you say?"

I watched my girl become exceedingly uncomfortable, the absolute last emotion I wanted her to feel right now.

"What do you think I said?" I tried to take the bite out of my question but failed miserably.

She frowned. "I wouldn't begin to know."

"Monet, you know where this is going for us. You *know*."

Instead of responding, she turned around, set her glass down, grabbed the dishtowel, and started wiping at the already clean counter. Deflection. Not a good sign.

"I know I love you, you love me, and that's really all I know."

I came up behind her, set my glass next to hers, and wrapped both my arms around her, allowing her to rest against me. "You know more than that. We're going for long term. I wouldn't have moved myself in if we weren't."

Her head dropped down, and she turned quickly. "It's still hard to believe that you want me, well...us. It's a lot to take on."

Needing her to connect with my words on a visceral level, I cupped her cheeks and ducked my head toward hers. "Monet, listen, and listen good. The second, the very second I think the time is right and you'll commit to me forever, without any leftover fears from what that bastard did to you mentally, I'll be putting a ring on your finger. We *will* go the distance. I've no doubt. When you know it too, that's when it will happen."

She nodded and wrapped her arms around my waist, resting her head over my heart. "I love hearing your heartbeat. It reminds me that I have somebody to hold on to. That I'm no longer alone."

"And I'll always be here for you to hold. Lily too. And just so you don't get your panties in a twist, I told the queen we needed to take our time, and if you and I got married, then I'd adopt her and I'd be her daddy. I hope that was okay. I kind of freaked out."

She snickered against my chest and rubbed her nose against my sternum. "No, I think that's fair to say. She'd asked Atlas one time to be her daddy, and we had to tell her that he needed to be Mommy's husband. So that's kind of the same thing. Although she didn't talk to Atlas for a week, which really broke his heart. That man loves her like his own."

A niggling trickle of the green-eyed monster bore down on me. "Yeah, well, he can back the truck up because I'll be taking on the daddy duties until something is official. And you mark my words, beautiful. It will be official."

I could barely recognize the force behind the words spewing from my lips. The singular thought that Atlas wanted to be Lily's father, even in the most peripheral sense of the word, slithered like a poisonous snake down my spine. I clenched my hands into fists until Monet placed her hands on my biceps and ran her warm palms down my arms to my hands. She deftly eased each finger out of lockdown so she could intertwine our fingers.

"I love that you are a little gonzo macho man about this,

but Atlas would never try to overstep his boundaries. He's her uncle, and he loves the role. He's also one of your best friends. Let's not get riled up over who loves who more." She grinned, rose onto her toes, and put her mouth on mine.

She tasted of wine and the sweetest sugar. My girl was whipped cream and cherries all mixed in one. I could not get enough. I ran my hands down to her ass and cupped it firmly. She moaned into my mouth. The second that reached my consciousness, I hefted her up, encouraging her to wrap her legs around my waist. My woman did not need to be asked. When her crotch touched my hardened dick, I was the one moaning.

"Fuck!"

"Mmm." She made that little sound that always went straight to my cock.

"We done talking?" I spoke around licks and nips of her sugary mouth.

"Um-hum," she murmured and slanted her head to the side and grinded her body against mine while taking my mouth in a deep kiss.

I didn't have to hear another sound. I locked her body to mine and led her to our room. Our room. I hadn't gotten over how good that felt, knowing I had a home to go to, a family that wanted me there every night. Fucking dreamworthy. And I was sharing that dream with the most delightful woman alive. I'd never take that right for granted.

When I made it to the room, I kicked the door shut. Thank God Lily was on the opposite side of the house or the noise surely would have woken her. I slipped one hand behind me and turned the lock. Lily could still come to the door if she was scared, but I did not want her little eyes to see me taking her mommy. No way, no how. That would devastate Monet and me more than the little one. Of that I was certain.

When I got to the bed, I turned around and planted my ass on the mattress; my woman adjusted without comment, her lips never so much as breaking a millimeter away from mine.

I kissed her hard, holding the back of her head and crushing her mouth. She mewled and rubbed her delectable body against my erection. I could feel her heat through the single layer of my cotton track pants. She was positively simmering in my lap.

Pulling away, I lifted the sleep tank she'd put on before dinner. Her breasts bounced free, the brown nubs already erect, seeking attention. I curled forward and took one succulent tip. I didn't lead up by flicking and laving it. No, I went straight for the gusto and sucked her peak hard, taking into my mouth as much of her breast as I could. Her hands flew to my head, gripping me to her chest. No way I'd leave heaven after one taste.

I became hungry. Positively starved for her skin. My animalistic side was coming out, wanting to take, rut, *claim.*

"So good, Clay. So, so good." Her head tipped back and that silky long hair of hers fell back behind her, trailing against my knees and thighs. Christ, I loved her hair. Thick, wavy, and sexy as fuck.

I switched breasts, still using my thumb to rub and circle around the one I'd left. I vacillated between plucking her brown tips to sucking them deep and biting down. She ground down so hard on my cock in my lap, I knew she was going to come. And I wanted that. Fuck yeah, I wanted it.

I twisted each nipple and kissed around the globes, pressing them together so I could rub my face and scruff all over them. Mark them with little red scratches showing I'd been there. I'd like seeing that tomorrow. On that thought, I bit down on the side of her breast, finally feeling free to leave my mark on her skin in a possessive but loving reminder.

She arched and gasped.

"You coming, beautiful? Just from me playing with your pretty titties?" I asked around a mouthful.

A thrust of her hips and a grind against my cock sent shivers skittering along every nerve ending. I plucked and tugged at each tip, trying to make her crazy.

"Clay...please," she mewled, chasing an orgasm that was just out of reach.

"No, no." I tsked and flicked my tongue against one tip but continued the barrage to the other oversensitive peak. "I want you to come. Get nice and wet for me. Soak those panties, beautiful, because the second you do, I'm going to rip them off and bury my cock so deep, you'll never forget our first time."

"Baby..." she whispered, closed her eyes, and lifted herself almost completely off my body. Her knees held her weight while she arched her chest, gifting me her breasts. And what a gift they were. Round, a perfect handful, but not too large on her frame. Mocha-colored, quarter-sized areolas that beaded up nicely under my hands and mouth.

Wanting her to skyrocket but also enjoying the fuck out of watching her go over the edge, I pinched each tip, twisted them—first right, then left—and enjoyed the show.

Monet slammed her ass down, her center to my crotch, and rode my erection through my pants. Her body was wild, bucking, adding that additional bite of pain to her tits each time she pushed back.

"I'm going to come..." she announced like she always did.

Cute and hot.

"Come for me," I urged, watching the most erotic display of a woman's sexuality I'd ever seen, and I had a front-row ticket as it was happening in my lap.

As Monet arched, she shoved one of her hands into her tiny sleep shorts and went to town on her clit. I grunted, thinking about thumbing that knot myself. That simple move had my balls drawing up tight and sweat pricking over my skin.

I continued the torture on her breasts until her entire body locked around my form and she cried out, tipping her head back and losing it all in several gasps.

"Fucking hell, you're a goddess." I let go of her breasts but kissed and licked all around them, avoiding the bruised tips. I ran my tongue up her neck and back down, biting into my spot until she started laughing.

I inhaled against her neck and shifted far enough so I could cup her cheek and see her eyes. Limitless pools of love stared back at me.

"How do you feel?" I asked, kissing her lips in a tiny peck.

"Yummy."

One of my favorite words. It wasn't something I'd heard regularly in bed, which made it all the more unique, because she was saying it and was adorable after having just gotten her rocks off on my lap.

I figured she might yawn and get sleepy after the day she'd had, but instead she gripped the hem of my shirt, yanked it up and off, and pushed me back until I was flat against the mattress, her legs still straddling me.

"My turn." She gave a sexy wiggle and I knew that meant my girl was going to wrap her perfect lips around the head of my cock and suck me down. I could not let that happen because tonight wasn't about that. No, it was about more, about finding together.

Her tongue came out and flicked against my nipple. A spiral of lust tingled from that spot and went straight down south to where my already painful erection stood loud and proud.

Shifting my weight around, she got the hint and scrambled back. She stood at the end of the bed, chucked off her panties and shorts in one go, and stood gloriously naked.

"Goddamn, you're gorgeous," I reminded her.

She smiled, and her eyes lit up as she reached out and tugged my pants down in one fell swoop. Once I too was naked, she ran her nails up my thighs and licked her lips.

I shook my head and backed up the bed so my head reached the cloud of pillows at the headboard. I crooked a finger. "Now come here." I pointed to my dick, a pearl of pre-cum leaking at the top at my excitement from her bucking-bronco routine on my lap. "Right here." I again gestured to my cock.

She moved fast. Faster than I would have anticipated, thinking we'd go slow the first time we made love. I should have known that Monet was unlike any woman on this earth. The moment she hit my thighs and straddled my width, she curled a hand around the base, centered it to her slit, and slammed down in one go.

"Oh Gaaaaaaaahhhhhhhd," she moaned.

I gripped her hips, preventing her from moving a single inch. If she did, I might go off on one fucking thrust like a pubescent high schooler taking a girl's cherry for the first time.

"You're so...oh my...so big. I knew it was large, but...Clay..." She shimmied her hips and stirred my cock within her. I gritted my teeth and bore down.

I needed her down over me, lying across me, skin to skin. "Get down here now, beautiful. Need your mouth on mine," I growled, and her eyes widened before she mewled like a content baby kitten and kissed me.

I plunged my tongue into her mouth, shifted my hips back as much as I could, and jackhammered home. She cried out, my kiss swallowing it down. Fucking bliss. Being inside Monet unsheathed was better than any dream I'd had, and I'd had many since moving in. A month of endless scenarios where I took her hard, fast, slow, sideways, from behind, in the shower, in the tub, on the floor, against the wall. Nothing could ever measure up to the real thing.

Without warning, I rolled us over, pulled back my hips, and slammed home. Her body bounced up the bed at the force of my thrust, but her arms locked around my back, her legs around my hips, and she didn't complain.

For a few minutes, I was lost to the carnal act of taking my woman. Rolling in deep, pressing my pubis against her clit so I could grind against that cherry pit over and over, and I too was gone. She liked that grinding move. I knew by the way her eyes rolled back into her head and how she tightened her legs around the small of my back with each thrust.

Fuck, my woman was hot. And wet. And tight. So goddamned tight. Like a mighty fist locked around my girth. My cock was happier than it ever had been, and she'd made him pretty fucking happy this past month with her mouth and hands. Those were great, but her pussy? My God, her pussy owned me.

Pussy-whipped by this woman? Sign me the fuck up.

"Clay...love you, Clay...so much," Monet whispered into my ear before biting down on my shoulder. "I'm going to come again. Come with me."

Hell, as if I could deny her anything. Gripping one of her knees, unlocking it from my waist, I pushed it up and out toward her armpit. "Want deeper. More of you. Need it. Gonna take it." I clenched my teeth and drove in hard to the end of her. "Fuck yeah!" I lived for the extra inch inside. Nothing quite like it. Nothing.

Her eyes went crazy wide, and she lifted her face to the sky. I watched as her mouth opened in a silent cry when it came over her.

She shook, and I trembled.

I took, and she shattered.

She locked me into her body, and I lost my soul.

My vision was nothing but color. The cherry red of her lips after so many kisses. The pink of her cheeks. The black waves of her hair flowing over white cotton sheets. Her brown nipples peaked and tight. The shimmering translucent silver of sweat that misted over her skin. Color dancing...everywhere. And all mine.

I smashed my mouth over hers as it came over me. "Love you, Monet. Fucking love you," I mumbled around her lips as a wall of pleasure so intense embraced me, coating every nerve ending with bliss and a blinding white light. I planted my cock deep and let it all go. Shot after shot of my cum roared through me and into the last woman I'd ever make love to.

"You're it for me, Monet." I whispered into her neck, my lips resting against my spot. "You're all I'm ever going to need in this lifetime."

My woman wrapped her arms and legs back around me and held me there. All of my weight was pressing her into the mattress, and she didn't complain. I bet if I tried to leave the safety of her arms, she wouldn't let go. I wanted her to never let go.

"You're it for me too, Clay. Before you came along, I thought I knew love and what a relationship should be like, what sex should be like. You've destroyed that. What we have is so much more than I'd ever thought possible. I'm going to hold on to you. Do whatever it takes to keep you because I never want to see you go."

I kissed her neck several times. "Not ever gonna leave you, beautiful. Not ever. I promise."

"Gonna hold you to that promise."

I rolled over, taking her with me so she didn't bear my weight again. She shifted up on me, crossing both of her arms over my chest and setting her chin into her hands.

"So what did you think?" I asked smugly.

She pretended to think about it and put a ho-hum placating look on her face. She couldn't hold it. Not tonight. Not after the magnificence of what we just shared.

"I think I'm going to have to experience it at least ten more times to give a worthy answer to that question."

Greedy girl. I loved it. I chuckled and planted my hands on her ass, gripping a nice amount of cheek. My cock was already hardening against her stomach.

"You may get the opportunity," I warned and thrust against her.

"Seriously? Again?" She ran a finger down my torso and lifted up to a sitting position.

"You're insanely hot, and I've waited over a month to be with you."

Her eyebrows shot up into her hairline. "You didn't wait for jack. You had me in other ways." She pouted prettily and placed her hands on her hips. If she hadn't been naked with her tits bouncing in front of my face, I'd have prodded at her a little more, but not when she was looking like my next meal.

Instead, I palmed both of her tits and swiped my thumbs across her nipples. She gasped and bit down on her bottom lip.

"Hurt?"

"A little. Sensitive."

"Well, how about this time, you ride me until you come all over my cock?"

She licked her lips and stretched her arms over her head in a yoga move I'd seen many times before but usually standing. Those succulent gobbles bounced enticingly, and I groaned.

"Well, it's a dirty job, but someone has to do it." She grinned gloriously.

"Yeah, and that's you, beautiful. Now hop on my cock."

Monet giggled. "That sounds like a nursery rhyme."

"If it is, we'll read it together."

She laughed, and I sat up and pushed myself back against the headboard at the perfect moment when my girl slid down my length.

"Yummy." She moaned, tipping her head back.

Instead of making a joke of her cute side, I slid my hand into her hair, allowing the long strands to run through my fingers like silk ribbons. "True," I said, taking her mouth with mine.

CHAPTER SIXTEEN

HEART
C H A K R A

When your heart chakra is open, you are flowing with love and compassion, you are quick to forgive, and you accept others and yourself. A closed heart chakra can give way to grief, anger, jealousy, fear of betrayal, and hatred toward yourself and others.

MONET

A warmth unlike anything I'd ever known surrounded me. A set of masculine hands were running down my rib cage underneath the covers. I woke more fully when the blanket crept down and the morning chill touched my bare back.

"Good morning," Clay rasped into my ear before kissing his way down my spine and back up. "You're back is healing wonderfully. I think you'll be pleased if you ever get up the courage to look at it," he teased.

And I hadn't yet. I didn't want to know what it looked like. Something inside me was afraid to see. I feared the happiness bubble I was currently living in would burst and I'd have to start all over again.

Noncommittally, I hummed and tucked my elbows under my chest to settle in while Clay caressed me. His lips touched down at the top of my wound.

"I'm going to kiss every inch of you until you understand you're beautiful. *Everywhere*." Clayton continued his mission, kissing featherlight along my scar. From the very top of my shoulder, down over my shoulder blade, and along my side until he ended at the top of my hip. Of course, then he got kinky. He slid one of his large hands under my front and zeroed right in on the tiny bundle of nerves aching for attention.

His fingers moved through the wetness that increased at his touch, and I bucked my hips back, encouraging. He pushed one finger inside and then used his thumb to circle blissfully around my clit.

I arched, lifted my head to gasp, and pressed into his movements.

"You like that, baby?" he cooed, shifting his weight and straddling my hips. Clayton worked his fingers magically, finding just the right spot to take me from tame to wild.

Without thought, he rested his ass on my thighs, keeping me pinned facedown to the mattress. Then he used his free hand to slide up my ribcage, over my shoulder, and into my hair, where he tunneled in and gripped me by the roots while at the same time he forced two fingers deep.

Any other woman, or a normal *me*, would have bucked into it and crooned in pleasure. That is not what happened.

Not at all.

I screamed at the top of my lungs. Loud enough to shake the windows.

And I was back *there*.

★ ★ ★

My attacker was on top of me, straddling my sides and crushing my hips into the pavement.

He dug a forceful hand into my hair and tugged my head back hard. Blood poured down my back and onto my hand as I lifted up, trying to get him off me. I screamed, kicked, and pushed off the concrete, but nothing would jar him loose.

That's when I heard it. Laughter. Kyle's laughter while he held me down. "Not so all-powerful now, are you, Monet..."

He put the knife to my throat and dug the tip in. It burned like acid dripping on my skin.

"No!" I screamed.

"Yes!" he growled, pulling my head back so hard that my back bent unnaturally and I thought for sure he'd break my spine.

"Any last words?" His tone was absolute. That was the end.

"Monet!" Someone called my name.

I jolted and screamed.

"Monet, I'm sorry!" A soothing voice. One I loved. Cared for. There to save me. To bring me back.

★ ★ ★

Clayton's voice entered my nightmare.

"Baby..."

I blinked several times. The room started to come into

focus. "Clayton!" I screeched, reaching, climbing, battling the smoke and black surrounding my vision.

"Monet! Monet! Jesus, I'm sorry. I'm so fucking sorry!" Clayton's entire form shook; his eyes, now a smoky blue, were filled with fear.

Tears poured down my cheeks, and I found myself huddled to the headboard with my knees up and my arms locked around them. I lifted my head, and Clayton held his hands out to me in a gesture of surrender.

"Okay, I'm far away. Nowhere near you. Please, Monet. Please, baby. I don't know what to do." Clayton's voice was ravaged by dread and panic.

I swallowed around the grit in my throat. "I... Clayton. Honey." The punch of embarrassment slammed my chest like a battering ram. "Oh no."

Clayton moved toward the bed, likely having sensed I'd returned to the here and now. He pulled me into his arms and wedged his face against my neck. "Oh my God. You scared the fuck out of me. I love you. Monet, I'm sorry. I love you," he repeated, obviously needing to make sure I knew it.

"It's okay. I'm okay now." I locked my arms around his strong back and tried to remember. For a long time, Clay held me and we did yoga breathing, in for four breaths, out for four breaths, until both of us were calm enough to speak. I settled my ear to his chest and listened to his heartbeat. My favorite place.

You are not alone, Moe. Clayton's with you. He'd never hurt you. It was just a flashback.

Clayton petted my hair and placed kisses on my forehead and wherever he could reach. One of his hands eased up and down my back in soothing gestures that put me into a trancelike state. Gone was the frightening moment of being back there in Kyle's clutches. Gone was the fear he'd caused. In its place was warmth, life, and love. Clayton could give me all of that, and I was finally able to accept it.

"Clay, tell me what you experienced. I know you're shaken up," I requested, speaking to his chest but not ready to look into his eyes.

His large frame trembled as if it was hard to speak. "We were, uh...having fun. I was behind you, with my hand otherwise, uh...busy. And then...fuck. Shit just went bad. Really fucking bad, Monet." His voice cracked, sounding like heavy boots over gravel.

I could feel wetness slide down the heated skin of my shoulder. I eased back and found his eyes red-rimmed and glassy. I cupped both of his cheeks and kissed him softly because I knew he needed it. Whatever I'd gone through had pained him as much as it had me.

Taking a moment to breathe, allowing my heart to settle at his concern, I finally spoke. "I had a flashback of when Kyle had me pinned down in the garage. He sat on top of me from behind and yanked my head backward by my hair in order to cut my throat."

Watching Clayton's expression crumble into one of sheer misery and then horror probably topped the list of the last things I'd ever want to see in my lifetime.

Seeing my big, strong, capable man break right before my eyes eviscerated me.

He shook his head. "I did that. I took you back there. Me. I hurt you." He stood up and started pacing.

As scared as I was and as shaky as the flashback had left me, we both needed to get past this.

Naked as the day I was born, I came up behind him, wrapped my arms around him, and pressed my lips into his back. "No. You do not get to take that on your shoulders." I cleared my throat. "Never. Not ever. Don't compare what we have to what that vile man did to me. You didn't know." I sucked in a harsh breath. "Honey, I didn't know that would happen. I'm sorry I scared you."

He turned around so fast it put me off-kilter, but he caught me and plastered my body up against his chest. "You're sorry? No. I should have known better." His jaw was firm, hardened in a way that reminded me of what he looked like when he first took in my features after the initial attack.

"But you couldn't..." I tried.

"My job is to know what you need, when you need it. I failed." He ran a shaky hand through his spikey hair. Blond layers fell every which way, making him even more ruggedly handsome.

I rubbed my hands up and down his chest. "Clayton, you do know what I need, because all I need is you. You being understanding as I figure this out. You here for me, for Lily. I'm sorry I scared you. It's very clear to me that I need to spend more time talking to my therapist about what happened. And perhaps, the next time we're in a particular position, we'll plan for it. You can help me get past it. Do you think you could do that? Work with me on crossing over that fear?"

Clayton fell to his knees before me. He wrapped his arms around my waist and hugged me close before kissing my belly. There he rested his forehead in supplication. "I'll be whatever you need. Anything. Anytime. Whenever."

I wiped at my tears. "I love you."

"I love you too. So much." He kissed my belly again and

laid his head there so he could look up. His eyes were a murky blue, unlike the startling sky blue they usually were when he held me.

"I'm sorry I scared you," I whispered as a tear fell onto his cheek.

"I'm sorry too. We'll get past this, beautiful."

I ruffled his hair. "Yes, I do believe we can get through anything as long as we're together."

★ ★ ★

I entered the kitchen to the sounds of Queen's "We Are the Champions."

"Queen?" I chuckled.

"Yes, Mommy?" Lily answered as if I'd called for her. My little girl was a riot.

Clayton grinned, bit into a carrot, and then tossed one to my love bug. She picked it up and crunched loudly the same way he did.

I shook my head and smiled and my two loves. They filled my heart with such joy, I should have easily been able to push aside all the latent negativity of my experience with Kyle, but I couldn't. My therapist said it would take time. Intellectually, I knew this. I'd said the same thing many times in my daily practice. It just didn't fit into *my* world. I had everything I'd ever wanted munching on carrots and dancing to Queen in my kitchen. Nothing should be able to bring me down.

"How'd your call go with, uh...your friend, the good doctor?" Clayton asked smoothly, being vague so that the littlest of ears wouldn't pick up on the fact that Mommy needed a doctor's help.

I went over to my big man and looped an arm around his waist. "Really good. Time heals all wounds, as they say. But you were right. I need to have more than a handful of sessions. We've set up a time every few days to go over some of the, uh... more repugnant details so that what happened today won't happen again," I assured him.

He frowned. "Did you tell her about today? Exactly?"

"Of course. She needed to know so I could get past it."

Clayton nodded, seemingly not altogether happy about me hashing out the finer details of what triggered the flashback.

He pursed his lips. "Did she say there was any specific cause...?"

I gripped him by the waist and turned him toward me so his gaze came directly to mine. "She said it was bound to happen at some point. Pushing those types of experiences to the back of your subconscious only delays them coming to the surface. The trigger was not you but the act of remembering a time where I was in a similar position. Trust me. You are not the problem. I am. Pretending what happened was a small thing did not do me any favors. I'm now suffering the consequences of that decision, but there is a positive side to this."

He gripped my hips. "Thank Christ. Lay it on me, because right now I could use a positive."

God, he was so sweet. My guy wanting me happy and healthy above all else.

"The fact that I have a big, strong, handsome, caring, and loving man to be there for me when I fall or have a hard time or a bad dream. Whatever it is, I've got you to lean on."

"And you always will." His response was quick and to the point.

I rose up on tiptoe. "Exactly."

He kissed me soundly and for a long, long time. So long that the queen had finished her carrots, the song had ended, and she wanted attention, as evidenced by her patting us both on the thighs.

"Um...hello. The queen wants dinner."

"You do!" Clayton ruffled her hair, picked her up, and tossed her in the air. Then he caught her, pretended to drop her, but stopped and caught her. It was frightening to see my baby hurling in the air several inches above his head and then him catching her while she squealed in delight, but it was also the type of thing a father would do with his child, so I didn't say anything. They needed to bond, and I had to allow it to occur organically and not butt in.

While they were playing, the phone on the wall next to the counter rang.

I went for it, figuring it was Mila asking what was for dinner. She did that often. Invited herself to dinner. Now that she was pregnant, she did it a couple times a week. She'd call, find out what we were having, and debate if she wanted that or something else. Neither Clayton nor I minded because we enjoyed having her around, and I loved petting the bump. Now closing in on four months, she had a perfect little cantaloupe going.

"Hello?" I asked with a smile in my voice, watching my man and my kid run around the island.

A broken, stuttered voice ripped through the line. "Monet..."

Instantly the hair on the back of my neck stood at attention. "Yes, this is she. Who is this?" I didn't recognize the voice.

"My God, Monet. He hurt me. So bad." The sob coupled

with sniffles allowed me to register the voice as one I knew all too well.

Matisse.

"Matisse, is that you?" I needed to confirm. I hadn't heard from my sister since she and Kyle left the lawyer's office, and that was a long time ago.

The sound of a hacking, wet cough came through the line. "I'm hurt. I need help."

"Help? What happened? Where are you?" I asked, a frantic energy zipping up my spine and making me jittery.

"In a hotel..." she croaked. "I don't know where I am. He hurt me and beat me. Left me for dead." Her sobs tore through the phone and went straight into my bleeding heart. Target obliterated.

Clayton put a hand to my shoulder. His eyes were hard at the mention of my sister's name.

"Can you look at anything on the desk or the end table that says where you are? I'll come get you," I rushed to offer.

Clayton shook his head. "Could be a trap," he gritted through his teeth.

I licked my lips and pressed my thumb and forefinger against my temples. "Anything?" I asked, my heart hammering out a beat so hard I could almost hear it myself.

"Um...yeah. It says Berkeley Inn."

My eyes widened and Clayton scowled. "The Berkeley Inn? That's not far from here. When did he leave you? Where did he pick you up?"

Matisse sobbed some more and howled in pain. "I don't know. Please, help me. I have nobody. He hurt me. He hurt me so bad. Monet, he *raped* me." She cried out with a new round of emotional distress.

He raped me.

I gripped the phone so tight my hand started to throb. Tears burned the back of my eyes, and I ground my teeth and mouthed rape to Clayton. His entire face went from concerned to heated anger in a split second.

"Matisse, I'm sending help. Look at the phone. What room number are you in?"

"Twelve."

"Twelve," I repeated to Clayton.

He had his cellphone to his ear, calling the detectives on our case.

"Yeah, Berkeley Inn, room twelve. Says she's wounded bad. And uh, she told her sister she'd been violated. Yeah, okay, we'll meet you there."

"Help is on the way, Matisse. We're sending detectives right now, and they're sending in paramedics. We're going to meet you at the hospital."

"It hurts...Monet."

"I know, I know. I'm going to get you help and I'll be there for you. I'll be there." All the times we weren't there for one another rushed to the surface, my sisterly desire raging strong.

"Stay on the phone with me. Please."

"Of course, honey," I cooed, even though my heart was unraveling with every word.

Another ten minutes of me whispering to her and finally I could hear the police knocking on the door. "That will be the help we sent. Go open it."

"Can't. Too painful to move," she whispered, her voice getting weaker.

"She can't open the door," I told Clay.

"Break it down," he uttered into his cell phone.

I heard what sounded like wood shattering and metal bending and then a variety of voices tending to Matisse.

"See you soon," I said.

She didn't answer.

"Let's go. We'll have Mila meet us at the hospital to pick up Lily," Clayton muttered, coats already in hand.

I just followed along with whatever he said. All I could think of was my sister as a child and her growing up into a lovely woman. Talking about boys while we watched silly chick flicks. Her big, cheery smile. And then her words over and over.

He hurt me.

Left me for dead.

He raped me.

★ ★ ★

The hospital was a madhouse, but we were able to meet up with Detectives Richardson and Bolinsky in the emergency room.

"Where is she?"

"Seeing the doctor," the taller detective replied.

"I need to go to her now."

One of the detectives led me to a private room and knocked on the door. A nurse opened it a few inches, her eyes turning hard.

"We need privacy."

"Victim's sister is here."

Victim. Again with that word. Couldn't they use *survivor*? Sounded more appropriate than victim.

"Your sister's here. Do you want to let her in?" The nurse spoke to someone behind her. I couldn't hear the reply, but she opened the door enough for me to slip inside.

On the other side of the room was my sister. Her black hair, so much like mine, was a disheveled mop around her sullen face. She'd lost a lot of weight since I'd last seen her. She couldn't have been more than a size two, if not a zero. Heavy bandages lined both her arms. Bruises were visible on her biceps and around her neck. Her lip was split and a dot of dried blood clung to the edge.

I went to her and wrapped my arms around her small frame. She folded her thin arms around me and clung to me like her life depended on it.

"Miss, you're going to have to stand back while I do the exam. It will only be a few more minutes. You can hold her hand if you'd like."

I nodded and held Matisse's hand. Hers was cold and frail. The nurse was efficient, and I watched while Matisse stared at the ceiling and tears fell down each side of her face. Anger simmered heavy in my veins, wanting an outlet, but I couldn't go there. I had to be strong for her. Regardless of what my sister had done and how she'd betrayed me, she was still my sister, and I loved her. Warts and all. And she'd been beaten and violated. No one deserved that.

Not being able to stop myself, I ran my hand through her hair and over her forehead, trying to calm her. She nuzzled into my palm, reminding me of better times when we were sisters who loved each other and told one another everything, not sworn enemies because of a manipulative psycho.

When the nurse finished, I stayed while she gave her statement to the detective. Clayton stood like a sentry in the back of the room, arms crossed, stance wide and imposing, not saying a word.

"After he strangled you, then what happened?" Detective

Richardson asked.

My sister swallowed and dipped her head down. "He pinned me to the bed and pulled out his knife. About this big." She held her fingers out, indicating several inches in length. Probably the same knife he cut me with, I thought but didn't share.

"Then he said he was going to play with me the way he played with my sister." Her gaze lifted to mine and she choked back a sob. "He cut one arm and then the next. He'd stuffed a pair of socks in my mouth so no one would hear me scream."

I ran my hand up and down her back, trying to soothe her the only way I knew how. When she was a little girl and scared of her new family, this was what I'd done to settle her when the nightmares came.

"Continue. We'll get through this in one shot, ma'am," Detective Bolinsky urged.

She nodded, and I held her hand.

The detective wrote down everything she said, including the details of her rape, into his notepad. "And where can we reach you if we need to follow up with you?"

Her eyes widened and more tears fell. "He stole my purse. He knows where I live. He'll come back. He'll kill me for sure!" Her voice rose and fell until the emotional turmoil took her over in heaping, wracking sobs. She turned in toward my body, and I held her while she cried.

"You'll come home with us. Clay and I will take care of you." I glanced over at Clay and his jaw hardened. That move meant he did not agree with my decision but wouldn't say anything until we were in private. Which was fine with me.

He'd get over it. My sister needed me, and I would take care of her. Then I'd figure out how to make my man not angry with me.

"Come on. Let's get you home."

Matisse nodded into my chest and then slid off the bed, plastering her body heavily against my side.

"Thank you, Monet. I don't know what I'd do without you."

And I vowed to myself right then and there that I'd fix this relationship with my sister, get past it all, and she'd never have to find out.

CHAPTER SEVENTEEN

HEART
CHAKRA

You can easily spot a person with a guiding heart chakra because they will be hard-working, responsible, and will spend their free time on activities that enhance their character and make them into better people.

CLAYTON

The next day, I left a cruiser in front of Monet's house while I went to pick up Lily at Atlas and Mila's place. Lily clung to my leg while I sipped a cup of coffee. She rubbed her face against my thigh, wiping away sleep. She wore a full-body pink pajama set with white rubber nubs on the feet and a white zipper running from her chest all the way down to her left foot.

I set my cup down and picked up my girl. "How'd you sleep, sweetie?" I asked, kissing her cheek.

"I haded a dream that someone snuck in the door of the secret garden." Her nose crinkled in concentration.

"And then what happened?"

She laid her head against my chest. "Then you gave them a taco and told them to leave."

Mila started laughing, perched on the stool at her island. Atlas blinked, a stupid look on his face, before he shook his head.

"A taco?" I asked.

"You make good tacos." She said it as if that was the only answer needed.

I petted her hair. "I'm glad you think so, my queen."

"How's about PowPow makes you some pancakes and fruit?" Atlas offered.

Her dark-blue eyes widened, and she kicked her feet to get down. "I help!" she said, eager to get to her uncle.

Atlas bowed. "Of course, Your Majesty. I am but a humble servant at your service."

"'S'right! Don't forget it!" she admonished, pointing one chubby finger at him.

Mila flicked her arm out toward the living area, and I followed her. She wore a man's silk robe over what had to be one of Atlas's T-shirts, because it came down almost to her knees. Her legs were bare, as were her feet. Her pregnant belly was just barely visible. A barefoot and pregnant joke sat on the tip of my tongue, but I didn't dare. With Mila, she was liable to lob something at me when I wasn't looking.

"How are you feeling, Mila?" I asked instead.

She lifted a hand and shook it from side to side. "Most of the time I'm fine. Hungry, pissy. Literally, I've got to piss all the time." She placed a hand over her belly. "For the most part,

I'm getting used to it. Weird though. You'll figure it out when Monet gets pregnant again."

Monet pregnant again.

The overwhelming happiness that flushed through my body was like an all-over feeling of rightness. I wanted to see Monet round with my child. More than once. I wanted a big family, and Lily would be an excellent big sister.

"Did Monet have trouble getting pregnant?" I found myself asking for information I hadn't realized I wanted to know.

Mila obviously didn't think it was an inappropriate question because she answered immediately. "Nope. The fucktard had bad sperm. Thank God she went to the sperm bank. Though it is kind of funny now that I look at you."

I frowned. "Why's that?"

"You fit the description of her donor. Over six feet, blond, blue-eyed, built. Monet wanted to pick a donor that resembled Kyle. Obviously, I encouraged her to embellish those traits a bit." She chuckled.

"Where did she go?" I asked, not really sure why I did.

She snorted and put her feet under her ass, getting comfortable on the side of the sectional. "Why? You think you need to use the services of Berkeley Health and Reproductive Services?"

The coffee I'd swallowed moments ago swirled acidly in my stomach, and my mouth started to salivate. I pushed back the gut reaction and breathed through the eerie feeling that made my skin feel moist and clammy. I had to get my shit together and fast. This was not the time to go there.

"No reason," I forced myself to mutter. It took everything I had not to ask more questions. Not because I didn't want to know. I fucking did. Still, I thought I should ask those questions of the woman I loved, not her best friend.

Mila fingered one of her brown curls and tipped her head assessing. She squinted and bit down on her bottom lip. "What's the deal with Matisse being at your house?"

I chuckled dryly. "Gotta love a woman who goes right to the point."

She shrugged. "Never pretended to be sugar and spice."

"More like hot sauce and a cold beer."

Mila smirked. "Spill."

I eased back, getting more comfortable on the couch, and sighed. "I don't want her there, but Monet is not budging on the issue. I don't know if she feels a sisterly pull or what the fuck it is. I just know I don't trust her. Her eyes are blank."

Mila frowned. "Clay, she was violated. I imagine that messes with the light in one's eyes."

I shook my head and rubbed at my face. I needed to shave. My whiskers were too long and abrading my woman's skin. I didn't want any more marks on her. That ex of hers had done enough damage. "I don't know. Why now? She called Monet instead of the police when she woke up after being beaten and raped. Does that sound normal to you?"

"No. It doesn't."

"And then the fact that they hadn't spoken since all the shit went down? He attacks Monet and makes it clear that he's doing so in order to get Matisse the money. So what changed?"

The more I thought about it, the more things didn't add up.

"I think those are all questions you need to ask Matisse. Only, go in gently. If she's hurt as bad as you say..." Mila offered what I already knew.

"See, that's the thing. He didn't hurt her as bad as he did Monet. She needed surgery and almost a hundred stitches. Could have bled out with the damage he'd already done, let alone what he planned on doing to her."

"Yeah. Sounds like knives must be his weapon of choice." Mila's jaw hardened, and one of her hands went into a tight fist on her lap.

"Still, the knife wounds on Matisse are superficial. They didn't even need stitches, just bandaging."

"But he didn't rape Moe," she whispered and glanced across the open loft toward the kitchen, making sure Lily was occupied. I respected her even more for that—thinking of Lily the way she always did.

Mila made an excellent point. I couldn't deny how devastated Matisse was while giving her statement. I just couldn't shake the feeling that things were off.

"I don't trust her," I admitted on a weighted sigh.

Mila stood up, walked around the coffee table, and placed a hand to my shoulder. "You don't have to. You look after Moe"—she flicked her eyebrows toward the kitchen—"and that little girl. That's what you do. They are your priority."

"Thanks, Mila." I placed my hand over hers.

"Anytime, bro." She winked and went toward the kitchen. "Baby wants pancakes and hot sauce," she announced dramatically to the room while rubbing her belly.

I burst out laughing and followed the crazy pregnant lady to check on my girl.

★ ★ ★

We were cuddled up in our bed, Monet's bare leg flopped over my thighs, my hand on her ass. "That was phenomenal, baby." She kissed my chest over my rapidly beating heart.

Damn, she was not wrong. "Yes, it was." I firmed up my grip on her ass cheek and hugged her close. I loved having her warm skin over mine like a blanket.

She mumbled something sleepily under her breath.

I figured it was the perfect time to dig for information. "What's Lily's blood type?" I threw out the question hoping she'd answer and not ask why.

"Huh? What?" She clung to my ribcage more tightly.

"Her blood type. I was just wondering what it is. Want to make sure I know the important details about our girl."

I could feel her grin against my chest. "Our girl."

"Yep. Our girl."

"Mmm. I like the sound of that." She kissed my chest in a way that didn't encourage after-sex cuddling and sleep; it said round two was well on the way.

I locked my arms around her. "So what is it?"

Her body relaxed and she rested against me again, her attention diverted for a moment. "It's actually really rare."

I knew it before she said it.

"AB negative."

Only one percent of Caucasians had AB negative blood, and less than half a percent of Asians, which Lily was, making the likelihood of that blood type far more rare.

"Mine too." I forced out the words, trying to make it sound calm, but my mind was raging with impossible scenarios.

She ran her hand up and down my chest methodically. "Well, that's good. You have something in common."

"Monet, there's something I gotta tell you. Something on my mind."

Her body stiffened in my arms. I moved both my hands up and down her bare skin to try and put her in a state of relaxation once again.

She nuzzled my chest and then rested her ear over my heart. I noticed she often did that. Said it reminded her that she wasn't alone. I didn't like the idea of my woman ever feeling alone. Not if I could help it.

"This is way out of left field, but Mila told me you got the sperm donation from Berkeley Health and Reproductive Services."

Her tension eased, thinking we were going into a topic that wasn't threatening.

"Yeah, I did. So?"

Gooseflesh danced across my forearms as I came clean. "I donated samples there on a few occasions while putting myself through college."

"Really? Why?"

"Remember when I told you that I'd gotten scholarships and put myself through college?"

She nodded against my chest.

"Well, I worked a lot and lived on my own. Donating sperm and plasma were awesome for extra money back in the day."

For a long while, she was quiet. Every minute felt like an acupuncturist putting one more needle directly into my skin.

"Clayton..." I knew that tone, and it was thoughtful but tired.

Something inside me flicked to life at the mere consideration that the amazing little girl, the one I'd come to love and care for as my very own, could actually be *mine*. Maybe that's why we'd bonded so quickly when she didn't bond as easily with others. Because she was my daughter.

"No, hear me out. Lily's donor looked like me. Correct? At least that was the description in the materials you chose from."

Monet thought about it for a moment before responding. "Well, yes, but we were purposely trying to find characteristics that were similar to my ex-husband as well. Blond hair and blue eyes is not an unusual combination." She didn't need to remind me that Kyle and I had something in common, even if it was superficial.

Still, giving it more thought, back when I was twenty, it hadn't dawned on me that the clinic would actually be generating life with my sperm. Being barely legal, I just needed the cold hard cash to get by while busting my ass in college. All I cared about was the payout. Now I wondered if I had a whole host of children out there. Instead of worrying about that possibility, I got my mind back on the matter at hand. Lily and her paternity.

"That I get. But her blood type is the same as mine. And it's rare, Monet. Very rare."

She sighed and lifted up on one elbow, her hair falling in over her shoulder and in between her breasts. I wanted to finger the silky waves but didn't want to distract Monet from what we were discussing. "Clay, honestly, what you're leading up to is ludicrous."

I scowled and couldn't bite back my hint of irritation. "Why? Because you wouldn't want me to be her biological father?"

She laughed out loud—tipped her head back, opened her mouth, and shook with it. Actually laughed when we were having a very serious conversation. So serious I got pissed. Mad as hell. Fire licked up and down my spine. I sat up, pressed my hands into my hair, and took several deep breaths, trying to bank back that fire.

Monet followed me up and placed her hands on my back. "You're misinterpreting my laughter, Clay. It's joy, honey. The fact that you would even come to such a conclusion is so unbelievably lovely. But you have to realize how unlikely it is. Sure, you have a rare blood type and donated at the same clinic I used several years ago, but the odds have got be astronomical. I mean..."

"A gift from God," I offered seriously.

She smiled and pressed the length of her body against my back, warming the sudden chill I'd felt. "A miracle. Yes." She kissed my back and flattened her mouth to my flesh so I felt her speak. "I'd love nothing more than to find out that Lily was indeed your child, but a piece of paper wouldn't mean anything to me. Not if you already plan on taking that role, which you yourself stated you have. Unless something has changed in your plans and I haven't been given the new information."

I cringed and ground my teeth. Maybe she was right. The idea that the cosmos had put this insanely gorgeous woman—my exact type—in my path, not to mention have her be someone who was artificially inseminated with my sperm from a sperm bank I donated to a decade ago? I sagged against her, my shoulders curling forward with defeat. I guess it did seem a little out into *Deep Space Nine* territory. Even so, the hope was there, and I didn't know how to turn that off.

Monet waited patiently while I came to terms with the ridiculousness of what I'd been suggesting. It may have sounded crazy, but it didn't change the fact that I wanted it to be true down to my very core. To know that Lily was mine and that I might've had claim to her biologically... At this point, it would be a fucking dream come true. Only, it was not often that dreams came true, and I'd already found my dream come true in Monet. I shouldn't be greedy for more.

"Clay, since we're talking seriously, can I ask you one of my own?"

I locked an arm around her form. "Ask me anything, beautiful. I'll always tell you the truth."

She nuzzled into my side. "Why did you bail on what we'd started last year when you helped move Mila in here?"

Unable to stop it, my entire body tightened. We'd just discussed some heavy shit, but if this woman was to be mine for good, she'd need to know why I was so spooked. More than that, she needed to know about my past. Hugging her close I inhaled her jasmine scent, reminding me that no matter what, I had her, I had Lily.

"Years ago I was engaged to a woman named Stacey."

Monet dug her fingers into my side and stiffened. I rubbed her arm and along her hip to soothe the reaction. "I'm okay, just surprised. Keep going."

I swallowed around the sour taste that hit my mouth at remembering Stacey and all that she represented.

"One day, my then girlfriend told me she was pregnant. Even showed me an ultrasound picture to prove it. We hadn't been together that long, but I was young, stupid, and in what I thought was love—but more importantly, I was a proud man. If my woman was pregnant with my kid, I'd be damned if I didn't put a ring on her finger and make an honest woman of her. So I asked her to marry me. Moved her into my house and started planning for a future." I ran a shaky hand through my hair, remembering how Stacey had smiled and accepted my ring instantly. Lies. All lies.

Monet's voice was raspy when she responded. "Why do I get the feeling this went bad really fast?"

I let out a frustrated breath, renewed anger at the memory of how fucked in the head that woman was. "Because it did. Not long after I moved her in, shared everything with her, including my money, she disappeared."

Monet gasped.

"Cleared my bank accounts, left me a Dear John letter telling me she'd lied about being pregnant, and just bailed."

"No." She lifted up on her elbows and locked her gaze on mine.

I nodded. "Took me months to find her. When I did, she was in Vegas. Gone through the money she'd stolen and had her body wrapped around a high roller."

Her mouth opened in silent shock.

"No baby. And believe me, she'd have been several months by then, and the skanky dress she was wearing when I found her left nothing to the imagination."

Tears built behind my girl's eyes. Tears for me. For my past. One fell down her cheek. I swiped it with my thumb and then tasted it.

"Hey, no tears for me. Sure, at the time that shit messed me up. But had it gone well, I wouldn't be here living the most beautiful life with the right woman for me. Now would I?"

She frowned and licked her lips. "I guess not."

Turning swiftly, I captured my woman and tumbled to my back, bringing her over me in one fell swoop. She settled over me, her frown turning into a smile.

"So now you know. You going to be okay knowing all my ugly?"

She nodded, flattened her body over mine, and hugged

me. "I love you," she whispered against my chest.

With my thumbs, I tilted her head back up so I could get to her. "I love you." I kissed her lips hard and fast but with intent and purpose.

"I love you for wanting to be my baby's dad." Her eyes were as dark as night but filled with a flash of yearning I was sure only I could fill.

Curling a hand around her nape, I brought her down so we were nose-to-nose. "One day, I will be." And that was a fucking promise.

"I like the sound of that," she agreed sweetly, taking my lips in a deep kiss. For long moments, our tongues danced. I alternated from deep lunges and soft flicks of my tongue against hers. Damn, my woman could make me hard as granite with a single kiss.

Being sneaky, I ran my hands up her thighs, which were straddling my waist. "You know what I like the sound of? You coming on my face," I growled and surprised her by lifting her ass up so that she had to reach for the headboard, her knees bracketing my head. Right where I wanted her, the promised land hovered over my face. Her center glistened in the soft light of the room, proving that she wanted me just as badly.

"Oh God!" she exclaimed at the first lap of my tongue from her tiny pucker to the sweet cherry-red knot. I flicked at her pleasure center, running my tongue around and around until her hips gyrated with each pass.

In that moment, I owned every inch of her body. She was lost to her pleasure and I was the one who'd found it. Hovering over me, rocking her hips against my face, she ran a hand down between her breasts, over her stomach, and slid her fingers along my cheek. This time, she surprised me by moving them to her center, where she opened the petals of her sex wider in offering.

"Need you," she whispered, her head falling forward as I sucked on her clit hard between her fingers, tasting her salty skin alongside her sweet cherry.

She let go and tunneled her hand into my hair, holding my head to the spot she liked best.

"Mine," I growled and then drank from her. I fucked her with my tongue and circled my index finger around her dark rosette, adding more stimulation in a place we hadn't gone before.

"Oh my God." She wiggled her sweet rump.

I growled. "You like a little ass play, beautiful?"

"Mmmm," she hummed.

"Is it yummy?" I flicked at her clit and shoved my finger into her ass up to my first knuckle.

Her body jerked, and I had to hold her down with my other hand on her hip to keep her in place while I doled out more stimulation.

"Yeah...yummy." She jerked against my face and started to get wild. I fingered her more quickly, lapped at her leisurely, until her body seemed to simmer with the need to come. I wasn't giving her enough to put her over the edge. I could have easily. Instead, I wanted her to beg. Loved hearing my woman asking for me to continue my assault on her body.

I stuck my tongue as far into her as I could and wedged my finger deep without moving it. She was sitting over my face with my tongue up her slit and my finger up her ass.

My cock was so hard I thought it would break in half if I so much as touched it, but I pushed those thoughts aside and focused on my sex goddess as she rode my face, searching for her blissful end.

"Please..." she finally uttered the words I wanted. They shimmered down over my chest and went straight to my dick, making it weep at the tip.

"Christ! That's my girl. You ask for what you need," I taunted.

"Need more. Oh, Clay, so much more," she mewled and swirled her hips.

With superhero strength, I pulled my woman off my face and my finger from her ass and settled her over my cock. She did not need to be told what to do. She sat on my dick so fast and so hard that my entire body spasmed right along with her.

"Fuck yeah!" I groaned. I lifted her up, curled one hand around her shoulder and the other on her hip, and helped her ride me hard, fucking me to within an inch of my life.

After a series of brutal strokes, her crying out with each one and me hitting the very end of her, over and over, I knew she was going to blow. Her eyes were pure black pools, and sweat misted her skin, tiny droplets coating both of our bodies. I licked the length of her neck, tasting the salt and sweet of her. I got up to my knees and took her with me. She wrapped her legs around my waist and let me forcefully pull her on and off my cock until we both found it.

Fire burned in my thighs as I pumped and poured into her. She locked her legs around me, so I couldn't move but an inch as she held me to her. For a long time, her body trembled with aftershocks. When I knew we'd both milked every last speck of pleasure from our coupling, I brought her back down to lie over my chest.

She fell asleep instantly. My dick softened still lodged inside while she snoozed against my chest, small puffs of air leaving her mouth contentedly. I decided I didn't care. Fuck being dirty. I liked dirty as long as it came with my girl. So we'd wake with a mess. Big deal.

After one of the most passionate and intense nights of lovemaking, nothing could get me to pull my length out of her. Nope. Instead, I gripped both of her ass cheeks and thrust my hips deeper so that I was planted as far as I could go, and then I too fell asleep.

CHAPTER EIGHTEEN

HEART
C H A K R A

The predominant color for the heart chakra is emerald green, and the gemstones associated with the heart are emerald, malachite, jade, and rose quartz. These gemstones promote wisdom, balance, and peace in all things. They can also be used to protect the heart against negativity and cruel intentions.

MONET

"He thinks what?" Mila sat on the couch across from me in the family room while Lily watched cartoons. Matisse sat silently in the armchair, her feet pulled up under her and a blanket around her shoulders. She stared blankly out the window.

It had been a week since her attack and seven weeks since

mine. Still, there had not been hide nor hair seen or heard from Kyle. He hadn't called the house or been located by cops. We were still at a dead end. Until that cockroach crawled out from under his rock, I feared we'd never catch a break.

I played with the ring on my right finger, twisting it around and around while I chatted with my best friend. "You're a smart cookie; figure it out."

Mila scowled. "Let me get this straight. Years ago, Clayton donated sperm at the same bank you used to get pregnant with Lily?"

I nodded.

"And he's an exact replica of what you and I picked out when we chose a specimen. The age requirement fits too. We chose someone in their twenties, which Clay was at the time. Basically, a young stud." She waggled her eyebrows dramatically.

"Yep." I sipped on my iced tea and watched as the ice cubes clinked against the glass.

Mila pursed her lips and cracked her neck from side to side. "And they share a very rare blood type. AB negative."

I let out a long breath of frustrated air. "Yes, but it's all just a coincidence."

"Huh. I guess it could be." She tapped at her lips with a finger. "The real question is, what are you going to do with this juicy information?" She cocked one of her eyebrows into a point.

Matisse glanced my way and looked down at her arms. The bandages were off and the wounds running down each arm from elbow to about two inches above her wrist were neat red lines, even from several feet away. They were scabbing over and didn't seem to bother her too much, which I figured was a blessing.

I shrugged and focused my attention back on my friend. "Absolutely nothing."

Mila's head jerked back as if she'd been slapped. "You're kidding, right? Tell me you are not serious?"

I shook my head. "Mila, I don't need to verify what is basically a shot in the dark. Clayton plans on being with us long term, and we're speeding down the highway toward church bells and forever. He has every intention of adopting Lily fully. It doesn't matter what a paternity test says."

Matisse's eyes widened, and she turned to Mila. "You think it's possible that Clayton really could be the biological father?" Her voice was a whisper, and it was probably the longest sentence she'd said since we returned from the hospital a week ago. I found this to be a mini-win but wouldn't dare address it out loud.

Mila pushed her curls out of her face, and yet they stubbornly bounced right back into place. "Uh, yeah. Why am I the only one who thinks this is awesome and a total possibility?"

Matisse looked down and away.

I stood, ignoring the question, and headed to the kitchen for a refill of my tea. "Anyone need anything?" I asked, and both women shook their heads.

Mila followed. Once she had an idea in her head, there was no going back. "I think we should check into this."

I gathered my wits firmly and shook my head. "No. It would ultimately hurt if a test revealed she wasn't his, and I don't want to do that to him. You don't know what he's been through in the past," I whispered, leaning over the counter toward where Mila was perched on a stool.

"What?" She glanced around in true best friend fashion, making sure the coast was clear.

I grabbed the sponge and wiped down the already clean counter. "His last serious girlfriend lied to him about being pregnant with his child. Even showed him a fake ultrasound."

"No!" Mila gasped and covered her mouth with her hand.

"Yes. Worse, he moved her right in, put a ring on her finger, and told her he was going to take care of her and the baby and they'd be a family."

Mila squinted and inched closer to me. "What'd the bitch do?" Her words were scathing and dipped in acid.

I gripped on to the counter, the emotional turmoil hitting me all over again. Clay had just told me the other night when we'd gone to bed and talked more about the future and what we both wanted. I had finally asked what drove him off from dating me last year and he told me the truth about Stacey. The story ate at my gut, but maybe repeating it to my best friend would help the heartache I felt toward his situation with his ex.

I took a deep breath and let it all out. Once done, I sat there gutted all over again while my best friend processed.

Mila flattened her lips into a hard, white line. "That's messed up." Mila's voice shook with anger. My best friend had a feistiness I loved but a temper I despised. She could go off half-cocked at any given moment.

I rushed to assuage the situation. "Yes, it is. As you can see, he loves kids. And as much as Clayton is a man's man, macho guy, he has a really huge heart. His ex did a number on him. I couldn't allow him to get his hopes up about Lily and then be let down. Not when things are so good between us and it doesn't matter what the outcome is anyway."

"You're a better woman than I," Mila offered.

"I doubt that very much. Still, that's why. Okay? I just needed to vent to you about it."

She nodded and pursed her lips. "It's cool. Crazy wild when you think about the potential."

"For now, let's just leave it alone and not bring it up." I placed my hand on hers. "All right?"

"You got it. I do have some wicked cool news for you."

I smiled because she was smiling.

Mila placed her finger on the table and traced random circles on the countertop.

"What? Tell me. I could use some good news."

Mila's amber-colored eyes were misty when she set her gaze on mine. "Atlas couldn't wait...and, well...we uh." She choked on her words.

A thrill rippled through me. "You eloped! Didn't you?"

Mila chuckled, hopped off her stool, and came around to where I stood. My emotions battered me like golf-ball-sized hail. I'd really wanted to have a little something for her. I'd live with her decision, but I wanted to see my best friend, my soul sister, get married to an amazing man.

Her grin didn't abate when she grabbed my hands and put them on her stomach. At four months, her tiny athletic frame made her look almost six months along.

"We couldn't wait to find out what we were having, so we went to one of those Peek-A-Boo Baby places and got a special ultrasound. Moe...we're having a girl." Her smile was huge.

A girl.

My best friend was having a baby girl.

"Oh my God! A girl. We're having a girl!" I jumped up and down and wrapped my arms around Mila and held tight. "I'm so happy!"

Right then Lily ran in the room, saw us jumping like silly schoolgirls, and jumped right along with us, clapping her hands. "Why we happy?"

"Love bug, Mimi has a baby girl in her belly!"

Lily's eyes widened and she wrapped her hands around her auntie and kissed her belly. "I loves you already."

Mila stroked Lily's hair while we both cried happy tears.

"I cannot wait to buy her pretty dresses." I could see it already. Mocha-colored skin, wild, dark curly hair. She'd look fantastic in red.

Mila frowned. "Why can't I just borrow all the clothes you have saved up in the garage, you hoarder!"

Laugher spilled easy between us. "You can and more! Now we plan the baby shower!"

"Actually, about that, I discussed it with Atlas and we both made an executive decision."

I frowned. "You promised I could have a party!" I reminded her. I wanted to stomp my foot but reined in my childlike desire. "You have to celebrate your love and your baby," I encouraged.

Mila nodded. "Yep, we agree. So we want to have a combo wedding and baby shower. Small, just our closest friends. We'll celebrate both our marriage and our baby on the same day." She lifted a wary gaze my way, probably expecting me to balk at the idea.

"Honey, that's really rather perfect." I bit my lip, imagining the options already.

Her entire face lit up so bright I might have needed sunglasses. "Really? You like the idea?"

I looped my arm around her neck. "I love it. Let's start planning right now!"

Mila shrugged and hugged Lily close. "No time like the present!"

* * *

Another week gone and no word on Kyle. The cops were baffled. We were angry. Matisse, two weeks into her healing, was still walking around zombielike. Clayton was ready for my sister to leave. Every time we went to bed at night, he made a point to tell me how uncomfortable he felt having her in the house. She hadn't fully shared what had happened between her and Kyle or whether or not she was still in a relationship with him when he attacked her. Of course, she'd gone into detail with the police, but they wouldn't share that information with us even if I'd asked. No, it was time for my dear sister and me to have a very serious chat.

Clayton was reading to Lily and putting her to bed, his deep rumble a comfort as I navigated toward the end of the hall where the guest room was. As I approached, I could hear my sister's hushed words.

"No. It's too soon."

I frowned and slowly walked up as quietly as possible.

"I don't know the codes." Her voice rose with what sounded like irritation. "I haven't been in a position to need them."

I crept up closer to the door. It was open enough that I could see she was standing facing the back window, her cellphone glued to her ear.

"Of course I love you. Why would you ever question that?" Her shoulders pulled back and she stiffened. "I don't know when a good time will be. I told you, I'll call."

Who did she love? Kyle? Could she be talking to my ex-husband, the man who beat, cut, and raped her? The man who almost killed her sister? It couldn't be. A sense of dread shifted the air around me and I couldn't wait any longer to intrude.

Just as I pushed through the door, she groaned, turned around, and tossed her phone on the bed, hanging up on whoever she had been talking to. Her gaze lifted to mine, and she stopped dead in her tracks.

"Who were you talking to?" I asked directly.

"A friend." She crossed her arms over her chest. A defensive move I recognized a mile away.

"A friend you love?"

Matisse scowled and glanced off into the distance.

"Answer me!"

Her head snapped back, her gaze locking with mine. "Yes." Her tone bordered on miserable before she turned and sat heavily on the end of the bed and put her face in her hands.

"Kyle?" I asked, not being able to keep the slice of anger out of my words.

Her head came up, tears flowing down her face. "Gosh, no! I haven't seen him in weeks. Months, even."

I rested my hand against the bureau to hold myself steady. "Then who?"

She shook her head. "No one you know. Just a coworker."

"So why wasn't he at the hospital or asking to come here?" I dug, needing more from her.

"Because I don't want him to see me. Not like this. He'll never get past what happened to me. I'm not sure I can get past it!" Tears welled in her eyes and poured down her cheeks.

I rushed over and sat down on the edge of the bed, placing a hand to her back while she cried. "I'm sorry, I know how hard this must be for you. I have firsthand knowledge."

A flash of anger fired bright in her eyes before something changed, and it was like closing the blinds on a window. Her expression went back to cold and blank.

"Matisse, please talk to me. I need to know what happened with Kyle. When he hurt me, he said some things I can't forget, and those things made it seem as if you were still with him."

She wiped at the tears on her cheeks and clenched her teeth. "I had nothing to do with your attack. As I told you, I'm seeing someone new. Haven't heard from Kyle in a while. Are you telling me that you don't believe me? Your own sister? After the man raped me? I hated him after I found out what he did to you. Leaving you is one thing, but trying to kill you?" She shook her head and let her question drop.

I petted her back and rushed to ease her worries. "Okay. I'm sorry. I'm sure you understand that I had to ask."

Matisse narrowed her eyes for just a second. The movement was barely perceptible, but still I saw it and had no idea what it meant.

"Yes, I understand. And I'll be out of your hair soon if that's what you're worried about. I can tell that your new boyfriend doesn't like me." Her nostrils flared and her lips curled minutely before she settled her features into her usual mask.

Regardless of what Clayton felt or didn't feel, Matisse was my sister. I wanted her here if this is where she needed to be. I also needed her to understand where Clayton was coming from. "Matisse, he doesn't know you. None of us do, really. You barely speak, you've not taken any time getting to know Lily, and you've spent most of your time hiding out in here."

"I just don't want to be a bother, but I can't go home. Not

when I know he could get to me. I'm so scared he'll come back for me and finish the job." A sob tore through her, and she tugged me into an embrace and cried on my shoulder. I held her for a long time. Long enough for the sobs to abate into small sniffles.

"You don't have to go anywhere. You can stay as long as you'd like. You're welcome here. You're my sister, and this is my home. Matisse, you're always welcome."

She nodded into my shoulder and made a choking sound. "Thanks. Thank you, Monet. You're the best big sister a girl could ever hope for."

I grinned. The feeling of doing something right soothed any nervous energy I'd had when approaching her. She hadn't had anything more to do with Kyle. She feared him and was evidently in love with someone new. All of that sounded really good.

I rubbed her back until she calmed down completely. "Everything is going to be okay. Soon Kyle will be caught and put behind bars."

"I know. It will all work out the way it's supposed to," she asserted, her voice monotone.

"Okay, well, I'm going to let you get some rest. See you tomorrow. Maybe we can spend some time talking more and getting to know one another again. As adults." I got up, went to the door, and laid my hand on the doorknob, ready to leave.

"I'd like that, Monet." Her voice was small and sweet, reminding me of how it was when she was little.

"I love you, Matisse."

"I know." She smiled.

"Okay, then." I finished pulling the door closed.

★ ★ ★

The next morning, I was greeted by a giggling love bug hiding under the covers in the empty space my man must have vacated.

"Wake up, beautiful. We have breakfast for you and a present," came the deep baritone of said guy.

Lily giggled under the covers. I opened my eyes and turned on my side. There was a Lily-sized lump next to me shaking with every new bout of laughter.

"Why is the queen hiding?" I asked Clay, pushing up into a seated position. Thank goodness we'd just gone to sleep last night or I'd be trying to find ways to explain to my daughter why her mommy was in bed naked. Since we hadn't had any hanky-panky, I was in a normal tank and sleep shorts.

Clay beamed, his smile alive and happy. "I don't know. I told her I had a surprise for you and her, and she decided that she wanted to surprise you in bed too."

On that response, my little one flung the blankets back and scrambled to stand on my bed. "'Prize!" she screeched.

I scooped her up and pulled her to my chest. "My goodness. What an amazing surprise you are this morning. And such a great hider!"

She nodded. "Yeah, PowPow taughted me. Now he says I'm the best."

I kissed her nose. "That you are. So what is this about breakfast and a surprise?"

Clayton set a tray on the bed beside Lily and me. The tray consisted of an array of pastries, coffee, milk, and two black boxes with gold filigree etching at each corner. They were identical in size and shape. The boxes were a sturdy wood with a unique gold latch that acted like a lever that notched into place to open and close it.

"This one is for you, and this one is for Lily." He picked them up and handed one to each of us. His eyes were a bright Caribbean blue and shining with love and admiration. I could stare into them all day, but I had a squirmy wormy excited child in my lap who wanted to open her present. As of yesterday.

"What it is, Mommy? What is it?" Lily said excitedly.

"I don't know. Let's find out." I showed her how to open the latch, and together we opened our boxes. Inside were identical heart-shaped pendants on white-gold chains.

"The stone is jade," Clayton announced proudly.

The stones were wrapped in white gold with marcasite curving on the top right corner and bottom of the hearts, giving the plain stones more sparkle and pizazz.

"I love green!" Lily squealed. "Mommy, can I wear it now?"

"Of course you can." Clayton came around the bed and sat next to her. She handed him the box, and he got to work removing the necklace. I did the same so I could see it sparkle in all its glory in the morning sunlight.

"Clayton, these are stunning. But it's not our birthday or anniversary." I'd not been given a present by a man when it wasn't for an anniversary, Christmas, Valentine's, or my birthday. Those were pretty much the only times I'd ever gotten a gift unless it was from Mila. She gave me little things all the time.

Clayton smiled. "Beautiful, I don't need a reason to get my girls something pretty to show I care. Want you both wearing something I gave you." He latched the necklace around Lily's neck, and it fit perfectly.

The chain on mine was a bit longer to suit an adult.

"Honey, they are magnificent. Thank you."

"And they're jade," he said with a tinge of pride.

"Yes, I see that."

"Jade is a stone that represents the heart charka. And Crystal at Lotus House said that the spiritual benefits of jade promote wisdom, balance, and peace. I figured none of that could hurt."

"You trying to protect my heart, Clayton?"

His eyes flashed to mine. "Always."

I held the stone right over my heart. "I love it so much."

"Me too, me too, me too!" Lily jumped on the bed, making the coffee container and silverware shake precariously.

"Easy, sweetie." Clayton scooped her up before I was sitting in a puddle of hot coffee instead of drinking it.

I stared at the dangling heart in awe. He'd bought jade necklaces to protect my daughter's heart and mine.

Then I remembered that day I got my stitches removed and Crystal and Jewel performed the grounding method on me in the bakery. She'd made a comment about my heart charka.

★ ★ ★

"And your heart chakra is hurting right now." Jewel frowned and ran a finger along my temple to my chin. "I sense that you're working on it, but there's still much more to be done."

"My heart chakra? How so?"

Jewel smiled softly. "In order to have a healthy heart chakra, darling, you must love yourself and be able to forgive yourself and others. I'm sensing there are some things you are not letting go of. Perhaps a person who wronged you. One you allowed in your life. Someone who continues to hurt you? Could *be a variety of things piling up."*

★ ★ ★

"You remembered that conversation about the heart chakra that we had with Jewel, didn't you?" I got out of bed and poked my man in the chest playfully.

He brought my fingers to his lips and kissed each one. "Maybe."

"I thought you didn't believe in their spiritual methodology? Hmmm?"

He shook his head and pulled me into his embrace, wrapping one of his thick arms around me and curling his hand around my side. Lily kicked to get down, but he held her firm. With both of his girls in his very capable arms, he seemed happier than he'd ever been. "I said I didn't *not* believe. If you remember correctly."

I rolled my eyes. "Yes, but that would lead one to assume you didn't actually believe in it yourself."

"I figured when it came to my girls, I would make sure you were covered either way."

"So even though you don't necessarily believe..."

He kissed my nose and then Lily's. She giggled and forced her head into the crook of his neck.

"I wanted you both covered anyway. Couldn't hurt. Now you both have pretty mother-daughter necklaces that your guy gave you. Win-win, right?"

"Yeah, honey, win-win. Thank you." I rose up on my toes and kissed his mouth.

"Eww, gross." Lily smacked at both our faces, trying to pull us apart.

Clayton ended the kiss, laughing jovially and trying to pin and tickle my daughter. I watched by the side of the bed and picked up the box that held my jade heart in it. I removed it from the packaging and put it on. It fell right above my cleavage, as close to my heart as it could get.

Yeah, my man was protecting my heart. Definite win.

CHAPTER NINETEEN

HEART
C H A K R A

To have a healthy heart, you must allow any suppressed emotions to surface and heal. Ultimately, you need to have love for yourself in order to feel real love for others.

M O N E T

"Beautiful, I'm hitting the gym. You and Matisse okay with Lily alone?" Clayton curled a hand around my waist from behind.

I had just latched my hoop earring in one ear and was working on the next. "Of course. It's been a full three weeks now since anyone has heard anything from Kyle. Matisse had even started talking about going home. I told her I'd have your security guy put a system in place at her house too if that would make her more comfortable. I also offered to help her move out of her current place and into something else." Personally, I hoped for the latter. Leaving a place Kyle knew about was the smarter move. Alas, it would be her choice, and I didn't intend to push her one way or the other.

"Yeah? What'd she say about that?" Clayton ran a hand through the spikes of his hair. It was getting longer on top, and he needed a haircut.

"Said she'd consider it and weigh her options."

He nodded, found his gel, put a dime-sized drop in his hand, and ran it through his spikes so they'd stand up more fully.

I watched with interest as he styled his hair. "Why do you get all pretty before going to the gym?" I asked, pressing a hip against the vanity while giving my man a full onceover.

He'd worn his usual track pants—this pair with two stripes running down the sides. Covering his cut chest was a matching black ribbed tank and nothing else. Though he did have a zip-up tossed on the counter near him, I knew he'd be taking it off within minutes of entering the gym, showing off the toned body he worked so hard for.

Clayton caught my gaze in the mirror. "Why? You jealous I'm looking super fly to work out? Worried about the cardio bunnies?" He plastered on an innocent expression.

"Cardio bunnies? What the hell is that?" The words flew from my mouth without a filter. Now he'd know I was jealous. Busted.

He grinned, quickly tugged me to him with one arm around my waist, and smashed me up against his long, hard frame. "Cardio bunnies are the chicks that spend day after day at the gym only working on cardio and nothing else. Sometimes, they are using it to scope out a target of the male variety." He waggled his eyebrows.

I scowled. "Really? And would you be taking them up on that offer?"

His playful smile turned into a grimace. "You know I get my ass to the gym and home as fast as possible when there's you to come home to. Besides, I got all the woman I can handle, and I like my *handfuls*." He proved this by cupping my left ass cheek in one hand and my right breast in the other. His skillful hand swiped a thumb across my nipple, which instantly made me melt in his arms.

"There's my sweet, sexy woman. Now, we'll pick this back up when I return. Yeah?" He clenched the goods one more time and kissed me soundly. So soundly I'd practically forgotten my name by the time he pulled away. His kisses were mind-bending every time.

"Hmpfh." I grabbed a brush and pulled it through the tangles in my hair. "You need a haircut. Do you want me to make an appointment for you with Viv?" Genevieve was one of the Lotus House teachers, but she also owned and operated her own hair salon, which our crew took advantage of. She did the best work, but it was also nice to support a friend.

Clayton checked out his hair in the mirror. "Could use a cut. Yeah, beautiful, that would be cool if you could. See what she's got available and just text me the date and time. I could take the queen for a trim if you think she needs it. Viv usually has Will in the playroom next to her chair, and I'm sure Lily would like to play with him."

Leave it to my man to not only think about my daughter possibly needing a haircut but wanting to bring her to one of our friends because they have a child she could play with.

"You just want to show off your queen." I pointed the

brush at his reflection in the mirror.

He grinned, pecked me on the side of my mouth, and nuzzled my nose. "I am the king." He winked, smacked me on the ass, and left the bathroom. He hollered out over his shoulder, "Be back in a couple hours."

"I'll make dinner!" I yelled out.

"Sounds good. Love you."

"Love you too!"

I finished getting ready, taking my time to curl my hair just so. I wanted to drive my man's mind away from any cardio bunnies when he arrived home later. About fifteen minutes later I made my way into the kitchen, looking for Lily and Matisse. I hadn't heard from my girl, and she was not usually quiet.

The second I entered the kitchen, I knew it had all gone to hell. A person can plan for and anticipate the worst, but when it came knocking at the door, or in this case, was sitting in the living room, all that planning went to the wayside. I knew in an instant that I was wholly unprepared.

Sitting in the one cozy chair in the living area off the kitchen was none other than my ex-husband, Kyle. Only, he wasn't alone. He had Lily on his lap with a knife pointed at her neck.

Oh please, God. No. Not my baby.

"Mommy..." she said in a broken, frightened voice.

Everything in my world narrowed down to one focus. This small space. Matisse sitting opposite Kyle on the couch, her legs bouncing up and down nervously. Her fingers twisting in her lap. The TV had a cartoon playing on it. *Dora the Explorer*, I think. The clock on the wall dinged loudly, announcing it was four o'clock in the afternoon. Clayton had just left fifteen minutes ago. He wouldn't be home for at least two hours. If I went for the phone to call for help, Kyle would kill my daughter.

"I suspect you've deduced how bad this situation is by now." Kyle spat his venom-coated words.

Now was not the time to freak out. I had to be smart. Find a way out of this. For Lily.

"How did you get in here?" I clenched my teeth tight, trying to think of a way out of this for all of us.

He huffed and glanced at Matisse. "Walked right through the front door, didn't I, Matisse?"

Matisse glanced down at her lap. I couldn't tell if she was being submissive to him or hiding her shame.

"Mommy," Lily cried again and wiggled.

"Baby, don't move. It's going to be okay. Kyle. Let her go," I ground out through my teeth. Tears pricked at my eyes, but I didn't let them fall. Wouldn't. I was scared out of my mind, but this bastard wasn't going to see that. Not in front of my daughter.

Still, fear like no other slammed over my body as if an entire vat of acid had been poured on me. My fight-or-flight instincts were pumping wildly under the surface, but it was nothing compared to my mothering instinct raging like a tornado of energy in the room. I locked eyes with Kyle. I sent over hate, disgust, and retribution in my gaze.

"Let. Her. Go," I warned again.

"Or what, Monet? What are you going to do about it? It seems that I'm the one who holds all the cards here. Isn't that right, baby?" He grinned evilly and glanced at Matisse.

I focused on my sister when she said, "Yeah, that's right." Her entire body shifted, and a calm seemed to have settled over her. No more bouncing of the legs, twisting of fingers. Oh no, Matisse had put on a mighty act. Her best performance yet. And I'd fallen for it. Her dark eyes lifted and locked on mine, her lips turning into a sinister smile.

"Why?" I gasped, not being able to contain this level of betrayal.

She tipped her head back and laughed. The sound bounced off the walls and pierced my ears. Lily cried out.

"Mommy... I want my Mommy." Lily tried to kick off her captor's legs, but he held strong.

My heart practically exploded in my chest with the need to go to her. "Baby, don't move," I urged again and fell to my knees, barely catching myself with my hands.

"Why are you doing this to me? We took care of you. Took you in!" I demanded, my anger barreling to the surface needing a target.

Again, Matisse laughed and shook her head. "You've always had it all. Beauty, brains, money. And you took it all for granted. Our father chose to be with *your* family. Hid us away for years. Years!" Her voice rose to a screech as she proceeded. "Until my mother gasped her last breath, he chose you and your mother. Then, of course, your mom just offed herself like the weak fucking bitch she was."

I wanted to cry, lash out. I trembled with the anxious energy to do just that, but I couldn't. *Show no fear. Don't give them anything more to use against you.* I had to figure out a way to get Lily away from Kyle.

"He hurt you. Cut you like he did me. Raped you!" I desperately tried to remind her of the attack she suffered three weeks earlier.

Never in all my days would I forget the look on her face as she smiled, looking like a villain from a horror movie.

"Kyle would never hurt me." She thrust both arms out so I could see her forearms almost perfectly healed, barely a line to see. Nothing like the knifing I'd suffered.

"I did this to myself with a steak knife, not the hunting knife he's got held to your daughter's throat." She grinned. "And the rape?" She scoffed. "Never happened. Just a hot round of hard fucking with a little breath-play action, and voilà! You got a certifiable rape."

I couldn't stomach one more word from Matisse, so I sat back on my heels and addressed my ex-husband, hoping to find some shred of decency. "Kyle, why not let Lily go play in her room. Do what you want with me. Just let her go. You don't want to hurt a child."

He scoffed. "You don't know what I want." He pulled Lily up into a standing position. I pushed forward and tried to reach out to grab her, but he pulled her away by the collar of her footed pajamas. She cried out, and I bit into my lip so hard the metallic taste of blood filled my mouth.

Kyle dragged my daughter close to me but not enough so I could reach her. Her eyes were beyond frightened and her lip quivered in fear.

"What I *want*, Monet, is to hurt *you*. Repeatedly, until you beg me to stop. Hurting her will do that. Besides, she and that steroid junky you've got living here seem to be your two soft spots." He twisted his lips into a maniacal sneer.

I got up on my knees and put my hands into a prayer position. "Kyle, this is me, *begging* you to let her go. Take me. Leave her here. Do whatever you have to do, but just leave her behind."

He shoved my daughter into Matisse's arms before getting up in my face. "I don't think you understand. If she's alive..." he whispered, his eyes black holes of nothingness, "then she gets the money. If you're both dead, the money goes to Matisse, your next of kin."

Money. This was all about the fucking money. Money that wasn't even theirs.

"I'll give you whatever you want. Take me to the bank right now. I'll withdraw whatever you want. You don't have to do this. Please. Kyle. You loved me once. I know you did. Please, please...just let my daughter go!" I begged.

Smack! An explosion of pain struck my cheek as Kyle punched me. "Shut the fuck up! Jesus Christ, I don't remember you being this chatty." He pressed his finger and thumb into his temples. "I need to think!"

"You need to think about letting my girls go before I kill you with my bare hands," came the rumbling deep voice I woke to every morning, fell asleep to every night, and kissed quiet every day.

Clayton stood at the edge of the room with his eyes zeroed on Kyle, his chest moving with his breathing as if he'd run a mile. Each of his fists were locked tight and ready for some serious damage. Clayton was beyond angry. The veins on his forearms and neck stood out beneath his otherwise smooth, tanned skin. He held his lips into a tight white curl, nostrils flared. This man was two hundred and thirty pounds of solid muscle ready to stampede my ex into oblivion.

Kyle's eyes widened when he saw Clay, as did my own. I wanted to jump for joy but kept calm as I moved slowly to stand. Once I got on my feet, Clay's arm wrenched out and shoved me behind him.

"Forgot my gym bag. Thank fuck," he said below his breath as I closed in on his back. I squeezed his biceps in gratitude and silently thanked the good Lord above for this gift.

Clayton's voice rose loud in the room as he addressed Kyle again. "You think for a second you can come into my home, put your hands on *my kid* and *my woman*, and threaten their lives?" he growled, his timber so threatening I was scared. For Kyle. My man would and could kill him with his bare hands.

Matisse's hands shook where she held on to Lily. My sweet baby was quiet, her eyes glued to Clayton. Her savior and mine. At least I hoped so. Right now, he was the only way we were going to get out of this situation alive.

"You think because you work out and inject your muscles full of 'roids, that makes you somehow stronger and smarter than me?" Kyle spat out.

Clayton didn't take the bait or respond to the attempted blow. "Put down the knife. Let's go head to head. Man to man." He lifted an arm and waved his hand as if to say, *bring it on.*

Kyle snickered, moved quicker than I thought possible, and grabbed my daughter from Matisse's hold, tugging her in front of him. Clayton got a step closer but not enough to get to her first.

That's when the tears came. Big fat drops sliding silently down my cheeks. I knew, regardless of the outcome, I wouldn't be able to live with myself if anything happened to her or the man I was head over heels in love with.

I watched as Matisse shifted behind Kyle.

"What are you going to do now? Huh, boy?" Kyle taunted.

While he focused on Clay, I reached into my back pocket where I had my phone. I couldn't let on what I was doing, but I hoped like hell I could hit the right buttons to call the police, or at the very least, someone who would pick up and hear the call. Using my thumb, I felt for the right spot and was pretty sure

I got it. I glanced over my shoulder, easing more fully behind Clayton so they couldn't see what I was doing. I punched the nine and the one and one as fast as I could and just left the line open.

When I thought for sure they were on, I announced as loudly as I could muster. "Put down the knife and let my daughter go, Kyle. She's an innocent. She has nothing to do with this."

Kyle shook his head. "You stupid people do not get it. I'm not leaving here until the three of you are dead, and I'll do it one at a time if I have to. Matisse. Gun, baby?"

When I heard the word gun, I lunged at my sister. She'd barely had a second to get the gun out from behind her where she'd tucked it into her pants. Her arms came up and I went right back to my training with Nicholas. I grabbed her wrist, spun, and shoved the arm holding the gun through mine so it wasn't facing me. I smashed my hand into her elbow, and she let the gun go. It clanged to the floor and bounced out of sight. Matisse clung to me and pulled me down, the couch breaking my fall before we hit the floor.

Clayton took the opportunity with the commotion I'd made to move on Kyle.

He went for him with hands out front. Out of the corner of my eye I could see he had no choice but to release Lily or he'd have Clayton's hands wrapped around his neck. Knowing my man, he'd never let go until Kyle passed out or was dead.

Clayton grunted and pushed Kyle into the wall, breaking the glass mirror behind his head. The glass shattered to the floor in big chunky pieces.

I scrambled with my sister, shoving and pushing, trying to get a better position. We rolled back and forth, ripping at one another.

Lily stood in the corner of the room crying, her hands by her face.

"Run outside, Lily!" Clayton yelled, and my girl did what she was told. Unfortunately, she stopped when she got to me, seeing me down with Matisse on top.

"Mommy..." She reached her hands toward us.

"Go!" I screamed and grappled with my sister, the gun on the floor somewhere I couldn't see. I prayed it would stay hidden and neither of us would find it before the cops arrived.

Lifting my arms, I got a good lock on Matisse's head and wiggled my thumbs into position. I pressed them right into Matisse's eye sockets and pushed as hard as I could. She let go, wailing like a banshee. I took a half second, pushed her over, and took my stance on top of her just as I was taught to get out of the rape hold. Her hands came up to protect herself, but she must not have gotten the same training I did, because she did all the moves Nicholas warned me not to do if I was caught under someone. As the good student I am, I took to heart everything Nick taught me and fisted my hands and wailed on my sister's face until she stopped fighting and her face was a bloody mess. My hands were no better.

Pushing off her, I found Clayton holding one of Kyle's arms up above his head. The other hand was wrapped around his jaw, where he pounded Kyle's skull against the wall. But Clayton made one crucial mistake: he forgot about the knife.

I watched in utter horror as Kyle's right hand came up from behind him and plunged the knife right into Clayton's side near his ribcage. My man roared in pain, his body bowing powerfully, the knife wedged in his side. Kyle pushed him back enough to get his hands off him.

"Police! Hands up!" came a cluster of voices behind me. I raised my hands on instinct.

I watched everything happening around me take place in slow motion.

There was no sound.

Clayton fell to his knees.

His powerful arms going to his side.

His fingers split between the knife still lodged inside him.

Blood poured out around his fingers.

He lifted his head, his eyes a startling navy as I watched the light in my man's eyes go dark and fade out as he fell to his back.

Finally, my ability to move returned, and the sounds of sirens and people yelling orders entered my consciousness. I ran to Clayton and fell to my knees at his side. "Clayton! Baby, hold on. Hold on!" I heard myself demanding. I placed my hands over and around his wound, attempting to stabilize the knife and stop the bleeding. The weapon was buried to the hilt. I was sure that he'd been stabbed with the same knife used on me.

Clayton's eyes flicked and his mouth opened and closed. "L-Love you. L-Lovvve Lilyyyy," he stuttered around a cough, and then his powerful bulk went completely slack in my arms.

"No, no, no, no!" I screamed. "Help! I need help!"

Paramedics with a stretcher appeared out of nowhere and pushed me back. "We've got him, ma'am. We've got him. Back up so we can help him."

Help him. Yes. Help him.

Someone put their hand on my shoulder. A woman with kind brown eyes and curly blond hair. "Ma'am. Come with me."

I nodded, following numbly until all that had occurred

rushed back to the surface. "My daughter! Where is she? She ran outside." I was panicked but continued to watch Clay as the men worked on him.

"He's got a pulse," one said.

"Oxygen!" another called out.

"Lift," I heard before seeing his bulk being placed on the stretcher.

The woman tapped on my shoulder. "She's outside with the neighbor. She needs her mommy. She's really scared."

I nodded. "Need him to be okay." She led me out the door. "Need him okay. I love him."

"Got that. We'll get you guys off to the hospital where he's being taken. Let's get your daughter."

As the cop led me outside, I watched as Matisse's head was shoved down as she was placed into a patrol car. Kyle had been handcuffed and was being led to a different one.

My neighborhood looked like something out of murder mystery. Neighbors stood at the edge of the sidewalk watching the train wreck that was my life unfold for all to see.

Kyle's pipsqueak voice entered my haze. "I'll get out," he mocked. "They can't hold me forever, and when I do...I'm coming after *you*," he sneered at me as the cop shuffled him past me and toward the patrol car.

The big burly cop leading him "accidently" pushed him so he ended up tripping over the curb and falling against the front of the cop car. "Shut the fuck up," he growled.

"Don't be afraid," the nice blond woman encouraged. "He's going to get at least forty-five years to life for two counts of attempted murder with special circumstances. He's never getting out of jail in your lifetime."

I nodded but didn't say anything as she led me around the

side of an ambulance, where my daughter was wrapped in a blanket and being held by the little old lady who lived across the street. Of course, my girl would go to her. Definitely the sweetest.

"Baby!" I cried out, and she jumped out of my neighbor's arms and into mine.

"Mommy, I so scawed!" she cried.

"It's okay, baby. Everything is going to be okay now. We have to go to the hospital and check on Clay."

"Clay's hurt? That bad man hurted him?"

"Yeah, baby, he did. Very badly. We need to go make sure he's going to be okay."

CHAPTER TWENTY

HEART
C H A K R A

People guided by their heart chakra feel inclined to fill their hearts with optimism and joy. They go out of their way to wish others well-being and are naturally involved in helping people, volunteering, serving the ones they love, and giving back to the community.

CLAYTON

I glanced out the window to our backyard. It looked like blue bells and white daises had exploded all over the place. Monet was in rare form, running from spot to spot making sure everything was just right for the "Powers Nuptials and Baby Shower." I laughed, holding on to my side as Monet placed a plastic bassinet on a fake lily pad to float across the pool. The woman was insane, and I loved her. More so today than ever before. She had taken on planning this party as if it was to be her living legacy. No expense spared. No amount of cake, candles, and booze was too much for her best friend. Made me wonder how she'd be when it came time for our wedding.

The ache in my side eased as I closed my eyes and pictured Monet wrapped in delicate lace and with Lily holding her hand, walking down an aisle toward me, both ready to be mine for eternity. I shook my head, reminding myself I wasn't a pansy-assed man, but I wouldn't deny being a pussy-whipped one either, if push came to shove. Monet and Lily had me wrapped around their fingers, and I did not care one bit. I welcomed it. They brought color to my life every day. Not a single person before her had done that.

And by God, my woman was a freaking saint for taking care of me all these weeks. After Kyle's knife pierced my spleen and tore into my stomach, I'd had surgery to remove the spleen altogether and patch up the stomach and surrounding muscle. I had about a six-inch scar running down my side where the surgeon had to open me up. I ran a finger down the puffed edge of the tissue. All things considered, I was lucky. Very lucky. The area ached now and again like it did today, but that was to be expected.

The best part of it all? Kyle and Matisse being hauled off to prison. Kyle was charged with two counts of attempted first-degree murder and two counts of attempted kidnapping. Matisse got a lesser sentence for conspiring to commit murder and accessory to attempted kidnapping. They both pled to lesser charges, but their sentences were to be served consecutively, so neither would breathe free air for the rest of their lives. Good riddance. Secretly, I hoped he'd get made someone's personal bitch. The way he hurt Monet, made her life a living hell, threatened her daughter... Both my fists tightened as if ready to strike a phantom threat.

Christ, my Lily still cried out for her mommy some nights, even months later. Both are in regular counseling and healing more every day. I'm back at the gym working with clients again but not doing too much in the way of lifting. Slowly but surely, things were getting back to normal.

This party would go a long way toward making my girls happy and solidifying the family unit. And so would my surprise. I fingered the black velvet box I'd been carrying around all week. Trying to figure out the best time to pop the question had me a nervous wreck. The right time hadn't presented itself yet, but today, seeing my girl so happy, running around making a wedding and baby shower something to remember for people we loved... Today was it.

I flicked open my phone and dialed Mila's number.

"What? Don't tell me bridezilla's at it again? We're almost there!" Mila growled.

Bridezilla. She called Monet that even though she wasn't the one getting married. Monet had been acting a little crazy with all this planning and making sure everything was perfect. She'd put Mila and Atlas through the ringer too. I just sat back and enjoyed every second of it.

I chuckled into the phone. "Naw, she's fine. Outside razzing the decorator, moving things around. You know the drill."

She sighed. "Yeah, I wish she wouldn't have made such a big deal. I mean we could—"

"Have just gone to the courthouse. I know. You've told us a hundred times." I modified my tone, letting her know what her sacrifice meant to me. "She needed this to take her mind off everything that's happened. So I wanted to thank you first and foremost for giving it to her. Meant a lot to her and to me."

A sniffle came through. From tiger to kitten in one second flat. "Don't make me cry. I'm the hormonal bride, and I can't take it."

"Eek. Well that's going to put a damper on what I need to ask now." I gripped the back of my neck.

"Eek? Clayton Hart, did your big manly man ass just use the word eek?" she taunted. And there was our feisty friend.

"Seriously. I need to ask you something important, and it's okay if you say no. This is your day and all..."

"Clay, get the lead out. I'm growing wider by the second. I'll be as big as your house when you finally ask me what it is you want."

She was not lying. The woman was only into her seventh month of pregnancy and her belly did seem to grow daily. Sometimes it was as if she'd had a basketball shoved under her top, and other times a watermelon. Weird as shit, the whole pregnancy gig, but I couldn't wait to try it out with my woman down the road. Sometime very soon.

Mila's groan broke me out of my musings. "Shit, this must be good if you're freaking out."

"I want to ask Monet to marry me," I said it quick, like ripping off a bandage.

"And?"

"And? You act like that's a small thing." Heat prickled against my neck and I began to sweat. I gripped the velvet box and flipped it open to remind myself the ring was still there. A thin platinum band with one center round diamond with two baguettes flanking it. The wedding band was in another box hidden in the back of my sock drawer. I knew the second I saw the ring it was perfect.

"No, it's not a small thing, but it's not like I'm surprised."

I sucked in a harsh breath and let it fly. "I want to do it today. At the party, after your ceremony, when everyone is giving the speeches. Would that be okay?"

She laughed heartily. "Curly, get this. Clay's gonna pop the question during his speech today."

"Right on, man!" I heard Atlas shout through the line. "Way to grab life by the horns!"

"Totally cool!" Mila gasped. "I love it. Unconventional, and so you to do it in front of everyone."

"Gotta stake my claim." I flicked the box shut and shoved it in my pocket.

"Oh, I think you did that a long time ago, but I'm going to enjoy the show. It will just make the day more special."

I shouldn't have been nervous. Mila and Atlas were our closest friends; hell, they were family. Of course they'd want us to be happy and share in their day.

"Cool. I just wanted to make sure. Now the second thing... Can I marry your best friend?" I asked once again, the nerves making my heart palpitate.

"Uh, Clay, I'm not sure I'm understanding. Are you asking *me* personally for my best friend's hand in marriage?"

"And I'm going to adopt Lily," I added matter-of-factly.

"So you're asking for my approval to marry my best friend and adopt my niece," she clarified, her tone indecipherable.

"Yes, I am. You're her only family. I think it's important that the other person who loves her as much as I do be on board with my plan to make them mine."

She cursed and laughed. "Classy brother all the way. Okay, sparky, I'll bite. Are you going to take care of her?" Her tone bordered on a warning.

"Until my last breath."

"And Lily?"

"Will never want for anything."

She hummed into the line. "That's what I like to hear. Then yes, you can marry my best friend, you crazy loon!" She laughed. "Now come outside and help us with the loads of stuff in the car. We're out front."

I chuckled and ended the call. Mila had given her permission. The ring was in my pocket, the sun was shining, and all things led to her saying yes. God, I hoped she'd say yes.

MONET

The ceremony was absolutely perfect. Mila looked a vision in her white shimmery sundress. I'd suggested an all white and blue party, so all the partygoers were in various shades of white and blue. Genevieve had pulled Mila's hair back into a bundle of curls on the top of her head with strategic locks falling down for the super soft effect. Atlas had worn khakis and a white button-down shirt open at the collar. They only had eyes for one another. The ceremony was quick—as requested—and then came the reception slash baby shower part of the night.

We weren't playing any games because we were keeping the day-to-evening event classy. The sun had just set, and a round of champagne was being passed out for the official toasts and speeches.

I stood at the microphone next to Clayton. He looked stunning in a pair of khakis and a pale-blue dress shirt. I wore a white lace sundress with a large blue sash at the waist that matched his shirt. Lily scampered by in her fluffy flower girl dress, chasing after baby Will. Will was in a baby suit looking incredibly adorable and moving surprisingly fast for a toddler.

My large deck and surrounding trees had twinkle lights. Candles lit every possible surface without being intrusive. I'd hired a DJ to play soft music while people mingled. A huge buffet table was laid out on one side of the deck with fresh fruits, cheeses, small sandwiches, and plenty of bite-sized gourmet appetizers. The bride wanted a variety of options, specifically one of everything. In her gestating state, she was like a baby herself, putting everything in sight into her mouth.

Holding the mic up, I tapped the top, gathering our guests' attention. "Hello, everyone. I want to first thank you all for coming. It means a lot to me to have you all here, as I know it does to our couple of the night, Mila and Atlas." I nodded toward the couple sitting ten feet from me.

Atlas had his arm wrapped around his now wife and beamed as though he'd just won the lottery. I guess in a way he had, because I couldn't imagine anyone who would love him more than Mila.

"Tonight, we celebrate the marriage and the new life that my best friend Mila and her husband Atlas share. She didn't want a big to-do; she just wanted Atlas. Atlas didn't care what they did as long as he had the woman he loved marrying him for life. I think that's what it's all about. The heart wants what the heart wants, and it doesn't matter in what form it comes, as long as we listen to it and follow it to our happily ever after." I raised my glass, and the thirty guests followed. "To happily ever after. Mila, I'm so glad you found yours in Atlas."

Mila smiled at me and blew me a kiss. Clayton wrapped his arm around me and took hold of the mic. "My turn."

I sniffled and smiled, wiping at my tears of joy, so thrilled that this day had finally come for my best friend.

Clayton's voice was strong and deep when he spoke. "Atlas and Mila are not only a great couple but are made for one another, because honestly, who else could handle their feistiness?" The crowd laughed, and several nodded in agreement at his joke. "But they are also going to be amazing parents in the very near future."

Atlas took that moment to rub Mila's belly affectionately, bent down and gave it a kiss, and then kissed his wife. "I wish them the best this life has to offer..." Clayton continued. "Because I know as long as they have each other, it's going to be amazing." He lifted his glass and everyone followed.

A chorus of "hear, hear" and "kiss the bride" rang out over our friends. Once they'd followed through on the requests, Clayton turned to me.

"And now, with the approval of our happily married couple, I'm going to do what I've wanted to do since the first day I took care of my sweet Lily all those months ago and laid eyes on her mother the next day. Monet..." Clayton took something out of his pocket and in front of God and everyone went down on one knee.

I broke out in chills, gooseflesh starting at my hands, running up my arms, over my chest, and spreading along my entire body. My hand felt clammy as I clamped it around my champagne flute so tight I worried it would break. Tears pricked at the back of my eyes as Clayton reached for my other hand.

"Monet, beautiful, you are the love of my life. I told you once before that you were it for me. You and Lily are everything I could have ever dreamed of having for my own. I want to make our love and our life together official. Will you be my forever?"

His voice shook on the last statement, but he held strong, his gaze never leaving mine.

I nodded through the tears pouring down my face and set the glass down on the nearby table so I didn't drop it.

Clayton grinned, his eyes shining with so much love and affection they stole my breath. He flicked open a small velvet box and presented it to me. The most gorgeous ring I'd ever seen stared back at me, sparkling under the twinkle lights above. And my goodness...the thing was huge! I covered my mouth with my hands, choking back the sob that threatened to tear through me at any second.

Clayton smiled softly and squeezed my hand. "Will you make me the happiest man alive and marry me? Allow me to adopt Lily as my own?"

I smiled wide and fell even more in love with him for bringing Lily into his proposal.

With perfect timing, my little one ran over to me and hugged my legs. She peered into the box and tipped her head, assessing the ring and Clay, as was her way.

"It's not a crown, but it will do the job," she said, tapping on her bottom lip.

The crowd laughed. Clayton grinned, and I shook my head.

"So, I'm wearing a hole in my pants here, beautiful..." Clayton grinned.

My eyes widened, and my cheeks flushed with heated embarrassment.

"What do you say?"

I looked around the space at all our friends, each couple holding one another. Happiness exuded around me in heaping doses, but nothing like the waves of love coming off the man kneeling before me.

"Yes! A million times yes!" The words spilled from my lungs as if they had gossamer wings.

Clayton pulled the ring out of the box, slid it on my finger, looped an arm around my waist, and hauled me against his chest. His lips crushed mine in the most important kiss I'd had to date. He kissed me long, hard, and so deeply I had to grip his shoulders so I didn't pass out. He pulled away, set me on my feet, and cupped both of my cheeks.

"I'm going to make you so happy. Big family, big life. Everything you ever dreamed of. I'm going to make it happen."

I knew down to the tips of my toes he meant every word, and it all sounded perfect.

I smiled softly and trailed a finger from his temple to his bottom lip. "Don't you see? You already have."

He grinned and kissed me again.

CLAYTON

The last of the crew sat at a round table. Me with my fiancée cuddled into my side, the happy newlywed couple snogging and whispering to one another in their own love-drunk world, Trent Fox and his wife, Genevieve—Will playing in the yard—and my buddy Dash Alexander and his wife, Amber.

I sat around, watching each of the couples at the table. I'd lay down my life for every person here. Monet might not have blood relatives in her life, but this was her family, right here, the people sharing in the beauty that was this day and evening. These people would be there for our wedding, any babies Monet would give me, and all of the happy times we would have down the road. School events, sports activities, recitals, family dinners, birthdays, anniversaries, graduations. Name it, and they would be there during the important times. The times I would want to remember.

And I would. Remember every minute of this day.

I sighed, watched the kids play tag, and sipped my beer. "Life couldn't get any better than this," I announced to the table.

"You think?" Atlas grinned, a lock of brown hair flopping over onto his forehead. The dude needed to cut that damn hair already.

"I know," I said with complete and utter confidence.

Mila laughed, maneuvered herself and her belly to stand, and went over to the DJ table and grabbed something. As she walked back, her caramel-colored eyes twinkled. "I'll bet there's one thing that could make this night abso-freaking-lutely epic."

Trent pounded the table jovially. "Bring it on, girl."

Viv smiled and hooked her arm around her husband, waiting to hear what Mila said.

"What have you got there, Mila?" Monet asked, leaning hard against my side.

She tapped her mouth with the envelope. "Let's just call this an early wedding present, shall we?"

She set the large white envelope in front of Monet and me.

"Go ahead, open it." She stood next to Atlas. Still seated, he looped an arm around her waist and rested his cheek against where their baby grew.

Monet picked up the envelope, ripped the seal, and then pulled out a stack of papers. She picked up the top single sheet and laid the rest on the table. I tried to read over her shoulder but couldn't really see in the low lighting. Instead, I sipped my beer and waited. Except, the woman in my arms went dead still and gasped as though she'd been stung. Her hand went to her mouth, and tears fell down her cheeks.

What the hell? Anger threatened my calm mood as I watched my girl become emotional.

"Oh my God!" she said through her fingers, muffling the sound.

"What the ever-loving fuck..." I snatched the paper away.

The top of the form read LabCorp Genetics. I knew a buddy of Atlas's who worked there. A guy by the name of Bradley Grover. Worked him over at the gym a couple of times, but he hadn't been back in a while. Probably scared him off with the hardcore workout.

"This your friend's company?" I asked Atlas, shaking the piece of paper.

He nodded. "Slow your anger roll, Clay. How's about you read it before you rip our heads off for making your girl cry." He knew me too well.

I clenched my teeth hard. Next to me, Monet was crying her eyes out. I held her close and scanned the letter quickly. There were a bunch of boxes lined up next to one another showing perfect matches. Getting to the bottom, I scanned the text. Then I read it again more slowly to make sure I wasn't misreading.

We compared twenty-one genetic markers by multiplying twenty-three paternity indexes derived from twenty of the genetic loci we test to determine paternity of one Lily Holland against the DNA of Clayton Hart.

Based on the testing results included within, the probability of paternity is ninety-nine-point-nine percent (99.9%).

It is confirmed that five-year-old Lily Holland is the biological child of Clayton Hart.

"She's mine." I gasped and rubbed at my chin. "Lily's mine. Really mine. How in the world?" Monet wrapped her arms around me and cried into my neck. I held her close and looked up at my friends. "How did this happen?"

Mila rubbed her belly. "Well, Monet told me about the conversation you had about you being a donor at the clinic Moe went to and that your blood type was rare and the same as Lily's, and obviously, you love her so much. I just couldn't let it go. Are you mad that we went behind your back?" Mila frowned and sucked in a breath she didn't let out for a long time.

"Not mad," I said the two words in a monotone.

"Happy?" Atlas goaded.

"Not happy."

Silence went around the table, and I lifted a crying Monet to stand. I curled both hands around her jaw and swiped away her tears. "She's mine."

Her chin trembled, and she bit into her bottom lip. Tears ran in a river down her face. "That's what it says." Her eyes flickered to mine and around as if she was afraid.

"She's mine," I repeated, letting the truth fill my pores and permeate my being. "My daughter. Of my flesh." I pounded my chest with my fist.

Monet just nodded, more tears falling.

"I'm fucking *ecstatic*. This is the best news of my entire life!" I pulled Monet close and roared. "Lily is my daughter!"

The table cheered along with us.

I hugged my woman, tears falling from my own eyes. I

skated my lips across her ear. "Never going to let you two go. You own my heart. You and our daughter own my heart."

Together we wept, we kissed, and we celebrated with our friends.

Lily ran up with Will hot on her heels.

"Baby, come here." I kneeled down to her. "Hey, you remember what you asked me a long time ago? And we told you that I had to marry your mommy?"

Her big blue eyes, darker than my own but still very much like mine, widened. "Are you my daddy now?"

"Yes, baby. I'm your daddy. And you know what we just found out?"

I scooped her up and held her between Monet and me. "You've always been mine. A test was done and we found out that I'm your *real* daddy."

"My forever daddy," she clarified simply.

Her forever daddy. That hugged my heart, and I felt it clench, the message seeping deep.

"Yes, love bug. Clayton is your forever daddy," Monet confirmed.

"King Daddy it is!" She clapped and hugged us both. "Can I tell my friends now?"

I chuckled and kissed her cheek. "You can tell everyone in the world, honey."

She kicked her feet to be let down. "Will...I gotta tell you somefing!"

Everyone around the table laughed, and each person got up to hug us one at a time, sharing in our bliss.

EPILOGUE

MONET

One year later...

The buzz of the needle pierced my skin for the millionth time that day. My lower back and hip were sensitive, but for the most part I'd been fine. I enjoyed the bite of the tattoo needle. There was something sexy and illicit about the pleasure pain of each new pinprick. I could see why people would get obsessed with getting them. Except, for me, this was my fourth and last session.

I found through my sessions under the needle that individuals came to get tattoos for different reasons. Some to sleeve their arms and legs with splendid things that reminded them of good times, or cherished totems, maybe even hope for the future. Some came to commemorate an important event or were symbols of unity and friendship. Then there were the people like me. The patrons who were getting something appealing to cover something ugly, to wash away the past.

Each new lily and leaf added to the vine of flowers on my back took another piece of Kyle's mark away and replaced it with beauty. Just like Clayton suggested. Once we'd become engaged, I immediately started the process of covering up the damage Kyle had done to me. Amazingly, it was extremely cathartic. Every inch that was covered took another pound of weight off my chest and released me from my past. Today it would be finished. Kyle erased from my life forever.

Besides marrying my man in a small wedding on the beach in Maui a few months ago, nothing could make me happier.

"How's it going over here, beautiful?" Clayton walked over to me, shirtless, cellophane wrapped around his own fresh artwork.

"Let me see?" I asked.

He got closer to where I lay on the table so I could take in the majestic art. He was adamant about getting the same lily flowers over his scar that he'd gotten from Kyle. Lilies for our daughter, the same flowers I had running up the entire right side of my back. He said it united us in letting go of our past. United in all things.

Two lilies, pale lavender with black trim, and swirls of black lines and leaves wove up the side of his waist and onto his ribcage. The flowers had yellow centers that burst with color, giving the flowers a very realistic appeal to them.

"Pretty cool, yeah?" He checked it out himself in the long mirror across from me.

"Very cool." I wanted to wax poetic about how much

it meant to me, but he knew. I didn't need to say anything to show my love and appreciation. My husband just knew. Like he always did when it came to me. To us.

"All right, Moe, you're done." The tattoo artist rolled his chair back and put down his gun. "I'm going to slap some salve on it and wrap you. Go ahead and take a look. I went over everywhere thoroughly, but if you feel anything needs a touch-up, you let me know and we'll knock it out free of charge."

I nodded. "All I want to know is if you covered every single inch of the scar. Entirely." I was adamant about that. Every speck had to be covered.

"I knew the rules. It's covered. Clay, man, take a look." He gestured to my newly tatted skin.

Clayton bent over me and ran his finger down the healed parts of the tattoo, sending a shiver of delight rippling through me. He glanced up at my face, knowing what he'd done, and gave me a wink. Then he focused on the new ink. He got close and inspected it thoroughly, knowing if he said it was covered, I'd believe him.

"Nothing to see here, beautiful, but a sexy-as-fuck tattoo down my woman's back." He shot me one of his sinful smiles that spoke of long mornings in bed and long nights of the same.

I shimmied up to a standing position. The artist handed me a mirror, and for the first time ever, I was excited to see my back. Usually the sight of the scar instantly took me back to that horrible day and the pain Kyle caused. Now I had something to look forward to.

I lifted the mirror and checked it out. Running from my hip all the way up in a wide, sweeping trail were bunches of lilies in varying sizes and shapes. Black lines swirled magically around the flowers, flowing in and out. Leaves of a bright green hugged the edges here and there, and the centers were a startling yellow as if, when touched, pollen would stick to my fingertips. Nothing had ever been so life-changing except my baby when the nurse handed her to me after her birth.

"My goodness, Clay." I reached for his arm to steady myself, gratitude and acceptance rolling over me in waves.

"Monet. Baby, do you see *now* how gorgeous you are to me?" He asked the question he repeated every day. My answer was always the same. No. Today, and every day after, that would change.

He wrapped an arm around me, his hand coming close to the new design but not touching it. I memorized that moment, seeing his tanned hand against my skin and the colorful flowers sweeping along my back.

"Yes, Clay. I finally do see." Because I was beautiful. Now I could look at myself with pride. I could wear a strapless dress and show off the beauty I'd given myself. "Thank you. Thank you for making me see."

He smiled and kissed me. "Love you, Mrs. Hart."

"I love you, Mr. Hart."

"So, Clay, man, when's your next one?" the tattoo artist inquired.

Clayton chuckled and twined his fingers with mine. "Don't know. Probably when I have another kid and need to add another flower." He shrugged.

The man laughed, and I clenched Clay's hand. His eyes flashed to mine.

"Better make your appointment soon, then." I lifted his hand to my belly.

His eyes widened and his mouth dropped open. "Are you saying what I think you're saying? That I should *plan* to make an appointment or I already need an appointment?"

I laughed and shook my head. Men could be so dense sometimes. We women always had to lay it all out for them.

"I'm saying in about seven months, you're going to be a daddy...well, a daddy again."

His mouth opened and closed. "I'm going to be a..." He ran his hands through his spiked hair twice and then turned to me. "You're carrying my baby?" he asked, awe coating every word.

I smiled wide. "I am. That's why I had to rush this appointment. I just found out and didn't want to wait to finish the last of the tattoo, so we'd be free."

"She's carrying my baby," he announced to the tattoo artist.

The man just laughed and walked away, giving us our space.

Clayton looked like he was completely mystified.

"You gonna hug me or what?" I laughed.

"Fuck yeah!" He pulled me in his arms. "You're carrying my baby," he whispered into my neck. "We're going to have a baby. Lily's going to be a big sister."

"I can't wait," I admitted, as happy as I could ever be.

Clayton pulled back and stared deeply into my eyes, and I saw it all. Our future was endless blue skies.

"Monet, before you, I was going through the motions. Work, gym, a couple of friends. Nothing gave me joy. Not like we have now. I had love in my life but not the love of a good woman. You came along and filled my heart with love, my days with laughter, my bed with a beautiful woman." He gripped me more firmly and brought his face a scant inch from mine so nothing could intrude on this moment.

"For you, my wife...my love is limitless."

THE END

Want more of the Lotus House clan?
Continue on with Honor Carmichael
and Nicholas Salerno's story in:

Silent Sins
Book Five in the *Lotus House Series*
Coming April 3rd, 2018

EXCERPT FROM *SILENT SINS*
A LOTUS HOUSE NOVEL (BOOK #5)

NICHOLAS

Lotus House is alive with energy when I enter, and my baby sis, Gracie, is hot on my heels. She's wearing a bright smile and the new yoga outfit I bought her to celebrate her first day.

"Hey, Nick!" Dara waves from the front desk where she's helping a blonde customer sign up for classes. Luna, the owner's daughter, is behind her, filing something away in the cabinets.

"Ladies, bringing in my baby girl Gracie to teach her first Vin Flow class. You pumped, Gracie?" I ask, knocking her shoulder playfully.

"So pumped!" She squeals and does a little touchdown jig.

Dara smiles huge. "Girl, you know you got this. I've taken your substitute classes. Just remember, when you lose your place, breathe through it and go into tree, warrior, or child's pose, depending on if you have them standing or on the mat."

Gracie leans into the counter, bumping the petite blonde next to her. "Oh, sorry."

The blonde looks up, but all I can see is her profile. And what a damn fine profile it is. Classic, proud chin, a small, straight nose, and bee-sting-reddened lips. Her skin is so pale I can see the light-blue veins running just under the surface of her long, swan-like neck. Her blond hair is a golden platinum that's bundled up on top of her head, making her look more like a ballerina than a yoga student.

She mumbles something and then tips her head down, just as I round over to Gracie's side so I can see her more clearly. Long, black, fanned eyelashes meet the top of her cheeks as she focuses on the initial new client paperwork in front of her.

Smoothly, or not so smoothly, I encircle Gracie's bicep and ease her around behind my body and to the other side so I can be next to the willowy creature who's yet to look up. Something about her is calling to me, forcing my hand as I touch her shoulder.

Her gaze flashes up, eyes a foamy see-through gray, like cloudy white quartz. With a mere glance, I'm lost. Gone.

Sorrow. Sadness. Pain. All those emotions flash behind her gaze before she licks her lips and looks back down. She drops the pen, her hand shaking when she picks it back up.

A barrage of images parades across my vision like a mini-movie. Looking at her eyes over dinner. Watching those eyes twinkle as I make her laugh. Staring into them, lust-filled with desire, as I press into her naked body. Sharing past sadness and helping her find peace while holding her in my arms. Her tears falling as she bares her soul.

For the first time ever, I've looked into a woman's eyes and seen my future, and it centers entirely around me being the man for her.

I stand there like a numbskull while she finishes her paperwork and enters the main entrance with her new lotus-shaped entry card.

"Fuck. Did that just happen?" I whisper under my breath and press the palm of my hand against my forehead.

Dara places her hand over my fisted one on the counter. My entire body is strung tighter than a drum, and I have no idea why. "Loosen up. She's taking your class in fifteen minutes." She chuckles.

I turn my head and focus on my friend. She's an exotic, stunning woman. Her brown skin and ocean-blue eyes are startlingly unusual and nothing like those of the delicate blonde I just blanked out on after a single gaze.

"Hmmm, I'm guessing that rule you've got about not dating clients..." she hedges.

"Out the fucking window," I growl, staring at the closed doors, wishing I could see through it and catch one more glimpse of her.

Dara laughs hard, followed by Luna, who snickers and wiggles around doing a little dance. Christ, these women are as bad as my own sisters. Speaking of which, I do a three-sixty and realize that Gracie is gone. "Where's my sister?"

"Cool your jets, man. She's setting up for her first class," Dara offers.

I hunch over and shake my head, trying to clear it of the woman I've just seen. "I meant to take her to her class." My big brotherly duty is feeling neglected as I stand stupidly, my feet stuck to the floor.

"Oh, how sweet. Like she's in kindergarten, and she needs her big brother to walk her in and protect her from the big bad yogis." Luna jabs me in the chest with a pointy finger.

"Ouch!" I rub at the spot and realize what she's said is the truth. Gracie doesn't need her big brother hovering. "Just wanted to make her feel supported. I'm proud of her."

Luna nods. "Then show her that by proving you know she can handle herself. No helicopter brothering at Lotus House. Got it?"

Her words are firm and brook no argument. I swear, if I had a dime for every time I was bossed around by a beautiful woman, I'd be rich as hell.

I toss my towel over my shoulder. "Fine. You sure the blonde is taking my class?"

Dara nods. "Yep. I offered Gracie's Vin Flow, but she chose Introduction into Aerial Yoga."

"Did you warn her that it's a lot of hanging from silks above a mat?"

Dara grins. "Yep. She said something like 'it sounds dangerous' and promptly signed right up."

"Huh. May be a risk-taker. I like it." Definitely wouldn't have assumed that from her hunched shoulders and lack of eye contact. If anything, she seemed extremely shy and introverted. Guess I'd have to figure her out.

"What's her name?" I ask Dara.

"Dara..." Luna warns in that motherly manner from over her shoulder.

"Seriously, Luna. I know you're vying for boss lady when the moms retire, but I'm just asking what the woman's first name is, not the code to the safe."

Luna purses her lips as her red bangs fall over her forehead. "Maybe she wants her name to be private?" She blinks innocently.

"Give me her freakin' name or payback is a—"

She waves her hands as if she's ringing off bad juju. "Okay, okay. Her name is Honor, but that's all I'm giving you. The rest you can find out the old-fashioned way. By asking her!" She looks down her nose at me.

"Honor." I let the name ping around in my head as I wave over my shoulder and head into the hallway leading to my assigned room. Good grief, if that isn't the perfect freakin' name for an angel like her.

Continue reading in:

Silent Sins
A Lotus House Novel: Book Five
Coming April 3rd 2018

ALSO BY AUDREY CARLAN

The Calendar Girl Series

January (Book 1)
February (Book 2)
March (Book 3)
April (Book 4)
May (Book 5)
June (Book 6)

July (Book 7)
August (Book 8)
September (Book 9)
October (Book 10)
November (Book 11)
December (Book 12)

The Calendar Girl Anthologies

Volume One (Jan-Mar)
Volume Two (Apr-Jun)

Volume Three (Jul-Sep)
Volume Four (Oct-Dec)

The Falling Series

Angel Falling
London Falling
Justice Falling

The Trinity Trilogy

Body (Book 1)
Mind (Book 2)
Soul (Book 3)
Life: A Trinity Novel (Book 4)
Fate: A Trinity Novel (Book 5)

The Lotus House Series

Resisting Roots (Book 1)
Sacred Serenity (Book 2)
Divine Desire (Book 3)
Limitless Love (Book 4)
Silent Sins (Book 5, April 3, 2018)

Intimate Intuition
(Coming Soon)
Enlightened End
(Coming Soon)

ACKNOWLEDGMENTS

To my husband **Eric**, my love for you is limitless too. There's really nothing else I need to say.

To my sister **Denise Pasion**, it's your fault that I love books so much. I'll never forget growing up and lying next to you in bed, hiding under the covers while you used a flashlight and read me O'Henry, whispering the tale to me so that our parents wouldn't know we were still up. I treasure that memory and had it not been for you countlessly buying me books over the years and being a voracious reader to look up to, I'm not sure I'd be where I am today. Your gift to me all those years ago keeps on giving. I love you.

To my editor **Ekatarina Sayanova** with **Red Quill Editing, LLC**... I might have made you work a bit harder for this one and for that I'm sorry. My emotions and tenses were all over the place. Thank you for having my back in all things and making me look good!

Heather White, I love that you always give me honest feedback even when you don't want to. I'm thrilled you enjoyed the suspense angle of this book. Your thoughts on each book really put things into perspective for me. Thank you.

Jeananna Goodall, Thank you for being the world's greatest personal assistant and knowing what I need before I need it.

Ceej Chargualaf, I can't tell you how excited I get to send you each chapter after it's written. Having someone to read and review my work as I'm writing it, cheering me on...it's such a blessing. You, dearest Ceej, are a true blessing. Thank you for all that you do.

Ginelle Blanch, You constantly amaze me with your ability to find errors even after two edits! I also so enjoy hearing about the parts of the book that tickle your fancy. I'm so thrilled you're one of my badass betas! Mad love, girl!

Anita Shofner, Every beta read you perform you crack me up. I so love experiencing my books through your chapter thoughts. I feel as though the joy you bring me is limitless.

Tracey Vuolo, Your passion with every beta read is by far the most intense. You live the characters' lives and breathe their experiences in a way I adore. Thank you for being part of my badass beta team.

To the Audrey Carlan Street Team of wicked hot Angels, together we change the world. One book at a time. BESOS-4-LIFE, lovely ladies.

ABOUT AUDREY CARLAN

Audrey Carlan is a #1 *New York Times*, *USA Today*, and *Wall Street Journal* bestselling author. She writes wicked hot love stories that are designed to give the reader a romantic experience that's sexy, sweet, and so hot your ereader might melt. Some of her works include the wildly successful Calendar Girl Serial, Falling Series, and the Trinity Trilogy.

She lives in the California Valley where she enjoys her two children and the love of her life. When she's not writing, you can find her teaching yoga, sipping wine with her "soul sisters" or with her nose stuck in a wicked hot romance novel.

Any and all feedback is greatly appreciated and feeds the soul. You can contact Audrey below:

E-mail: carlan.audrey@gmail.com
Facebook: facebook.com/AudreyCarlan
Website: www.audreycarlan.com